Karen Ch
THE POISON
The Detective Lav

THE POISONED QUILL

Visit Karen Charlton's website to learn more about her historical novels and sign up for her occasional newsletter for the latest news about her writing, competitions and events.

www.karencharlton.com

Published by Famelton Publishing
Cover design and illustration by Jessica Bell

FOR MY GRANDSON, BRUCE

LOVE YOU TO SCARBOROUGH AND BACK, DARLING

GRANDMA XXX

ALSO BY KAREN CHARLTON

The York Ladies' Detective Agency Mysteries

The Mystery of Mad Alice Lane (short story)

Smoke & Cracked Mirrors

Dancing With Dusty Fossils

The Detective Lavender Mysteries

The Heiress of Linn Hagh

The Sans Pareil Mystery

The Sculthorpe Murder

Plague Pits & River Bones

Murder on Park Lane

The Willow Marsh Murder

The Resurrection Mystery

The Mystery of the Skelton Diamonds (short story)

The Piccadilly Pickpocket (short story)

The Death of Irish Nell (short story)

Death at the Frost Fair (short story)

Other Works

February 1809 (short story)

Catching the Eagle

Seeking our Eagle (non-fiction)

Chapter One

August 1814
The Vicarage, Ealing

'Love divine, all loves excelling...'

Fifteen-year-old Flora Kilby sang the Wesleyan hymn softly as she dusted the China ornaments on the mantelpiece in the parlour, smiling at her act of rebellion. The master didn't permit any kind of music except Anglican hymns in the house; he loathed those favoured by Methodists.

But he wasn't here today. He was at a funeral in Brentford with the rest of the servants and there was only her poorly mistress, Baby Ruth and the wet nurse in the vicarage.

The thought made her confidence grow. Her sweet voice rose to a crescendo as she sang the next lines:

'Joy of Heaven to Earth come down,
fix in us Thy humble dwelling;
all Thy faithful mercies crown!'

Her rebellious streak satisfied, Flora smirked and hummed the next verse quietly.

When she moved across to the carved cabinet between the two tall windows, she enjoyed the sensation as her shoes sank into the thick pile of the Turkey rug. It muffled sound. Just like the blanket of pearly-white mist outside the window muffled the quack of the ducks on the village pond and the rumbling wheels of the local farm carts and carriages.

She trailed her hand across the walnut cabinet. Dusting and polishing the beautiful things in this room was her favourite part of her job. The cook, Mrs Minskip, had told her this furniture was made by a man called Mr Chips. She didn't believe that for one minute but whoever the carpenter was, he was a clever man.

Outside, the mist swirled in the slight breeze.

For a moment, she thought she saw someone lurking beneath the trees across the road on the village green, and she tensed with unease. The roads were full of desperate and homeless soldiers these days. Many of them were sick or injured, and it wasn't unusual to see them hobbling towards the hospital or find them gaunt and starving at the kitchen door. She knew she should be more charitable, but their battle scars and their pain-ravaged faces scared her.

The fog swirled again, and the figure – whoever or whatever it was – melted away. She dismissed her unease as nought but fancy and turned to the vase of flowers on her favourite little rosewood table. She scooped up the dropped petals and dried leaves and decided to replace the flowers with a fresh bunch from the garden.

The mistress would like it. The poor lady had barely left her room since the birth of little Ruth four weeks ago and deserved something nice. Mrs Langford loved the scent of roses – even though the master complained about the insects that came into the house in their wake. The master hated flies.

At the thought of her master, Flora tensed and paused.

The Reverend Langford was admired by his parishioners for his knowledge of the scriptures and his genial nature. But here in the claustrophobic world of the vicarage, she'd seen – and heard – the other side of the man. She knew it was wrong to dislike a man of God, but her Ma had taught her to be wary of men.

She winced as she remembered how angry the vicar had been when the doctor told him he had a third daughter. And that wicked, wicked note that was pinned to the wooden porch of the church had made everything ten times worse. Flora recalled how viciously the Reverend had yelled at his poor wife afterwards. She'd felt so sorry for the mistress. No one in their right mind would believe those shocking lies – but it seemed the vicar did. His temper lately had scared Flora out of her wits.

Her thoughts were interrupted by the sound of a loud thud. The baby screamed. She dropped her feather duster and raced up to her mistress's bedchamber. The baby's screams were now joined by the yells and shouts of two arguing females.

Mrs Annette Snelling, the wet nurse, stood at the end of her mistress's bed, her face dark red with anger and liquor. She held the bawling infant in her arms.

'I ain't never been spoke to so disrespectfully!' the woman yelled. 'Who do you think yer are with yer airs and graces? Vicar's wife or not – I've 'eard what they say about yer!'

Flora gasped. She'd never liked the sly-eyed wet nurse who reeked of gin, but this went beyond the pale.

Mrs Langford's pretty eyes blazed with anger. She raised herself up from her pillows and leaned forward. 'Give me my child and get out of my house, now! You're drunk!'

The woman laughed.

Flora strode forward and snatched the baby from the woman's grasp. 'You heard the mistress. Leave!'

'Yer nowt but a fancy strumpet!' the vile woman yelled at Mrs Langford. Then she barged past Flora, nearly knocking her over.

Mrs Langford sank back against her cotton and lace pillows, breathing heavily. Her thin arms shook as she reached out for Ruth. Tears rolled down her pale cheeks. 'Thank you for intervening, Flora.'

Flora gave her the child and watched Little Ruth nuzzle into her mother's breast, her tiny mouth opening and closing as it sought the nipple. Mrs Langford gently examined the infant's limbs.

'What happened, Ma'am?'

'She dropped Ruth on the floor.'

Flora's hand fluttered to her mouth in shock. 'Oh, Mistress – I'm so sorry! Is Ruth hurt? Shall I fetch Doctor Morton?'

'No, I think she's well. There's no bones broken.'

'My Ma always says babies are more robust than we think.'

'Your mother is very wise. I think Ruth will be all right now. Dear God! Why on earth did the Reverend employ that dreadful woman?' Mrs Langford added angrily.

'I don't know, Ma'am.'

And she didn't. She didn't understand any of it. She'd even asked Mrs Minskip about it.

'Why can't the mistress feed her own baby? And why is the master so set against the idea of a wet nurse?'

The cook laughed as she kneaded the dough between her fat fingers. 'It's the way of the gentry. They employs others to do everythin' for them. The vicar's first wife, God rest her soul, fed her babes and he wants the second Mrs Langford to do the same.'

'But it must be lovely to feed a child. My sister always looks so content when she's feedin' Lily.'

'It ain't our place to question our betters,' Mrs Minskip reminded her. 'And don't forget Mrs Langford has all the chinks.'

Flora nodded, still confused about the nursing. But she understood the cook's reference to the money. Her mistress was a wealthy heiress, far richer than the vicar. She could easily afford a wet nurse. Eventually, he'd backed down and sought out a wet nurse himself. But they'd been shocked when he'd brought that disgusting woman to the vicarage. It was like he wanted to punish his wife.

Mrs Langford's voice interrupted her thoughts. 'Flora, I need you to make sure Mrs Snelling leaves the house. I don't trust her.'

'I will, Ma'am.' She turned to go, but another wail from Baby Ruth made her turn back. The infant's face was puckered with distress as she repeatedly tried – and failed – to find a nipple.

'I think she's still hungry,' the mistress said. 'And I've no milk for her.'

'Are you sure you don't want me to fetch the doctor?'

'No. I'm in good health, Flora – and I'm sure Ruth is, too. Just pour me a glass of water from the jug.'

By the time Flora had poured the water and put it on the bedside table, a notion had popped into her head. 'If it ain't too forward to mention it, mistress, my sister has just had a baby – a healthy little girl called Lily. My sister's a polite and God-fearin' woman. She could help with the feedin', if you'd like.'

Clara Langford's thin face lit up with sudden hope. 'That's kind, Flora. What a wonderful idea! Please make sure that dreadful woman leaves the house, then fetch your sister.'

Flora hesitated. 'It might take me a while to find her,' she confessed. 'It's market day in Brentford. She'll be shoppin'.'

'The sooner you leave, the better. I'll try to settle her now, but Ruth will need another feed in a few hours.'

'I'm not sure I should leave you alone after such an upset.'

Mrs Langford smiled. 'Thank you for your concern, Flora, but Ruth's needs must come first – or *I* won't settle.'

Flora nodded and hurried down the stairs after the wet nurse, determined to give her a piece of her mind.

But there was no sign of the woman in the kitchen – or in the servants' quarters in the attic. She'd gone and so had her belongings.

Remembering the mist outside, Flora grabbed her shawl, descended the stairs and was almost at the front door when she heard something in the front parlour.

Mrs Snelling was standing in front of the walnut display cabinet. The glass door was open, and she was fingering the precious items inside. Her filthy carpet bag was on the Turkey rug by the muddy hem of her cloak.

Flora drew herself up to her full height and strode into the room. 'What the devil do you think yer doin'!'

The woman smirked, half turned and dropped something shiny into her cloak pocket. 'Just sayin' goodbye to these little beauties. It'll be a while before I see such pretties again.'

Flora's sharp eyes scanned the contents of the cabinet. A silver baptism cup, belonging to Mr Langford, was gone. 'Put it back – the cup you've filched!'

The woman scowled, closed the door and picked up her bag. 'Get out of my way, chit!'

She moved quickly, once more knocking Flora out of her way.

Flora screamed, staggered, and grabbed the back of a chair to steady herself.

'Lord! I'll be glad to get away from you lot – I don't think I've ever met a bigger bunch of wheedlin' hypocrites!' The woman threw open the front door and stormed out – straight into the man who was standing on the doorstep with his arm raised towards the door knocker.

Flora heard the commotion and the surprise in the gentleman's voice as he apologised for their collision. Flora wanted to go after the wet nurse, but the woman was already running, her boots crunching along the gravel path.

Then, Mr Ashfield strode into the parlour with his confident gait and a waft of the fresh outside air.

He was the last person in the world Flora wanted to deal with right now. She burst into tears and sank down on the sofa.

Despite his recent illness, which had left him gaunt, and his skin tinged with yellow, Ashfield was still a handsome man with fine cheekbones and a strong jaw. His high forehead creased with concern at the sight of her distress. 'What's the matter, Flora? And who was that woman?' He pulled his handkerchief out of his coat pocket and held it out towards her.

She opened her mouth, but no words came out. For a moment she was mouthing like a stranded fish on the bank of the River Brent. She took the handkerchief and tried to pull herself together.

'What's happened?' Ashfield asked again, his tone more urgent now. 'Are Mrs Langford and the baby well?'

She found her voice and her words came out in a torrent. 'It's all gone wrong. That were the wet nurse. She dropped the baby and Mrs Langford's dismissed 'er. Now she's stolen a silver cup, and I couldn't stop 'er.'

'Do you want me to fetch the constable?'

'Can't you just go after 'er? Catch 'er and get it back? The Mistress wants me to fetch a new wet nurse.'

Ashfield frowned and glanced at the thick fog outside the window. 'I didn't see which way she went – and I'll never find her in this fog. That's a job for the parish constable, Flora. Where the devil is everyone else?'

'Mr and Mrs Minskip are at the funeral of Reverend Finch in Brentford – and the master has gone with them. It's just me and Mrs Langford in the house.'

But you knew, didn't you? she thought. *Half the parish is at the former vicar's funeral. You'd never have called on the mistress if you thought the master was here...*

'Good God – and you've had to deal with this on your own? Look, I'm here now, Flora. You fetch this new wet nurse for Mrs Langford, and I'll sit with her until you get back. Then I'll fetch the constable to catch that damned thief. I hoped to have a quiet word with Clara anyway.'

'You can't,' Flora snapped. 'The mistress is still a-bed – and the master's out. It wouldn't be proper.'

Ashfield's smile was charming and gentle. ''Oh, come now, Flora! You know Mrs Langford and I are old friends. She'll be delighted to see me. I tell you what, why don't we let Mrs Langford decide? You go upstairs and ask her if she'll meet me in her parlour.'

Flora sighed. She'd done her best. *God help them all if the master came back early.*

Mrs Langford was delighted to learn Mr Ashfield had called to see her and Baby Ruth. Her cheeks flushed like a young girl's. She climbed out of bed and asked Flora to help her dress. She chatted happily while Flora brushed her long white-blonde hair with the mother-of-pearl hairbrush from the dresser.

'This is excellent news, Flora! Mr Ashfield can stay with me while you fetch your sister.'

But it ain't right, Ma'am, Flora thought, pinning her mistress's cap into place.

Finally satisfied with her appearance, Mrs Langford picked up her baby and went into the adjoining parlour.

Flora led Mr Ashfield upstairs and hovered outside the door for a while, listening to their laughter and the warmth of their conversation.

Careless, she thought, shaking her head. *They're so careless.*

She put on her cloak and bonnet and walked out into the fog to find her sister.

She'd no notion this would be the last time she'd see her mistress alive.

Chapter Two

The knock on the door came when Ned Woods and his family had just sat down for their supper.

The kitchen was filled with the delicious aroma of Betsy's lamb stew and dumplings and the heat and steam from her latest frenetic round of laundry.

Woods didn't know why his wife insisted on such a frenzy of washing and scrubbing just before they departed for their annual trip to see his brother. But after twenty-five years of marriage, he knew better than to question how Betsy ran their household – unless he wanted to be called a muttonhead and get slapped with a ladle. But he did wish she'd use a little less starch. His shirts were so stiff they could walk to Market Harborough on their own.

Smiling, Woods reached down to stroke their little dog, Alfie Bobbin, who sat at his feet. 'Are you lookin' forward to havin' a new place to sniff, little fella?'

Twelve-year-old Rachel was describing Uncle Alby's tavern, The Angel Inn, to her little sister and her foster brother, Georgie.

'And there's ducks?' Tabby asked. 'Will there be ducks for Alfie Bobbin to chase?'

Young Georgie just looked amazed. He'd been abandoned by his mother after his father died and had never set foot outside of Southwark. But the poor little nipper didn't want to come with them. He still hoped his Ma would come back for him and wanted to stay in London so she could find him. Thankfully, Betsy's sister had offered to move into their house and care for him while they were gone.

But this arrangement hadn't pleased their two eldest sons, Eddie and Dan. They'd looked forward to a bit of freedom in their parents' absence. They hadn't stopped sulking since they found out Aunt Ginny was coming to stay.

Despite this, Woods was proud of his boys. They were both tall, powerful young men who were doing well in their jobs and making their own way in the world. They were just a bit too independent, he thought wistfully. If he wanted to spend time with his sons these days, he had to bribe them with a tankard of ale down at the local tavern. It was the only time they'd sit still long enough to talk to him.

He suddenly remembered his wedding anniversary would fall while they were away. He scratched the greying stubble on his chin and pondered how to make the day special for Betsy. Perhaps Alby's wife, Rosie, would take care of the girls while he took Betsy out for a treat?

But where to take her?

Alfie Bobbin leapt to his feet, barking. He dashed through the door into the hall. The little dog was half blind with cataracts but there was nothing wrong with his ears. The next second there was a loud, insistent hammering on their front door.

Woods pushed back his chair and rose to his feet. 'Gawd's teeth! Who the devil's that?'

Betsy glanced back from stirring the pot. 'Go quickly, Ned. They'll have the door off its hinges!'

But he didn't get a chance; someone had already opened the front door and entered the house.

A deep male voice hollered: 'Ar do! Neddy? Are you there?'

There was only one person in the world who called him bloody *Neddy*.

'Heaven and hell! *Alby?*'

Young Georgie whimpered in alarm when a colossus appeared at the kitchen door, with a battered hat pulled low over his bushy eyebrows and wrinkled forehead. This giant had Alfie Bobbin tucked under his arm. The little dog was trying to lick his face. Alby blinked at the light and steam of the kitchen and raised a huge paw to remove his hat and wipe the sweat off his brow. 'There you be, Neddy! Ar do.'

Betsy recovered the quickest from the surprise appearance of her brother-in-law. 'Well, where else would Ned be at supper time?' she quipped lightly. 'Sit down, Alby, and join us. I'm about to serve the stew and dumplings.'

Delight sparked in Alby's eyes, and he hurried to take off his coat. 'Thank ee, Sister Betsy – and ar do to you, too.'

The children jumped to their feet and clamoured around their uncle, asking him a dozen questions all at the same time. Rachel took the dog from him and Tabitha held up her arms until he hoisted her up into the air. Eddie and Dan grinned and shook his free hand. Rachel shoved the nervous Georgie forward to do the same and introduced him.

Woods finally found his voice. 'Gawd's teeth! What the devil are you doin' here, Alby?'

'Ain't you pleased to see me?'

'I'm allus pleased to see you, you daft cork-brain… but it's dangerous for you in London!'

'I've important tidings. We men need to speak.'

There was a 'humph!' from Betsy as she ladled out the stew. But Woods had more important concerns at that moment than his wife's indignation.

Nearly forty years ago, young Bert Woods had mixed with a local gang of thieving coves run by a violent bastard called Yabsley, who'd killed another gang member called Tash. When Bert tried to walk away from the gang, Yabsley had set him up to take the blame for the murder.

A hue and cry was raised, but with help from their mother's Kilby relatives, Bert fled London. He changed his name to Alby Kilby and settled down with Rosie as a tavern landlord. But the villains of London had long memories – and so did the law.

Woods finally managed to reach through his children and shake Alby's hand. 'Why didn't you wait until we got to yours?' he asked.

'And why didn't you write to us, Uncle Alby?' Rachel asked.

Alby threw back his large head of white curls and laughed. 'I don't know my letters, Treacle. My Rosie does all that.'

'Did you get here without bein' seen?' Woods asked. 'Are you sure you weren't followed?'

'I'll check the front and back, Da,' Eddie whispered quietly to his father.

Woods nodded gratefully to his eldest son.

'I came down the Oxford cut with my boy on his barge, *Adelaide*,' Alby told them. 'I waited till it got dark. He's loadin' up grain now and leaves at ten. I ain't got long.'

'Then we'd better eat,' Betsy said. 'Sit down, everyone.'

By the time Eddie returned, Alby had helped himself to a second helping of stew, a great achievement because he was eating with only one hand. The other still held Tabitha, who was perched on his knee.

Woods raised his eyebrows in enquiry to his son. Eddie shook his head and slid down into his seat at the table.

Woods breathed a sigh of relief and turned his attention to his food. But even Betsy's excellent stew and a pudding of treacle tart and custard couldn't dislodge the feeling of unease that had walked through the door with his brother.

Something was wrong.

Woods wiped the custard off his chin with his shirt sleeve and cleared his throat. 'So why are you here, Alby? What's so important to tell us that it couldn't wait? We'll be in Market Harborough in a few days.'

'Ah, about that.' Alby scooped up another spoonful of custard. 'I'm afraid you can't come to stay. The canal board 'ave taken over our inn fer a few weeks fer their engineers – there's trouble with the locks at the bottom staircase at Foxton. Their chinks were too good to pass by.'

A shocked silence fell over the entire family. Woods didn't dare look at his wife. But Alby seemed oblivious to the family's disappointment.

'So, these are your *important tidings*?' Dan said sarcastically.

'Part of it. I thought I should tell you meself. Ye'll have to come another week.'

Betsy's voice caught in the back of her throat when she spoke. 'That might not work out, Alby. It's difficult for Ned to get time away from work. His new magistrate is a weasel. If we put it back a few weeks, he might turn round and say "No".'

Unperturbed, Alby grinned at his sister-in-law. 'Then it's a blessin' I've sorted out another cottage fer you.'

Woods' eyes narrowed with suspicion. 'In Market Harborough?'

'No. In Brentford, at the start of the Grand Junction canal.'

'Brentford? Why the deuce would we want to go there?'

Alby's face was suffused with surprise. 'Why, it's a grand place, Brentford – and the fishin' is good. There's shops for Sister Betsy and the girls and the wharves are allus busy.'

Rachel turned to her mother. 'Didn't you and Da used to go there when you were courtin'?'

Betsy nodded. 'Yes, your father proposed to me on Hanger Hill.'

Alby grinned again. 'I bet that were a day to remember, Sister Betsy! Our Neddy down on one knee!'

'She turned me down,' Woods said abruptly.

'Who owns this cottage, Alby?'

'Our Kilby cousin Dora. She's widowed now and runnin' a tidy business. Do you remember her, Neddy?'

Woods shook his head. Their dead mother's Kilby relatives were a vast tribe who lived or worked on the coal and grain barges on the canals and navigable rivers of England. Swarthy-skinned with black hair, their features were made even darker by the coal dust lodged in the lines of their leathery, weathered faces. He couldn't tell one from the other.

'Dora has a small cottage in Brentford – just a couple of rooms – and said you were welcome to 'ave it fer a week fer a small token. I thought it would be handy like, for when you did your detectin'.'

'Detectin'? What detectin'?'

'For findin' Da.'

'Da!' Woods jerked back in his chair.

'He's bin seen.'

'Gawd's teeth!' An unpleasant shiver ran down Woods' spine.

The children exchanged puzzled glances. It was Dan who voiced what they were all thinking. 'But Grandpa Woods is dead. You told us both of our grandpas were dead.'

'It were easier that way,' Betsy murmured.

Another silence filled the kitchen. Dan threw up his hands in irritation. 'I think you need to tell us the truth.' His siblings nodded in agreement.

The words came easiest to Alby. 'He walked out on us and your Grandma when your own Da were just a nipper.'

'Desertion?' Eddie muttered darkly. 'That's against the law.'

'And a horrible thing to do,' Rachel said.

Betsy cast a worried glance at her silent husband. 'We never thought to see him again. It were the simplest thing to do, to tell you he'd died. I'm not sure Ned wants to see him again, Alby.'

'But surely…' Dan interrupted. 'Surely, Grandpa Woods must be about a hundred years old by now?'

Woods snapped out of his shock. 'He'll be in his late seventies, you cheeky rascal. He were only nineteen when Alby were born.'

'Oooh! That's the same age as our Eddie.' Rachel turned to her oldest brother. 'Don't you be gettin' any cork-brained ideas about startin' a family, Eddie Woods!'

Eddie blushed and scowled.

Woods turned to Alby. 'When did this happen? Who says he's back?'

'It were Nathan Kilby. You remember him, Ned? Our cousin; Tod's brother.'

Woods shook his head again.

'He'd just gone through the Thames lock and were at the tiller when he saw Da sat fishin' on the tow path. He were already past the old fella when it dawned on him who it were. He shouted out but Da ignored him.'

'Did Cousin Nathan moor up the barge and speak to the man?'

Alby's broad forehead wrinkled in confusion. 'Of course he didn't! He'd got cargo to get to Leicester and had to be nippy.'

Woods rolled his eyes. 'So, the only evidence you've got that our Da has returned is the word of a distant cousin, who reckons he caught a glimpse of him in Brentford.'

Alby's huge moon of a face broke out into a broad grin. 'Aye, that's about right, Neddy. That's why you need to do some detectin'.'

Dan opened his mouth to ask a question, but Woods held up his hand to stop him. 'And if I do find him, Alby,' he said sharply, 'exactly *what* do you want me to say to him?'

His family held their breath. Woods rarely used that tone with them; they knew he was on the verge of losing his temper.

Alby gave a short laugh that caught in his throat. Pain flashed through his eyes, which moistened with tears. He blinked them back and mumbled, 'Ask him why he left us.'

After supper, Woods, Eddie and Dan escorted Alby back to the wharf. Woods didn't think there'd be anyone abroad who might recognise his brother, but he wanted his strapping sons by his side in case there was any trouble.

When they returned home two hours later, young Georgie and the girls were already in bed. Betsy sat alone by the kitchen hearth with her needlework. She rose and made Woods a cup of tea. 'Is Alby safely away?'

'Aye. The *Adelaide* were already loaded. There were only time to shake my nephew's hand before they pushed off. They've gone. Leave us alone, lads. I need to speak to your Ma.'

Eddie and Dan nodded and went upstairs. Woods sank into the battered old armchair opposite his wife.

Betsy frowned and picked up her needlework again. 'It'd have been bad for you if anyone had recognised Alby. None of you would have had jobs tomorrow if someone had seen him with you.'

Woods nodded. 'Aye, he took a huge risk comin' back to London – and we did too, harbourin' him.'

'Yes – and all for a fool's errand!'

'Maybe – maybe not. But this matters to him, Betsy. He were only thirteen when Da left us – still a nipper himself – it hit him hard.'

He paused for a moment before he asked: 'What do you think about this daft notion of goin' to Brentford and stayin' in there for a while?'

She sighed. 'I don't think we've much choice if we want a change from London. That weasel Magistrate Conant will use any excuse to keep you in the city, and we can't go to Market Harborough now. 'Tis a pity. I were lookin' forward to seein' Rosie again.'

'It might not be so bad in Brentford,' Woods suggested.

'Ha! But you won't be with me and the children, will you? You'll be out lookin' for this ghost who everyone thinks is your da.'

Woods smiled. 'Have more faith, woman. I'm a damned good detective. I'll find this fella in ten minutes. Once we know his name is Fred Smith, my time will be for you and the gals.'

'Do you think Alby is gullin' himself with this tale?'

'I do. Our Da is long dead – but he won't accept this notion.'

'Well, I suppose Brentford will be a change – and at least I'll be able to take the girls to Ealing to see Magdalena and Sebastián while you do your fishin'.'

Woods' greying eyebrows rose in surprise. 'Why is Doña Magdalena in Ealing?'

'She's visitin' her friend, Lady Caroline. Stephen thought the fresh air and quiet might help her recover from whatever malady has been botherin' her.'

Woods' broad face creased with concern. 'Aye, sir has said a time or two she weren't well. What do you think it is?'

Betsy laid down her needlework. 'I don't know, Ned. It seems to be in her mind – not her body. She keeps cryin' and fussin' over the children. And not just the two little ones, either. She even frets over Sebastián. Women get like this sometimes after a birth. But I think it's somethin' more. And I'm worried she's turnin' back to her popery. Our Rachel saw her last week talkin' with some of those Catholic sisters from that nunnery down Carmine Street.'

Ned's frown deepened. 'She might just have been passin' the time of day with them nuns.' Then he roused himself. 'Well, the fresh air of Ealing will help – as will spendin' some time with that aristocratic doxy. As for us, I've a notion to do somethin' special in Brentford.'

Betsy eyed him suspiciously. 'And what's that?'

'I were thinkin' about our weddin' anniversary. We should take a little trip to Hanger Hill again – for old times' sake. Just you and me, with a picnic. And this time you might say *yes.*'

'You daft muttonhead,' she said primly, although the sides of her mouth twitched with amusement. 'I *did* marry you in the end. There's no need to propose again.'

Woods grinned and his eyes twinkled. 'Who said anythin' about a marriage proposal, Mrs Woods? It'll be a different question this time – but I'm still hopin' you'll say *yes.*'

She threw her pin cushion at him when he winked.

Chapter Three

Despite the warmth of the summer evening, Detective Stephen Lavender quickened his step as he turned into the quiet and leafy West Castle Square in Marylebone. His pristine white cravat was stuck to the back of his neck with sweat.

He was late. And this was one night when he should have been home on time.

Had they already left? His guts churned with his old curse: indigestion.

He sighed with relief when he saw the hackney carriage standing outside his home and the familiar skinny figure of coach driver Alfie Tummins.

Good. Magdalena and the children were still here.

Lavender had met Tummins four years earlier when the lad was still an immature, pimply youth who was barely shaving. But the young man was trustworthy and honest, and his sharp eyes and observation had once saved Magdalena's life.

The pimples had long gone, and Alfie now sported a fine beard on his thin but pleasant face. He'd been courting Teresa, Magdalena's maid, for years; his carriage was a regular feature outside the Lavender home. But he was here on business tonight; Lavender had booked him to drive his family to Ealing.

His wasn't the only carriage in the square tonight, Lavender noticed. A second hackney cab and two patient black horses waited further down the street, the driver swathed in scarves despite the warmth of the evening.

Lavender raised his hand in greeting to Alfie.

But the young man didn't respond. His shoulders were slumped forward, and he looked wretched. Lavender stopped beside him. 'Good evening, Alfie. What on earth is troubling you? Are your parents well?'

Alfie nodded his head, sadly. 'Yes, sir, Ma and Pa are well. But no – everything ain't right. Teresa turned me down again. She won't wed me.'

Lavender grimaced. He was desperate to get inside the house and see his family, but he knew he couldn't walk away from the distraught young man after a comment like that.

'I'm sorry to hear this, Alfie. In my opinion, you'd make a wonderful husband for Teresa. If it's any consolation, Mrs Lavender turned me down the first time I asked her to marry me. You must keep trying.'

'But it ain't the first time, sir! I asked 'er last year but she said she didn't want to live with my Ma and Pa.'

Lavender nodded. He understood Teresa's objections there. Alfie's father, who owned the hackney carriage company, was a decent enough fellow but he was also gruff and irascible.

'So, I've saved up me chinks and got us the chance of a nice little 'ouse all of our own near the livery stables. It's even got its own wash 'ouse and bread oven! But she's still knocked me back!'

Lavender opened his mouth to offer condolences, but Tummins' next words took his breath away.

'She says she might move back to bloody Spain!'

'Spain? Are you sure?'

What the hell was going on here? Teresa might still have a few maidenly doubts about marrying Tummins; it was a huge decision for any woman. But surely if she remained unwed, she would never leave Magdalena's side?

The two women had fled Spain together when the French invaded, and the danger and subsequent poverty they'd endured had drawn them close. They were more like sisters than a mistress and a maid – and Teresa adored the Lavenders' children.

Spain was still ravaged after the invasion of the French. Why on earth would she return alone?

Unless… unless she wasn't going back alone?

Lavender's stomach churned again, and he fought back his rising panic. He'd known there was something wrong for weeks now. His strong-minded, intelligent and loving wife had become sad, distant and weepy. She'd lost weight, and sometimes he'd caught an expression on her face that spoke of so much suffering, it made his heart break.

But surely she didn't plan to leave him?

He reached out and grabbed Tummins' arm. 'Don't worry, son. I'll get to the bottom of this and see what I can do. Are you sure you still want to drive them to Ealing?'

Hope surged in the young man's eyes, and he nodded. 'Don't you worry, sir, I'll get them there safely – and Teresa has promised to write.'

Lavender hesitated; he wanted to ask Tummins if Ealing was still the planned destination? He wanted to make him promise not to take his wife anywhere near a seaport, no matter how much she begged…

But embarrassment held him back. *Stop being so stupid. There's a simple explanation for everything.* He braced himself and entered the house.

The hallway was stacked with luggage trunks and bags. The poisonous, niggling devil of doubt who sat on Lavender's shoulder whispered that there was rather a lot of it…

Then he remembered that travelling with small children required a ridiculous amount of paraphernalia. He consigned his demon to the back of his mind and went upstairs to join his family in the parlour.

'Papa! Papa!' Little Alice raced across the carpet on her chubby legs and threw herself into his arms. Teresa sat on the sofa with Baby Jack in her arms and Sebastián, now a tall and gangly fourteen-year-old, lounged in the chair by the fireplace.

Magdalena stood by the window. She looked pale and thin, and her smile of greeting was half the smile it used to be. But her violet-blue eyes still turned to him with softness and love.

Still holding Alice, he pulled his wife into his arms. The little girl squealed with delight as she was squashed between her parents' embrace.

'I'm so sorry I'm late, *querida.* That damned trial at the Old Bailey dragged on interminably. I spent hours in the corridor of the courthouse, waiting to give my evidence.'

'All is well, Stephen,' she said gently, her Spanish accent softened now by years of living in London. 'We've only just finished packing. Travelling anywhere with two small children seems to require a vast hillside of luggage.'

He smiled. 'The saying is a *mountain of luggage* – not a hillside.'

'Fuff!' She waved a dismissive hand at his correction, but he knew she'd not make that mistake again.

Her mood is already lighter, he thought. *This trip will do her good.*

'But we must leave now if we're to reach Ealing by dark.' She turned to her son. 'Sebastián, please will you tell Mr Tummins we need to load the carriage. And perhaps you can help him?'

Sebastián García de Aviles Morales del Castillo, known to his school friends at the Catholic boarding school he attended simply as *García*, rolled the dark eyes he'd inherited from his mother. He untangled his gangly limbs and rose to his feet. His jet-black fringe fell across the high cheekbones on his thin olive-skinned face when he moved. He flicked it back before he spoke. 'I think you need to employ more servants, Pa. Mamá keeps mistaking me for one.'

Lavender smiled and put Alice down on the carpet. 'There'll be plenty of servants at Lady Caroline's home at your beck and call, Sebastián.'

'I think Master Sebastián be an idle skelpie-limmer,' Teresa observed from her seat on the sofa.

Lavender bit back his laugh. Teresa's grasp of English had never been as good as Magdalena's and, thanks to her association with Alfie Tummins, it was far more colourful.

Sebastián frowned. He and Teresa often argued these days, and Lavender sensed they were on the verge of another spat.

'Are you looking forward to this trip?' he asked.

Sebastián shrugged. 'I'll miss a jaunt to Vauxhall Gardens with Lewis minor, but it might be fun for a day or two in Ealing. And that old sea dog, Captain Sawyer, tells me there's good cricket on the village green.'

When he moved towards the door, Teresa rose to her feet with the baby and reached out for Alice's little hand. 'I shall come too with *los infantes*,' she announced. 'And we shall see that you and Mr Alfie Tummins load the carriage in the correct manner.'

'We don't need you to supervise, Teresa!' Sebastián complained.

But Teresa was adamant. Their bickering continued as they descended the stairs, and by the time they reached the hallway they'd switched to Spanish and were yelling and cursing each other in a manner that would make a docker blush.

Lavender closed his ears to them and embraced Magdalena again. 'I think you'll have a lively time with those two – and I feel sorry for poor Alfie.'

Magdalena smiled and broke away from him. 'Alfie's used to Teresa telling him what to do. I think he likes it.'

'Did you know he'd proposed again – and she's turned him down?'

Magdalena turned away to look out of the window at Sebastián and Teresa, who were still arguing. 'It's only a matter of time, before she accepts him.'

'She told him she might return to Spain,' he said cautiously.

Magdalena still had her back to him, and he couldn't see her expression. 'No, she mustn't do that…' she said vaguely. 'Silly girl.'

And it was there again… that distance.

He reached out and pulled her back into his arms. 'What is it, *querida?* What the devil is wrong?'

She pecked him on his cheek and ran her fingers across his face, pushing back his fringe. Her eyes were moist. 'You and Sebastián both need a trip to the barbers.'

'You're changing the subject.'

'There's nothing wrong with me, Stephen, except a little melancholy. It's quite natural at my age after the birth of a child. I miss my mother.'

Lavender frowned. 'Surely you mean your father? I thought your mother died when you were a child?'

'All women need their mothers when they become mothers themselves.'

Confused, he changed tack. 'Please just promise me you're not hiding anything? That you're not seriously ill?'

She gave a half-smile. 'I promise. I'm not seriously ill.'

'I love you, *querida.*'

'And I love you too, Stephen – more than you'll ever know. But now we must leave.' She picked up her portable rosewood writing desk with its sloped top from the windowsill. 'I'll need this. I'll write to you every day, my darling.'

He nodded but eyed the locked box suspiciously. Magdalena kept her correspondence in there, including the letters from her lawyer in Spain, who managed her estate and her tenants. She usually shared every detail of those letters – especially when she was frustrated by their contents.

But he felt she'd been secretive about her Spanish correspondence recently. One night after she'd gone to bed, he'd almost pulled out his lock picks to open the damn box and read the latest letter for himself.

But the thought had filled him with self-loathing. He was disgusted he doubted his wife.

He accompanied Magdalena out to the carriage.

He kissed his little children and jokingly offered to kiss Teresa goodbye too – from which she recoiled in horror. Then he ruffled Sebastián's hair, shook his hand and told him to look after his mother. Alfie Tummins shook the reins, and the carriage lurched forward.

Lavender stood for a while, staring after them. But his view was soon blocked by the second carriage that had been waiting in the square. It also chose that moment to move off.

Sighing, he returned to the house and his cold supper. With Magdalena, the children and Ned Woods all out of London, it would be a long, lonely week.

Chapter Four

Lavender still found it strange to see Nathaniel Conant sitting in James Read's chair, especially as Bow Street's latest magistrate was such a tiny figure. With his head of curly pure white hair, Conant looked like a black-cloaked and curious lamb peeking over the inlaid top of that massive oak desk of authority.

But at least there was less animosity in the office these days. And for that he was grateful.

Bow Street was the biggest and most famous of the London magistrates' courts and police offices. Under James Read, it had run like a well-oiled pump engine. The principal officers, nicknamed 'runners' by the public at large, were all loyal and experienced men; they knew exactly what to do and when. And should they forget their duty, the dour chief clerk, Oswald Grey, was always on hand to keep them on track. No one ever risked upsetting the man who organised their wages.

Conant's appointment had initially thrown them into turmoil; nobody liked the changes he'd tried to instigate. But after some tactful intervention from Lavender, things had settled down to a new order. Conant focused on his magisterial duties in court and Lavender and Woods, in their new roles of Chief Constable and Assistant Chief Constable, organised the workload of the runners and the horse patrol, ably assisted by Oswald Grey.

But Conant was still possessive of Lavender's fame. He craved constant newspaper exposure for Bow Street and pandered to their wealthy, aristocratic London clients at the expense of Lavender's patience.

Lavender was sick to the back teeth of solving the petty problems of the ton. Tasks like helping Lady X work out which one of her maids had stolen her tortoiseshell hairbrush bored him. And he'd spent most of last week soothing the nerves of Baron Y, who thought he'd seen an intruder climb over his orchard wall.

He craved mystery – and was desperate for a decent murder to solve.

And his instincts told him that the worried man who sat opposite Conant might be the one to provide it.

'This is Doctor Clive Morton,' Conant told him. 'He wishes to hire one of our detectives to solve a particularly nasty murder.'

Lavender felt the back of his neck tingle with anticipation. He recognised Morton's name from an article he'd read in the *Morning Chronicle*. He knew about this murder – and more importantly, where it had occurred. But he kept his face impassive as he shook the doctor's hand. He'd need to use guile to persuade Conant to let him go.

Morton was in his early forties, with receding dark hair. Wire-framed spectacles perched on his wide nose, covering intelligent and anxious brown eyes. Slightly overweight, his face was fleshy, the wide mouth loose and the lips full.

The man dressed in Lavender's own style: a plain black coat worn over black pantaloons with a pristine white cravat. But the tailoring of his coat was exquisite, and beneath it he wore a black velvet waistcoat with a tasteful silver stripe. Everything about him suggested Morton's medical practice was full of affluent and grateful patients.

'I've told Doctor Morton we might be able to send Principal Officer Vickery to his aid,' Conant said. 'But as you organise the men, I thought you should hear about the case yourself.'

'Alas,' Lavender lied, 'Detective Vickery is on his way to Somerset to deal with another case. However, *I* might be able to help.'

Morton's mouth widened into a pleasant smile. 'That's excellent news, Detective. I've read about you in *The Times,* and I hoped you were available.'

'I'm not sure I can spare Detective Lavender,' Conant blustered. 'Our Assistant Chief Constable, Ned Woods, is also out of town this week.'

More lies tripped off Lavender's tongue. 'I'm sure Bow Street can manage for a few days without me. Things are quiet downstairs, and Mr Grey has everything under control.'

'They are?' Conant asked with surprise. 'He does?'

'So, please tell me your problem, Doctor Morton. Is this anything to do with the mysterious death of the vicar's wife in Ealing? I read about it in the *Morning Chronicle*.'

'Yes, it's related to the death of Mrs Clara Langford, God rest her poor soul.'

'I thought Sir James Clitherow had already issued a warrant for the arrest of a man,' Conant said. 'A man called Ashfield.'

'Yes, the man charged with her murder is Mark Ashfield.'

'But if a man has already been arrested, why do we need to be involved?'

Morton sighed and shuffled uncomfortably in his chair. 'I'm not convinced they've arrested the right man.'

Conant's black bushy eyebrows, so at odds with his pure white hair, gathered in sharp consternation at this statement. 'I'm sure your Justice of the Peace made the right decision. I've a lot of respect for Sir James.'

'So have I,' Morton explained hastily. 'Sir James did what he had to do based on the facts that were set before him. But not all the facts were presented to the inquest – and there are too many loose ends that need further investigation. I don't think the local constable has made sufficient inquiries. There's more to uncover.'

Lavender nodded sympathetically. He and Woods had met a vast number of parish constables over the years. They were a mixed bunch, with varying ability. Some were sharp-eyed, intuitive detectives like himself and Woods; others were primarily employed for their muscles, and their main role was to break up drunk and brawling farmers on market day and drag them to gaol.

'Weren't you the doctor who gave evidence at the inquest?' Lavender asked.

'Yes – much to my regret.'

'Why's that?'

'Because I'm uncomfortable with the idea it'll be *my* evidence that will send Ashfield to the gallows.'

'I still can't spare Lavender,' Conant said shortly.

'I understand Ealing is a wealthy and pleasant suburb, noted for its fine air and handsome residences,' Lavender said casually.

His interest sparked renewed hope in Morton. 'Oh, yes! Apart from Baron Clitherow and his family, our neighbours include the Duke of Kent, two generals, several Members of Parliament and an admiral. For many years, Sir John Soane, the respected architect, owned Pitzhanger Manor and used it as his country residence. And there are many other prominent gentlemen live there. The whole village is in shock over this affair.'

Lavender smiled to himself. Conant's interest had piqued at this illustrious roll call. 'I understand there are also several prominent ladies among your neighbours,' he said. 'Doesn't Lady Perceval, widow of the late Prime Minister, also live in Ealing with her daughters?'

'Yes, and Lady Caroline Clare, sister to the Earl of Kirkleven, is the latest addition to our parish.'

'With such eminent residents,' Lavender said, 'I suspect you've little crime. I imagine your local constable would be out of his depth with the brutal murder of such a prominent member of the local society as Mrs Langford.'

'That's exactly my point, Lavender! And there's far more to this tragic story than meets the eye,' Morton continued. 'I was born in Ealing, and I know *all* the people concerned in this case intimately.'

Lavender crossed his booted ankles and flicked a piece of lint off his breeches. The sound of wagons rolling over the cobbles towards Covent Garden, and the muffled shouts of hawkers, drifted through the open window. 'All in all, sir,' he said to Conant, 'I think it exactly the kind of case I *should* take on, considering the influence wielded by the residents of Ealing. If there's more to discover, it'll only raise the profile of Bow Street with the ton. I think we should hear the full story.'

Conant sighed and surrendered. 'Pray continue, Doctor. Tell us what happened on the day of the murder.'

'Mrs Clara Langford was the youngest daughter of another prominent and wealthy resident of Ealing: Mr John Daniels. Daniels made a fortune with the East India Company. Clara married our new vicar, Thomas Langford, last year and was recently brought to bed with their first child. It was a difficult birth, which left her ill. But I visited her the day before her death and, although she was in low spirits, she was recovering.

'On the day of the murder, I was eating my luncheon at home when her brother, Mr Frederick Daniels, arrived in a terrible state with the news that Mrs Langford had been found dead at the vicarage. My first thought was that the cause of death was some terrible – but belated – complication of childbirth.'

'Who found her?'

'It was her husband, the Reverend Thomas Langford. He'd been at a funeral in Brentford but met Daniels on his journey home. The two men returned to the vicarage together.'

'The newspaper report said she'd died of arsenic poisoning.'

'Yes. When I walked into the bedchamber, I quickly realised she showed the classic symptoms of poisoning. There was vomit and diarrhoea and blistering around her mouth.

'I asked the maid what she'd eaten that day. Apparently, the family had eaten kippers for breakfast, but Mrs Langford only managed a few mouthfuls.

'Then I saw the remains of a glass of water on the table by her bedside. It had no smell – and I suspected arsenic poisoning immediately. I took it – and the water jug – back to my surgery to examine them further.

'I keep a few caged rats for experimental purposes back at the surgery. I gave two of them the last few drops of the water from the glass to drink. They both died, writhing in agony, within an hour. But further experimentation showed the water in the jug to be uncontaminated.'

'I congratulate you, Doctor,' Lavender said. 'You've shown better skills of detection than half the parish constables of England. But what happened next? How did the vicar take the news his wife had been poisoned?'

'He and Daniels were devastated, horrified. Neither of them could make any sense of it. But it turned out that while I was back at the surgery, the maid admitted she'd left her mistress alone in the vicarage with the baby. She'd arrived back a few minutes before them. They concluded Mrs Langford administered the poison to herself.'

'Good grief!' Conant exclaimed. 'Why on earth would a young woman with a new baby – a vicar's wife, for heaven's sake! – commit such a sinful act?'

Langford shook his head, sadly. 'She had been melancholic since the birth of her little girl.'

Lavender's thoughts flashed to Magdalena. 'Is this common? Do melancholic new mothers often kill themselves?'

'Not in my experience,' Morton said. 'It has happened – but in my professional opinion, Mrs Langford wasn't that distressed. That's what I told both her husband and her brother – and the jury, at the inquest.'

'Who had the opportunity to poison her?' Lavender asked.

'The maid admitted she'd poured the water for her mistress from the jug on the washstand and left it by her bedside and she swears Mrs Langford was in good health when she left the vicarage to fetch a new wet nurse.'

'Why did they need a new wet nurse?'

'There'd been some trouble with the old one – a woman called Annette Snelling. After a nasty argument about the woman's incompetence, Mrs Langford had dismissed her.'

Lavender frowned and leaned forward in his seat. 'That sounds like a possible motive. Has this Snelling woman been questioned?'

'No, that's one of the loose ends in this case. She's disappeared; the parish constable has been unable to find her.'

'Was there arsenic kept in the vicarage?'

'Yes, for rat poison. I asked Langford to show it to me. The package was kept at the back of the locked shed by their manservant, Minskip. There are two young girls in the house – Langford's daughters by his first marriage – and Minskip was conscious of the dangers of arsenic. It was a new packet and hadn't been opened.'

'Is this Minskip fellow trustworthy?' Conant asked.

The doctor gave a short laugh. 'I suppose so, although his wife – who is the cook and housekeeper at the vicarage – is rather a scold and famous for her strong opinions. They were both at a funeral wake in Brentford when the murder happened, and no suspicion has fallen on either of them. The funeral was for the former vicar of the parish. The Minskips had worked for him for years and Reverend Langford gave them both the day off to pay their respects.'

'That's a strong alibi,' Lavender observed. 'Was the vicar at the wake?'

'No, he attended the church service but after the ceremony he went to see one of his elderly parishioners. He didn't attend the wake. He never met his predecessor and felt his presence there would be uncomfortable for the grieving family.'

'That was sensitive of him,' Lavender said. 'So, the arsenic must have been brought into the vicarage. How does Mark Ashfield fit into this? Why was he arrested?'

'After questioning the maid further, the village constable discovered that Clara Langford wasn't left alone on the day of her death. Mark had arrived to visit Clara and was sitting with her when the maid went to find the new wet nurse. The vicar was furious she'd held back this information and dismissed her from her post.'

'So, the maid's testimony isn't to be trusted,' Lavender said, 'and she had the opportunity to kill her mistress. Does she have a motive?'

Morton shook his head. 'No. She was very fond of Mrs Langford. She also claims she caught a glimpse of someone watching the house earlier that morning, but this has not – to my knowledge – been investigated. Inevitably, suspicion turned on Mark, who was the last person to see Mrs Langford alive. Sir James Clitherow had no choice but to arrest him and send him to Newgate to await trial.'

Conant nodded in support of his fellow magistrate. 'Naturally, I would have done the same.'

'What did they determine to be Mark Ashfield's motive for the murder?' Lavender asked.

Morton threw up both hands in frustration and despair. 'He doesn't have one. You *have* to believe me, gentlemen, when I say they've arrested the wrong man. I've known Mark all my life and there isn't a harmful bone in his body. Yes, he loved Clara – the whole parish knew this – and Mark was devastated when she married the vicar. But he would never harm a hair on her head – or anyone else's, for that matter.'

Lavender wondered why this intelligent and rational medical man was suddenly so irrational.

'I still don't understand why her husband and brother were so quick to assume she'd killed herself,' Conant confessed. 'Why would someone with so much to live for even contemplate such a terrible thing?'

The doctor's flaccid face darkened. 'Unfortunately, an unpleasant shadow had been cast on her happiness – and her reputation – a few weeks earlier.'

'What do you mean?'

Morton pulled a folded piece of paper out of his coat pocket. 'Three weeks before, someone had nailed this to the wooden post of the church lychgate. It was a Sunday, and I went early to church that morning; I'd been up all night with a dying patient and wanted some quiet reflection. But there was already a small crowd of parishioners gathered around the gate reading this disgusting note. I tore it down, but it was too late. It was the main topic of gossip around Ealing within a couple of hours.'

‘What does it say?’ Lavender asked.

Morton handed the paper to Lavender. It was thin, cheap paper – easily accessible to anyone for a few pennies. The vile message was written in capitals. He read it aloud:

THOU ART A WHORING HOBBY-HORSE CLARA LANGFORD AND THAT CLINKER ASHFIELD DOTH RIDE YOU LIKE HIS NAG. THY BIRD-WITTED VICAR BE A HORNED CUCKOLD AND HAS A BASTARD IN HIS CRIB.

Conant grimaced. ‘That’s vile! The poor woman! The Langfords must have been devastated.’

‘They were. Someone told the vicar, and he came to see me that evening to ask if it was true. He wanted to see the note, but I didn’t want to add to his distress, so I told him I’d burned it. He was deeply upset and embarrassed.’

‘But you didn’t burn it,’ Conant pointed out.

‘No, it crossed my mind that at some point whoever wrote this note might be caught, and the constable would need evidence. I would like to see this person caught,’ he added, with a meaningful look at Lavender.

Lavender stroked the paper between his fingers thoughtfully. ‘Someone obviously held a festering grudge against Mrs Langford.’

‘This fiend has targeted several of us,’ Morton told him. ‘I’ve had a libellous letter written in the same style – and several of my patients have also received them.’

‘Such a vicious shrew deserves to be caught and whipped!’ Conant announced sharply. ‘Was this disclosed at the inquest?’

‘No. I think the vicar asked for it to be suppressed as evidence and Sir James agreed.’

‘In my experience,’ Conant said, ‘the writers of such calumny are cowards who hide behind their quills. They’re troublemakers who relish causing distress and anxiety for their victims – but I’ve never known one who turned to murder.’

'There's always a first time,' Lavender said thoughtfully. 'Which brings us back to Mark Ashfield and his motive for the murder.' Lavender's tone sharpened. 'Was he Mrs Langford's lover? Was he jealous and enraged by her marriage to the vicar? Did he decide that if he couldn't have her, no one else could?'

Morton winced. 'Clara was the love of his life. But their relationship has always been chaste. He worshipped the ground she walked on.'

'Why should we believe you?' Lavender asked coldly. 'How can you be so sure?'

'Because Mark Ashfield is my brother. I know the man better than anyone.'

Chapter Five

'Gawd's teeth!' Woods' eyes narrowed with alarm as he scanned the heaving mass of frenzied humanity in Brentford marketplace. Instinctively, he pulled his wife and daughters closer when another speeding stagecoach, crammed with a dozen passengers – mostly on the roof – hurtled past.

'It's changed a bit since we were last here,' Betsy said sadly.

Woods nodded grimly and searched the faces of the crowd for a middle-aged woman he'd never met: his distant cousin, Dora Kilby. The sooner they got away from the marketplace and found their lodgings the better.

Woods had lived all his life in the heart of London and was used to noise and the stench of the river in Rotherhithe and Southwark. Even the crush of the crowds in Smithfield market, the yelling of the street hawkers, the cursing of the dockers and the filthy squalor of Seven Dials failed to shock him.

But Brentford, this new Brentford, was a shock.

The town lined the main road between London and Bath. It always was a bit squashed, he remembered, trapped as it was between the high, forbidding walls of the Boston Estate in the north and the Thames in the south. And there'd always been a poorer side to the town, especially in the dark and stinking alleys behind the high street where small, cramped houses had been squeezed into every available space.

But back in his courting days with Betsy, there was a quaintness about the cobbled corn market and shabby weatherboarded cottages. Members of the ton would often break their journey here to visit the genteel and handsome shops.

He'd heard that the arrival of the canal had brought new industry to Brentford, but it seemed to have changed its character for the worse. A flour mill and a turpentine factory now loomed up behind the tiled roofs that, along with the belching chimneys of the breweries and brickworks, dominated the skyline.

'That's nineteen coaches I've seen drive by, Da,' Rachel said.

'I've seen a hundred and two,' Tabitha boasted.

Woods nodded and tightened his grip on their luggage.

Little Tabby didn't understand her numbers yet, but his gals were right about the amount of traffic. The fast, churning wheels of the coaches created dust clouds that added to the general filth of the town and settled on everything. The once gleaming windows of the taverns and the brass bell in the turret of the marketplace building had lost their sheen behind a thick layer of grime. Even the haggard faces of the people looked grey.

There was nothing *genteel* about the drunks staggering along the high street from one tavern to another. And there were beggars. Beggars everywhere. Many of them with missing limbs and wearing frayed army greatcoats.

'Pick up Alfie Bobbin before someone stands on him,' Betsy told Rachel.

'Or tries to steal him for the pot,' Woods snapped.

Tabitha gave a horrified squeal.

Then a fight broke out on the steps outside the Three Pigeons.

Two drunken women – both whores, by the look of their garish and revealing dresses – had rushed out of the open door of the tavern and were followed by a baying crowd who still carried their tankards of ale.

'Yer a scabby sow!' screeched one of the women.

'You tell her, Peg!' yelled one of the men in the crowd.

'And yer a pox-ridden harlot!' the other replied.

Peg launched herself on the other woman, who raised her arm to fend her off. Peg sank her teeth into it. Squealing in pain, the other woman grabbed handfuls of Peg's hair and ripped it out at the roots.

Betsy and the girls stepped back in alarm. Woods stood his ground but resisted the urge to interfere. He'd rather pull two dogs apart than separate two scrapping whores.

'Let's move away, Ned,' Betsy said.

'But what about her?' Rachel asked. She pointed at a well-dressed young woman standing on the edge of the fight.

The young gal was about sixteen and obviously gentry. She had neatly brushed dark-auburn hair and smart leather buttoned boots peeking out beneath her silk dress. Behind her stood a terrified maid, who looked about twelve. Neither of them should be here, watching and listening to these drunken whores.

Woods moved forward. 'Come away, Treacle. This ain't the place for a young lady like you.'

The girl jumped in surprise at the sound of his voice but quickly recovered. 'It's all right, sir. My maid is with me.'

He was about to insist when Peg launched a vicious right hook into the other woman's face. Blood splattered everywhere. The other whore dropped to her knees on the cobbles, clutched her nose and wailed.

'You both need to leave, Treacle.'

The young woman shrugged and glared at him. 'I don't welcome your interference, sir.' She had a long pale face and light insipid eyes that were too close together and framed by invisible eyelashes. 'But it's over now anyway. Come along, Mabel.'

Woods was taken aback by her hostility, but made sure the two girls were safe on the other side of the road before he returned to his family.

Betsy and the girls had been joined by a short, plump woman in a faded purple dress. Her badly dyed black hair was frizzy and rose up over her high forehead. It gave her the look of one of those poodle dogs. Heavy gold rings stretched her earlobes and made her look like a gypsy. She was sucking on a chipped bone pipe and emitted a billowing cloud of tobacco smoke.

'This is Mrs Kilby, Ned,' Betsy informed him.

'You can call me Dora seein' as we're kin,' the woman said in the deep gravelly voice of a heavy smoker. 'I see you've been enjoyin' the entertainment, Neddy.' Her dark eyes glinted with intelligence and amusement.

'I've seen better,' he said, smiling. 'It's a pleasure to meet you, Cousin Dora. Just call me Ned, by the way.'

The woman's smile broadened, revealing her tar-stained teeth and the gaps in her gums. 'Your Alby said you'd say that – but 'e reckoned you're more partial to *Neddy*.'

Woods rolled his eyes. He'd have words with his brother next time he saw him. 'How did you find us in this crowd?'

'Alby said I'd find you easy enough. 'E stopped by on 'is way back up the cut the other night. 'E told me you was a big, ugly fella with a great round moon of a face, who'd 'ave three pretty gals and a mangy flea-bitten pup by your side.'

Betsy's lips flickered into a smile. 'That sounds about right. These are our daughters, Rachel and Tabby – and our dog, Alfie Bobbin.'

Cousin Dora patted the little dog. ''Tis a bad case of mange the little fella 'as.'

Betsy bristled. 'I've done my best with him. I've spent a fortune at the apothecary on salves.'

'We rescued him from the street,' Woods added.

Dora stood up, nodding. 'The apothecary's herbs won't be fresh. I'll fetch you some of my own later.' She gave the girls a warm look of approval. 'What lovely chestnut curls you both 'ave. You've pretty 'air. You won't need no love potions. You'll break 'earts when you're older.'

'Fuff! Boys!' Rachel blushed and scowled. 'I don't want none of that nonsense.'

Dora laughed and turned back to Betsy. 'Gals are such a blessin'. I've two of my own.'

Her eyes flicked across to the crowd outside the Three Pigeons. The argument between the two women had started up again. Raising her voice, Dora said: 'We'll get away before those two hellcats kill each other.'

Peg spun round angrily. 'I 'eard you, Dora Kilby! Yer better watch yer mouth, you old witch!'

Dora laughed, faced the woman and raised her fist into the air. Slowly and deliberately, she twisted it round to show off the pentagon tattoo on the back of her hand. Then she released her chubby index finger and jabbed it twice in Peg's direction. 'Watch your mouth, Peg O'Connell.'

The whore screamed in terror and dived behind one of the drunken men in the crowd. 'She's 'exed me!' Yer all saw it! The bitch 'as 'exed me!'

Laughing, Dora pushed her pipe back in her mouth and marched through the crowds, which hastily parted before her. The startled Woods family hurried in her wake.

'Are you really a witch, Aunt Dora?' Rachel asked, once they'd left the crush of people.

'Of course I am, sweetie.'

Tabitha was flexing her chubby wrist while she walked, trying to copy Dora's dramatic hand movement. 'Will you teach me how to do an 'ex, Aunty Dora? I want to 'ex our Dan.'

'Who's Dan?'

'My brother. He's mean to me.'

'Is 'e? Well, don't worry, you little poppet. I'll show you 'ow it's done before you go 'ome.'

Satisfied with the promise, Tabitha fell silent.

Betsy glanced around the filthy town with unease. 'Are our lodgings nearby?'

'No, your lodgin's are further away – on the butts.'

'The butts!' Rachel laughed. 'That sounds rude!'

Dora smiled. 'You're a little character, ain't you? No, the butts is nice.' She turned to Betsy. 'You'll like it there. But I've got an errand to do at the wharf first. Come on.'

They crossed a narrow-arched brick-and-stone bridge that crossed the Grand Junction Canal, pausing at the top of the bridge to stare at the scene below. The wharves that ran alongside the canal were lined with grimy warehouses and heaving with activity. The towering soot-stained walls amplified the metallic clang of the machinery and yells and curses of the men. The noise bounced backwards and forwards across the canal in that confined basin.

Downstream was a pair of locks, side by side. Each contained a barge, low in the water due to the weight of the cargo beneath the tarpaulins covering their hulls. Two men had their backs to the beams, straining to open the lock gates. More barges and a couple of narrowboats waited their turn, floating mid-stream in the black and oily water.

But, as always, it was the horses that drew Woods' attention.

Several of them stood patiently on the tow path beside their barges. The ropes between them and the vessels were slack and dipping into the water. Only their matted tails moved, swishing away the flies. Like everything else in Brentford, the horses were filthy, but their stillness gave them a quiet dignity among the chaos.

'Those horses are well trained,' Rachel said, 'considerin' the noise.'

'They're enjoyin' the rest, Treacle,' he replied. 'Them's heavy barges they haul.'

Dora pointed to the double lock below them. 'That's the gaugin' lock – the Ham weigh dock.'

'What's a weigh dock?' Rachel asked.

'It's where Big Jim Kilby uses weights and a long stick to measure 'ow low the boats are in the water. Then 'e works out the toll and collects the chinks off the bargees.'

'Is he another cousin?' Woods asked.

'Lord knows,' Dora said, 'I've lost track of Kilby's relatives – God rest 'is soul. 'E used to know them all – but 'e's been dead five year now.'

'May he rest in peace,' Betsy murmured.

Dora shrugged. ''E were a good fella, my Kilby – and a sharp businessman. When 'e 'eard the canal were comin' to Brentford 'e says to me: 'I sees an opportunity 'ere, Dora – in property. This town will boom. 'Tis an easier life than 'auling coal from one end of the cut to the other. 'E came off the cut, sold his barges and bought a few tumbledown cottages that needed a lot of work to make 'em 'abitable. 'E left me a tidy legacy to manage.'

Woods noticed a few derelict weatherboarded houses squashed here and there in gaps between the warehouses, and he wondered if any of them belonged to Dora Kilby.

But he didn't have time to ask. She turned abruptly at the end of the bridge and disappeared down a flight of steep stone steps that led them to the tow path and the weigh dock.

Big Jim Kilby was one of the men operating the weigh dock and he was as big as his name suggested. A colossus of a man with skin weathered like a piece of old leather by the sun, he wore a filthy collarless shirt rolled up at the sleeves, braces and a wide belt to protect his stomach muscles.

Woods couldn't gauge his age, but he seemed to be plagued with arthritis; every now and then he rubbed his right shoulder, and he limped when he moved. His brawny forearms were heavily tattooed. The compass rose and braided rope curled around his massive wrist told Woods this man had spent time in the navy. And the anchor suggested he'd crossed the Atlantic at least once.

Big Jim had his back to them as they approached. He was hollering at a bargee who was opening the lock gates. 'Put yer back into it, man! I've seen more strength in a cabin boy!'

Dora waited until he noticed her, then she held out a small package in her hand. 'I got yer baccy, Jim. You owe me tuppence.'

'Thank you, Dora.'

She pulled a small jar out of her pocket and gave it to him. 'I've got another salve fer yer shoulder pain. It's arnica and comfrey.'

'I hope it don't smell as bad as the last one,' he said.

She smiled. 'No. There ain't no turmeric in this one.'

The man's unsmiling eyes flicked over Woods and Betsy. Beneath the dust, his thick unruly hair was pure white, a stark contrast to the wrinkled and creased brown leather of his face. 'These your new lodgers?'

Dora took another puff of her pipe. 'Aye, this is Mr and Mrs Woods, and these pretty gals are Miss Rachel and Miss Tabitha.'

The big fella scowled when the two girls inched closer to the lock edge to peer down at the barge and the greasy black water below. 'They won't be so pretty if they fall in and get themselves crushed between the wall and a barge.'

Woods bristled at the fella's attitude - and Betsy pulled the girls back.

'I'm sure they'll 'ave more sense than that, Jim,' Dora said. 'They've grown up by the river in Southwark.'

'And no walkin' across the locks to get to the other side,' the old fella snapped at the girls. 'If you fall in, I ain't divin' in after you.'

'We're not cork-brains,' Rachel told him angrily.

He grunted and turned back to watch the barge exit his lock.

'What's the fishin' like in these parts?' Woods asked.

Big Jim shrugged. 'It ain't bad towards Osterley Lock' he said over his shoulder, 'but pull your line in before a barge gets to you or they'll tek it and yer rod with them. Bargees with cargo don't give a damn.'

Woods thanked him, and Dora led them across another bridge and on to the opposite bank of the canal. Tabitha skipped happily beside her. 'Is Mr Kilby a pirate?' she asked. 'He's got a lot of tattoos.'

Smiling, they soon left the shadows of the high buildings. Clear blue sky, with its bobbing white clouds, spread over them along with the warmth of the sun. With every step they took away from Brentford, the air became cleaner and the noise abated.

The edge of the canal was lush with its summer greenness. A low wall separated the tow path from a well-tended market garden where vegetables bloomed in rows. There was still a niff arising from the sluggish, oily waters of the canal, but it was overwhelmed by the heady smell of the rich loam.

'I can smell apples!' Rachel announced, pointing to an ancient orchard on the opposite bank, the gnarled boughs of the trees weighed down with summer fruit. Her voice alarmed a grey heron that had stood unseen on the opposite bank. It unfurled its huge wings and rose into the sky.

Alfie Bobbin, who'd had his little nose to the ground, happily sniffing at a huge pile of horse manure, suddenly turned into a wolf. He leapt into the canal after the huge bird. But the cold shocked him. Whimpering, he turned back but was unable to scramble up the steep bank.

Woods dropped to his knees to scoop the frightened little animal out of the cut.

'Put him on his leash, Ned,' Betsy said, smiling.

Where there were herons, Woods thought, there were fish. This might be a good place to set up his rod.

Maybe Brentford weren't so bad after all?

Their lodgings were lovely. The Butts lived up to Cousin Dora's glowing description. It was a quiet, clean and pretty place of broad, leafy tree-lined streets full of small brick-built houses with bow windows.

Their cottage was at the end of a row. It was small: just three rooms stacked on top of each other and joined with a twisting wooden staircase, but it was clean and comfortably furnished. Woods put down their heavy bags and sank gratefully into a well-upholstered armchair by the fireplace.

Betsy was delighted. 'It's perfect, Cousin Dora! Thank you.'

'If you don't favour Brentford for your provisions, there's Ealing just up the road, along Windmill Lane.'

'Thank you. I might go there tomorrow to see a friend.'

'I've left you a packet of tea, a loaf, some milk and there's coal in the yard fer cookin',' Dora told them. 'I can stay a while and read your tea leaves, if you'd like? I only charge thruppence.'

Betsy politely declined.

'Well, 'ave a good evenin'. I'll pop round with some apple cider later. If you mix it with vinegar, it should ease your dog's mange. I live just over the square in the end 'ouse wi' the large garden. If I'm not 'ome, my gal Flora will be.' She turned to Woods and gave him a flash of her yellow teeth as she smiled. 'Are yer fishin' tomorrow, Neddy? Or will you visit yer friend as well?'

Before Woods could answer, Rachel said: 'Da's got business in Brentford. He needs to find a very old man.'

Dora arched a black and suspicious eyebrow. 'Be this police business? Alby told me yer were a runner.'

'No,' Woods replied. 'I'm havin' a rest from that.'

'The old man's called Woods,' Rachel said, 'same as us.'

Dora laughed and winked. 'Ah, a family matter then. Well, there's an old chap called Woody squattin' in one of them ruined weatherboarded cottages you saw back at the lock. Do you reckon 'e'll be the one yer after?'

Woods smiled and stretched out his legs. 'I don't know. Maybe in a couple of days I'll pay him a visit and find out.'

Chapter Six

'Only three days? Magistrate Conant wants you back in Bow Street after only three days?'

Doctor Morton's face creased with anxiety as he sat back on the scuffed leather seats of the hackney carriage they'd hired to take them to Newgate. 'He must have a lot of faith in your ability if he thinks you can solve this dreadful mystery so fast.'

Lavender smiled and glanced out of the window at the familiar sights and sounds of Covent Garden: the heaving crowds and the bellowing hawkers at their stalls on the side of the street. Dray horses strained as they hauled the heavy wagons laden with fruit and vegetables. Straw drifted over the filthy cobbles in the slight breeze. 'We're lucky he's permitted me to come to Ealing. He likes to keep me close. Now, tell me more about your brother.'

Morton sighed heavily before he began. 'My father died when I was twelve and a few years later my mother married again. Mark was born soon after that. The age difference between us meant we weren't close as children. He was five when I left home for medical school – but he was always a sweet child, and I loved him dearly.

'After I qualified as a surgeon, I spent many years working in Manchester. I saw very little of Mark as he grew up, but I visited Ealing occasionally, and my mother kept me informed of Mark's progress through Cambridge and his first years at work. She also told me of the deep attachment he'd developed for one of our neighbours, Clara Daniels, whom I knew to be a lovely young woman.'

'Why didn't they marry?'

'Her father intervened; he wouldn't give permission for their union. He didn't feel Mark was good enough for her.'

Lavender raised his eyebrows. 'How so?'

'Old man Daniels was a wealthy man after his time in India – a self-made man – a *nabob*, I believe they're called? Clara was due to inherit a fortune. Daniels didn't want any man to live off his daughter's money.'

'After he left Cambridge, Mark had trouble settling to a career. He tried a few professions like the law and accountancy but didn't relish any of them and drifted in and out of employment. In short, he…' Morton struggled with the next words. 'He lacks ambition.'

Lavender thought of his own little Alice and his own hopes for her future. 'I can understand that, to some extent,' he said gently. 'All fathers want their daughters to marry a man with good prospects and financial independence.'

'There was more to it than that. John Daniels was the most controlling man I've ever met; he kept his children on a tight rein. In the end, he gave Mark and Clara an ultimatum. He'd found a lucrative position for Mark with the East India Company in his former office in Calcutta. He told Mark if he did well, he could return in a year and claim Clara for his bride.'

'So, Daniels held a carrot over his head.'

'Yes, and both of them were too naïve to realise Daniels was playing a double game.'

'How so?

'The Reverend Thomas Langford had already arrived in Ealing. He was a widower with two small daughters. He'd impressed the old man with his determination, piety and ambition. He impresses everyone. I understand he's a great favourite of the Bishop, and there's a rumour Langford has one eye on the Bishop's mitre and wants one for himself. With Daniels' blessing, Langford began to court Clara when Mark left England.'

'How do you know this if you were in Manchester?'

'I'd come back to Ealing with my daughter to set up my practice. My own wife and my stepfather had died. My mother was ailing; it made sense to return.'

Lavender nodded, sympathetically.

'But Mark was back within a few months,' Morton continued. He'd barely set foot on the Indian subcontinent before he contracted malaria and became seriously ill. The East India Company shipped him back home.'

Lavender grimaced and thought of the suffering Ashfield must have endured – and would still endure. Newgate was one of the vilest and most brutal gaols in England. It was no place for any man – never mind a sick one. 'Has he made a good recovery?'

Morton shook his head. 'He has recurring bouts of the fever, which lay him low. He bears it bravely, but his health is frail, and I doubt he'll ever be able to hold down a professional position again.'

'Daniels told Clara she might as well marry the vicar because he'd never let her wed my brother. She was distraught, and pleaded with her father to change his mind, but he threatened to cut her out of his will unless she obeyed him.'

'So, she married the Reverend Langford because her father made her?'

'In short, yes. But Mark did the honourable thing. He knew he'd come back from India half the man he was when he left England, and he would spend the rest of his life as a semi-invalid. He released Clara from her promise and told her to find happiness elsewhere – with his blessing. They became great friends. Her father passed away soon after her marriage.'

'That's all very romantic, Doctor,' Lavender said slowly. 'But I wonder how the vicar felt, knowing his wife was in love with another man.'

Morton chose his words carefully. 'A wealthy wife is a great asset to any man with ambition, whether his ambitions lie within the Church or elsewhere.'

'Do you suspect he married Miss Daniels for her money?'

Morton shook his head. 'I can't say. That's between the vicar and his conscience.'

'You said your brother had come back from the East Indies only *half a man.* In your medical opinion, can *half a man* still father a child?'

Morton's face wrinkled in disgust. 'I don't like your suggestion, Lavender – but I understand why you've asked. Yes, Mark could still father a child. But he didn't. That baby girl is the vicar's child.'

As far as you know, Lavender thought.

Their carriage slowed as it approached the overcrowded streets around Smithfield market. Ahead, the great dome of St Paul's Cathedral bulged into the sky behind the grim and menacing façade of Newgate prison.

'Who benefits financially from Mrs Langford's death? Who will receive the rest of the inheritance she gained from her father?'

Morton sighed, his eyes fixed on the prison gates ahead. 'John Daniels split his money equally between his three children but left the family home, The Laurels, to his elder daughter, Elizabeth. She'd moved home after her husband died. On her death, the house is to pass to her own son. Daniels was fond of his grandson.'

'What about Mrs Langford's brother, Frederick? How did he feel about this?'

'Father and son had a poor relationship. Frederick Daniels wasn't happy with this arrangement about the house, which he felt should have been his. But there was nothing he could do about it. He has the money his father left for him in trust. And it's a tightly controlled trust, which only pays out a fixed amount at certain times of the year.'

'And does the Reverend Langford inherit his wife's share of this trust?'

'No. Daniels made it quite clear in his will that if either of his two youngest children, Frederick or Clara, died without a male heir, their share was to be divided between the other siblings.'

Lavender's eyebrows rose in surprise. 'So, Mr Langford doesn't inherit a penny of his wife's money? And her baby daughter won't benefit from it either?'

'No. It reverts back to Elizabeth and Frederick.'

'You do realise, don't you, this gives them both a strong motive for murder?'

Morton nodded, and his tired brown eyes stared back at Lavender, full of concern.

'Where were these siblings at the time of their sister's death?'

'I don't know. I don't think the constable asked them. But Lavender, don't waste your time investigating Elizabeth. She's a wonderful woman who was fond of her sister.'

Lavender raised a cynical eyebrow but kept his thoughts to himself.

The carriage had stopped in the dark shadows cast by the grim and imposing walls of the squalid gaol. Lavender braced himself for the stench, squalor and misery he knew lay ahead. Morton had already pulled his handkerchief out of his coat pocket and rolled it into a ball, ready to cover his nose.

Lavender reached for the door handle, then hesitated and turned back. 'Why did Daniels have a poor relationship with his son?'

'Frederick has no ambition. He's content to live the indolent life of a country gentleman, which infuriated his father.'

'And?'

'He lives his life beyond his income. He's only one step ahead of the bailiffs and debtors' gaol. His gambling debts made his father despair.'

Doctor Morton had paid for a small private cell in the gaol for his brother, with a high window, a narrow pallet bed and a desk and wooden chair. But the privacy didn't shield Mark Ashfield from the horrors of Newgate. The window was barred, but unglazed. The screams of the insane, the angry murmur of brutal and bestial men and the desperate cries of tortured souls still drifted through. And the vile stench of Newgate, a horrific mix of urine, faeces, unwashed bodies and desperation, rose from the damp straw on the cell floor and seeped through the heavy studded door every time it opened.

It wasn't cold in the cell; a small fire burned in the grate, but Ashfield sat on the bed, shivering beneath a thin blanket.

Morton crouched down beside his brother, opened his bag and pulled out a flask of red wine. 'Here, drink this. It's laced with quinine.'

While Ashfield uncorked the bottle and lifted it to his lips with a shaking hand, Lavender observed him.

Ashfield had once been a good-looking fair-haired man with excellent bone structure, high cheekbones and a strong, square jaw. But malaria, grief and the insanitary conditions of Newgate had ravaged his features. His yellowing skin clung tightly to his face, neck and hands, and made him skeletal. His clothes hung loosely from his emaciated frame. His sad eyes, the same soft brown as those of his brother, glanced curiously at Lavender.

Morton gave the man his coat to wear on top of his own, sat down beside him on the pallet and explained Lavender's presence.

Ashfield gave a short hollow laugh. 'You should have saved your money, brother. There's no help for me now. Even the great Detective Lavender can't save me. They'll hang me for killing Clara – and I'll be glad to join her in death.'

'Don't talk like that!' Morton snapped. 'God damn it, man! If you stop fighting for justice, it'll just make you look guilty.'

Lavender pulled out the chair from the desk and sat facing them both. 'There's always hope. But I can't make you any promises except to investigate this case thoroughly. I'll do my best to find out the truth.'

'You're wasting your time. If the hangman doesn't get me, the fever will.'

'But I'm not only doing it for *you* – I'm also doing it for Mrs Langford,' Lavender reassured him.

'You want justice for Clara, don't you, Mark?' Morton asked.

The distraught prisoner didn't reply. Lavender took this as an affirmative.

'Right, let's start at the beginning. What time did you arrive at the vicarage, what happened and why were you there?'

Ashfield shivered again beneath his blanket. His brother put a comforting arm around his thin shoulders.

'It was about ten o'clock in the morning. I was desperate to have a quiet word with Clara. I knew she'd been melancholic since the birth of her child. There'd… there'd also been some unpleasant rumours spread in the village. I wanted to make sure she was well and offer her my help and support.'

Lavender nodded. 'Your brother explained to me the nature of those rumours. Did you know the Reverend Langford was away from home that day?'

Ashfield nodded. 'Yes. That's why I went to see her then. Langford had made it plain I wasn't welcome at the vicarage because of my past association with Clara. Sometimes we'd meet socially at other people's houses or while walking through the village. But I hadn't seen Clara for weeks and was worried about her.'

'Did you see anyone else outside the vicarage? Their maid claimed she saw someone lurking under a tree. Or was that you, waiting for the right moment to knock at the door?'

Ashfield gave another hollow laugh. 'I'm not devious, Detective. I simply tied my horse to the gatepost and walked up the path to the front door. But before I raised the knocker, the door flew open, and the wet nurse ran out into me.'

'What happened next?'

'I spoke to Flora, and she led me up to Clara's sitting room. When Flora left to fetch a new wet nurse, Clara and I sat and talked.'

'Did this maid bring you refreshment? A pot of tea, perhaps?'

'No. Clara offered me tea, but I knew she was desperate for the wet nurse, so I refused, and Flora left us to fetch her.'

'Why is this relevant, Lavender?' Morton asked.

'I need to know if Mrs Langford ate or drank anything else that morning besides the kippers she had for breakfast and the water in the glass.'

Morton nodded. 'Of course. Please carry on.'

'How long did you stay with Mrs Langford?'

'Only about forty minutes. After this, the baby woke up from her slumber, crying for nourishment. Clara struggled to calm her and became distressed. She asked me to leave, and I did. I felt helpless; there was nothing I could do.'

'Had the maid returned at that point?'

'No.'

'So, you left sometime around eleven o'clock?'

'Yes, I heard the church clock chime the hour when I rode away.' His face creased with emotion. 'I keep thinking that if I'd stayed longer to help her with the infant... she wouldn't be dead.' He bowed his head once more and covered his face with his hands. 'I can't sleep at night when I imagine her suffering.'

'Was Mrs Langford in good health when you left?'

'Yes, she was well. Upset about the baby – but well.'

'And where was she when you last saw her?'

'In her sitting room, with the baby.'

'Not in her bedchamber, where they found her body?'

'No.'

'Did you see her drink the glass of water by her bedside?'

Ashfield looked shocked. 'I never went into her bedchamber!'

'Did she go into that room? What about when the infant was crying? Did she return to her bedchamber to pick up the child?'

'No, she'd already placed little Ruth into a rocking crib in the parlour with us. She was sound asleep when I first arrived.'

'Where did you go when you left the vicarage?'

'I rode my horse for a while; it needed exercising. Then I returned home. I didn't learn about Clara's death until several hours later when Clive' – he pointed to his brother – 'came to tell me about the tragedy. I was distraught.'

He paused for a moment, then added: 'The constable called at the house to interview me the next day. I told him everything I've just told you.' Ashfield's teeth chattered.

Morton rose and poured more coals on the fire in the grate.

'He... he asked me to make myself available for... for the inquest, which I did. I realise now I was... was the last person to see Clara alive. But I never expected Sir James would turn on me and have me arrested!'

'Why did he think you'd killed Mrs Langford? What did he suggest motivated you to poison her?'

Confusion flickered over Ashfield's face, and he glanced at his brother for help.

'He said he thought it was a crime of passion,' Morton said. 'He suspected disappointment and unrequited love had poisoned Mark's mind and he'd poisoned Clara in revenge.'

Lavender sat back, faintly surprised. He had the sense he'd walked into the pages of a sentimental romantic novella.

'Everyone in the parish knew about Mark and Clara's unresolved love affair,' Morton added.

Lavender rolled his eyes. 'I doubt the prosecuting counsel will be able to make a convincing case with a motive as weak as that. The lawyers at the Old Bailey are notoriously unsentimental and callous.'

'So… do you think… I… I've a chance of an acquittal?'

Lavender nodded. Ashfield was exhausted and suffering. He knew he'd have to end the interview soon. 'Yes, I think you stand a good chance of an acquittal – but it would be even better if I uncovered the real murderer. I just have one last question for you, Mr Ashfield. Is there anything else you remember about that morning? Anything unusual, or out of the ordinary?'

The two brothers glanced at each other.

Then Morton said, 'I'll tell him, Mark. You save your energy. There's only one thing, Lavender – which neither of us understands. When Mark spoke to Flora, she told me the wet nurse had stolen a silver cup before she left the house. She wanted Mark to go after her, but the damned woman had already disappeared in the fog.'

'This is the same woman who had just been dismissed by Mrs Langford? The one who's vanished?'

'That's right. But when Mark told the constable this, the vicar checked the cabinet and said there was nothing missing. The girl was mistaken.'

Chapter Seven

Sebastián was grateful when Rachel and her parents turned up at Cedar Court unexpectedly.

He badly missed his school chums and needed company of his own age. Rachel was two years younger than him, but they'd always had an easy friendship. She liked doing the same things as him and in so many ways she was as good as a boy – especially when it came to playing cricket.

Within minutes, they'd slipped away from the adults and set off to explore Ealing.

It didn't take long; it was a small village. They soon got bored of skimming stones in the duck-pond. The slow, meandering River Brent was a dull place, and the village seemed to consist of miles of cobbled lanes lined with high impenetrable brick walls, behind which stood dozens of large houses or orchards where the tree boughs drooped under the weight of juicy fruit.

Now, the children were hot and thirsty – and the smell of the forbidden fruit was tantalising. The sweet scent made Sebastián's stomach tighten with hunger.

All they needed was a few loose stones – or – please God – a gate.

'There!' Rachel broke into a run, and it took him a moment to understand what she'd seen.

Fifty yards ahead, the lane turned to dry, parched earth and widened to veer round the thick trunk of a gnarled oak. Its leafy branches reached out over the orchard wall.

He caught up with her at the base of the trunk and his heart fell with disappointment when he saw the height of the lowest branches. 'We'll never climb that.'

'We will if we work together. Give me a leg up.'

He laced his fingers together, then grunted as she raised her boot into his hands and transferred her weight on to that foot. He pushed her upwards as hard as he could.

Rachel hauled herself on to her stomach on the lowest bough and inched forward. A small flock of starlings who'd been sheltering from the sun among the branches rose wheeling into the cloudless sky, squawking out their indignation at the intrusion.

It was only when Rachel's flailing boots and stockinged ankles disappeared over the wall into the dense foliage of the tree that he suddenly felt a guilty pang of responsibility. She was two years younger than him; he should be up there, not her. 'Be careful, Rachel. Your Pa will belt me if you fall out and hurt yourself.'

A muffled, unladylike snort came out of the rustling leaves. 'He ain't ever belted anyone.'

There's always a first time, Sebastián thought.

Rachel called out again: 'I can reach some of the apples. Be ready! I'll throw them over.'

'Just don't fall!' Sebastián braced himself and, when the apples began to fly over the wall, he caught them with a precision that would have impressed his cricket master.

'That's enough. Shuffle back.'

The leaves rustled again, and Rachel's boots reappeared. Her stockings were snagged and torn to shreds.

Suddenly, there were shouts and the sound of a large dog barking.

'Heaven and hell! There's someone comin'!' Rachel yelled.

He held up his arms to help her down. But she let go too soon and caught him a glancing blow on his chest with her boot when she fell.

He yelped with pain but stood his ground, caught her round the waist and broke her fall. They shoved the apples into their pockets, then raced towards the end of the lane. Their feet pounded on the dry earth as loudly as his thumping heart. He risked a furtive glance over his shoulder. No one had followed them.

The lane opened out on to the meandering riverbank. They went around a bend and threw themselves, laughing, into the long, sweet grass beneath the shade of a tree.

For the next few minutes they devoured their prize in silence, listening to the song of the crickets in the tall grass rising and falling in the summer heat. They attracted the attention of a group of ducks, who paddled lazily towards them.

Apart from a young boy in a ragged shirt, with a fishing rod, there was no one else around.

'We're eating the evidence of our crime,' he said, grinning. 'Even our fathers wouldn't be able to clap us in irons now.'

She smiled back. 'You've got juice dribblin' down your chin. That'll give you away.' Her faded summer dress was filthy, and she had leaves and twigs stuck in her curly hair. 'Do you want to be a detective like your pa?'

He shook his head. 'No, I want to join the army and fight for my country.'

She gave him a wry sideways glance. 'Which country? Spain or England?'

He tutted. 'I shall enlist in the best army in the world – the British army of Field Marshal Wellington. I've already told Pa I want him to buy me a pair of colours when I finish school.'

'What did he say?'

Sebastián shrugged. 'Well, he didn't say "no". He just listened, nodded, muttered something about Cambridge, and said we'd talk later when I was older.'

'Do you ever think about your other pa – the soldier who died?'

'Not really. I can barely remember him. Mamá doesn't talk about him much. But I know he was a great soldier who fought alongside General Cuesta. He died a hero at the battle of Talavera.' He paused for a moment, wistfully imagining the glory and pride this brought to a man. 'Mamá says he was a handsome fellow, so I must take after him.'

Rachel laughed and elbowed him in the ribs. He was about to push her back when the scruffy boy with the fishing rod approached them. Skinny, with dark-brown hair, he was shading his huge blue eyes against the sunlight with a grubby hand. He had a length of frayed rope tied round his waist, holding up his breeches.

'I say, would you fellows mind sharing your apples? It's like a blacksmith's furnace out here today and I'm parched.'

Rachel smiled, tossed him an apple and patted the grass beside her. 'It's better in the shade. Have you caught any fish?'

The boy sank down beside them and shook his head. 'No, they're not biting today. I say! These are *excellent* apples. Where did you get them?'

Their new friend had an educated speaking voice, Sebastián noted, despite his filthy and ragged appearance. He waved his hand back in the direction of the orchard they'd raided.

'Oooh!' the boy said. 'That's Farmer Gilbert's land – he'll skin you alive if he catches you.'

'They're worth it,' Rachel said. 'I just wish we'd got more.'

'Are you still hungry? Would you like some juicy plums?'

Rachel and Sebastián nodded in surprise.

'Then come with me.'

When they stood up. Sebastián saw the boy was slightly taller than Rachel. He guessed he was about thirteen.

'I'm Bruce, by the way. Bruce Charlton.'

Sebastián held out his hand. 'This is Miss Rachel Woods and I'm Sebastián García de Aviles Morales del Castillo.' He let the name hang for a second until he saw the respect and awe wash over the younger boy's face. 'But my friends call me García.'

'May *I* call you García?' Bruce asked.

'You may.' The two of them shook hands solemnly while Rachel rolled her eyes.

Bruce led them back into the maze of narrow lanes and paths that wound through the market gardens and orchards of Ealing. Eventually, he stopped next to a low, broken wall. 'A farm wagon took the corner badly and knocked this wall down last week.'

On the other side of the loose stones and damaged masonry stood rows of low trees, all laden with clusters of fat plums. Against the dark leaves of the plant, their smooth skins were every shade of purple, amethyst and crimson. A few plums, too ripe to cling any longer, had fallen to the ground, their soft flesh split open. Bees hummed lazily around the fallen fruit, drunk on the sugar.

‘They look like jewels!’ Rachel exclaimed. She started to scramble over the broken wall.

But Sebastián grabbed her arm and pointed up the slope to the farm buildings, whose windows looked directly out at the orchard. ‘What about the farmer?’

‘Don’t worry about him. He knows me,’ Bruce said. He clambered over the wall and reached up to the nearest tree. His fingers curled around a warm plum and, with a careful twist, he snapped it free and handed it to Rachel. He removed a second plum and tossed it to Sebastián. ‘This is one of our tenant farms.’

Sebastián laughed. ‘No offence, Bruce old chap – but you’re jesting with us, surely? You don’t look like a country gentleman.’

Bruce smiled. ‘What are they supposed to look like?’

‘I don’t know. Fat? Gouty? Dressed in hunting scarlet with a pack of beagles sniffing at their heels?’

Bruce’s smile widened. ‘You’ve mistook me for my grandfather. He was like that. But he’s dead now and the estate belongs to us. Well, to my mother – but I’ll inherit it next.’

Rachel paused in her eating. A trail of golden juice was already snaking down her chin. ‘I’m sad to learn of your Grandpa’s demise, Bruce. What happened to your father?’

The boy shrugged and snapped off another plum for himself. ‘He’s dead too – a long time ago. But he never liked Ealing and the countryside.’

‘How sad,’ Rachel said.

Sebastián smiled to himself and bit down on the plum. The skin split instantly, and juice flooded his tongue, sweet and tart all at once.

Their new friend was a good storyteller, he decided. It happened sometimes when you lost a parent when you were very young: you made things up – especially about the dead parent. He’d seen it so often among his bereaved school chums; they invented a fantasy world. He was glad he’d never been tempted to do that.

‘What about you?’ Bruce asked shyly. ‘Why are you in Ealing?’

'We're visiting the area with our families,' Sebastián replied. 'Rachel is here with her parents. I'm here with Mamá. My Pa – sorry, my stepfather – is back in London, working.'

'Oh, so you've got a stepfather, have you? Is he good to you?'

Sebastián nodded. 'Yes, Pa's a decent man.'

'Do you think your ma will marry again?' Rachel asked.

Bruce shrugged his thin shoulders. 'It's hard to tell. The doctor keeps calling on her. But she likes animals best and she doesn't like men much. Apart from me,' he added with a beaming smile. 'She likes me.'

Sebastián nodded wisely. 'Stepfathers can be tricky. Lots of my school friends have them. If your mother wants another husband, tell her to get one like mine. He sort of disappears into the background, but he listens when I want to tell him something. He can be a bit dry and prefers reading books to playing cricket—'

Bruce's eyes lit up in delight. 'Cricket! Do you play cricket?'

'Yes, is there any chance of a game?'

'Yes. I attend the Great Ealing School.' Bruce's words poured out in excitement. 'I'm a day pupil because I live so close, but most of the chaps are boarders and have gone home for the summer. But there's a few still here, whose parents are abroad or dead or something. I can organise a game.'

Sebastián smiled again. Lady Caroline and Captain Sawyer had told his mother about Great Ealing School last night over dinner. They'd said it was a good school – on a par academically with Eton. He didn't think it was the kind of place that would let in pupils who were the sons of common farmers.

But if Bruce could rustle up a few boys for a game of cricket, he didn't care if they were farm boys or urchins from the back streets of Brentford.

For the next few minutes, they munched on the fruit and made their plans.

'Naturally, Rachel shall be on my team,' Sebastián concluded.

Bruce's large blue eyes widened in surprise. He turned to Rachel. 'You play cricket?'

'Yes, she's quite a hoyden,' Sebastián said. 'You should see her on horseback. She rides like a neck or nothing.'

'You'd be surprised what girls can do,' Rachel said dryly. 'We're every bit as good as you boys.'

A loud whistle suddenly rent the air. The children spun around.

Two swarthy men in dirty black coats were standing in the dusty lane on the other side of the wall, gesturing to them to come back to the road.

'*¡Aquí! ¡Ven aquí!*' one of them called.

'Who are they?' Rachel whispered.

'Vagrants,' Bruce said. 'We get a lot of beggars.'

'Vagrants?' she queried. 'They sound like Frenchies to me. Are you sure they're not escaped war prisoners?'

'*¡Ven aquí!*' The man raised his voice angrily.

'They want us to go to them. Do they want our plums?'

'Don't trust them,' Bruce said quietly. 'If they climb over the wall – run to the farmhouse.'

The children braced themselves and stared defiantly at the gesturing foreigners.

A horrific and guttural animal scream suddenly rent the peaceful air of the orchard. Starlings flew out of the trees, screeching. Sebastián's blood turned to ice at the sound of cloven hooves clattering at great speed along the cobbles of the lane towards the two men.

The men spun around and recoiled in shock. One yelled: '*Jabalí!*' Then they turned and ran.

The creature let out another great roar.

Rachel grabbed Sebastián's arm. 'What is it?'

'Don't worry,' Bruce said calmly. 'It's only Boris. He must have broken out of his pen again.'

A huge head, a hulking mass of muscle and bristled fur, appeared above the low wall. Small, deep-set eyes burned like embers beneath a heavy, furrowed brow as it observed the children. Its tusks, long and wickedly curved, jutted from its lower jaw, yellowed with age and sharpened by years of rooting and fighting.

'Gawd's teeth!' Rachel clutched his arm tighter. 'I've never seen such a big pig!'

The creature exhaled a snort, sending a spray of dust and spit into the air, and its nostrils twitched as it caught the sweet scent of the fruit.

'He won't hurt you. He's just hungry. He's a wild boar – but he's tamed now,' Bruce explained.

Sebastián stood his ground. His heart was pounding like the pistons in the looms of a cotton mill, but he was determined not to show any fear in front of the younger boy.

The animal heaved its huge bulk over the tumbled-down wall on its thick and powerful legs, and the hairs stood up on the back of Sebastián's neck.

'I didn't know they could climb,' he said, alarmed.

Bruce reached up and snapped off clusters of the fruit. He threw them into a pile between them and the approaching boar. 'Once he's eaten, I'll wrap this rope round his neck, and we'll lead him home. He often gets out and is tame as a poodle when his belly is full. My mother rescued him from a travelling menagerie.'

The animal was gorging on the fallen fruit at the base of the first trees in the row. His whiskery snout disturbed the bees, who flew upwards in an irritated cloud. It grunted constantly.

Rachel went to help Bruce add to his pile of fruit. But Sebastián's eyes were still on the lane beyond the wall, where the foreigners had stood.

His mouth twitched with amusement. 'So, your mother is a pig farmer, is she?'

Bruce stopped for a moment to contemplate this question. The young boy had an even temper, Sebastián realised. It wouldn't be easy to rile him.

'I suppose so, but she has dozens of animals, including a zebra.'

'A zebra!'

'Yes, she rescued it from the same travelling fair.'

'Can you ride a zebra?'

'I don't know. We haven't tried. It runs free with the horses.' The boar moved closer. 'The show man claimed Boris was a wild boar from France, but Mama says he's too small and light to be pure bred – and his ears are too small.'

'*Small?*' Rachel's voice was sharp with disbelief.

'Yes, Mama thinks his mother was a domestic farmyard sow.'

'In the shade of the lane, he must have looked darker,' Sebastián said thoughtfully. 'Those Spaniards thought he was a wild boar.'

'Spaniards?'

'Yes. He said "*Jabalí!*". That's the Spanish word for a wild boar. They called out to us in Spanish too.'

'What are Spaniards doing in Ealing?'

Sebastián stared back at the lane, then shrugged. 'I don't know.'

Chapter Eight

Lavender breathed in deeply when he stepped outside the prison on to the cobbles of Smithfield market.

Newgate always left him feeling dirty and contaminated. The air in his nostrils and even in his lungs seemed rank. Instinctively, he brushed the dust off his coat. The turnkey slammed the studded and spiked gate shut behind them.

Not that Smithfield meat market smelled any better than Newgate. The cobbles here were always smeared with dung, animal fat and blood from the slaughter. But at least the ferrous tinge of the blood was better than the stench of despair that seeped out of the damp stone of Newgate.

The two men hailed a hackney carriage, clambered aboard and sank back in the cracked leather seats.

Morton looked wretched. 'I've not seen him so ill since he first returned from India,' he said. 'I fear he might not survive long enough to be tried – never mind hanged.'

Lavender nodded. 'I'll do my best to bring this case to a speedy resolution.'

'Are you convinced of his innocence now you've met him?'

'I'm convinced of his naivety and romantic nature,' Lavender said cautiously. 'Staying alone in the vicarage with a married woman – whom he loved – was inappropriate and a mistake. It may prejudice the jury against him. However, such foolishness doesn't make him a murderer.'

Morton sighed with relief and nodded.

'Tell me again, Doctor, what time did Frederick Daniels come to your house to fetch you, and what was the scene when you arrived at the vicarage? I need to work out a timeline of the events.'

'It was after one o'clock – perhaps a quarter after the hour? Daniels and Langford had arrived together at the vicarage about one o'clock.'

'Why was Daniels there?'

'He wanted to see his sister, so Langford went upstairs to tell her she had a visitor. That's when he found his wife dead on the bed and Daniels rushed over to fetch me. I live five minutes away. I grabbed my medical bag and went back with Daniels.'

'And where was the infant when you got there?'

'She was downstairs with the maid and her sister, the new wet nurse.'

'What about the Langfords' two young daughters?'

Morton shook his head. 'They're little girls. They were in the school room over at Boston Manor. Lady Clitherow lets the vicar's daughters share their governess.'

'What time did the two women – the maid and her sister – return to the house? Were they already there when Daniels and Langford arrived?'

Morton sighed. 'Initially, the maid said she'd left her mistress alone with Mark for just half an hour—'

'Which doesn't fit with your brother's account.'

'No. When the constable challenged her version the next day, she changed her story. Apparently, she'd struggled to find her sister. She'd been absent from the vicarage for over two hours. The two women arrived back just before the vicar returned.'

'Presumably, this maid and the new wet nurse went straight upstairs to see Mrs Langford and the baby. Why didn't they discover her body?'

'Everything was quiet upstairs when they returned. She assumed Mrs Langford and the baby were asleep. She took her sister into the kitchen and made a pot of tea.'

'Quiet?' Lavender exclaimed. 'There was a starving child in that bedroom. Babies aren't quiet when they're hungry. This doesn't make sense.' His eyes narrowed as a new thought leapt into his mind. 'Did you examine the baby, doctor? Had it been hurt in any way?'

Morton nodded. 'I gave the child a cursory examination and established she was unhurt. To be honest, Lavender, I was distracted by the dead woman and my suspicions about the poison. It was only later I realised the infant was unnaturally sleepy. I think she'd been drugged to keep her quiet.'

'Drugged!'

'Yes, possibly with laudanum. Mrs Langford had a small supply, which I'd left for her. She may have administered the drops herself, while waiting for the new wet nurse to arrive.'

'Isn't it dangerous to give laudanum to tiny infants?'

Morton looked uncomfortable. 'Yes, too much could be fatal.'

'Were you able to establish a time of death for Mrs Langford?'

'Post-mortem rigidity had already begun to stiffen her joints and the bruising from livor mortis was visible to the naked eye on her back. She'd been dead at least two hours by the time I examined her at half past one. Mark claims he left the vicarage about eleven o'clock. I think she was murdered soon after that.'

If Mark has told the truth, Lavender thought. 'Did you mention the issue of the drugged baby at the inquest?'

Morton shook his head. 'I didn't think it was relevant to the murder inquiry and – to be honest – I wanted to protect Clara's reputation. The poor woman had been through enough.'

'What do you mean?'

'I didn't want her remembered as a woman who drugged her child, like one of those vile creatures who run baby farms for profit.'

'Which brings us back to that disreputable wet nurse. The woman who's vanished. Women like her will know exactly how much laudanum to administer to quieten a child.'

Their carriage slowed as it approached the doctor's lodgings. 'I'll see you in Ealing soon, Doctor, but I've one last question: you said you'd also received one of these poisonous letters. What did yours say?'

Morton pulled a fragile and folded sheet of cheap white paper out of his pocket. 'I meant to give it to you earlier when we were in Magistrate Conant's office.'

Lavender took the paper, unfolded it and read:

MORTON THOU ART A NIM GLIMMER A FAKE QUACK WITH AN ICE TONG WHO CUTS THE MUFFS OF HARLOTS AND SCRAPES OUT THE BASTARD TO STIFLE THE SQUEAKER

Lavender frowned. 'An abortionist? This person accuses you of child murder?'

Morton nodded sadly. 'It arrived about six months ago. It's all nonsense, of course. I kept it for the same reason I kept the other one: I'd like this woman found and stopped. You must focus on clearing Mark's name – but if you stumble across the bitch who spews out this calumny during your investigation, I'd be grateful.'

Morton opened the door and left the carriage.

Lavender nodded and pocketed the note.

Everyone seems to assume it's a woman, he thought.

The grim, poorly lit entrance hall of Bow Street Magistrates' Court and Police Office heaved with activity. A motley crew of drunks, pickpockets and whores waited at the main desk with their arresting officers. Some of the manacled felons were slumped on the floor, others – mostly the whores – greased the flaking walls with the back of their filthy rags.

Lavender ignored the crush and the catcalls and climbed up the stairs two at a time to the magistrate's office.

'What's your impression of this case so far?' Conant asked.

'I've my doubts about the murder charge against Ashfield. He's a gentle soul – a bit of a cork-brain, but gentle. He's no clear motive for the murder. The motive suggested by Sir James Clitherow is ridiculous – I don't think it'll stand up in court once the jury see the accused, who's a sick man. Apparently, her siblings have the most to gain from her death; they're due to inherit the wealth she received from her father.'

'Not her husband?'

'No, the old man's will stipulated that his money stayed in his family. But of course, her husband also has a motive to kill her. Even the most devout vicar has his pride. That vile accusation of adultery must have upset him.'

Conant nodded. 'I agree. But deal with him gently, Lavender – the man has just lost his wife.'

'Yes, his second wife. Morton mentioned the first Mrs Langford died some years ago, before Langford obtained the living at Ealing. Can you contact your friend, the Bishop, and ask him about the circumstances of her death?'

Conant looked shocked but made a note of Lavender's request.

'We can't afford to assume anything, sir,' Lavender continued. 'I don't want to ignore any avenue of inquiry.'

'No one could ever accuse you of being a sentimental romantic, Lavender,' the magistrate said, as he made a note.

'To be honest, sir, I think there's something in the water at Ealing that has filled them *all* with romantic and sentimental notions – and Sir James Clitherow has drunk it too, hence his arrest of Mark Ashfield.'

Conant bristled at the criticism of his fellow magistrate but said: 'Don't offend Sir James. You'll have to meet with him to tell him about your investigation, and I've no idea if he'll be pleased to see you or find your intervention intrusive.'

'I understand. I also think Doctor Morton was half in love with the deceased woman. Do we know any surgeons in Manchester? Morton practised medicine in the town for years. I'd like to know some more about his background.'

Conant's black eyebrows rose in surprise. 'Our client won't expect you to investigate *him* – I'm not sure he'll like it.'

'All information is valuable in a case as complicated as this.'

'Your former employer, Magistrate Read, has a brother on the board of the Manchester Infirmary. He's in London now. I can write to them both, if it'll help?'

'Yes, sir, thank you. I'll stay at Cedar Court in Ealing while I'm there; it's the home of Captain Sawyer, a family friend. Please send any replies to me there.'

Conant made a note of the address and handed across a letter of introduction to Sir James Clitherow. Lavender rose to leave.

'Don't forget, Lavender – I want you back here in three days' time.'

Lavender's jaw tightened, but he said nothing and continued towards the door.

'And keep your wits about you – don't drink that damned water. Sentimental officers are no use to me.'

Chapter Nine

It was a journey of only ten miles to Ealing, but the traffic was heavy, and Lavender frequently had to pull his horse into the side of the road when coaches thundered up behind him. It wasn't until he turned north, past the vast estate of Gunnersbury Park, that he left the worst of the carriage congestion behind.

He relaxed and admired the scenery. The sun-baked road wound gently between hedgerows thick with wildflowers and brambles. Butterflies flitted from bloom to bloom, their wings catching the light, while bees droned drowsily among the foxgloves lining the verge.

On either side of the road, field after field of golden wheat swayed in slow, lazy waves, rustling in the slight breeze and shimmering in the heat. The scent of dry hay and sun-baked earth filled the air.

It was late in the afternoon by the time Lavender reached Ealing and its market gardens with their long, neat rows of vegetables and orchards.

To Lavender's delight, the first person he saw when he entered the picturesque village was Sebastián. His son was ambling along Windmill Lane, scything off the heads of wildflowers in the verge with a stick.

Lavender hailed him, dismounted from his horse and was pleased to see the warm grin of welcome on the boy's grubby, olive-skinned face.

'Mamá will be so pleased to see you!' Sebastián exclaimed. 'And little Alice. Can I ride your horse?'

'I'm here to work,' Lavender warned gently. He helped Sebastián up into the saddle. 'But I hope to enjoy some time with you all.' He took the reins and led the horse towards Cedar Court. His son was hot and sweaty, and there was a niff of the farmyard about him. Curiously, he also had a dirty boot print in the middle of his white shirt.

'Will you watch our cricket match? Our new friend Bruce is organising a couple of teams from boys still left at the school. I don't know how good they'll be, but I'll have Rachel on my side.'

Lavender stopped in surprise. 'Rachel? Rachel Woods? I thought they were supposed to be in Market Harborough.'

'No. There was a change of plan. The whole family is down the road in Brentford. Will you watch the match?'

'Of course I will.' This was good news, Lavender decided. A curious turn of events, but still good news. He knew Woods was having a much-needed break from work and wanted to spend time with his family. But if he had the time to spare, it would be good to talk about the case with Ned over a tankard of ale in a tavern. 'Are you enjoying your time here?'

'Oh yes. Captain Sawyer took me fishing the other day. It was a bit dull, and I didn't catch anything. Today was better. Bruce has a wild boar. We had to put a rope on it and take it home when it escaped. I saw the other strange animals his Mamá keeps, including a zebra.'

Lavender blinked and glanced up at his son to see if he was jesting. But his animated young face was sincere.

'They've got a menagerie at The Laurels,' Sebastián continued. 'Bruce and his mother love animals. Bruce says it'll all be his when his Ma passes on. He'll buy an elephant then.'

The Laurels? The home of Mrs Elizabeth Charlton? Lavender had a sudden twinge of unease about his son's association with this family. 'Did you meet Bruce's mother?'

'Yes, she's kind. She gave us refreshments once we returned Boris the boar. She's in mourning, of course, because her sister has just died, but she wasn't crying or anything like that.'

'Do she and Bruce live alone at The Laurels?'

'Yes. His Uncle Fred has to live in the gatehouse on the estate because his mother doesn't like him. She says he drinks too much. He's always complaining too – especially about the ostrich peering in at his window and crapping on his doorstep.'

A million questions were on the tip of Lavender's tongue, but he decided to let Sebastián's chatter flow. His son was at a difficult age now and had become rather languid – and argumentative – of late. Today his eyes were bright, and his skin flushed with excitement. He wasn't prone to lying or flights of fancy, so there must be some truth in this bizarre account of his day.

'I walked Rachel home to Brentford afterwards. We saw a couple of vagrants earlier and I thought it was best to accompany her.'

Lavender nodded. 'That was the right thing to do, son.' The end of the war had brought poverty and mass unemployment to Britain. Thousands of soldiers had returned to England to find there were no civilian jobs for them anymore. Vagrancy and crime were on the rise. It seemed even quiet, leafy Ealing wasn't immune.

'I heard them speak Spanish.'

Spanish?

But before Lavender could question Sebastián further, they'd turned a corner, and Cedar Court stood before them.

Two storeys high, with double-fronted bay windows and attic windows in the roof, the elegant house dated back to the early 1700s and was surrounded by a well-kept flower and vegetable garden. At the rear of the property, he saw the coach house and stables, and a building he thought might be a dairy.

'It's got seven bedrooms and a long gallery where Lady Caroline displays her paintings!' Sebastián informed him.

Lavender thought of Lady Caroline's cramped and cluttered apartment in Lincoln's Inn Fields and smiled. Twice widowed and left almost destitute by her second husband, she'd used her considerable talent to earn her living as a portrait artist but had still spent most of the last few years dodging her creditors. Her association with Captain Sawyer, who also owned a property in Portugal, had improved her comfort and lifestyle. The couple had recently returned from a lengthy stay in Portugal. Although what the good parishioners of Ealing thought about her – the daughter of an Earl living openly with the retired sea captain – was another matter.

'If I take your horse to the stable, will you tell Mamá I won't be in for dinner? I've got to get back; Bruce wants to show me the owls. Mrs Beavis the cook will feed me in the kitchen.'

Smiling, Lavender nodded.

Magdalena was in the sunny drawing room with the children. Her dark eyes lit up with joy when she saw him. They embraced warmly while little Alice clung on to his legs, begging to be lifted up. She was sleepy and already in her nightgown. He pulled her up into his arms.

'Lady Caroline and Captain Sawyer are resting before dinner,' Magdalena said. 'I know they'll be delighted you've joined us.' She looked much better, Lavender thought. Already, the fresh air, the company of her friend and the change of scenery had done her some good.

'Unfortunately, I'm here on a case, Magdalena. Conant will drag me back to London as soon as he can. But let's make hay while the sun shines, shall we?'

'Make hay?' she said, laughing. 'Are we to be peasants now?'

He smiled. 'It's just an English expression, Magdalena, about having fun.'

'Fun? Ha! That is a word I *do* understand. As for your work? Fuff! Tell us about it over dinner and we'll help you to solve it quickly – then you'll have more time to spend with me and the children.'

Alice snuggled into his shoulder. 'I smell a horsey, Papa,' she said sleepily.

He laughed. 'I need to wash and change for dinner, but I'll put you to bed first, little princess.'

'Story, Papa.'

'Yes, story.'

Forty minutes later, the adults gathered in the yellow dining room, which had been decorated in the Adam style with elaborate white plasterwork and neoclassical friezes along the high walls and long ceiling. Large gilt mirrors added extra depth to a room that was already generously proportioned. Tastefully arranged between them were some of Lady Caroline's most beautiful landscape paintings.

Magdalena looked resplendent tonight. Teresa had curled her glossy black hair, swept it back and held it in place with jewelled hairpins. She wore a burgundy satin dress trimmed with black lace, which showed off her glowing olive skin to perfection. The neck was low and enhanced her magnificent decolletage. Lavender remembered her buying this dress early in their marriage. It would please her that despite the birth of two more children, it still fitted.

Captain Sawyer, a man of short stature with twinkling blue eyes, huge bushy white whiskers and a head of wild snow-white hair, hobbled towards Lavender on his wooden leg and shook his hand warmly. 'Glad to see you, Lavender. There's always a berth for you here.'

'And not a hammock in sight,' Lavender replied, smiling. 'You've a beautiful home, Captain.'

Sawyer glanced around the room, and Lavender saw sadness flit across his face. 'Aye, well, my mother – God rest her soul – did a good job getting the place shipshape. I was never supposed to inherit this pile – I had two older brothers, which is why I was shipped off to sea at seventeen. But they didn't last the course.'

Lavender nodded and murmured his condolences.

'I feel a bit guilty sometimes,' Sawyer added.

'You've nothing to feel guilty about, my dear,' Lady Caroline said gently from behind him. 'You fought long and hard for your country for years, wallowing in the bowels of filthy and stinking warships. You deserve a little luxury in your retirement.'

Lavender smiled and went to greet his hostess, who was already seated at one end of the gleaming oval rosewood table. Her silver-topped walking cane rested beside her. Meanwhile, Sawyer pulled out a chair for Magdalena.

Lady Caroline was a strikingly attractive redhead in her late forties, and tonight she wore a yellow pearl-studded turban with a pale-green ostrich feather. Her silk gown was the same delicate shade of pale green and trimmed with more pearls. Lavender bent over to kiss her cheek.

'Excuse me for not standing to greet you, Stephen,' she said, 'but my old injury is plaguing me again.'

He nodded with sympathy and took the chair beside her. When Lady Caroline was eighteen, she'd scandalised her family and the ton by eloping to the continent with Victor Meyer Rothschild, a younger member of the great European banking family. Sadly, their marriage was short-lived. It ended in a horrific coach accident that killed Rothschild and left Lady Caroline maimed for life.

'That's a shame, Lady Caroline, but I have to say you look wonderful. Portugal obviously suited you. You're radiant.'

'Bless you, Stephen. That's kind of you.' She turned to the footman and instructed him to pour the claret and serve the roast beef.

Magdalena smiled. 'Yes, Caroline, you're glowing – just like a bride should.'

Lavender looked up in surprise. 'A bride?'

'I've only just discovered it myself, Stephen,' Magdalena continued. 'Captain Sawyer and Lady Caroline were married while they were in Portugal.'

'*Married?* That's wonderful! Congratulations to both of you! But why the secrecy? Why haven't I read about it in *The Times*?'

Lady Caroline waved a dismissive hand. 'Oh, for heaven's sake, Stephen – you're as bad as Magdalena, who *berated* me for not writing to her with the news. This is my third marriage; it's hardly newsworthy.'

Lavender chuckled and thought back to the string of young men who'd fallen hopelessly in love with this irrepressible aristocrat over the years. 'I think most of the ton will disagree with you on that point. But why hold your nuptials in Portugal?'

She sighed, lifted her fork and indicated that they should eat. 'Portugal is so lovely and warm, unlike dreary England. The vineyards, the meandering rivers, the orange trees… the country can quite turn your head with romance. Besides which, it's full of Catholic priests. For the first time, I was able marry in my own religion. I hope this time God will smile on me.'

'Here, here.' Sawyer raised his heavy crystal glass of Madeira. 'I'll drink to that.'

Lavender raised his own glass. 'I'd like to propose a toast. To our newlyweds: Lady Caroline and Captain Sawyer.'

Smiling, Magdalena joined him in the toast.

No sooner had Lavender put his glass down than Sawyer lifted his up again and gave a tender look across the table to his wife. 'Another toast – to the two most beautiful women in England, who are both sitting at this table.'

Lavender lifted his glass again.

'To our wives and sweethearts…' Sawyer proposed.

'To our wives and sweethearts,' Lavender echoed.

'…may they never meet.' Sawyer added.

Lavender and Magdalena burst out laughing.

But Lady Caroline gave her husband a disapproving look. 'Behave yourself, Joshua. You're not a salty bachelor in the Navy now.'

But the Captain chuckled; he'd enjoyed his little joke.

The meal passed in pleasant conversation about family matters, news of old friends and the latest scandals in London. The roast beef was excellent and was followed by gooseberry tart and a rich vanilla-flavoured cream. The Claret flowed freely, and the fine wine and company of good friends left Lavender more relaxed than he'd felt for weeks. He reached out and squeezed Magdalena's hand.

It wasn't until the servants had cleared away the dessert plates and fetched out the port that the conversation turned to Lavender's latest case.

'I feel Magdalena and I should leave you and Joshua to enjoy your port,' Lady Caroline said. 'But I do so want to know what has brought you to Ealing, Stephen. Is it something to do with the terrible murder of Mrs Langford?'

Lavender explained how Doctor Morton had asked Bow Street for help to investigate the case against his brother.

'Ah, so our good doctor thinks they've got the wrong man?' Sawyer said.

'But who else could it be?' Lady Caroline asked. 'Young Ashfield was the only person in the house once the maid left. Do you suspect the maid? Or the husband?'

'It's often the husband,' Lavender said slowly. 'But poison is usually the weapon of choice of a woman – and there's a lot of unexplored avenues in this case. Did you hear about the note someone pinned to the church lychgate?'

'Of course!' Lady Caroline threw her hands up in distress. 'What a terrible, terrible thing for someone to do! My maid rushed to tell me about it. The whole parish knows. The Langfords must have been in great distress.'

'I can only assume,' Lavender said, 'that because of the contents – and the way it was made public – the writer bore a strong grudge against the Langfords.'

'So, the writer might be the killer?'

'The shame it elicited gave the vicar a strong motive to get rid of his wife,' Magdalena said quietly. 'Most men would be horrified at such humiliation.'

'Doctor Morton told me several of his patients have also received anonymous letters in the same vile tone. You and Captain Sawyer haven't been a victim of this prankster, have you? I would like more samples to compare.'

'No – but until recently we've been out of the country.'

'Has anyone in the parish voiced suspicions about whom this vicious person may be?'

'Oh, yes,' Lady Caroline said. 'Ealing is full of gossip and speculation. The main suspect appears to be a woman called Kilby – Dora Kilby – who lives halfway between here and Brentford. She's reputed to be a witch.'

'There's plenty fear the woman, hereabouts,' Sawyer added. 'They don't like to cross her because if they do, she'll cast her evil eye on their cow, and its milk will dry up.'

Lavender glanced at Magdalena. 'Kilby? Wasn't that the maiden name of Woods' mother?'

Magdalena nodded. 'Yes. Dora Kilby's a successful businesswoman. She owns and rents out several properties. Ned and Betsy are staying in one of them. I asked Betsy about her this afternoon, and she said Dora was kind to them but seemed to enjoy her wicked reputation. She likes riling people.'

Lady Caroline indicated to the footman that she wanted her chair pulled back. 'We'll leave you two gentlemen to enjoy your port now, but if there's anything you think we can do to help with your case, Stephen, please don't hesitate to ask. If the murderer is still out there, the sooner they're caught the better.'

Lavender nodded his thanks and he and Sawyer rose to their feet as the ladies retired to the drawing room.

'Pour yourself another port,' Sawyer said. 'I'll be back in a moment; I've something to show you.'

Intrigued, Lavender watched his host hobble out of the room on his wooden leg. The captain was back a few moments later with a crumpled piece of cheap white paper in his hand, which he gave to Lavender.

'Caroline doesn't know about this. It arrived a few days ago and I've kept it from her.'

Lavender braced himself and opened the paper.

The letter was as bad as he feared, but mercifully it was short:

THOU ART A CAPTAIN QUEERNOBS WITH RANK BOWELS AND THY TROLLOP IS THE BASTARD DAUGHTER OF A TRAITOROUS PAPIST

'Disgusting,' Lavender murmured, shaking his head.

Sawyer gave a short laugh. 'I was more upset I paid the post boy tuppence to receive it! Don't let it ruin your evening, Lavender. I know you and Magdalena are close to Caroline, but she doesn't know about it, so there's no harm done.'

'I've seen three of these now. It's like the writer has scooped up every foul phrase they can find from the gutters of the Seven Dials and spewed it out on to paper – and this person obviously doesn't know you and Lady Caroline are married.'

Sawyer shrugged. 'Not many folks do. Caroline thinks it'll be fun to keep it to ourselves and tease the neighbours for a while.'

'May I ask an intimate question? I need to establish how well this libellous writer actually *knows* you.'

Sawyer burst out laughing. 'Is it about the bowels? Well, it ain't a good idea to stand downwind sometimes – but I reckon I'm no worse than any other man.' He slapped Lavender on the back. 'Come on, shipmate, let's forget this nonsense and join the gals.'

Chapter Ten

Lavender rose early the next morning and left for Boston Manor as soon as he thought it was an appropriate time to make a call.

He'd heard Sir James Clitherow was a serious man with a dour nature who patronised many good causes and ran his estate and affairs with a firm but fair hand. He doubted such a man lay in bed until noon.

He enjoyed the ride through the quiet country lanes with the blackbird song and the scent of the wildflowers drifting on the slight breeze. The cool morning air cleared his head, which had been a touch groggy after Captain Sawyer's generosity with the wine decanter the previous night. The sun rose steadily into the cloudless blue sky above; it was going to be another scorching hot day.

Boston House was a magnificent seventeenth-century building and the opulence of the grand hallway suggested the interior was as elegant as the exterior. However, when the footman led him to Sir James's study, he was surprised to find it was a small, plain and rather dreary back room, panelled up to the ceiling with dark, ancient oak.

The baron sat behind the huge mahogany desk that dominated the room and was cluttered with piles of letters, an inkwell and silver quill, and an open ledger filled with looping and precise script. He was in his late forties, sombrely dressed in a black suit. His domed pate was bald apart from a ring of greying blond hair at collar level. He had a round face with wide-set intelligent eyes that observed Lavender with distaste.

'A Bow Street runner, eh? It never bodes well, when you fellows come a-calling. You'd better sit down and tell me what you want.'

Lavender sat, handed Sir James the letter of introduction from Magistrate Conant, and explained his business.

Sir James's scowl deepened. 'Well, this is a rum do. I can't see why Bow Street wants to poke its nose into our affairs.'

He threw the letter on to his desk and for a silent moment it lay there between them like an accusation.

'Doctor Morton would like the case investigated further,' Lavender said cautiously. 'He feels there is more to uncover in the mystery of Mrs Langford's death.'

'Of course he does!' Sir James snapped. 'The accused man is his bloody brother! Still, if he wants to waste his money…'

'Magistrate Conant thought it wise to apprise you of the situation and let you know I will be in the parish asking questions.'

'Mm, Nathaniel is a tactful man. I hope you are too, Lavender, especially if you intend to question our vicar – the poor fellow has suffered enough!'

'It *is* my intention to question the Reverend Langford.'

'Treat him with respect – not as a suspect. He has a sound alibi for the day of the murder, and he's been a broken man since his wife was killed. I can't think why Morton won't accept my judgement about the case. His brother was the only one who had the opportunity to poison the poor woman according to the medical evidence he gave himself!'

'There are some loose ends Doctor Morton wants me to investigate, for example the whereabouts of the missing wet nurse. I hope to work with the local constable on this matter. And then there's this spate of poisonous anonymous letters that have circulated around Ealing—'

Sir James interrupted him brusquely and waved a dismissive hand in the air towards the door. 'Oh, do what you need to, Lavender. I'll give you a copy of the inquest report and instruct Constable Hinge to assist you.'

'Thank you. I'm staying with Captain Sawyer while I'm in Ealing. He and his wife, Lady Caroline, are friends of my family. Constable Hinge can contact me at Cedar Lodge.'

Sir James's grey eyebrows rose sharply. 'His wife? Did he marry the jade?'

Lavender frowned at the slur. 'I think it was the other way around. After several proposals, Lady Caroline consented to be Captain Sawyer's wife last winter. They were married in Portugal.'

Sir James laughed. 'Well, they've kept that quiet. They've been the subject of rife speculation for months.' He walked to a cupboard and extracted a buff-coloured file.

Lavender took it, stood up to leave, then hesitated. 'Before I go, sir. I would like to know if you or any of your family have received one of these unpleasant letters?'

Sir James narrowed his eyes and paused. Lavender remembered what Morton had said about how most people refused to discuss their contents.

'As a matter of fact, I did – but it went straight on the fire. Can I trust you to be discreet, Lavender?'

'Yes, sir.'

'It was a nasty piece of filth. It cast aspersions on my manhood and accused me of being an agent of Satan, who beat his tenants and practised unchristian acts on his wife.'

'Did you ask Constable Hinge to investigate this libel?'

'I did not. The man has more important matters to deal with than searching for some bitter, mad woman who hates her neighbours.'

'One last question, sir. Is Doctor Morton highly regarded in this parish?'

'Yes, he's the best doctor we've had here for years. His reputation is stainless.'

Lavender thanked him again and left.

A curious contraption arrived at the door of Cedar Court just as Sebastián finished his breakfast.

His sharp ears were the first to hear the rattling metal and the bells jingling. He dashed to the tall window that overlooked the immaculate gravel drive and burst out laughing. 'Mamá! Come here! You must see the trap Uncle Ned's hired!'

The others joined him at the window and burst out laughing.

'Oh, look at poor Betsy – she doesn't look happy!' Magdalena giggled.

The trap was drawn by a black horse with its mane carefully braided with white fluttering ribbons and tiny wildflowers. Silver bells were fastened to the bridle. They jangled sweetly with each flick of the horse's ears.

A garland of fresh roses and ivy was draped over the gleaming blue paintwork at the side of the trap. Next to it was a large sign that announced to the world the occupants were 'JUST MARRIED'. Dozens of horseshoes dangled from the cart sides, which swayed with the movement and clashed noisily into each other.

Ned and Betsy Woods sat on the driving seat together in their Sunday best, with Alfie Bobbin between them. The girls were perched on the back step with their legs dangling. Ned was beaming from ear to ear across his broad face. But Betsy looked like she wanted the ground to open up and swallow her.

Still chuckling, the household went outside to greet the arrivals.

Woods and Rachel had already climbed down from the vehicle and were helping little Tabitha.

'How wonderful!' Lady Caroline exclaimed. 'What a magnificent vehicle for your trip to Hanger Hill on your wedding anniversary.'

'It ain't *quite* what I ordered at the livery stables,' Woods admitted, grinning. 'I don't think the ostler heard me right. I reckon the fella's a bit deaf. He fancied I were gettin' wed rather than celebratin' twenty-five years of wedded bliss.'

'There won't be another twenty-five years if you ever pull a ruse like this again, Ned Woods!' Betsy snapped from above them. 'Oh, Magdalena! Lady Caroline! Folks have been cheerin' and clappin' us all the way from Brentford. I've never been so embarrassed in my life!'

'I think it's magnificent, Betsy,' Lady Caroline said. 'I hope this is a truly memorable day for you both. You deserve it.'

But Betsy wasn't convinced. 'One fella read the sign on the side and shouted out that lookin' at the age of our gals, we should have wed years ago! I were mortified.'

‘Well, sweetness, we’re leavin’ the gals here for the day,’ Woods said. ‘So, it won’t happen again. And by the time we’ve eaten that delicious picnic you’ve packed, and drunk the ale I’ve brought, you won’t care about *anything* on the way home.’

‘Don’t worry about the girls, Betsy,’ Magdalena said. ‘Tabitha and Alice play so well together and Sebastián and Rachel are good company for each other. You have a wonderful day with Ned.’

Betsy muttered something inaudible.

Still grinning, Woods climbed back up on to his seat and took up the reins.

Everyone cheered and waved them off. ‘Have fun!’ ‘Enjoy yourself!’

Rachel joined Sebastián as the adults went back inside with Tabitha.

‘What do you want to do today?’ Sebastián asked.

‘I’ve got a notion to go to Brentford to try an’ find my Grandpa. You can come with me if you like.’

‘Grandpa? I thought you didn’t have any grandparents?’

‘Ma and Da have lied to us for years. Grandpa didn’t die, he deserted my Granny and my Da when he were only tiny.’

‘What?’

Quietly, she told him about her Uncle Alby’s surprise visit and the news someone had seen her long-lost grandfather fishing at the side of the canal.

‘That’s an extraordinary story! Do you think it’s true?’

Rachel shrugged her shoulders. ‘Mrs Kilby, our landlady, told Da there were a man called “Woody” livin’ near the gauging lock. I think he might be the one. But Da doesn’t seem bothered about doin’ any detectin’. All he’s done since we got here is lark about with Ma and fish.’

Sebastián realised he was rubbing his chin, a gesture he knew his own father often made when thinking about a mysterious case. He nodded sagely. ‘In that case, Rachel, it’s up to us to track down your rogue of a grandfather. Let’s take Bruce too.’

Bruce was milking a goat when they arrived at The Laurels. He hastily rose from his stool and asked a dairy maid to complete the task. He had on a clean shirt but still wore his ragged trousers with the frayed rope for a belt.

'Brentford's a slum,' he told Sebastián. 'It's not the kind of place a young gal like Miss Rachel should go on her own.'

Sebastián smiled to himself. He was beginning to think Bruce was sweet on Rachel.

They went to the canal and followed the tow path towards Brentford. Wherever possible, they sought relief from the relentless August heat beneath the shade of the fruit trees overhanging from the orchards.

'My mother says there'll be a storm tonight,' Bruce said, wiping the sweat from his brow. 'Some of the horses have become nervous.'

Sebastián glanced up at the vivid blue of the cloudless sky. 'Gosh. She can forecast the weather from the mood of the horses?'

Bruce nodded.

A young woman of Sebastián's own age walked along the tow path towards them. She wore a fashionable straw hat with a brim over auburn hair to protect her pale skin, but it cast her eyes into shade. As she approached, Sebastián realised she was glaring at Bruce in disgust.

'Good morning, Miss Amelia,' the younger boy said pleasantly.

'I see you're out of school for the summer, Bruce Charlton,' she replied haughtily. 'Can't your mother afford to buy you some decent clothes? Or do you only possess your scholastic uniform?'

Before he could reply, the young woman cast her eyes over Sebastián and Rachel and frowned. 'And I see you've found yourself a pair of scruffy urchins to spend your summer with.'

Sebastián laughed and gave a deep and mocking bow. 'Pleased to meet you, Ma'am. Sebastián García de Aviles Morales del Castillo at your service.'

Her light, insipid eyes blinked in surprise, but she continued to glare. 'A foreigner?'

'I was born in Spain, Ma'am. But I'm British now and plan to join the Duke of Wellington's regiment as soon as possible.'

'Ha! And no doubt you're a papist too?'

'Of course.'

'And what are you doing here, Mr García? Looking for converts to Catholicism?'

'My mother and I are visitors to Ealing. We're enjoying its delights and the hospitality of Captain Sawyer and Lady Caroline at Cedar Court.'

'Delights! Ha! You must be easily pleased, Mr García. It's boring in Ealing. It's a place where old people come to die – and Captain Sawyer and Lady Caroline are old.'

'That's not true, Amelia,' Bruce protested. 'Ealing's not boring. There'll be a cricket match on the village green tomorrow.'

'You'd be more than welcome to come and watch, Ma'am,' Sebastián added.

'I'd rather poke myself in the eye with an embroidery needle.' She turned and flounced down the tow path.

'Who's that?' Sebastián didn't know whether to be amused or offended.

'She's the doctor's daughter, Miss Amelia Morton,' Bruce told them. 'She's a blue stocking and very clever.'

'I saw her in Brentford when we first arrived,' Rachel said. 'She were watchin' a brawl outside one of the taverns.'

Bruce nodded. 'That'll be for her novella. She's writing a great novella full of excitement.'

'Is she always so cross?' Sebastián asked.

'Yes – she's not a pleasant person.' Bruce sighed. His shoulders slumped and his gentle features were swamped with misery.

Rachel glanced at him sharply. 'What's the matter?'

'I think they may make her my sister.'

Sebastián and Rachel stopped in their tracks. 'What?'

'The doctor… he's been courting Mama. His wife is dead, just like my Papa.'

Sebastián mulled over this impending disaster. 'It can be useful to have a doctor in the family.'

Rachel was more forthright. 'But this can't happen, Bruce! That gal is a bad-tempered shrew! You'll have to tell your Ma she can't marry the sawbones. Make her pick someone else.'

'I don't think there is anyone else. Mama giggles like a young girl when the doctor is around and is always rushing inside to brush her hair. Although she's sadder now since my aunt died.'

Sebastián remembered some talk he'd overheard the previous night. 'Is this the vicar's wife who was poisoned?'

'Yes. The lady who died was my aunt, Mrs Langford. She was my mother's sister.'

'How awful for you,' Rachel said gently. 'To have lost your aunt like that.'

'Don't worry,' Sebastián reassured him. 'My Pa – Detective Lavender – is here, investigating the case. He'll make sure the right man hangs for the crime.'

Bruce visibly brightened at the news.

'Why is Amelia such a highty-tighty tabby?' Rachel asked.

'Mama says she's known disappointment,' Bruce explained. 'When she turned sixteen they stopped her going to the governess at Boston Manor, which was hard for someone so bookish. The vicar's two daughters took her place. There wasn't room for Amelia anymore. She's been out of humour ever since and moans about how no one takes the education of girls seriously. Do you like your schooling, Miss Rachel?' he asked as an afterthought.

Rachel gave him a sweet smile. 'I'm happier spendin' my time in a stable.'

Chapter Eleven

On his way to the vicarage, Lavender left Windmill Lane and followed a narrow path through a sweet-smelling hayfield. It wound its way along the banks of a deep and meandering tributary of the River Brent. This longer route gave him a chance to plan the questions he needed to ask the Reverend Langford.

Sir James was right: this was a delicate situation. Whenever a woman was murdered, suspicion always turned immediately to the husband – and God knows, this man had a strong motive to rid himself of his wife. Innocent or not, Mrs Langford had dragged his saintly reputation into the gutter through her association with Ashfield. But apparently Langford had a strong alibi. Lavender knew he had to tread carefully and not exacerbate the man's distress.

Lavender dismounted and led his horse to drink from the stream. He took off his hat, wiped the sweat from his brow and pushed back his dark hair. Magdalena was right – he needed to find a barber.

While his horse wandered off to munch on the long grass, he sat on a stile to read the file Sir James had given to him. Sparrows chirped from the hedgerows, their chatter blending with the distant call of a woodpigeon hidden among the trees. A grasshopper sprang into sight, before vanishing into the tangle of green.

The inquest report didn't tell Lavender anything he hadn't already heard from Doctor Morton. Collecting his horse, Lavender remounted and rode towards the interview he dreaded more than the rest.

The vicarage was a large and attractive building on the far side of the village green, opposite the church. The exterior, with its double bay windows, had been whitewashed, and gleamed in the sunlight.

The door was answered by a young maidservant, who showed Lavender towards the drawing room. There was a large pile of packing cases in the spacious hallway.

Lavender heard the vicar before he saw him. He was muttering angrily to himself and appeared to be slapping something with a newspaper.

When Lavender entered the room, he saw a fair-haired man in his late thirties killing flies in one of the tall windows. Flushed with the exertion, the vicar was scowling. But when the maid introduced Lavender, a rueful smile lit up his face.

'You've caught me at an awkward moment, Detective. If there's one thing I can't stand, it's flies. I know they're God's creatures – but they're everywhere at this time of year.'

'They can be annoying,' Lavender sympathised.

'Fetch me some more fly papers,' Langford instructed the maid. He pointed towards the pile of little dead bodies on the windowsill. 'And a dustpan and brush to clear up this mess.'

The girl nodded and left.

Langford put down his rolled-up newspaper and held out his hand. 'How can I help you, Detective?'

Lavender shook the vicar's hand and gently explained why he was there. To his relief, Langford didn't complain about his interference in the case. He merely nodded and offered Lavender a seat. 'Doctor Morton loves his brother,' he said simply. 'I understand why he wanted a thorough investigation.'

'Before we start, I want to offer you my sincere condolences. Your wife's death is a tragedy, and I know it must have been horrific for you.'

Langford winced but took a deep breath and composed his features. He was long-nosed but had high cheekbones, a firm jaw and good skin. He had taken his jacket off and was sitting in his waistcoat and shirt sleeves. Instinctively, his hand went up to the clerical collar at his neck. 'It's ruined my life. And the life of my family.'

'I noticed the packing cases outside in the hallway. Are you leaving?'

'Unfortunately, yes. On top of everything else, this terrible incident has cost me my living here and my daughters their home.'

'How so?' Lavender asked, shocked.

Langford's voice rose sharply with anger. 'The Bishop believes it's untenable for me to remain here as the vicar after everything that has occurred.'

'But surely your parishioners are sympathetic?' Lavender protested.

Langford held up his hands to stop him. 'It's no use. The Bishop is resolute on this matter – and I've come to the same conclusion. God is testing me. I'm tainted by events that are not my fault. It's a challenge I can't overcome and – no matter how galling – I need to accept the inevitable.'

'I'm sorry to hear this.'

'Yes,' Langford snapped. 'But you – like my parishioners – still suspect me of killing my wife, don't you?'

Lavender was surprised at this sudden change of attitude in the man.

'Thank God Sir James is a compassionate man and can look beyond the obvious,' Langford continued. 'The sooner Ashfield is tried and hanged the better, as far as I'm concerned. There's a vacant living in Lancashire and the bishop has put my name forward. Hopefully, the scandal won't follow me up there.'

'I've heard parts of the north are beautiful.'

'Not this part of the north. It's a poverty-stricken mill town, full of filth, rats, consumption and strong liquor. I had thought my days working at the rough edge of society were over after I left my last parish in Rotherhithe, but no. It seems God has a different plan for me.'

'Rotherhithe?' Lavender was impressed. This was a tough London borough full of poor immigrants, drunken dockers and whores. 'How long were you there?'

'Three years. The gentler pace and people of Ealing have been a blessing – until someone decided to ruin my wife's reputation with a notice pinned to the church lychgate and then someone murdered her.'

'Do you think it was the same person?' Lavender asked.

Langford gave him a hard stare. 'Mark Ashfield murdered my wife, Detective, because he couldn't have her. As for this degenerate letter writer, I assume it's a hysterical woman.'

There was a timid tap on the door, and the maid came back in with the dustpan and brush. 'I'm afraid there's no fly papers left, sir. Mrs Minskip says she'll buy some more when she goes on her errands later.'

Langford didn't respond. He sank back into his armchair and stared gloomily at the empty grate in the hearth.

While the maid swept up the dead flies, Lavender glanced around the spacious, elegant room with its luxurious Turkey carpet and Chippendale furniture. Everything about it, from the Sèvres porcelain on display in the gleaming walnut cabinet to the gilded ormolu clock on the mantelpiece, suggested comfort and wealth.

Despite his better judgement, Lavender sympathised with Langford. To lose his wife and her income was bad enough, but to be forced to leave affluent Ealing, where he was obviously so much at home, for the filth and poverty of a northern mill town, must be a double blow.

Once the maid left, Lavender cleared his throat. 'I appreciate this will be painful for you, Reverend, but I'd like to hear your own account of the day of the murder.'

'I don't know what else I can tell you, Detective, that I haven't already told the inquest. Have you seen the report?'

'Yes, Sir James gave me a copy. I think it would be helpful if you just told me, in your own words, what happened.'

Langford sighed and sank back in his chair. His face became stern with melancholy. 'I went to a funeral. My predecessor, the Reverend Finch, had recently died and myself and two of the servants went to his funeral in Brentford. It was a sombre, miserable day. Quite suitable for a funeral. A thick fog descended overnight and hung motionless in the trees.'

'How did you travel?' Lavender asked. 'By horseback?'

'Yes, I rode my horse, but the Minskips went in the cart. I intended to leave after the service and visit a parishioner, so I needed to make my own way home.'

'Where was the funeral service held and what time did you leave?'

'It was held at St Paul's. The service finished just before eleven o'clock. I left immediately.'

'Did anyone see you leave?'

'I've no recollection of that.'

'Why did you leave immediately?'

'I'd never met my predecessor or his sister. I was a stranger and didn't want to intrude on her grief. I only went to represent the parish.'

'Where did you go next?'

'I went to visit one of my former parishioners, an old and frail man called Abel Jupp, who recently moved to Brentford. He'd been ill and is a deeply pious man – scared of death. I hoped to bring him some comfort.'

Lavender was tempted to point out that Mr Jupp was now the responsibility of the vicar of St Paul's in Brentford. But he bit his tongue. Langford had been cooperative so far, but the man was unpredictable, veering between anger, self-pity and grief. 'How long were you there?'

The vicar gave a short laugh. 'Ages. Probably a good hour or more. Abel might be frail, but he can still talk the hind leg off a donkey. He missed Ealing and wanted to reminisce.'

'Then you came home? Which route did you take?'

Confusion flickered in the vicar's grey eyes. 'I'm not sure how this is relevant, Lavender? But if you must know, I came up Windmill Lane and cut across the fields on a path. I was deep in thought and needed some solitude, so I left the main road. I didn't want to run into any of my parishioners.'

Lavender nodded. 'I think I may have taken the same route myself, today. At what point did you meet Frederick Daniels?'

Langford's forehead creased as he tried to remember. 'I think it was at the start of the path. He was coming away from the village, across the fields, but turned back to ride to the vicarage with me.'

'I understand he wanted to speak with his sister. What did he want?'

Langford rolled his eyes. 'What did he always want with my rich wife?'

'Money?' Lavender suggested.

'Yes, he was on his uppers again and wanted another loan.'

'None of this was mentioned at the inquest.'

'There was no need to – and no one has asked about it except you. It would embarrass Daniels.'

'You obviously care about his reputation.'

Langford shrugged. 'He's a tiresome man but he was my wife's brother. When we marry, we inherit our wife's relatives to add to our own, don't you think?'

Lavender nodded. It wasn't the time to point out his own wife barely had any relatives left after the French invasion of Spain.

'Daniels was the black sheep of his family long before I married Clara. His fast living gave the gossips plenty to prattle about. I didn't want to embarrass him further by mentioning the reason for his call at the vicarage.'

'That's a commendable sentiment, Mr Langford. But Daniels' insolvency gives him a strong motive to murder his sister because of the terms of his father's will.'

'Oh, for heaven's sake, Lavender! The man was coming here with his tail between his legs to *beg* his sister for money – not to *murder* her for it!'

'How did you feel about that? It can't have been pleasant watching him sponge money off your wife?'

Langford shrugged his broad shoulders. 'Clara's allowance from her father's trust was Clara's money; she was free to fritter it away on her wastrel of a brother if she wished.'

'Did you know her income from the trust would revert to her siblings in the event of her death if she hadn't produced a male heir?'

'Of course,' Langford snapped. 'Her father made sure I understood this before I married her. All she had to do was produce a son.' He paused, shook his head, then added quietly: 'She couldn't even manage that.'

'What happened when you arrived home?'

'Our maid, Flora Kilby, came out into the hallway. She'd been with her sister in the kitchen. She told me Clara and the baby were asleep upstairs. I went up to tell Clara that her brother was here—' His voice broke and his face contorted with anguish.

'And you found her dead,' Lavender said gently.

'Yes. I'm sure you know the rest from the evidence in the inquest report and from what the doctor has already told you.'

Lavender nodded and said carefully: 'There's one thing that surprised me in Doctor Morton's account of the events of that afternoon. It's how quickly you and Mr Daniels assumed Mrs Langford had taken her own life.'

'That was before we knew Ashfield had been in the house!'

'Still, it's quite a leap to jump to such a conclusion.'

Langford shrugged dismissively. 'Clara had been low since the birth of her child – and that damned note on the lychgate didn't help matters.'

'That must have been distressing for both of you.'

'Absolutely. But I understand there's been an unpleasant spate of similar letters circulating through the parish. My family have not been the only target of this vicious hatred. Sir James told me he'd received a letter in a similar tone through the post about a year ago.'

Yes, but no one else had theirs broadcast to the entire village, Lavender thought. 'Have you received a similar letter?'

'No.'

'Have you any thoughts about who was responsible for the note left on the lychgate?'

'Most of the parish assume it's the work of some witch in Brentford called Kilby.'

A thought suddenly struck Lavender. 'Is your former maid, Flora Kilby, related to her?'

'I don't know. Clara hired the girl, not me.'

'What about the wet nurse whom Mrs Langford dismissed and who's since disappeared?'

‘She was an unpleasant woman – and a drunk. Clara made a mistake hiring her.’ Langford sighed. ‘I don’t think there’s anything else I can tell you, Lavender, and if you don’t mind, I’d appreciate it if you left me to my solitude. I hate talking and thinking about that day.’

Lavender stood up. ‘Of course. But before I leave, please allow me a few moments with your housekeeper, Mrs Minskip.’

Langford gave a short, hollow laugh. ‘Do you need to check my alibi, Detective?’

‘It’s my job to check everything.’

‘Be my guest.’

‘Thank you.’ Lavender paused beside the walnut display cabinet on his way out and scanned the contents. ‘Where’s the silver cup the maid claimed the wet nurse stole?’ he asked.

‘I’ve removed it to a safer place in case any more of my staff develop thieving habits. Oh, and Lavender …’

‘Yes?’

‘If you intend to pursue my late wife’s brother as a suspect, you might as well interview her eccentric sister as well. Elizabeth also stood to gain financially from Clara’s death. And there’s a rumour in the village that Doctor Morton is infatuated with her. His expertise in arsenic poisoning quite surprised me. They might have colluded in my wife’s death.’

Lavender tried not to let the surprise show on his face. ‘I’ll make sure I speak to Mrs Charlton.’

‘Good. I hope both Elizabeth and Frederick find your questions as unpleasant as I have. I can’t believe they’ll inherit *all* Clara’s money, while I move to a poorer living with two daughters to feed and clothe,’ he added in a bitter aside.

‘I thought you now had three daughters, Mr Langford?’

The vicar waved a dismissive hand in the air. ‘Yes, yes, of course. I keep forgetting about Clara’s brat.’

Chapter Twelve

Sebastián wrinkled his nose in disgust as the children walked along the tow path towards the gauging lock at Brentford. He didn't like this place and felt hemmed in between the grim, smoke-stained warehouses that towered over them on one side and the black and oily waters of the canal on the other.

'It reeks,' he complained, pointing to the filthy, garbage-strewn water. There were old rags, pieces of timber and several indeterminate objects he preferred not to examine too closely. 'Do the people who live here use this as a latrine? And what the devil's that?'

They stopped to examine a piece of shredded and bloodied fur floating on a piece of wood. It had a long tail and half a face.

'I think it's a dead rat,' Rachel said.

Bruce picked up a stick from the bank and poked at the creature until it plopped into the water and disappeared.

'Good Lord,' Sebastián said. 'If the rats can't survive in this water, there's no hope for the rest of us. If you fall in, keep your mouth closed, Rachel. Don't swallow it.'

She glared at him through narrowed eyes. 'Stop tellin' me what to do or it'll be you that takes a dip in the cut.'

He laughed. 'I'm not going to fall in.'

'You will if I push you.'

'Now, now, chaps,' Bruce said, grinning.

Sebastián glanced down one of the dank alleys that ran between the warehouses and was surprised to see rows of limp laundry on lines. Hanging these clothes out to dry had been an act of optimism rather than common sense; they were already covered with a layer of brown dust from the belching smoke from the brickworks. 'I can't believe people live here.'

Rachel nodded. 'Cousin Dora says houses have been crammed into every yard and alley since the canal came.'

Sebastián's heart sank at the hopelessness of their search. 'Your Grandpa could be anywhere.'

Bruce pointed to the low, arched bridge ahead that took the traffic on the busy high street over the canal. 'The river's still tidal over there and sometimes it floods up to their doors.'

They stopped to watch a crane haul a tea chest out of one of the barges. It was powered by a gang of sweating men, their shoulder muscles taut beneath their filthy jackets as they heaved on chains and ropes. One of the men spotted the children and yelled at them to clear off.

They quickened their step and moved further downstream. Here, another gang was shovelling coal from the hull of a barge into barrows. They wheeled them across a narrow plank and added their load of coal to a mountainous pile of glistening fuel on the wharf. Each barrowful shimmered down the side of the coal heap, releasing a choking cloud of black dust that stung the back of their throats and made them cough.

'How will we find him, Rachel?' Sebastián asked.

She nodded and pointed towards the gauging lock where a huge man was pushing back the balance beam to open the lock gate. 'That's Big Jim Kilby, he's a relative of Da's. He might know where Mr Woody lives.'

She led them forward. But the moment Kilby saw them approaching, his lined face contorted with anger. 'I told you nippers to keep clear of my locks! Bugger off! I ain't fishin' you out of the cut!'

Sebastián and Bruce stepped back, muttering an apology.

But Rachel stood her ground and put her hands on her hips. 'There's no need to be so rude!' she shouted back. 'I only want to ask you somethin'.'

'Rachel, come away,' Sebastián said.

'I ain't got no time to answer yer damned questions!'

'And there ain't no reason to cuss in front of us children, either,' Rachel told him angrily. 'You need to get some manners, Mr Kilby. Manners maketh the man.'

Kilby stiffened. And for one horrible minute, Sebastián thought he would grab hold of Rachel and give her a good thrashing. Then the man threw back his huge head of white hair and burst out laughing. 'Well, you're a feisty little gal, that's fer sure.'

'All I want to know is where Mr Woody lives.'

Kilby reached up and rubbed his stubble. 'And what do you want with that old cove?'

'I think he may be my Grandpa.'

Kilby laughed again. 'Now, why ain't I surprised?' He pointed to one of the dank alleys. 'Down there – the old lecher lives in the last 'ouse. If you can call 'is sheep shed an 'ouse.'

'Thank you. Now that weren't so hard, were it, Mr Kilby? If you were nicer, maybe more people would like you.'

Sebastián grabbed her and dragged her away. 'For God's sake, Rachel! You shouldn't speak to a man like him like that!'

'He deserved it,' Rachel protested. She shook her arm free from Sebastián's grip. Her round cheeks were flushed with anger, which made her freckles stand out.

Beside them, Bruce chuckled. 'Kilby's a real brute. He's worked those locks forever and guards them jealously. He knows all the tricks the bargemen use to cheat the tolls. Everyone's afraid of him.'

'Everyone except Rachel,' Sebastián said, sighing.

The children arrived at the entrance to the alley and stared in dismay at the filth that greased the ground.

The high, windowless walls of the warehouses dripped with water and blocked out the sunlight, but they could still see the discarded slops, buzzing with flies. It stank even worse than the canal.

'Come on.' Rachel led the way, carefully picking a route around the worst of the effluent.

Behind the warehouses, two rows of ancient cottages faced each other. This extended the narrow alley, which was blocked by a high and crumbling brick wall at the end. The windows of the cottages were cracked, broken, and hung with rags on the inside.

The end house – or '*sheep shed*' as Kilby had called it – was the worst of them all. It was a one-storey lean-to. Tall weeds grew out of the sloping roof, which butted up against the last cottage in the row.

The warped door was open, and an old man sat on a low stool peeling potatoes. The vegetables were still encrusted with soil and Sebastián wondered if he'd stolen them from a field.

Short, filthy and skeletal, the old man had matted grey hair and an unkempt beard. Small eyes, too close together and encircled by rings of angry, sore skin, stared at them suspiciously. His shirt was ragged, and his breeches were so caked in filth they were glazed and shiny. But it was when he opened his mouth to speak that Sebastián got the biggest shock. His teeth were all made from wood, worn smooth from years of use. Rachel walked right up to him.

'What you want?'

'Good morning, are you Mr Woody?'

'I maybes. Whose askin'?'

'My name's Rachel Woods. I think you might be my Grandpa.'

The old man's upper body suddenly convulsed, and he coughed violently. Sebastián hurried to Rachel's side, his nose wrinkling again at the musty stench of stale sweat, old clothes and old age that emanated from the choking man.

'Are you sickly, sir? Do you want me to fetch you some water?'

Woody nodded and pointed a filthy finger into the house.

Sebastián dashed into the one-roomed shack, recoiled from the smell and grabbed a pitcher of water from the small table in the centre of the room. There was a battered tin mug lying next to a plate on which lay a muddy brown river fish. Ignoring its glassy dead eyes, the boy poured out the water and hurried back outside.

Woody gulped the water and stopped choking. Now his old, lined face creased with misery. 'I ain't a well man,' he told the children hoarsely. He patted his thin chest with a bent and arthritic hand. 'I 'ave palpitations of the 'eart and don't take well to shocks.'

'I'm so sorry I startled you,' Rachel said.

'Aye, I were at death's door last winter. Only the kindness of my friends kept me alive. They'd turn up wi' a bit o' broth and maybe a crust to dunk in it. It's all I can eat with these damned ivories.'

'How dreadful,' Sebastián murmured.

'Aye, they'd bring me food and a few pennies now and then fer some baccy and to pay fer the surgeon. I've a great longin' fer a piece of meat and potato pie.' He glanced at Bruce and Sebastián. 'You fellas don't 'ave some baccy with you, do you?'

Sebastián stiffened with surprise. 'I… we don't smoke.'

'It were too much to hope fer, ah suppose. It eases the pain and gives me peace from my sufferin'. I'm not long fer this world,' he added in a plaintive voice. His wooden teeth clicked when he spoke.

'I've a few pennies.' Rachel reached into the pocket of her apron. 'Will this help?'

She handed over the coins and the old man took them eagerly.

'That's kind of yer, little lady. I could see yer were a kind gal the moment ah clapped my peepers on yer. Yer take after yer Granny.'

'So, you *are* my Grandpa?' Rachel's voice rose with excitement.

'Aye, ah reckon so. But ye'll 'ave to forgive an old man 'is poor memory. I've been so sick of late, it's all muddled. 'Tis a good job yer've found me. I'm not long fer this world.'

'My Da will be so pleased I've tracked you down – and Uncle Alby.'

A look of shock passed over the old man's eyes. 'Alby? Did yer Granny 'ave twins?'

'No,' Rachel said, laughing. 'Uncle Alby is years older than Da, but he wanted us to find you. Don't you remember them?'

The man's smile was careful, almost measured, as if he had practised it many times before. His chapped lips stretched just enough to be polite, but not so wide as to reveal too much of his hideous teeth. 'Ah, it's all comin' back to me now. *Alby* – that were Albert, weren't it? The oldest boy?'

'That's right. And you christened my Da Edward.'

'But did we call him *Ned*?' Woody asked.

Rachel clapped her hands in delight. 'Yes!'

'And yer Granny?' he asked. 'Were she Ann or Mary?'

'Matilda. But everyone called her Tilda.'

'That's right, I recall her now. I knew it began with an "M". She were a gentle soul.'

Rachel smiled. 'She died when I was a baby, so I never knew her, but everyone said she was kind.'

'Ah can see 'er likeness in you – and 'er kindness.'

'I can't wait to tell Da I've found you. I'll bring him back with me tomorrow.'

A shadow of unease passed over the old man's face. 'I'll be 'onest with you, little lady, I'm not so well. I need time to mull this over. It's been a shock meetin' you today – and my 'eart's all of a flutter again. I don't think yer should bother yer Da wi' the news just yet.'

'Oh.' Rachel's face fell with disappointment.

'Yer wouldn't want to 'urt an old man who's not long fer this world, would yer?'

'No, no. Of course not. But can I visit you again?'

'Aye, that'll be grand. But don't forget to fetch a bit of baccy wi' yer next time. Or maybe a piece of pie?'

'Of course! Bye for now, Mr Woody.'

Sebastián breathed a sigh of relief when they left the old man and his stinking hovel. He wondered if Rachel had lost her sense of smell. They hurried back down the alley but once they reached the sunlight of the tow path they slowed their pace.

The wharves were as busy as ever. Big Jim was talking to a man in a barge and had his back to them when they emerged. They slipped away from the lock without him noticing.

Rachel walked beside Sebastián. Her round face beamed with happiness.

Sebastián sighed and watched the mooring ropes of the stationary barges tighten as the boats drifted out from the bank, then slacken as they drifted back again. Something was wrong, and he felt he had to say something to Rachel.

But before he could speak, Bruce pointed across the canal. 'Look – it's those foreigners again.'

Sebastián glanced up. The two Spaniards were leaning against the side of a warehouse, smiling at them. One raised his hand and waved. They both had dark, lank hair and swarthy skin. One sported a moustache and had a red kerchief around his neck. The other had a fraying green coat with brass buttons.

Sebastián frowned and turned away.

The next moment, a huge shadow bore down on the children. It was a powerful horse led by a thin and sweating man. Behind them, a taut rope hauled a barge, low in the water under the weight of the glistening mound of coal in its hull.

After the horse had passed, Sebastián's mind returned to his problem. 'You forgot to ask his full name, Rachel.'

She frowned. 'It's Woods – same as mine. Woody.'

'Don't you think it's a bit of a coincidence that a man with wooden teeth is called *Woody*?'

'What do you mean?' she asked irritably. 'What's a *coincidence*? You sound like Uncle Stephen.'

'I think *Woody* is a nickname. His real name might be Henry Smith.'

'Fuff! He's my Grandpa. You heard him – he knew about Da, Granny and Uncle Alby.'

But did he though? Sebastián frowned. He sensed Woody had known very little and had made some lucky guesses.

'Are you jealous because I've got a Grandpa, and you haven't?'

'No!'

'Is this because Big Jim called him a lecher?'

'No!'

'But why would he say he were my Grandpa if he weren't?'

Sebastián sighed and wiped the sweat off his brow. It was so damned hot, his fringe was stuck to his forehead. 'I don't know. I just don't trust him, Rachel.'

'Well, that's just mean!' she snapped. 'The poor old man!'

'I say, chaps,' Bruce said gently. 'You're on the same team tomorrow – don't fall out.'

That brought them both up with a start. Of course. There was nothing more important than cricket.

'Shall we go back to Ealing and practise for tomorrow's game?' Sebastián asked.

The others agreed and they quickened their pace.

'I can stay until the weather turns,' Bruce told them. 'Then I'll have to go home and help my mother bring in the horses. They're not easy to handle.'

'If you harness the stallion and lead him away, the mares will follow,' Rachel told him. 'I'll come and show you if you like?'

'We've two stallions,' Bruce told her. 'They're both mischievous and work together to confound us. The minute we approach them with a harness, they scatter in a different direction. This confuses the mares, who don't know which way to turn.'

Rachel laughed. 'There's an easy cure for naughty boys. I'll show you how to trick them tonight, if you like.'

Bruce accepted her offer of help and they walked along quietly for a moment.

Then Rachel said: 'What's a lecher, García?'

Sebastián blushed to the roots of his damp hair, and he started to hurry ahead. 'That's something girls shouldn't ask,' he snapped.

Chapter Thirteen

The vicarage kitchen was as spacious as the rest of the house, although far less opulent. A pair of tall, shuttered windows let in columns of streaming sunlight that angled down towards the flagstones on the floor. A large black range with raised polished-brass hearth fenders dominated the far wall, which also contained a built-in bread oven and a row of brass bells for summoning the servants. There were shelves of cooking pots and a plain dark-oak glass-fronted cabinet with a gilt-edged China dinner service.

Three women were sipping tea at the large dark-oak table that ran down the centre of the room. One was the young housemaid who'd answered the door to Lavender. The second, he assumed from the stains on her white apron, her floury hands and the scowl on her broad face, was Mrs Minskip, the cook. She was a rotund woman with broken veins on her flushed and fleshy face.

But the third woman was unknown. Tiny and painfully thin, she was dressed in an old-fashioned and faded mourning gown and a black hat with fraying ribbons. She looked up with excitement at Lavender's appearance, the eyes behind her round spectacles bright with curiosity.

He hesitated before he spoke and felt a pang of regret that Woods wasn't by his side. His easy-going and jovial constable had always been far better at dealing with the servant class than he was. Woods had the common touch and quickly put everyone at their ease, while Lavender always sounded too severe.

'Mrs Minskip? I'm Detective Lavender from Bow Street Magistrates' Court and Police Office. I need to ask you some questions about the day of Mrs Langford's murder.'

The cook's lips tightened in annoyance, but she turned to the little maid and said: 'Go and dust the bedrooms, Mary. This ain't for your ears.'

The young girl pushed back her chair and left the room.

'You should probably leave too, Miss Finch,' the cook said.

But the tiny old woman beside her remained firmly in her chair.

Lavender wondered if the cook would feel more comfortable if her friend remained. 'This lady can stay if she wishes. This shouldn't take long, ma'am.'

The tiny old woman smiled but the scowl deepened on the cook's face, and he suspected he'd said the wrong thing.

'I merely want to hear your own account of that day, but I know you spent most of it in Brentford at a funeral.'

Mrs Minskip sighed. 'This is Miss Jane Finch, the sister of the deceased. 'Er brother were our vicar 'ere for nigh on thirty years before 'e were afflicted with bad 'ealth. Miss Finch kept 'ouse for 'im and nursed 'im to the end.'

Lavender nodded and realised that although the cook wasn't comfortable with her former mistress in the room, Miss Finch might be a useful witness. She was well named. The tiny, quick movements of her head and hands reminded him of a wary bird who'd landed in a ploughed field to peck out a juicy worm. 'My condolences, Ma'am. But it may be fortuitous you're visiting Mrs Minskip. You can confirm who attended the funeral.'

Miss Finch nodded her head furiously. 'Of course, Detective! I'll do anything to help with the investigation into this terrible tragedy. Poor Clara! To have met such a dreadful end at the hands of that fiend!'

Mrs Minskip still looked annoyed, but she poured out an extra cup of tea and indicated Lavender should take the seat vacated by the housemaid. He preferred coffee but he was parched with thirst due to the heat and was grateful for the beverage.

'Did you know Mrs Langford well?' Lavender asked Miss Finch, as he replaced his cup in the saucer.

'No. But of course, I know *of* her. I moved with my brother to Brentford when he became too ill to continue with his pastoral care. It was sad to leave the vicarage, but it felt right to leave it to a young family. This vicarage *needs* young life.'

'Where do you live now?' Lavender asked.

'We moved in with our old parlourmaid, Nelly. She worked for us for over twenty years. My faithful Nelly married a stonemason, and they've a large house on the high street with the wood yard behind. She was *most* insistent we joined them. I've three lovely rooms on the top floor. I'm most comfortable there – and can barely hear the traffic!'

Lavender nodded sympathetically. Such lodgings would have been quite a shock after the vicarage. Despite their ailing health and encroaching senility, most clerics tried to keep a roof over their family's head until the last possible minute to avoid the genteel poverty now faced by Miss Finch. Some had even dropped down dead in the pulpit rather than give up their living.

'When I heard of the tragic death of poor Mrs Langford,' Miss Finch continued, 'I thought it only right and proper I should try to bring some comfort to dearest Brigit.'

Dearest Brigit was still scowling. Lavender sensed the little woman was a gossip who'd arrived unwanted on the vicarage doorstep to extract information about the scandal from her former cook.

Lavender turned to Mrs Minskip. 'How long have you worked here?'

'Seventeen years, sir. Minskip and I arrived shortly after we were wed to work for the Reverend and Miss Finch.'

'They're excellent and loyal servants,' Miss Finch interrupted.

For the first time, a glimmer of a smile curled at the edge of the cook's lips. 'Reverend Langford let us attend the funeral to pay our respects. We went in the cart.'

'Did you travel down to Brentford with the Reverend Langford?'

'At first, yes. Then 'e spurred 'is horse forward and vanished into the fog.'

'When did you next see him?'

''E were at the church door when we got to St Paul's. 'E were talkin' to the vicar there.'

'And after that? When did you see him again?'

She gave him a sharp sideways glance. 'I didn't. I were watchin' and listenin' to the funeral service. I weren't nosing' about who were, and weren't, there.'

'Did you see the Reverend Langford in the church, Miss Finch?'

The woman's thin hands fluttered to her face. 'I'm afraid I can't recall, Detective.'

'Miss Finch was buryin' 'er brother,' Mrs Minskip said sternly. 'She were in no fit state to count the congregation.'

'Oh, so true, my dearest Brigit! But it was such an *excellent* turnout!'

'If you want to check 'is whereabouts,' Mrs Minskip continued, 'ye'll need to ask someone else.'

'My apologies, Ladies. Unfortunately, it's my job to ask these questions. Please tell me what happened next.'

The cook shrugged. 'Minskip and I went to the wake. We left Brentford mid-afternoon and came 'ome to the vicarage to find the mistress dead and all 'ell 'ad broken loose.' Her eyes moistened at the memory. 'I liked Mistress Langford,' she added. 'She were a kind woman, allus smilin' and kind.'

'And what about Mr Langford? Do you like him?'

She broke eye contact and looked away towards the other side of the kitchen. 'He's a serious man with an important position. He's allus fair to me.'

Lavender noted her evasion. 'I understand he's about to take up another living in Lancashire. Will you and your husband lose your positions here?'

She shrugged. 'We'll 'ave to see about that. The new vicar may keep us on.'

'What do you think happened that afternoon, Mrs Minskip?'

'I think it were what they said at the inquest – Flora left the mistress alone with Ashfield and fer reasons best known to 'imself, 'e poisoned 'er.'

Lavender knew by her choice of words that she didn't believe Ashfield was a killer. 'What about the maid, Flora? She was also alone in the house with Mrs Langford for most of the morning. And her evidence is vital to this case. Is she trustworthy?'

'I allus found 'er a good gal. She's got spirit and ain't as meek as some in service, but she worked well. I never caught 'er tellin' lies. She knew there'd be 'ell to pay if she said Ashfield were in the 'ouse alone with the mistress, so she kept quiet about that at first.'

'She also claimed the wet nurse, Mrs Snelling, stole an item from the drawing-room cabinet.'

The woman shrugged again. 'I know nothin' about that. She may 'ave been mistook. But Flora didn't tell lies.'

'What do you think happened to Mrs Snelling?'

The cook's lips tightened in disapproval, and she frowned. 'I suppose she's drunk in some gin shop somewhere. I never liked 'er – and neither did the mistress.'

'But I thought Mrs Langford employed her?'

'No. 'Twere the master who brought that lush 'ere. They'd argued about whether a wet nurse were necessary, or not. I reckon he wanted to punish 'er.' She hesitated a moment, conscious she'd just criticised her employer. Then added: 'Like I said, he can be stern sometimes.'

'I'd like to ask about the vile notice that was nailed to the lychgate.'

'Ha!' exclaimed the cook, making Miss Finch jump nervously. 'I'd like to know who holds the quill behind that vile calumny too! I'd wring their bloody neck! Never in my life 'ave I 'eard of such evil!'

'I can see it was a shock to you, ma'am.'

'That sweet young gal would never plant a cuckoo in the nest of the vicar! She were *blameless*, I tell you – blameless! She were a godly woman and there were no wrong-doin' in *this* 'ouse.'

'I believe you, Ma'am. But what about the poisonous letters?'

'What letters?'

Lavender blinked. 'There's been a spate of unpleasant anonymous letters delivered to several homes in the village.'

'Oooh! Miss Finch leaned forward in excitement. 'What do they say?'

Lavender ignored her. 'Have you – or Mr Minskip – received one? Or maybe the vicar?'

'I don't know nothin' about the vicar's private letters and as for Minskip, no one would waste the time writin' to 'im – 'e can't read.'

Lavender frowned. 'What about your friends and the other people you know who are in service? Have any of them received unpleasant letters?'

Mrs Minskip shrugged and shook her head. 'No – and I 'ear about most things in Ealing.'

Lavender nodded; he could believe that. But how had this woman *not* heard about the letters? Was it only the gentry who were attacked by the poisoned quill, not the servant class or the tradesmen?

Mrs Minskip's eyes narrowed. 'These letters… are they by the same evil 'and?'

'I believe so.'

'And what do they say?' Miss Finch asked again.

Mrs Minskip rose to her feet and started to gather up the dirty crockery. She looked thoughtful. 'If yer don't mind, Detective, I need to visit the general store. And it's time yer went back to Brentford now, Miss Finch.'

Lavender stood up and picked up his hat. 'Ah, yes. I understand you need to buy some more fly papers for the vicar. Do you use a lot of them?'

She shrugged her broad shoulders. 'More than most, probably. 'E has no patience with flies – though I'm surprised there's none left. I'm sure there was four boxes in the pantry. I don't relish goin' out in this sun but needs must.'

'I'd like to speak to your husband before I go.'

''E's in the stables. I'll show yer the way.' She placed the crockery by the sink and led him to the back door.

Lavender sensed she wanted to speak to him alone.

He was right. Once they were outside in the sunlit back yard and out of earshot of Miss Finch, she turned towards him, her broad, veined face etched with concern. 'I ain't got what you'd call evidence – but if yer looking for the 'and behind all this trouble causin', you might want to look closer at Miss Finch.'

'Your former employer?'

'Aye, she's a nosy old tabby and the jealous type. She enjoys gossip and she's allus been a bit odd. She were put out when she 'ad to leave the vicarage. I can see 'er wantin' to cause trouble between the vicar and Mrs Langford.'

'Thank you for your suggestion.'

She pointed a fat finger towards the stables. 'Minskip's in there.'

She turned to go.

'One final question, if I may? Were the vicar and Mrs Langford happily married?'

She hesitated just a fraction too long before she replied. Her hesitation told him more than words could. 'They were companiable enough until the trouble started with the notice at the church.' She strode back to her kitchen.

Mr Minskip was rubbing down a glossy chestnut stallion with a handful of straw. He was older than his wife and slower of mind and speech.

The man's account of the day of the murder tied exactly with the one given by his wife. It only took a couple more questions for Lavender to ascertain that on the day of the funeral, he hadn't seen the vicar inside St Paul's Church either.

Chapter Fourteen

Woods sighed with contentment as he lay with his arm around Betsy and stared up at the leafy canopy of the sweet chestnut tree above. Little Alfie Bobbin lay at their feet, snoring soundly. The old dog was exhausted after their climb up Hanger Hill.

The branches of the tree stretched wide, casting dappled shade over them and the soft grass below. The summer air carried the scent of warm earth and wildflowers. Woods' stomach was pleasantly full after an excellent picnic, and he and his wife were flushed and tipsy from the strong ale. In fact, Betsy had even undone the top button of her gown, revealing the soft, milky flesh of her neck and cleavage.

He forced his eyes away, pulled her closer and whispered: 'I'm the luckiest man alive, Mrs Woods – and my greatest fortune in life was persuadin' you to join me at the altar in St Saviours twenty-five years ago.'

'Oh, Ned, that's so lovely,' she murmured. 'And thank you for arrangin' this surprise.'

'Am I forgiven for that fancy weddin' cart?'

She giggled. 'You daft muttonhead.'

He squeezed her tighter. 'And thank *you* for the picnic, Betsy – it were a real feast.'

Why does food always taste so much better in the fresh air? he wondered. He salivated at the memory of the thick wedges of cheese, the flaky crust of the pies that melted in his mouth and the fresh-baked bread.

A welcome breeze rustled the leaves above, sending a few early chestnut husks tumbling to the ground with soft thuds. He saw the quick flash of a red bushy tail and realised there was a squirrel up there as well. Bees hummed lazily among the wildflowers at the edge of the clearing.

'This is the life I want. We'll stay here for ever. Just you and me, Mrs Woods.'

She giggled again. 'Magdalena will be shocked if we don't go back for the girls.'

He kissed her soft, greying curls. 'They'd manage without us. They're nearly grown up now. The lads barely have any time for us anymore.'

'Except when they want feedin'.'

He smiled. 'Aye, there's that.'

Betsy pulled out of her husband's embrace and raised herself on her elbows to look back at the view.

Beyond the trees, the hill sloped gently downwards, revealing a glimpse of the countryside beyond: rolling fields stretching towards the horizon, golden in the late afternoon sun. Hanger Hill was the highest point in Ealing and the views of the meandering silver ribbon of the Thames and the distant city were magnificent.

The lighters and sailing boats skimming over the glistening surface of the river looked as small as insects. While they'd eaten their food, Ned and Betsy tried to pick out the towers of Westminster Abbey and the great dome of St Paul's beneath the shimmering heat haze hovering over London.

'Do you think we've been good parents, Ned?'

'Oh, I reckons so. This motherin' and fatherin' business don't come with instructions. It seems to me that often there's no right way of doin' things.'

'But I do worry about them so much.'

'What's botherin' you, Betsy?'

'It's our Rachel. It's the state she were in when she came home last night.'

'A bit of muck never hurt anyone, Betsy.'

'No – I meant how happy and excited she was after visitin' that menagerie of the Charltons. What's to become of her? She prefers muckin' out horses to the school room and can run faster than most boys.'

'She'll find her way. And we've agreed to pay the dame school for another year, remember? Perhaps she'll stay on there as an assistant and help out with the little nippers?'

'Her heart's not in learnin', Ned.'

'Perhaps she'll go into service. You've taught her how to clean and cook, and you've done it well.'

She frowned. 'Her heart ain't in that either, but there's so little choice for girls like Rachel.'

'Hoydens, you mean?' he said, smiling.

'Do you think we were too soft with them, Ned? They say if you spare the rod, you spoil the child. Should we have beaten them sometimes?'

Woods roared with laughter and pulled her back down beside him. 'That's the ale talkin'. Stop your frettin', Mrs Woods. What's done is done with our nippers and we can't change that. And today is about *us*, not them.'

He kissed her gently. 'Have I told you how fond I am of you today, Mrs Woods?'

'Several times. That ale's too strong for you, too.'

He laughed, and they fell silent for a while. Woods had a fancy that here, beneath the chestnut tree, time had slowed and stood still. There was a quiet magic to these ancient woodlands that made the world beyond feel distant and unimportant. Although he also had a fancy that the squirrel above his head was deliberately aiming her chewed nut shells in his direction.

'It's like the clock's turned back a quarter of a century. Just you and me canoodlin' at the top of Hanger Hill,' Betsy said. And not for the first time in their marriage, he wondered how she could always read his mind.

'Except this time we *are* married.' He gave her a cheeky wink. 'Now we can do more than just canoodle.' His hand reached out hopefully to stroke the creamy flesh at the top of her gaping blouse.

She slapped it away. 'Behave yourself, Ned Woods. We'll have none of that in public.'

'Aww.'

'Did you see the large house on the way up the hill? It weren't there the last time we came.'

'Aye.'

'You don't think they own this land, do you? Are we trespassin'?'

'Don't fret. If anyone comes, I'll tell them I'm a police constable interviewin' a dangerous suspect.'

She laughed and slapped him again. 'Lady Caroline said the house is owned by a family called Woods who'd made a fortune with a gelatine factory. You don't suppose that's your Da, do you?'

He snorted. 'We're lucky folks, Betsy, but not *that* lucky.'

'I suppose tomorrow you'll start on this wild goose chase and search for your Da.'

He sat up and shrugged. 'No, I reckon I don't need to. I'll deal with that on the last day.'

'You'll leave it until then? But what if you don't find him, Ned? Won't it sadden you?'

'There's no fear of that, my sweet. I already know where he is.'

Chapter Fifteen

Lavender first glimpsed The Laurels through the tall – and padlocked – wrought-iron gates at the entrance to the drive. A crudely painted sign hung on the gate that said: *Warning! Wild animals! Do not release!*

It was an elegant house built on a small rise in the distance. Its stone walls and towering chimney stacks gleamed like melted butter in the sunlight.

It was also tantalisingly out of reach; he struggled to find a way into the property. Eventually, he found a small side gate in the wall, half obscured by ivy. It bore another sign: *Tradesmen's Entrance. Close the door!*

He pushed it open, led his horse inside and found himself by the gatekeeper's lodge. He remembered that Sebastián had told him Frederick Daniels lived here. He rapped on the door. There was no reply or sound of any movement inside. He walked around the small house. The drapes were closed at every window; Daniels must be a late riser.

Frowning, he remounted and set off through the parkland towards the house. The gravel driveway was full of weeds and littered with animal dung. The gently sloping lawns were unmown and had returned to nature. The tall grass was full of grazing horses of different breeds and sizes. A tiny Shetland pony grazed in the shade of a giant Shire horse.

And in the middle of the horses a black-and-white-striped zebra munched on the tall grass and wildflowers, his coarse tail swishing away the flies.

Closer to the house, a flock of geese waddled noisily across what once was a flower bed, their long white necks stretched upright, heads swivelling this way and that as they searched for tender shoots.

Four goats had taken refuge from the strong sun in the shade of the trees. Three of them had long glossy coats of burnished orange but the fourth, a shaggy black and white animal with a formidable set of horns, was standing on its hind legs stripping the bark off an old oak.

Disappointed that he hadn't seen the ostrich, Lavender entered the impressive stone porch at the front of the building and rang the bell. He heard it jangling inside but once more he got no response.

Frustrated, he tied up his horse and walked around the side of the building. Here he found a derelict Italianate garden, edged with tall, conical cypress trees and full of colourful chickens of a variety of breeds. Some were perched on the crumbling marble statues and pecking around the base of a small, circular fountain.

Among the lily pads in the fountain, a duck whose plumage was a mix of brilliant orange, iridescent green, deep purple and white glided gracefully across the still water. Its large, sail-like orange feathers arched elegantly from its back and shimmered in the strong sunlight.

Lavender walked to the end of the terrace. Over the balustrade, he saw another expanse of overgrown parkland, sweeping gently down towards a woodland. It was dotted with grazing cattle, horned and shaggy Highland beasts rubbing shoulders with Jerseys among the long grass.

He heard the low murmur of female voices to his right. He followed the sound and found a flight of worn stone steps at the edge of the terrace. They led down through the trees to a large, cobbled farmyard surrounded by buildings that served as stables, animal byres and pens. The air was thick with the mingled scents of hay, animal musk and dung.

Two women were standing chatting next to the largest pig pen Lavender had ever seen, which contained a huge, black, grunting boar with an evil set of tusks.

One of the women had a red skirt and dark frizzy hair and looked like a gypsy with the huge gold hoops in her ears. She was puffing on a small clay pipe.

The other woman was dressed in mourning. Her dark hair was combed up into a bun on the back of her head. The curious eyes that turned towards him were a beautiful and vivid shade of blue and fringed with the longest black eyelashes he'd ever seen on a woman, apart from on Magdalena.

A large wolfhound lay at her feet. It raised its head when Lavender approached and growled. She silenced it with a word.

'Good morning, Ladies. My name is Detective Lavender. I'm looking for Mrs Elizabeth Charlton.'

The woman in the black dress nodded. She was tall and slender and had a sun-bronzed but clear complexion. 'I'm Mrs Charlton. Is this about my sister? Doctor Morton told me he planned to fetch a runner to investigate her murder.'

'Yes, Ma'am, that's why I'm here.' Lavender took off his hat and wiped the sweat from his brow with his handkerchief.

'I take my leave now,' the gypsy woman said. She handed Mrs Charlton a small jar of salve. 'Make sure you rub it into the wound twice a day.'

'Thank you for your help, Dora.'

So, this must be Dora Kilby, Lavender thought, and he watched the alleged witch as she strode off out of sight behind a row of stables in a billowing cloud of tobacco smoke.

'One of my goats has injured itself in a fight,' Elizabeth Charlton explained. 'It's a pygmy goat who took on a rather large Alpine billy. He's a feisty little thing. Are you thirsty, Detective?' Without waiting for an answer, she walked to a nearby pump, picked up a tin mug and worked the handle to pour him a drink. The hound rose and lolloped after her, then went and lay in the shade.

Lavender was impressed at the strength in Elizabeth Charlton's arms when she worked the pump handle. He also noted the muddy hem of her gown and the sturdy boots she wore beneath it. She clearly embraced the outdoor life.

He took the water, and she led him to a gnarled wooden bench in the shade of one of the buildings.

'You're Sebastián's stepfather, aren't you?'

'Yes, Ma'am.'

'My son, Bruce, seems to like him a lot – and that funny little girl, Rachel. Sebastián's a polite and charming young man. He's a credit to you.'

Lavender smiled. 'Thank you. That's always a relief to hear.'

'I'm glad they're in Ealing to distract Bruce. He's a day pupil at Great Ealing School but most of his friends are boarders and have gone home to their families for the summer. He's a sensitive boy and found the loss of his Aunt very distressing.'

'My deepest condolences on the death of your sister, Ma'am. It's a terrible tragedy for you all.'

The woman stiffened, blinked back her tears and nodded. 'Yes. It's awful. Clara was a silly young girl sometimes, but she was my little sister, and I loved her. She didn't deserve to die. I hate to think what she might have suffered.'

Lavender waited respectfully for her to continue.

'I just don't understand how anyone could do that to another person.'

'That's what I hope to discover.'

Her intelligent eyes scanned his face. 'So, you don't believe Ashfield killed her?'

'I'm not sure. Do you?'

'No, not really. I don't think he's capable of killing Clara.' Then her voice hardened. 'But those who make justice and retribution their business tell me he did it. And who am I, a mere woman, to argue with their deep wisdom?'

Lavender smiled. 'Sebastián's mother is the most intelligent person I've ever known – and the wisest. I never underestimate women.'

Elizabeth Charlton observed him sceptically. 'I see you're that rare breed, Lavender – an enlightened man.'

'And I can see you're an expert on rare breeds, Ma'am. By the way, what's that beautiful bird swimming in your fountain?'

Her features softened. 'I don't know. I bought it from a family friend who owns an estate in Surrey. He was a director with the East India Company.'

Lavender nodded and remembered that Morton had told him her father made his fortune with the East India Company.

'He said it came from Japan,' she continued. 'But I believe its common name is the Chinese Teal.'

'How many animals do you have?'

A large tabby cat jumped on to the wall of the boar's pen. Its arrival caught the attention of the wolf hound, which raised its head for a moment before lying back down.

'I don't know. But there still seems to be enough space for them to live in harmony – and enough money in my trust to feed them. I find animals so peaceful to live with – and inspirational. They're happy to share the resources of this parkland. It's a shame humans can't live like this.'

Lavender pointed to the pot of salve in her hand. 'I think that's proof it's not all harmony.'

She laughed. 'Yes, occasionally they fight for dominance and will attack – and kill – if they feel they, or their young, are threatened. But there's no hatred in the animal kingdom. No malice, envy or greed.'

She sighed, and her beautiful eyes drifted back to the cat, who was now washing himself. 'To be honest, Detective, I envy my animals. They live a simple, uncomplicated life – and I want that too.'

'I can understand that. I know you also lost your father and your husband recently. After that, your sister's death must be especially hard to bear. Life has been cruel to you.'

Her eyes moistened again at the mention of her sister. Then she shook herself out of her introspection and laughed. 'My husband died several years ago now – and to be honest, I don't miss him.' She turned her head and eyed him coquettishly. 'Does that shock you, Detective?'

'Not if your marriage was arranged by your father and was a loveless affair. I understand that's what happened to your sister.'

'Yes, I too was pushed down the aisle. My father had no time for us girls. He spoilt my brother – and adored my son – but women, especially daughters, were an inconvenience to him.'

'I'm sorry to hear it. Men like that don't know what they're missing. I adore my own daughter.'

'You *are* a rarity among men, Lavender. I shall have to catch you in a net and add you to my menagerie of rare breeds.'

He smiled. 'I'm not sure if my wife would be relieved or annoyed about that.'

Elizabeth Charlton turned and stared into the distance. Another cat, a black female this time, wandered into the farmyard trailing a pair of fluffy kittens behind her. In her mouth she carried a dead rat. The kittens took turns to pounce on its long, limp tail as it dragged over the cobbles.

'Does this unusual lifestyle of yours cause you problems with your neighbours?'

She laughed. 'Oh, there are critics. I think I'm considered an eccentric. Half the gentlewomen in Ealing raise a disapproving eyebrow every time they see me. Some even cross the road to avoid me.'

'I was wondering if you've heard about the poisonous and libellous letters some of your neighbours have received?'

'Yes. I received one too, about three weeks ago. I destroyed it.'

'What did it say?'

She shrugged. 'Nothing specific. Just that I'm a dirty moll, with a grubby son, and we both stink like a pigsty. The language was vile but the content just nonsense.'

'Have you any idea who sent it?'

'No. Most of the village know I keep a tame wild boar. It might be any of them – well, any of the men anyway. To be honest, I thought it was unimaginative.'

He frowned. 'Why did you think it was written by a man?'

'I don't know. I suppose because it was so *generalised.* Women enjoy gossip and make it their business to find out all sorts of tasty morsels of scandal about each other.'

She paused for a moment, thoughtful. 'Whoever it was knows little about me except the obvious: that Bruce and I spend a lot of time with smelly animals.'

Lavender remembered the letter sent to Captain Sawyer and decided she'd made a good observation. Lady Caroline never kept her Catholicism a secret and most elderly men suffered from flatulence. 'So, you feel it would have been a lot worse and more personal if written by a woman?'

'Yes. I suspect it's a man – or a very odd or immature woman. The writer could have accused me of unnatural, unwomanly behaviour – or desertion. Why didn't he – or she – do that?'

'*Unwomanly behaviour?*'

'Oh, yes, Detective. I hated my life with my husband in London. Once I found out I was with child, I left him to his gaming tables, his whores and racecourses and retreated to the Charlton estate in Scotland.'

Lavender was amused by her frankness. 'Your husband's death must have been… convenient for you.'

'It was.'

'I'm sorry you were so unhappy.'

She shrugged again. 'Bruce was the best thing that ever happened to me. I stayed up in Scotland with him for the duration of my marriage and only came home to England when I heard Charlton had succumbed to the smallpox.'

His mind returned to the vicar's comments about her and Doctor Morton. 'Would you ever consider marrying again?'

'Are you proposing, Detective?' she teased. 'Mrs Lavender won't be amused. No. I don't think so.' A shadow passed over her face. 'I'm unsure. 'On reflection, I think I fared better than Clara,' she continued. 'I wasn't happy but at least I wasn't in love with another man when I married.'

'Was it your impression the vicar loved your sister?'

'No. He was always polite, but he didn't love her. He wanted a mother for his little girls, so he could concentrate on advancing his career – and I think Clara's money was important to him.'

Lavender nodded. Doctor Morton had hinted at the same thing.

'And your brother, Frederick? I understand that like your late husband, your brother also gambles and has many creditors. He had much to gain financially from your sister's death.'

'Frederick only harms himself. And if you suspect him, Detective, you may as well suspect *me*,' she added with a smile. 'Half of Clara's share of the family trust is now mine.'

He fixed Elizabeth Charlton with a steady gaze. 'I do need to know where you were on the morning of your sister's murder. This way, I can eliminate you from my inquiries.'

'Ha!' She laughed and stared back at him. 'So now we come to the nub of it – the real reason for your visit. To find out if I killed Clara for her money.'

'It's my job to ask these questions, Ma'am.' He pointed to the cat and the kittens. 'I also need to ask you about any rat poison you keep on the premises. We're still trying to find the source of the arsenic.'

Fortunately, Elizabeth Charlton seemed more amused than offended. She pointed towards one of the stables. 'My groom keeps the rat poison in there. You're welcome to examine it if you wish. But you won't find much. I've eight cats and six kittens who do an effective job of pest control. As for my own movements that day, I spent the morning outside, riding with my son.'

'Can anyone else – one of your servants, perhaps? – verify this alibi?'

She shrugged. 'I doubt it. We were out in the fog exercising some of the horses. It would have been hard for anyone in the house to even catch a glimpse of us in mist that thick.'

'Did you only ride on your estate?'

'No. We went out into Ealing village for a while.'

'Did you see anyone else connected with this case while you were in the saddle?'

Elizabeth Charlton gave a short laugh and pulled a pair of tortoiseshell spectacles out of her skirt pocket. 'Even without such a thick mist, Detective, I need these to recognise anyone at a distance. I would be a poor witness for you.'

'And what about your brother? Where was he at the time of the murder?'

She pushed the spectacles back in her pocket. 'You'll have to ask him yourself. I let him live in the gatehouse.'

'I tried to rouse him, but he doesn't seem to be at home.'

She chuckled. 'Oh, he'll be there. But he doesn't answer the door in case it's the bailiffs. You might catch him at The New Inn, opposite St Mary's Church. When he's in Ealing, he goes there every night to play card games with the locals.'

'Thank you, that's helpful. I'll go tonight. I understand on the day of the murder he went with Reverend Langford to the vicarage to ask your sister for another loan.'

'Did he?' She gave a short laugh. 'Why am I not surprised?'

'Had he approached you for the same?'

'Yes. In fact, it was the day before Clara died. Frederick asked me for a considerable amount of money and was furious when I refused. I should have known he'd pester Clara next.'

'Did you see him on the day of the murder?'

'He came over to the house in the afternoon to tell me Clara was dead.' Her eyes moistened with tears again.

'What about earlier in the day?'

She shook her head. 'He was out early. When Bruce and I went out to the stables, one of the grooms told me Frederick had already arrived to collect his horse and had ridden off into the mist.'

'How early was this?'

'I'm not sure, but this was unusual for him. He's rarely out of bed before mid-day. He must have been desperate to see Clara.'

Lavender frowned and cast his mind back to what Langford had told him. The two men hadn't met each other in the fields until one o'clock.

Where had Frederick Daniels been that morning?

Chapter Sixteen

Before he left The Laurels, Lavender visited Elizabeth Charlton's groom in the stables. He was an ugly fellow, bald, with a nasty scar down one side of his face. But he was helpful enough.

He showed Lavender where they kept the rat poison and was adamant that it hadn't been touched by anyone except him. He also confirmed that both Frederick Daniels and Elizabeth Charlton had ridden out early on the morning of the murder and that Mrs Charlton was accompanied by her son.

When asked about the time, the man was less sure. He scratched his greying stubble and pondered the question for a while.

'The problem is, Detective, I'm short of a man and so bloody busy with all these animals the mistress keeps. I'm allus rushin' from one job to another.'

'Even an approximate time would be helpful.'

'A what?'

'Can't you guess what time it was?'

He scratched his chin again. 'Master Frederick came first – sometime after nine o'clock, I reckon. Then the mistress and young Master Bruce came a few minutes later.'

'And you didn't see any of them again?'

'No, sir. Mind you, it were like a pea soup out there in that mist.'

Lavender thanked him and left.

The sun was now at its highest in the sky and blazed down on his head. The heat was oppressive. His shirt stuck to his back with sweat and even Lavender's horse seemed to be suffering as it trudged wearily along the lane. He decided to ride back to Lady Caroline's home. Both Lavender and his horse needed refreshment.

He was becoming irritated with this case. Confirming the alibis of the suspects in a murder inquiry was standard practice, but no one had asked either of the dead woman's siblings about their movements. Yet they were the two people who'd the most to gain from the death of Clara Langford.

He also needed to visit Abel Jupp tomorrow and confirm the vicar's alibi. He sighed with frustration.

One thing was for certain: Lavender wouldn't be returning to Bow Street for some time. With so many suspects to interview, the alibis to check and the distances involved in the countryside, he needed help. Investigating this case was a two-man job.

When he arrived back at the stables at Cedar Court and dismounted, Lavender was relieved to be told by the groom that Constable Hinge was waiting for him in the house.

Good. Now at least I'll find out exactly how thoroughly – or not – this case has been investigated.

Constable Hinge was a scruffy, wiry man with unkempt whiskers, a hawkish nose and shifty, sludge-brown eyes. He swayed nervously from foot to foot when Lavender introduced himself.

'It's a rare 'onour to meet a runner, sir. A rare 'onour. Sir James 'as told me why yer 'ere.'

I wouldn't have to be here if you had done your job properly, Lavender thought angrily.

He led the constable into the sitting room belonging to the housekeeper, divested himself of his coat and sank into the comfy chair beside the hearth. Hinge went to the seat opposite and perched on the arm like he wanted to keep half upright in case he needed to leave quickly.

'I'll get straight to the point, Hinge. I need you to find that missing wet nurse, Mrs Snelling. Do you work alone, or do you have help?'

Hinge scratched his whiskery cheek and frowned. 'I can get 'elp from Norbert, if needs be. We've done our best to find the old tabby, sir, but she ain't been back to 'er lodgin's in Brentford and is nowhere to be found.'

'Does she have any family?'

'Not that we know of, sir – apart from 'er child, of course.'

'Her child?'

Hinge gave him a quizzical look. 'Aye, her little son. The mite's now livin' with a neighbour.'

Lavender nodded and quietly admonished himself for forgetting. Of course she had a child; the woman was a wet nurse. A disreputable tabby or not, it was strange she'd abandoned her baby.

'Where else have you looked?'

'All 'er usual haunts: the gin shop down Catherine Wheel Yard, The Six Bells on the high street and The Magpie and Crown.'

'Those are all taverns.'

'Aye, sir. She's a lush. But she ain't been seen anywhere.'

'What about the Brent and the canal?'

Confusion flickered across Hinge's face. 'Is that a new tavern, sir? I ain't 'eard of it afore.'

Lavender sighed. 'I meant the River Brent and the canal. Have you searched their banks, or done any dredging in the water? And what about some of the quieter country lanes between here and Brentford? I noticed this morning many are tree-lined – have you searched through the local woodland and shrubbery?'

'Do yer think she may be hidin' in the woods, sir?'

'No, Constable. I think she's dead.'

Hinge's mouth gaped open in surprise. 'Do yer think Ashfield 'as done fer 'er, as well as Mrs Langford?'

'I think *someone* has killed her and dumped her body. It's the only explanation for her disappearance.'

'Ooh.'

'She might be in the river, the canal, or half buried in the woodland undergrowth. We know she was heading back to her lodgings in Brentford when she left the vicarage on the morning of the murder. If she *had* been filching valuables from the vicarage, she probably wouldn't want to meet anyone and may have left the main path.'

'But the vicar said nothin' were missin'!'

Lavender ignored the constable's outburst. 'I want you and your fellow Norbert to scour every path and bridleway between here and Brentford, especially where they go close to the river or the canal.'

Hinge leapt to his feet. 'Aye, sir, I'll get right on to it. Straight away.'

'Just before you go,' Lavender said hastily, 'I need to know if you checked out the alibis of the Reverend Langford, Mrs Elizabeth Charlton and her brother.'

'Aye, sir. I thought it were wise to speak to Abel Jupp, seein' as how women is normally murdered by their 'usbands. But Jupp confirmed the vicar 'ad called on 'im that mornin'. It definitely weren't 'im as did for 'er.'

Lavender nodded but decided he would still speak to Jupp himself. 'And Frederick Daniels? Where was he at the time Mrs Langford, his sister, was murdered?'

Hinge's hands fluttered again. 'I don't know, sir. Once the maid told us Ashfield 'ad been with the poor woman when she died, there didn't seem much point in askin' Daniels.'

Lavender bit back his anger. 'Yet Frederick Daniels had a strong motive to kill his sister and was out riding in the parish from early in the morning. As was Mrs Charlton, who would also inherit half of her fortune.'

'Were she out, too?' the man stammered. 'I didn't know that.'

'In future, Constable, you don't leave a job half done. You turn over every stone and examine *everything* that crawls out from beneath it. Do you understand me?'

Hinge shuffled from one foot to the other and spoke to the rug beneath his boots. 'Yes, sir. Turn over all the stones.'

'And if Sir James has asked you to report back to him,' Lavender snapped, 'you can tell him I'm unhappy about how this case has been investigated so far.'

'Unhappy. Yes, sir,' the man mumbled.

'Now go and find me that wet nurse.'

'Yes, sir!' Hinge leapt to his feet, but when he reached the door he turned back. 'Don't you fret, sir. When I'm searchin' the riverbank, I'll turn over every stone.'

Lavender put his head in his hands and groaned.

Was it worth risking Betsy's wrath and asking Ned to join him in this investigation?

Chapter Seventeen

Lavender asked the cook to provide him with a plate of bread and cheese and a tankard of ale, and went in search of Magdalena.

She was in the panelled hallway of the house, examining a row of small but exquisite sketches hung on the wall next to the dining-room door. She wore a dark-red summer gown with a high waistline, which clung to her voluptuous figure in all the right places. The rich fabric caught hints of burgundy and wine with every movement and her warm olive skin glowed against the deep hue of her dress.

The sketches were drawn in pencil or charcoal and showed naval sailors at work on the deck of warships. One group were sitting on barrels mending a sail; in another, half a dozen burly men were pushing the bars of the capstan to haul up the anchor.

They were incredibly detailed. The artist had captured the strain on the sweating faces of the men and the outline of their powerful arm and thigh muscles bulging beneath their uniforms. Shadowing indicated the soft drape of the sailcloth, the braided weave of the rigging and the individual markings of the seabirds perched on the gunwale.

Magdalena greeted him with a smile and a kiss and pointed to the sketches. 'Aren't these wonderful? Captain Sawyer drew them while his ship floated idle in a windless sea. He has dozens of them.'

'He's a talented artist. I can see what our hosts have in common.'

'He's also very modest. Lady Caroline has tried to persuade him to exhibit some of them in London, but he won't. I think it's the cause of tension between them.'

Lavender smiled. 'Well, if that's all they have to argue about, I think they'll have a long and happy marriage. Where is everyone?'

'The younger children are out in the garden with Teresa. Sebastián has disappeared with Rachel. Lady Caroline is painting in the conservatory, and I think Captain Sawyer has gone out. How does your case progress?'

Grateful to have her to himself for a while, Lavender led her into the dining room. He needed her counsel. They sat at the table, and the housemaid brought him his food and ale. While he ate, he told her about his frustrating morning.

Her glossy black hair was pinned up with an effortless grace. Loose curls framed her face, and a few rebellious strands caught the light pouring in through the high windows. The contrast of her dark colouring and the deep red of her gown against the soft lemon walls made her seem even more vivid, more alive. She was an exotic hothouse bloom transplanted into the pale, pastel – and sometimes insipid – world of an English country house. The dark, reflective pools of her beautiful eyes shone with compassion and sympathy as he talked.

'Mrs Charlton sounds like a fascinating woman,' she observed. 'I'd like to meet her. But would that be appropriate when she's a suspect in your case? In fact, should Sebastián and Rachel spend so much time with her son?'

He shrugged and raised his hands in a gesture of helplessness. 'I doubt the children will come to any harm – and I wouldn't dare interfere with their plans for this cricket match tomorrow. But it's the scale of this inquiry that bothers me the most; there are so many loose ends, unchecked alibis and unexplored lines of enquiry – and Magistrate Conant wants me back in London as soon as possible. I need help, Magdalena. I need Ned.'

'Ha!' she exclaimed. 'Betsy will be furious.'

'That's what I fear.'

'Is there anything I can do to help?'

'Well, if you do meet Mrs Charlton tomorrow, see if you can discover her true feelings for Doctor Morton. The vicar suggested there's affection between them and they colluded to kill Clara Langford. If it's true, this complicates things and means I've now got to investigate my client as well.'

'Sebastián told me last night that according to his friend Bruce, your client, Doctor Morton, *is* wooing Mrs Charlton. The boys were discussing stepfathers and Sebastián advised him to tell his mother to find a quiet one like you.'

Lavender laughed. 'That is a very welcome compliment.'

'Teresa told me the servants in the kitchen have also been gossiping about Doctor Morton's pursuit of Mrs Charlton. They think he may be after her fortune.'

Lavender's eyebrows rose in surprise; his client didn't seem to be short of money. But, of course, no one could ever tell from such a short acquaintance.

'Oh, I forgot. We've received some letters. Yours is from London.' She rose to her feet and went out into the hall to fetch them.

His own letter was from his former employer, Magistrate Read. No doubt this was his reply to Lavender's request to learn more about Doctor Morton. He was about to open it when he saw the second letter in Magdalena's hand and recognised the cheap white paper and the rudimentary capital letters that spelled out her name and address here at Cedar Court.

'What's that?' A leaden sense of dread materialised in his stomach.

She smiled and passed it across to him. 'It would seem your anonymous writer knows my son and I are in Ealing, and we're Catholics. But you'll have to explain the rest to me. My English is not that good.'

Frowning, he unfolded the sheet of paper.

THOU ART A FAT HATCHET FACED PAPIST TROT AND THY BRAGGART NOCKY BOY IS A CODS HEAD

'Fat? Hatchet-faced!' he exclaimed angrily. 'Has this cork-brain even *seen* you? You're neither of those, Magdalena. And as for the rest, this fiend suggests Sebastián is a dull and stupid fellow – which is also a ridiculous thing to say. You mustn't take any of this to heart. The writer has a grudge against the local gentry and enjoys insulting them.'

She laughed. 'It hasn't upset me. To be honest, I feel flattered I've been noticed. I'm now part of the commune.'

'Community,' he corrected absent-mindedly, his mind still on the foul words in his hands. 'Elizabeth Charlton made an interesting comment today about how generalised her own letter was. She feels the writer is a man because women know and notice so much more about people and are more intuitive. The language is vile but by the sound of it, the one sent to Sir James Clitherow was also just a string of generalised insults.'

'Did you see their letters?'

'No. But I've collected a few other samples.'

'Show me.'

He reached into his coat pocket and pulled out the letters given to him by Doctor Morton and Captain Sawyer, along with the notice that was pinned to the church lychgate. He opened them out and laid them on the table. 'Lady Caroline doesn't know about this,' he warned her. 'Captain Sawyer asked me to keep her ignorance.'

Magdalena nodded. 'I'm not surprised. He's very protective.' A small frown gathered between her eyebrows when she finished the letter. 'I agree with Mrs Charlton. I'm not sure they're the work of a woman. And are you sure they're all written by the same person?'

'As sure as I can be,' he replied, frowning. 'Although I've wondered why this one was pinned to the church gate and the rest were sent by post. Why? What have you seen?'

'The punctuality.' She pointed towards the accusations made against Clara Langford and Ashfield. 'There are end stops.'

He read it again. It took a moment for him to understand what she meant.

THOU ART A WHORING HOBBY-HORSE CLARA LANGFORD AND THAT CLINKER ASHFIELD DOTH RIDE YOU LIKE HIS NAG. THY BIRD-WITTED VICAR BE A HORNED CUCKOLD AND HAS A BASTARD IN HIS CRIB.

'They're full stops and they're *punctuation*, *querida*, not punctuality,' he told her.

She rolled her beautiful eyes to the ceiling then leaned towards him and whispered sensuously: 'That's what I love about you, Stephen. You always correct my English.'

Lavender smiled and stroked her arm. 'I may be annoying, but you never make the same mistake twice, my clever darling. And I think you've seen something here I missed.'

'Is that possible?' she teased. 'Has the great Detective Lavender, Chief Constable of Bow Street… missed something?'

'I don't know if it's relevant,' he confessed. 'It might just be the writer forgot their usual guise and inserted the full stops by accident. But I'll visit the general shop that distributes the post. They might be able to tell me who posted the letter addressed to you.'

Their peace was suddenly shattered by a screaming child and the frantic patter of tiny shoes on the tiled floor of the hallway outside. 'Mamá! *Estoy herido*! I fell in doggie dung!'

Laughing, Magdalena rose to her feet. 'You finish your food, Stephen. I'll help Teresa with Alice.'

Lavender took another bite and washed it down with his ale. Outside in the hallway, young Jack began to wail. He heard a harassed Teresa trying to reassure everyone and Tabitha's clear little voice: 'It's not doggie dung Alice. It's mud.'

But Alice wasn't placated. Sobbing, she was led upstairs to change her gown.

Chapter Eighteen

Smiling, Lavender chewed his last mouthful of food and turned his attention to his letter from James Read. It was longer than he expected.

Read had asked his brother about Doctor Morton's history and had received a glowing account. Apparently, Doctor Morton was an exemplary physician and surgeon who'd run a valuable practice in the poorest part of the city. He often waived his fees in order to help his most destitute patients and gave his services to the Infirmary.

Mm, that wouldn't have made him rich, Lavender thought.

Read also told him that when Doctor Morton returned to Ealing, he'd been greatly missed by his colleagues. The only blight on his career had occurred a year before he left. A rumour began to circulate that he'd assisted some female mill workers with removing unwanted infants from their wombs.

Lavender grimaced and read on.

But nothing had been proven; no charges were made, and the authorities had deemed this vicious gossip started by a jealous colleague.

Lavender thought about this for a while, then turned his attention to the second half of Read's letter – and all thoughts of Morton went out of his head.

Mrs Read and I were delighted when Mrs Lavender called on us last month, but we were saddened to see how ill and wretched she looked. Charity assures me this can be a consequence of childbearing, and it will pass, but it was distressing to see her like this. Please give her our fondest regards and best wishes for her return to good health.

I was surprised when she asked me for more details of the death of her first husband, Don Antonio García de Aviles. She wanted to know the whereabouts of her husband's grave in Spain and asked me to make further enquiries.

I have now done so and am grateful for this opportunity to share them with you initially. I feel, in the light of your wife's ill health, you're best placed to break these unpleasant tidings to her.

De Aviles' body was never found and identified.

As I told you when you first enquired back in 1809, our agents on the Peninsula reported that de Aviles died at the Battle of Talavera earlier that year. He fought alongside his regiment and did not rejoin them when dusk fell.

You may recall from the newspaper reports that Talavera was a horrific military engagement. Sparks from the cannon fire and artillery ignited the parched grassland and started numerous fires. The heat from the blaze was intense. Many of the injured who lay in the path of the flames were burned to death and their bodies were impossible to identify. Their screams still haunt the soldiers who survived. Likewise, those who were already dead were burned beyond recognition.

It is assumed that de Aviles, whether dead or merely injured, was caught up in this conflagration. What is certain is that his body was never found and identified. Our agents believe he was buried in a mass grave along with the rest of our poor soldiers who died in this horrific battle.

I'm sorry to be the bearer of such grim and morbid tidings. Please inform Mrs Lavender what you think is appropriate from the information above...

Lavender put down the letter and stared at the verdant green of the tranquil English countryside outside the windows. But he didn't see any of it. His senses and his imagination were fixed on the blazing wall of flames and searing heat that bore down on the injured at Talavera. He heard their screams and smelt the stench of roasting human flesh, mingled with the acrid smoke and gunpowder fumes.

It must have been a hellish scene, unsurpassed by the horrors depicted in Dante's *Inferno.*

But why did Magdalena want to know what had happened to Antonio? He sighed, pushed his hair out of his eyes and wished he understood women better than he did.

In the five years he'd known Magdalena, she'd barely mentioned her first husband, except with anger. Theirs had not been a happy marriage and she resented how he'd ridden off to war leaving her and Sebastián at the mercy of the invading French.

When she escaped to London with Sebastián, her correspondence with Antonio had been acrimonious. He'd briefly sent money for Sebastián's education but refused to support his wife. She and Teresa were destitute when he'd first met them. They moved around the country, living off the charity of one set of Spanish émigrés after another, unaware that de Aviles was already dead.

For a moment, he had a nasty flash of jealousy. Why had Magdalena never mentioned her visit to James and Charity Read? Was she unhappy with her life with him and hankering after her first husband? This would explain her secrecy.

Then his common sense reasserted itself.

Magdalena's enquiry was a symptom of her recent melancholy: nothing more, nothing less. He remembered how after his father's death earlier in the year, he kept reliving the moment his father died every night when he closed his eyes – and again every morning when he awoke. He'd also been plagued with a morbid fear that Magdalena and their children might die.

He thought back over the last hour. He remembered Magdalena's smiles, her serenity and her grace when she'd sat with him at this table. There was a calm confidence in her posture, the stillness of her hands resting lightly in her lap. This visit to Ealing was healing his troubled wife.

He folded the letter and put it in his coat pocket. He'd no intention of sharing any of its contents with Magdalena today.

The general store stood in the centre of Ealing, opposite St Mary's Church and next to The New Inn, where the coaches to and from London left and arrived three times a day. A painted sign above the doorway announced that the proprietor was Mr J. Blake.

Lavender's eyes were drawn to the large iron postbox nailed to the outside wall next to one of the store's bow windows. Watched by her mother, a small girl was standing on her tiptoes posting a letter through the slot.

The air inside the large shop was thick with the mingled scents of sawdust, tobacco and spices. Cloves, cinnamon and coffee beans were stored in open barrels on a creaking wooden floor worn smooth by decades of boots and shoes. Next to them were barrels, crates and baskets filled with potatoes and apples. With so little floor space, the customers, mostly housewives and uniformed maids, were forced to huddle together.

Shelves lined every wall, stacked high with goods: bolts of fabric in muted florals and checks; glass jars full of preserves and pickles in brine; soap, lamp oil and patent medicines with grandiose labels. Three white-capped and aproned women worked behind the counter, flitting between the customers, the wooden drawer where they deposited the coins and a large ledger where they entered the sales.

Behind the counter stood a small, bespectacled man in a black waistcoat and rolled-up sleeves, weighing flour on a brass scale. Lavender attracted his attention and discovered he was the proprietor. He explained who he was and asked Mr Blake to take him into the privacy of a back room to talk, away from the curious eyes of the customers.

'I'm investigating this spate of anonymous and spiteful letters that have been delivered to several Ealing residents.'

Blake nodded, took off his spectacles and cleaned them. 'Yes, I've 'eard some of the gentry have had 'em. One of my customers came into the shop and asked for 'is tuppence back after 'e opened it. 'E sed 'e weren't payin' for such filth.'

'Who was this man?'

Blake narrowed his eyes. ''E asked me not to say.'

Lavender silently cursed the damned secrecy in the village around these letters.

Is it worth making a public announcement? he wondered. Should he let it be known he was investigating this affair? Should he ask people to come forward with their information?

'What's the system with the post? How do you operate?'

'The mail coaches bring letters from London to the inn next door, three times a day. They come 'ere to be sorted.'

'What about the local post? Letters written by one Ealing resident to another?'

'They go in the box outside. I empty it twice a day, put it with the rest, and my boys tek it round the village.'

'How many letters are posted into your box every day?'

Blake thought for a moment, then said: 'I've never counted 'em but I'd say between twenty and forty. Not all of 'em are for the folks in the parish, mind.'

Lavender's hopes sank. The affluent residents of Ealing were obviously literate and great letter writers. This wasn't going to be easy.

'One of these vile letters was delivered to Cedar Court just after one o'clock.'

Blake nodded again. 'Aye, it'll 'ave been young Tim as delivered it. 'E takes the post there for the second delivery.'

'So, it would have been placed in your postbox sometime this morning.'

'Yes. I empty the box at eight and twelve on the dot. That letter will 'ave been posted between eight and noon.'

'Is there any way of finding out who posted it?'

Blake shook his head. 'There's folks postin' letters all the time.'

'But you can see the postbox from behind your counter. Did you notice anyone in particular? Someone who may have been acting in a furtive manner?'

Blake laughed. 'We're too busy to notice who posts letters and who don't, Detective.'

Sighing, Lavender thanked him and left the shop.

His spirits lifted a few minutes later, however, when a curious and noisy contraption came into sight.

A flower- and ribbon-bedecked horse and trap, dangling dozens of clanging horseshoes, was driving down the road. The ruddy-faced man behind the reins, wearing his Sunday best coat, was his constable, Ned Woods. Cuddled up against his arm was Betsy. Both were flushed with ale – although Betsy looked the worse – and to the delight of the other pedestrians and shoppers in the street, they were singing.

Despite slurring the odd word, Woods' deep baritone was perfectly in harmony with his wife's faultless soprano as they belted out the final lines of a popular ditty:

'Let them ask as they cross the street,
Of any young virgin they happen to meet,
And I know she'll say from behind her fan,
That none can love like an Irishman!'

Smiling at the applause they drew, Lavender stepped out into the street and hailed the couple.

Woods reined in the horse and leapt down from the cart to shake Lavender's hand. His broad face beamed with his smile. 'Gawd's teeth! This is well met, sir! What the devil are you doin' here?'

'It's a long story, Ned. One I'd like to share with you, if Betsy doesn't mind.'

'Yoo-hoo, Stephen!' Betsy waved at him from her perch on the trap.

Smiling, he waved back. 'Good evening, Betsy – and a happy wedding anniversary to you. Have you had a suitably celebratory day?'

'It's been a day to remember, Stephen. Really s'lovely,' she slurred.

'Are you here about that shockin' murder of the vicar's wife?' Woods asked.

'I am. It's a real mystery, Ned.' He pointed to The New Inn. 'Can you meet me here after supper? We can talk over a tankard of ale. I need your help.'

Woods gave his hand another vigorous shake. 'I'll be there, sir, don't you fret. But I'd best collect the nippers and take them and Betsy home first.' He climbed back on to the trap and shook the reins.

The vehicle lurched forward, and the happy couple began to sing again.

Smiling, Lavender watched them go.

In the distance, he heard a rumble of thunder and felt the temperature drop. He glanced at the sky and saw the ominous black clouds of a storm gathering in the north over the gently rolling hills.

Still grinning, he set off back to Cedar Court.

Even a torrential downpour couldn't dampen his spirits now.

He'd got Ned back at his side.

Chapter Nineteen

The storm was in full force by the time Lavender took the short walk to The New Inn.

Black clouds rolled and swirled overhead and the rain slammed down, reducing visibility to a few feet. Blinding flashes of lightning revealed eerie, frozen-still images of the buildings and trees around him and the puddles boiled with raindrops. Most sensible people would stay at home on a night like this, but Daniels wasn't sensible. His gambling addiction would drive him to the tavern.

The New Inn was an old stone building that had been converted from a farmhouse into a tavern. Inside, it was a rabbit warren of smoky taprooms with low ceilings and uneven flagstone floors worn smooth by the centuries of boots. A musty hint of damp mingled with the smell of warm ale, tallow candles and tobacco.

Thankfully, the innkeeper had lit a fire in one of the cavernous arched fireplaces, and Lavender found a small table nearby. He removed his sodden hat and spread his greatcoat on the back of the chair to dry. He glanced around, looking for Daniels.

Despite the atrocious weather outside, the tavern was still busy. Many of the men had the collarless shirts, brown leathery faces and grubby clothes of farmworkers. Several large hounds lay on the floor by their masters, which accounted for the stink of wet dog Lavender had also noticed. But there was a surprising number of well-dressed local gentry among the drinkers. Two men, one wearing an old-fashioned wig, were poring over a pile of legal papers while sipping their ale.

His head turned at the sound of dice being cast upon a wooden table and he found his man. Daniels stood out among the other three dice players because of his claret-coloured velvet coat and pristine black mourning cravat. His clothes contrasted sharply with the homespun jackets and spotted neckerchiefs of his fellow gamblers.

Daniels looked remarkably like his dark-haired, blue-eyed sister. But his face, frowning and intent on the game at hand, was thinner and sharper than hers. The skin stretched tightly over his cheekbones. He was aged about twenty-five and tall. But he was too thin and angular for his height.

Lavender took a tankard of ale from the barmaid and sat back to watch the game. Judging by the gleaming piles of coins next to his opponents, Daniels was losing – and losing badly. His fellow gamblers were hard-featured, whiskery older men, who talked with the local accent and sipped their ale. They were quietly spoken and respectful towards 'Master Frederick', as they called him, but were steadily fleecing him of every coin in his pile.

Lavender gauged his moment and when it looked like the latest round was about to end, he called over the barmaid and asked her to invite the young man to join him. When she relayed her message, Daniels rose, came across with his glass of brandy and threw himself into the chair opposite.

'That was well timed, Lavender. A few more rounds of dice and I'd have been dished and pawning my horse!' His eyes shone with the strong spirits, but he seemed sober. Dark shadows of sleeplessness and anxiety beneath his eyes spoiled his good looks.

'Did you expect to see me tonight?'

Daniels nodded and took another swig of his brandy, while his eyes flitted nervously around the room. 'Yes. I saw Elizabeth at dinner, and she said you might look for me.'

Lavender revised his opinion of Elizabeth Charlton. The woman obviously had a softer heart than he'd expected. She might force her troublesome brother to sleep in the gatehouse, but at least she fed him. 'I need to ask you about the day of Mrs Langford's murder.'

Daniels winced and sadness passed over his face. 'Yes. That was a bad show. Poor Clara.' He gestured to the barmaid to refill his empty glass. 'I can't understand what got into Ashfield. I always liked the fella. It's unrequited love and all that, I suppose. Not that I know much about love, unrequited – or otherwise.'

'What happened that day?'

'I've already told the constable, and everyone at the inquest. I was out riding when I met Langford just outside the village. I needed a word with Clara, so I returned with him to the vicarage. But when we got there, Langford found her dead. I fetched the doctor and... well, you know the rest.'

Lavender nodded. 'When you say you were *out riding*, exactly where were you riding?'

Daniels looked confused. 'Here and there. Round about. To be honest, Lavender, I had a lot to think about. I've had a run of bad luck at the horses and I'm dodging my creditors. It worries a man. I just gave my filly her head and let her roam.'

'So, that's why you wanted to see your sister – to borrow money?'

'Yes.'

Lavender paused for a moment and assessed the young man. Daniels shared the same disarming frankness displayed by his sister, which made them both likeable. But this young man was desperate for money and had a strong financial motive to kill Clara Langford. It was imperative Lavender confirmed his alibi. He needed to push him harder.

'Your sister's groom told me you collected your horse soon after nine o'clock. It was nearly four hours later when you met Langford. That's a long time to just roam around the parish.'

Daniels looked confused. 'Was it that early?'

'Yes – and I understand you rarely rise before noon.'

The young man's eyes flashed with anger. 'God damn it, Lavender! Surely you don't suspect that I killed Clara?'

Lavender shrugged. 'You've a strong financial motive and, by the sound of it, plenty of opportunity.'

'But why would I kill Clara for her money when I could just borrow it from her?'

'We only have your word that she was so amenable – and like everyone else in the parish, you knew she'd be alone because of the funeral in Brentford.'

Lavender paused for a moment then continued: 'The housemaid claims she saw someone loitering at the other side of the village green, watching the house. She believes it was a man. Whoever it was, they'll have seen Ashfield, the parlour maid and the wet nurse leave. They'll have known Mrs Langford was on her own. Was that you?'

'No.'

'I'm not sure I believe you. Were you hesitating, trying to pluck up the courage to approach your sister for money?'

Daniels gave a short laugh – but his eyes weren't smiling. 'I didn't need to find the courage to speak to Clara. She's – she was – very kind.'

'Did anyone see you out riding?'

'No, not in that damned fog. One horseman would look like another in that murky pea-souper.'

'I understand your sister and nephew also went riding that morning. Did you see either of them?'

'No. I can't believe you're asking me these damned questions!'

Lavender sighed. 'Look at it from my point of view, Mr Daniels. You were gone for hours, have no alibi and we know a man was loitering outside the vicarage that morning. Your elder sister had already refused to loan you money, and I can't help wondering what might have happened if you'd called on Mrs Langford and she'd also refused to help you. Maybe you felt you had no other choice except to kill her for her share of your family trust?'

Daniels' face turned red with anger. 'Oh, for God's sake, Lavender! I wouldn't kill my own sister! I didn't go near the damned vicarage until I met Langford and rode back with him.'

'But that's part of the problem I have, Mr Daniels. The Reverend Langford told me when he met you in the fields outside the village, you were riding *away* from Ealing towards Brentford.'

Daniels mouth dropped open in surprise. 'No. No, that's not true!'

'Are you sure?'

'Yes. It was the other way round. Tom Langford was the one riding *away* from the vicarage when I met him. He was heading *towards* Brentford across the fields.'

Lavender paused for a moment, then said: 'How did he react when he saw you?'

'Well, he wasn't pleased to see me… but he rarely was. He turned his horse round and rode with me. Good grief! He was supposed to be in Brentford. Why was he…? Do you think…?'

'I don't know,' Lavender replied calmly. 'But I do know that one of you is lying.'

Daniels pushed his chair back abruptly and stood up. His face was contorted with emotion. His voice broke as he spoke. 'I can't take any more of this. It's bad enough that a chap loses his sister in such a dreadful fashion, but to be suspected like *this*?'

'I offer you my condolences, Daniels, but I have to get to the truth.'

The young man gave an almost imperceptible nod, then said slowly, 'There's something else you should know. My sister Elizabeth wears her late husband's riding jacket and hat when she's on horseback. She prefers to ride astride like a man and claims that if any of the neighbours saw her at a distance, they'd mistake her for a man and be less shocked.'

Then he turned and left.

Woods arrived about twenty minutes later, soaking wet and – as usual – starving hungry.

'Did Betsy mind you joining me tonight?'

Woods grinned and winked. 'She don't know I'm here, sir. She's in bed snorin' off the ale. With her abstemious nature, the strength of it took her by surprise. Rachel's promised to keep an eye on her and Tabby. She's a good gal, is our Rachel – and clever too. She helped the Charltons round up their hosses to get them in the stables before the storm broke.'

'How did she do that?'

Woods' broad chest puffed out with pride. 'Just like her Da taught her. The problem is, they've two stallions: a Shire horse and a Shetland pony. When they try to round them up, they scatter in different directions, which confuses the mares. Rachel put a harness on them both and tied the little pony's reins to the bridle of the Shire horse. Your Sebastián gave her a leg up and she rode the Shire to the stables with the pony and mares trotting quietly behind.'

'Well done, Rachel,' Lavender said, smiling.

While Woods ordered a bowl of stew and a tankard of ale, Lavender told him everything he knew about the case and explained its complexity. He'd only just finished when the food arrived. Woods fell on it eagerly.

'As far as I can tell, no one has checked on the alibis of any of the suspects or made any real attempt to find that missing wet nurse. She's an important witness – if she's still alive.'

Woods was happy to talk with his mouth full. 'So, Sir James and his constables arrested Ashfield simply because they think he was the last person to see Mrs Langford alive?'

'It seems that way.'

Woods nodded sagely. 'This sounds like a bafflin' case, sir, and I've a notion that weasel, Conant, wants you back in London soon?'

'Yes, he does. I need help, Ned.'

Woods laughed, then coughed as he choked on a hunk of bread. 'Gawd's teeth, sir! I spent years teachin' you everythin' I know – but you *still* need my help?'

Lavender smiled. 'I'm lost without you, Ned.'

'Tell me again, sir – who has the most to gain from Mrs Langford's death?'

'Her brother and sister inherit her share of the family fortune between them. Neither of them has a good alibi and Frederick Daniels is badly in debt.'

'What about the husband? That's what's confusin' my old noggin.'

'Financially, Langford will be poorer because of her death.'

'How so?'

'Mrs Langford's share of the trust reverts to her siblings. And – thanks to the scandal – he's to lose his living here and move to a mill town in the north.'

'It don't sound like he had a motive to kill her.'

'My instincts tell me it's not simple, Ned. Because of that dreadful note pinned to the church lychgate, Clara Langford had become an embarrassment to her husband. I don't think he ever cared for her – or is mourning her loss. Yes, he's miserable and unhappy – but I felt most of it was self-pity. He made snide comments about his wife's siblings, and his parting comment to me left me in no doubt he believes his new daughter was fathered by Ashfield.'

Woods scowled. 'Heaven and hell. This wicked scribbler has a lot to answer for. What about that sawbones, Morton? Where does he fit into this?'

'I'm not sure, but something's not quite right and I can't put my finger on it. He's been *too* helpful throughout this inquiry at every stage. I don't think he's as wealthy as he appears. Allegedly, he's fond of Elizabeth Charlton.'

Woods grinned and winked. 'So, he's *fond* of the wealthy widow woman, eh?'

'He's also an expert on arsenic poisoning and, ironically, it's *his* evidence that's put his brother in gaol.'

'Do you think he may have set his brother up to take the blame while he swans off into the sunset with the woman and all the chinks?'

'I don't think so, but I can't afford to dismiss any line of enquiry in this case – no matter how fanciful.'

Woods paused with his spoon halfway to his mouth and stared at him. 'But why employ *you* and pay for his brother's private cell in the gaol if he wanted him there in the first place?'

Lavender shrugged. 'Guilt, perhaps? Or to impress Elizabeth Charlton?'

Lavender took a sip of his ale then added: 'I've also noticed there are many young widows and widowers in this case. I wonder if one of them has murdered before? Morton, Langford and Mrs Charlton have all buried their first spouse. And there was a rumour in Manchester that Dr Morton helped factory girls remove unborn babies.'

Woods grimaced. 'It seems to me it's a good job I'm here, sir. You're pullin' yourself into a messy tangle with this case. I can see you don't have evidence for any of your suspicions. *And* it sounds like your suspects are leadin' you in a merry dance that would grace the stage in Drury Lane.'

Lavender sighed and nodded. 'They keep blaming each other.'

Woods put down his spoon, gave a small belch and wiped his mouth on his coat sleeve. 'Then it's not all bad – you must have rattled their cages. Just remember, sir, sometimes the simple answer is the right one. Now, what about them sick letters? Have you got 'em?'

Lavender nodded and pulled out the papers from his pocket. He spread them out over the table. Woods read them, glowering.

'From what I've learned so far, these missives are only aimed at the gentry. Someone clearly holds a grudge against them. And their hatred of Clara Langford was particularly strong.'

'Which means this scribbler is also a suspect in your murder inquiry.'

'Exactly.'

'It's the language of the docks, the brothels and the gutter,' Woods observed. 'Yet there aren't many stevedores or harlots who can form their words with a quill.'

'That's true,' Lavender said thoughtfully. 'This writer is literate at least. But if the writer *is* part of the educated gentry of this parish, where on earth did they learn such slang?'

'Have you any notion if it's a man or a woman?'

'Not yet, although several names have been suggested – including,' he added with a smile, 'that of your Cousin Dora.'

Woods chuckled. 'Our Dora's a feisty filly – and she don't care who she upsets. I can see how her name might come up. Do you want me to have a word with her?'

'I'd like us both to go and see her, if possible. I also need to speak to her daughter. Flora was the housemaid at the vicarage at the time of the murder. You're always so much better at interviewing the common folk than me.'

'That's because you scare them, sir. I've warned you about this before.'

'I'll ride to Brentford tomorrow and fetch you,' Lavender continued. 'I'll borrow a horse for you from Captain Sawyer's stable. I need to speak to the vicar of St Paul's and some old man called Abel Jupp who has provided an alibi for Langford.'

'Why do you want to speak to the Brentford vicar?'

'No one saw Langford inside the church during the funeral service. I thought I'd ask the vicar if he saw him.'

'Do you think Langford slipped back to Ealing when the service began?'

'Possibly.'

Woods downed the last of his ale. 'We'd better have an early start tomorrow. Especially as we're both watchin' a cricket match in the afternoon.'

'Oh, God! I'd almost forgotten! Sebastián will never forgive me if I don't watch him play! But are you sure you don't mind helping me, Ned? This week is precious time alone with your family.'

Woods smiled. 'I've a notion I'll be thrown out of the lodgin's tomorrow mornin' anyway. Apart from nursin' a sore head, Betsy has pies to bake – she's agreed to help with the tea at the cricket match. She won't want me under her feet.'

Chapter Twenty

When Lavender arrived at Woods' lodgings the next morning, the door was wide open.

Two things wafted out.

The first was the delicious smell of warm, fresh pastry mingled with apples simmering in sugar and cinnamon.

The second was Betsy's irritated voice: 'For God's sake, Ned! Stop hoverin' over them apple turnovers! You've only just had your bread and drippin'!'

Smiling, Lavender knocked on the door jamb and stepped inside the hot kitchen, where a perspiring and red-faced Betsy was pulling another tray of golden pastries out of the oven.

Alfie Bobbin rushed over to greet him, and he bent down to stroke the little dog. 'Good morning, Betsy. Ned.'

'Stephen!' Betsy straightened up and brushed flour off the front of her apron. 'Thank the Lord you're here! Take this muttonhead away before I end twenty-five years of wedded bliss by beatin' him to death with a ladle!'

He laughed. 'I'm happy to oblige, Betsy. I've one of Captain Sawyer's excellent roans outside, Ned.'

Betsy waved her ladle in a menacing manner at both men. 'And don't the pair of you forget that cricket match!'

Lavender grinned and glanced around the tiny kitchen. 'Where is the heroine of the hour? Apparently, most of Ealing is agog to see the girl-who-plays-cricket.'

'She's disappeared – and I need her help too,' Betsy grumbled. '*And* she's taken sixpence out of my purse, so don't forget to arrest her for theft when you see her.'

'She's probably already in Ealing with Sebastián, checking the pitch,' Lavender said. 'He was worried the village green would be waterlogged after last night's storm. He was the first up for breakfast and darted out of the house.'

Betsy humphed, leaned over the oven and muttered something sinister but indistinguishable.

Outside, the sun blazed in a cloudless blue sky. The storm had long since passed but it had left the air heavy with the pleasant scent of wet earth, crushed leaves and rain-soaked grass.

Dora Kilby's neat brick house was across the square on the end of a terrace. Beside it, a tall and ancient wall enclosed her herb garden. It had a separate entrance through an archway with a rusty wrought-iron gate. When they passed, they saw Dora standing with a young woman in the far corner of the garden, beside great golden orange blooms of calendula and the unmistakable ferny leaves and pale flowers of the valerian plant.

Lavender and Woods dismounted, tied up their horses and went through the gate towards the women. The path between the well-tended beds was narrow and lined with clover and creeping thyme. Their legs brushed against the fragrant purple spikes of a lavender bush that hummed with bees. Tall foxgloves rose like towers beside unruly clumps of camomile, while comfrey and mullein offered their broad, soft leaves up to the sun. Against the sunniest, south-facing wall was a huge swathe of purple and red opium poppies with their distinctive wavy petals.

Everything here was grown for its medicinal properties and although Lavender recognised many of the plants, there was a large number he didn't know. He kept his hands well away from anything he didn't recognise in case it was poisonous.

If she'd had a motive, Dora Kilby would have been Lavender's main suspect for the poisoning of Clara Langford. He understood why dark rumours circulated about her in the community; no doubt she had the ability to kill as well as cure. Knowledge like hers was powerful.

Woods greeted his cousin warmly and introduced Lavender. She reached out a tattooed hand to shake his. The young woman who'd been standing with her gave them a curious glance then left with her small pouch of valerian.

Dora took them into her kitchen, bade them sit at the table and made them a cup of tea. Then she settled her plump hips down on a chair beside them, pulled out a pouch of aromatic sun-cured small-leafed tobacco and lit her chipped clay pipe.

She looked like a prosperous farmer's wife, he decided, and her pretty kitchen was full of sunlight and feminine knick-knacks and ornaments. But her large earrings were solid silver and her rings also looked expensive. Her seat was well upholstered and comfortable, and she soon enveloped them in a cloud of Turkish tobacco smoke – a rare variety. Dora Kilby was a woman who was prepared to pay for her luxury. Lavender was amused to hear her call Woods 'Neddy'.

'I've been asked to investigate the tragic murder of the vicar's wife, Mrs Kilby,' Lavender told her. 'I need to speak to your daughter, Flora.'

'Flora is out on an errand for me. She'll be back soon enough. I've 'eard about the trouble up in Ealing. Arsenic poisonin' is a terrible way to die, the poor woman.'

'Did you ever meet Mrs Langford?' Lavender asked.

'Aye. I were midwife at 'er confinement.'

'You were there? I'd assumed Dr Morton attended her when the child was born.'

''E weren't needed. It were a simple enough birth for a midwife to 'andle. That baby gal came out easy – which surprised me, on account of her bein' so large.'

Lavender saw something flicker in her dark-brown eyes – and heard the slight edge in her voice.

'Was the child unusually large?'

She sighed heavily. 'I've said nothin' to no one. But now Mrs Langford's passed, I don't suppose it matters if the truth comes out.'

'What truth?'

'She weren't no seven-month babe. I've seen many of them before. They've no fat beneath their skin; it's thin and glows red with the blood veins. And their 'eads seem too large for their little bodies. Baby Ruth were perfect: full grown and full term.'

Lavender frowned. 'Why did you expect a seven-month baby?'

She laughed and took another puff of her pipe. 'Because I can count, Detective, that's why. According to my Flora, the vicar and Mrs Langford were wed in November. But her waters broke in June, and young Ruth were born then.'

'Gawd's teeth,' Ned murmured when the significance of this revelation sank in. Meanwhile, Lavender's thoughts flashed back to Ashfield.

Dora rolled her eyes to the ceiling. 'It's not a crime, Neddy – even among the gentry. I can't say I've ever 'eard of a vicar swivin' with 'is wife before they're wed, but there's no accountin' for some folks and 'e's a young and lusty fella.'

Except... what if it wasn't Langford who'd been swiving with Clara before their wedding?

'Did you tell anyone about this?' Lavender asked.

'Lord! No! It weren't my place. I took my chinks and left them to their peace.'

Ned leaned towards her, frowning. 'Did the vicar know the child were full term?'

'No. I don't reckon 'e knew the difference between a full-term child and a seven-month babe.'

But he'll have had his suspicions, Lavender thought. *What if Clara was carrying Ashfield's child and married Langford to protect her reputation?*

'And Doctor Morton?' he asked.

She shrugged. 'If 'e did 'ave a notion, 'e never said.'

But he wouldn't, would he? If Morton suspected anything, he'd keep quiet about it to protect his brother.

'And you left the vicarage on good terms with the vicar and Mrs Langford?' Woods asked.

'Yes, Neddy. I've already said.'

'It's just that your name has been mentioned with regard to that vile note that was pinned on to the church about Mrs Langford.'

'Well, of course it has,' she replied calmly. 'Folks allus think of me when somethin' is amiss.'

'Why's that, Mrs Kilby?' Lavender asked.

'Because I'm a businesswoman, that's why – and a successful one too, despite not 'avin' a man. There's a meanness in a lot of folks that makes them try to pull you down and 'old you back, when you're a woman on 'er own who earns a lot of chinks.'

Lavender couldn't fault her logic. He'd known several successful widows and spinsters in his time, including Lady Caroline – and Jane Scott, who ran the Sans Pareil Theatre in London. Neither of them were strangers to the bitterness and jealousy of other people.

'But you've just told us you were probably the *only* person who knew for certain little Ruth Langford wasn't conceived in the marriage bed,' he persisted. 'That vile note called the child a *bastard* and her mother a *whore*.'

She nodded, calmly. Her huge silver earrings glinted in the sunlight when she moved her head. 'Aye, but it doesn't mean I wrote it.' She smiled and her eyes twinkled. 'In fact, I couldn't have wrote it even if I wanted to.'

'Why's that, Dora?' Woods asked.

'I'm dead sharp with my numbers and the countin', Neddy. You 'ave to be in business. But I never learned my letters. There were no schoolin' for the likes of Kilby and me.'

'You can't write?' Lavender asked sharply.

'No, she can't,' said an angry female voice behind him. 'If she needs somethin' read, or has writin' to do, I do it for 'er.'

A tall, slim girl of about fifteen stood behind them, with a straw bonnet on her sleek black hair and a basket over her arm. She was a slimmer version of her mother but without the earrings and tattoos. Her dark eyes flashed with anger. 'And I'll thank you, Cousin Neddy, not to cast suspicion on my Ma.'

'Now Flora, don't take on so,' Dora said. 'They're just doin' their job.' She rose to her feet and went to the teapot in its cosy. 'Sit down, gal, and 'ave a brew. Cousin Neddy and 'is pal want to ask you some questions about Mrs Langford.'

'I'm sorry if I've caused you grief, Treacle,' Woods said. 'But this is Detective Lavender, a friend of mine, and he's been charged with gettin' to the bottom of this horrible murder of Mrs Langford.'

The girl gave them both a filthy look, but she took off her bonnet, joined them at the table and thanked her mother for the tea.

When Lavender questioned her, she soon gained her confidence. She spoke clearly and in an orderly manner about the events of that day. At times she was upset – she'd obviously been fond of Clara Langford – but she was critical of her former mistress's decision to remain alone in the vicarage with Ashfield and send her out to fetch a new wet nurse.

'I knew there'd be a fuss. They'd been arguin' a lot over the previous weeks and sometimes I'd 'eard Ashfield's name mentioned. The vicar 'ated 'im.'

'Do you know why, Treacle?' Woods asked gently.

'The whole parish knew why,' she retorted. 'That damned notice posted at the church caused a lot of trouble between the Langfords.'

'Flora knows about men and women and what they do,' Dora told them. 'I don't 'old back with my daughters. I've seen too many young gals ruined because of their innocence. I reckon that forewarned is forearmed.'

Woods nodded in agreement with his cousin and was about to launch into a discussion about the dangers of rearing daughters, but Lavender interrupted them.

'Flora, did you mention these arguments between the Langfords at the inquest?'

'They didn't ask me. All I 'ad to do were describe what 'appened on the day she were killed. No one said a bad word about the vicar.'

I'm sure they didn't, Lavender thought angrily. The man's position in Ealing society had put him above suspicion.

'It were an awful time, and they'd 'ad a blazin' row about the wet nurse too. 'E didn't see as she needed one and in the end 'e went into Brentford and came back with that dreadful lush, Mrs Snelling. The mistress were upset. I think 'e did it on purpose to spite 'er.'

Lavender frowned. Mrs Minskip, the cook, had hinted at the same thing. Langford had lied to him about who'd hired the wet nurse. 'And did you definitely see Mrs Snelling take an object from the cabinet in the drawing room?'

'Yes. It were a small silver baptism cup, engraved with the vicar's name. But it were 'eavy – solid silver – and worth a few chinks. I know this because I'd picked it up often enough to dust it. She put it in 'er cloak pocket and barged past me out of the 'ouse. She nearly knocked me over.' Her pretty face creased with anguish. 'I don't understand why the vicar said nothin' had been stolen. 'E told me I were mistaken – but that's not true!'

'Do you think there's any chance Mrs Snelling came back later, while you were out of the house, and put it back?' Woods asked gently.

Flora's eyes flashed again. 'Not 'er. She's no conscience.'

'What happened when the constable questioned you the next day?' Lavender asked.

Flora grimaced at the memory and her words tumbled out in a rush. 'At first I didn't tell them Mr Ashfield had come a-callin'. I didn't want to cause no trouble. But the constable wheedled it out of me. The vicar got angry and said I were a disgrace and a bad servant for leaving the mistress alone with a man and 'e sacked me.'

'I'm just glad she's out of there,' Dora said angrily. 'That vicar is a viper.' She turned her head and spat on to the flagstone floor.

'But it ain't over, Ma!' Flora exclaimed. 'They've told me I 'ave to go to the Old Bailey and give evidence at Mr Ashfield's trial. I 'ave to speak against 'im!' Then she burst into tears.

Lavender sat back in his seat while Ned and her mother did their best to comfort her. She was right to be alarmed. She'd already changed her story once and would have a terrible time in the witness box. The defence lawyer would tear her apart, and the confusion about the missing silver cup would be brought up to prove her a liar and an unreliable witness.

'It might not come to that,' he said gently. 'Not if I find the real killer first.'

She stopped crying and looked at him hopefully.

'Tell me, Flora, do you think Mr Ashfield murdered Mrs Langford?'

'Of course not! 'E worshipped the ground she walked on – everyone knew that! And she loved 'im too. She were laughin' with 'im like a young gal when I left the vicarage. 'E'd never 'urt 'er.'

Dora put down her pipe and rose to her feet. She collected up the used cups and stared into their depths.

Suddenly, her swarthy complexion blanched with alarm. 'Neddy, you and the Detective 'ave to leave – now.'

'I'm all right, Ma,' Flora said. 'They ain't upset me.'

'No, it's 'im.' She jabbed her smoking pipe in Lavender's direction. 'There's danger swirlin' round you and your kin. Great danger. Yer need to go. Now!'

'Heaven and hell!' Woods exclaimed.

Lavender froze in his seat like he'd been doused with a pail of cold water. Then his rational mind clicked into place, and he smiled, cynically. 'Does this threat come from a man with a burnt face, by any chance?'

She nodded, and continued to stare into the teacup. 'I see ye've been told before… by 'er that's long dead. Yes, I see 'im now. 'E's 'ere.' She glanced into Woods' teacup. 'And you, Neddy – you'll 'ave to say goodbye to your daughter.'

Woods nearly choked. 'Which one?'

'That's enough.' Lavender rose abruptly to his feet and hauled his horrified constable up with him. 'You're wrong, Mrs Kilby. The man with the burnt face died when a tunnel collapsed on him in Ely. We're leaving now.'

Chapter Twenty-One

Clenching his jaw, Lavender strode down the garden path towards the gate where they'd tethered their horses. His stomach churned with the shock. He took a deep breath and reminded himself that Magdalena had warned him Dora Kilby enjoyed alarming people with her alleged powers.

Woods followed him, deep in his own thoughts. They mounted their horses in silence and rode towards Brentford down a path between two lush fields that glistened a vivid shade of green after the downpour the night before. In places, mist rose from the warm, saturated ground, curling around fenceposts and hedgerows like a ghostly veil.

Woods finally broke the silence. 'I know you don't believe her, sir, but she knew about Nidar.'

'She didn't. I deliberately fed her the information about a man with a burnt and scarred face to see what she said. Nidar's dead, Ned. That tunnel in Ely collapsed on his head. Your cousin was out to shock us, and fished for information.'

'But she knew about the dead gypsy gal who first warned us about him – she knew the poor lass were dead.'

This was harder to refute. Many years ago in Northumberland, they'd wanted information from a young gypsy and let her read their palms. They'd got their information, but it was a mistake. She made some disturbing predictions that still bothered Ned.

'That was a lucky guess,' Lavender soothed. 'Everybody dies eventually. Either the girl was alive – or she was dead. And many people visit a spiritualist more than once. Your cousin has a vivid imagination, Ned, and she's clever. She likes to make people fearful of her – it enhances her reputation.'

Woods reined in his horse and turned to face Lavender. 'Don't it bother you what she said about your family bein' in danger?'

Lavender sighed. 'Not enough to make me abandon my investigation and hurtle back to Cedar Court. Magdalena and my children are safe with Lady Caroline and Captain Sawyer.'

He glanced at Ned's worried face, and added: 'Nothing will happen to either of your daughters, Ned. In fact, I suspect our families are safer here than they would be back in London.'

'Except there's a damned murderer on the loose,' Woods growled. 'This place might look like the Garden of Eden – but there's evil here.'

Lavender silently agreed with him. Ealing was picture perfect, a pastoral idyll where nature gently dictated the rhythm of life. But many of those who trod its fertile soil lacked something – what did they lack? – Morality? Integrity? Honesty?

It was a place where well-brought-up young men led indolent lives, and a pregnant young woman appeared to have tricked an unsuspecting vicar into marriage. And somewhere, hidden from sight, another vicious soul composed vile letters designed to upset and horrify their neighbours. Even the sweetness of the birdsong and the chirping crickets couldn't mask this level of moral ambivalence and degeneracy.

'And I'll tell you somethin' else,' Woods snapped, wiping the sweat from his brow with his sleeve, '*all* these charmin' gentry you're interviewin' are bloody lyin' to you. That sawbones will have known about the seven-month babe – but he still told you his brother didn't lie with the dead woman.'

'I've worked that out,' Lavender murmured. Woods' tone was angry but at least his thoughts had returned to the case, rather than Dora Kilby's vile predictions.

'And what about the vicar, eh? He claimed he'd never met Cousin Dora – yet she went to the vicarage to deliver his child.'

'Yes, that's another time he's lied to me.'

'They're all at it,' Woods persisted. 'Not one of these genteel, church-goin' folks has an honest bone in their damned body.'

'You're right, Ned. It's time we checked out the vicar's alibi.'

They stopped at a fork in the path. One way led to the heart of Brentford, the other to the canal wharf and the home of Abel Jupp.

'If you're still willing to help me – you speak to Jupp, and I'll seek out the vicar of St Paul's.'

Woods nodded, but his eyes were glazed. His thoughts had returned to the Kilby woman. 'I'm mortified about my cousin's behaviour, sir. I reckon it were uncalled for.'

'It's all right, Ned. I know you hardly know her and you're only here because Alby asked you to come.'

'The thing that's botherin' me the most, sir, is she normally asks for thruppence to read the tea leaves – and she didn't ask us for money.'

Lavender smiled. 'We'd offered to help her daughter. Perhaps she felt she had to repay us.'

Woods shrugged his broad shoulders. 'Either way, the sooner we get back to our families the better.' He dug his heels into the flank of his horse and set off at a canter. 'Don't be late for the cricket!' he called over his shoulder.

Lavender watched him go, sighed… and then cast a worried glance back in the direction of Ealing.

He'd done his best to calm Ned, and he knew Dora Kilby's words were just part of a grotesque performance… but why couldn't he shake off this feeling of unease that weighed so heavily on him?

Lavender had found Abel Jupp's address in the inquest report and passed it on to his constable. Woods knew it was near the wharf, so he left his horse at the stables used by the bargees and asked the ostler for directions. Big Jim Kilby was leaning on a balance beam, smoking his pipe. Woods gave him a cheery wave, but the leather-skinned old misery didn't wave back.

Woods turned down the dark alley towards Jupp's cottage, grimacing at the stench. Side-stepping the dubious puddles of stagnant effluent, he made his way towards the ramshackle cottage where Jupp lived. There was a battered wooden chair by the door, which had a hole in the rattan seat. Despite the heat, the cracked windows and the door were shut.

Woods wondered if Jupp was at home. Then he remembered that according to the vicar, Jupp was an invalid who'd recently been ill and narrowly escaped being carried out of this hovel in a wooden surcoat.

He rapped on the door and heard scuffling. Something heavy and metal was being dragged over flagstones. 'Hold fast!' a querulous old voice shouted from within. 'I'll be wi' you by and by!'

Eventually, the warped door jerked open. 'What you want, big fella?' Jupp snarled. 'I ain't got nothin' worth stealin'. And I don't buy from pedlars.'

A disgusting smell wafted out that made Woods wince. But he was immediately distracted by the fella's mouth. Or rather his teeth. The old man had a full set of worn, wooden teeth that clacked when he talked.

'My name's Woods, Assistant Chief Constable Ned Woods from Bow Street Magistrates' Court and Police Office. I need to ask you some questions.'

The fella's eyes were small, too close together and encircled by rings of angry, sore skin, but when Woods introduced himself they widened like saucers. 'She didn't say owt about you bein' a runner!'

Woods hesitated in surprise, then decided Jupp must have heard about his arrival in Brentford from Cousin Dora.

'I ain't done nothin' wrong!' Jupp continued, wailing in terror.

'Easy, fella,' Woods soothed. 'I just want to talk to you about the Reverend Langford and his wife's murder.'

''Ah didn't top 'er!'

'No one said you did,' Woods said patiently. 'I need to ask you about the time the vicar called here.'

'I already told that other shoulder-clapper, Constable Hinge.'

'I know that, but I want to ask you again.'

'Well, ah ain't lettin' you in! And as for that other thing, it were only sixpence fer a bit of baccy!'

Woods frowned. He wondered if the old fella was touched in the head. He was as thin as a rake, but he looked healthy and had a ruddy glow in his cheeks. He didn't look like he'd been close to death's door and needed a comforting visit from the vicar. The fella needed a good wash, yes, but the last rites? No.

Woods felt it was best if he stayed on the doorstep of the hovel anyway. The old fella smelt bad enough, his rooms would be worse. 'What other thing are you talkin' about?'

Jupp's jaw slammed shut and his teeth cracked as they clashed against each other. The words tumbled out of him in a rush. 'The three of 'em just turned up at the door, askin' questions. It ain't right, pesterin' an old man! I ain't a well man. I've palpitations of the 'eart and don't take well to shocks.'

His teeth clacked like a pair of those Spanish maracas used by a dancer Woods had once seen.

'*Three* of them?' he asked, confused. 'I'm sorry you're ailin', fella, but I need to ask you about the vicar. Did the Reverend Langford bring others with him when he visited you that day?'

Jupp's small eyes narrowed. 'You want to know about the vicar?'

'That's why I'm here,' Woods said slowly. He'd begun to doubt Jupp's suitability as a witness; this fella was a cork-brain.

'So, she didn't send you?'

'No. Detective Lavender sent me.' Woods' patience was running out. 'We're investigating the murder of Mrs Langford. I need you to tell me what time the vicar arrived here and how long he stayed.'

Relief flooded across Jupp's gaunt face. 'You should 'ave said from the first. Aye, the vicar were wi' me that day. 'E's a kind and decent fella to pass the time wi' an old invalid like me. 'E arrived just after eleven o'clock and stayed for over an 'our.'

Woods stared at him thoughtfully. There was something too smooth about what he'd just said, like he'd rehearsed it for a turn on the stage at Drury Lane. 'How do you know?' he asked.

''Ow does I know what?'

'How do you know it were just after eleven o'clock and he stayed for over an hour? Do you have a pocket watch? Or a clock?'

For a moment, Jupp looked alarmed – then his expression creased into a sneer, and he bared his hideous wooden teeth. 'A clock? 'Ow should a poor old fella like me own a clock – or a fancy pocket watch? Look, see.' He pointed a filthy finger at the crumbling brick wall that blocked off the end of the alley.

Woods turned to look and swallowed down his disappointment. Beyond the wall towered the smoke-blacked walls of an ancient church, which also had a ruddy clock tower. As if to compound his frustration, the damned thing chose that moment to chime the hour.

'That's 'ow I tell the time. That's 'ow half of bloody Brentford tells the time. The vicar came just after eleven o'clock and when he heard the clock chime for mid-day 'e said 'e 'ad to leave. I asked 'im to fetch me a pail of water from the standpipe, and a few other things. Bein' a carin' man, 'e obliged. Then 'e left.'

Woods nodded. Lavender would be disappointed. This was a perfect alibi for Langford. He would never have been able to get back to Ealing and murder his wife in such a short time.

'Now if yer don't mind, Mr Runner, I need to go out and get some more baccy!'

Woods thanked Jupp and walked back down the fetid alleyway. Behind him, he heard the old fella's door bang shut. But as he emerged into the searing heat of the wharf, Betsy's earlier complaint about a missing sixpence stopped him in his tracks – and his old nose started to itch. Somethin' weren't right.

'It were only sixpence fer a bit of baccy!'

'Gawd's teeth!' Another of Jupp's comments suddenly made sense.

'The three of 'em just turned up at the door, askin' questions.'

He glanced across the canal at the shadowed alleys of the warehouses and chewed his lip thoughtfully. He reckoned he had time before he needed to head back to Ealing for the cricket match, but he had to get to the other side of the cut, preferably without alerting the big fella. A quick glance reassured him that Kilby had his back to him.

Woods walked swiftly to the gates that were stretched out across the water and angled like a pair of hinged arms holding back the current. Except there wasn't a current. Recently emptied to let through a barge, the level of the water was low and lapped gently against the slimy stone. The air here was damp, tinged with the smell of algae, grease and old wood.

Atop the gates was a narrow walkway with no handrail. He stepped nimbly across.

A few seconds later he slid behind a huge piece of rusting machinery, melted into the shadows of the warehouses and watched for Abel Jupp to appear.

He didn't have long to wait. Jupp came out of the alley and turned towards the town centre. For an old invalid who'd recently escaped death, he had a sprightly gait. Woods watched him climb up to the road, cross the bridge and disappear before he made his move.

On his return trip across the lock gates, he was less lucky. Big Jim spotted him and cursed him loudly.

Woods gave the fella another cheery wave and hurried back down the dank alley.

It only took one good shove to force open the door to Jupp's hovel. Woods' eyes watered from the stench as he glanced around the filth and the squalor. The few remaining patches of plaster on the stone walls were covered with black mould. A mattress and a pile of dirty blankets lay on a low wooden pallet, next to a battered chest. There was one chair by the tiny hearth with its meagre pile of coal. It didn't take him long to search the unlocked chest, which contained soiled clothing.

But two other things caught his eye.

The first was an iron box shoved beneath the pallet. It was solid iron, relatively new, chained to the floor and locked with a shiny new padlock. This must be what Jupp had dragged across the flagstones when Woods first arrived. He knew everyone needed somewhere to store their chinks and precious items… but that was an expensive iron box for an old man who lived in poverty.

The last time Woods had seen one like this it had belonged to a fence called Wilkinson, who kept it in his stalling-ken in a slum in the Seven Dials.

The second thing he saw made him gasp with anger.

On a chipped plate, in the middle of the battered old table, stood a golden triangle of mouthwatering beauty.

It was one of Betsy's flaky pastry apple turnovers.

Chapter Twenty-Two

Lavender was irritated when he arrived back at Cedar Court in Ealing. His mission to confirm Langford's alibi had failed.

He'd found the vicar of St Paul's easily. The elderly gentleman confirmed he'd shaken hands and conversed with Langford before the funeral but admitted he didn't see his colleague again. He estimated that about seventy mourners attended the funeral and suggested Lavender sought help from the sexton, who'd also been part of the congregation. Maybe he saw Reverend Langford inside the church?

It took Lavender ages to find the sexton and, when he questioned him, the man shook his head and murmured that he didn't remember the Ealing vicar being there.

Lavender was convinced Langford never set foot inside that church. He'd shown his face at the church door, but when everyone was distracted with the arrival of the coffin, he'd slipped away unnoticed.

This was peculiar behaviour for a respected vicar from the Church of England but there could be many valid reasons why the man had walked away. After all, he'd never met the dead man or his sister. And he still had the testimony of Abel Jupp that formed part of his alibi. He wondered how Ned was getting along with Jupp?

Lavender needed to speak to Langford again and challenge him about his absence at the funeral and the other blatant lies he'd told. But that must wait until tomorrow. The detective had a far more important matter to attend to: his son's cricket match.

When he dismounted in the stable yard of Cedar Court and handed the reins of his horse to the groom, Lavender was surprised to learn that Ned still hadn't returned. There was no time to wonder about this – the rest of the household had already walked across to the village green. But before he joined them, he had to dress the part. If Captain Sawyer was to be believed, a cricket match in Ealing was quite a social occasion.

Lavender hurried upstairs to his bedchamber, stripped off his sweat-dampened clothes and washed. Next, he pulled on a clean shirt, tied his best burgundy silk cravat around his neck and pulled on his gold-striped waistcoat. Fortunately, his best boots were already gleaming by the door after a good polish from Lady Caroline's efficient footman.

He hurried outside and to the green, squinting against the sunshine.

This flat expanse of closely scythed lush grass, encircled with ancient trees, was at the heart of Ealing. The trees had been strung with colourful bunting, which fluttered like ribbons in the gentle breeze. Beneath the dappled shade of the boughs, a considerable crowd of spectators had arrived and settled down with chairs and picnic blankets.

Among them were the uniformed schoolboys and black-gowned masters from Ealing Great School and most of the gentry from Ealing. Captain Sawyer stood talking to Dr George Nicholas, the headmaster of the school. The pair were supervising some boys who were wheeling a large wooden scoreboard into place. He knew Sebastián and Bruce had asked Captain Sawyer to referee the match, and the headmaster to keep score. The captain wore a battered straw hat and was surprisingly agile, despite his missing leg.

Sir James Clitherow and several elegantly dressed ladies had gathered at the far side of the pitch. While the ladies sat fanning themselves, a group of excited little girls ran up and down the boundary line. Behind them, a white-clothed table had been set up with a silver tea urn. Liveried footmen moved between the guests with China cups and saucers.

Lavender's eyes narrowed when he spotted the diminutive figure of Miss Finch flitting along the row of ladies. Her black mourning gown stood out against the colourful silks and bonnets of the ladies from Boston Manor.

Is she collecting more gossip to turn into vile accusations with her poisoned quill? he wondered.

An awning with more fluttering bunting had been erected to shade the wooden table of refreshments. Lady Caroline and his family were seated here, along with Betsy. He hurried towards them.

Sebastián's face lit up when he arrived. 'Pa! You made it!' His cricket whites enhanced the healthy glow of his sun-tanned olive skin. Animated and athletic, Lavender's gangly son was turning into a handsome young man.

'Of course I did. I wouldn't have missed this for the world.'

'We're going to win.'

'I've no doubt about that – good luck and enjoy yourself. How's the pitch? Has it dried out from last night's rain?'

Sebastián grinned with relief. 'Yes, it's perfect.'

Beside Sebastián, Rachel tugged unhappily at the collar of a pristine white dress. The cricket bat she leaned on seemed too big for her – but Lavender knew she wielded it like a deadly weapon. Betsy had tied white silk ribbons into her curly hair but they'd both already come undone and trailed down her shoulders. Rachel scowled. 'I can't turn my head, Ma!' she complained. 'And why the deuce do I have to wear a sash? It'll come off and trip me in the first five minutes.'

Betsy murmured soothing words to her daughter and removed the offending sash.

A third child stood with them – a skinny, dark-haired boy, also resplendent in cricket whites. Sebastián introduced him as their new friend, Bruce Charlton. The young boy solemnly shook Lavender's hand, then turned back to the others and they began a heated discussion about tactics.

Elizabeth Charlton sat next to Magdalena. Lavender bowed politely to her, and greeted Betsy and Lady Caroline at the same time.

'I invited Mrs Charlton to join us,' Magdalena whispered when he bent down to kiss her. 'It only seemed right as our children are on the same team.'

He sat in the vacant chair next to Magdalena and smiled at little Jack, who lay in a basket at Magdalena's feet. A parasol had been sunk into the ground beside him, to keep the sun off the infant.

Meanwhile, Alice was with Tabitha and Teresa over by the duck-pond, pointing at the ducks. Alfie Bobbin was patrolling the boundary, his tail wagging as he collected pats from the other spectators.

Lady Caroline pointed towards her husband. 'I told Joshua not to wear such a ridiculous hat,' she complained, 'but he claims it's his lucky cricket hat.' She had abandoned her customary turban today and wore a large straw bonnet decorated with green silk flowers that were replicated in the floral pattern of her poplin gown. The colour set off her flame-coloured hair to advantage.

Lavender grinned. 'Sailors are superstitious men.'

He settled back into his seat. There was an air of eager anticipation across the village green, which was infectious. What was about to unfold wasn't just a match, he realised. It was a ritual, a story retold every summer across England, woven into the very soul of every village.

Sir James Clitherow ambled across the green towards them, his bald head gleaming with perspiration. He bowed before Lady Caroline. 'How do you do, Mrs Sawyer? Lady Clitherow and I would like to extend our felicitations to you and the Captain on your recent nuptials. We're delighted for you both. Lady Clitherow hopes to call on you at Cedar Court soon.'

Lavender winced at the slight and wondered if it was deliberate.

But Lady Caroline nodded graciously and said: 'Thank you, Sir James, that's kind of you and Lady Clitherow. I shall look forward to her visit. Although may I remind you that the daughter of an earl is always referred to as "Lady", no matter whom they marry.'

The baron's round face flushed with embarrassment. 'Ah, my apologies, Lady Caroline. I should have remembered. I'm a friend of your brother, the Earl of Kirkleven.'

'Oh, poor you,' Lady Caroline murmured.

'In fact,' the baron continued, blithely unaware of her sarcasm, 'he recently invited me to join a hunting party up at Kirkleven Castle.'

'Goodness! And you think that's something to anticipate with delight?' She leaned forward and tapped him playfully with her fan. 'I grew up there, Sir James, and would strongly advise you *not* to go. Kirkleven is a crumbling, freezing cold pile of old stones – and the local stags are *vicious*. They've even been known to invade the castle kitchens. If you do accept this invitation, I recommend you take an extra pair of wool flannel drawers and keep two pistols about your person – both primed.'

Sir James's mouth twitched with amusement. 'I shall bear your advice in mind, Ma'am. I look forward to meeting you again at Boston House.'

Beside Lavender, Magdalena giggled and whispered in his ear: 'Is it acceptable amongst the British aristocracy for a woman to mention men's undergarments?'

'No,' he replied, smiling. 'But Lady Caroline makes her own rules.'

After a few more pleasantries, Sir James took his leave of Lady Caroline and asked Lavender to join him for a quiet word. The two men walked out of earshot of the women.

'How do your enquiries progress, Lavender?'

Lavender hesitated for a second, then decided blunt truth was the best policy with a man like the baron. 'To be honest, sir, I find myself frustrated. I believe your constables have done a poor job with this investigation. Neither of Mrs Langford's siblings have an alibi for the time of her murder and even though they had the most to gain from her death, neither of them have been questioned by Constable Hinge.'

Sir James looked shocked. 'But surely you don't think Mrs Charlton or young Daniels—?'

'I suspect them all – including the vicar.'

'Good grief! Why?'

'So far I've been unable to find a single person who remembers seeing Reverend Langford inside St Paul's during the funeral service. He arrived at the church – but no one saw him inside the building.'

'Oh, this is preposterous, Lavender! You're wasting your time. Langford is an innocent man with an excellent alibi!'

Why was he so sure about this?

'I think you should leave Langford alone to his grief.'

Lavender stiffened but before he could respond, Sir James added: 'And Hinge tells me you also believe the Snelling woman is dead in a ditch.'

'Yes, I do. It's the only thing that makes sense of her disappearance. I believe she witnessed something – or someone – connected to the murder of Mrs Langford and has been silenced by the killer.'

The baron shrugged. 'She bumped into Ashfield when she left.'

'Yes, but there was a second witness to his arrival at the vicarage – the housemaid, Flora. If he'd killed the wet nurse to silence her, he'd have gone after the girl as well.'

Clitherow's eyes narrowed. 'We'll talk about this later, Lavender.' He turned and strode back to his family.

Lavender frowned and didn't notice Doctor Morton until the man was by his side. Morton was accompanied by a scowling, red-haired young girl in a straw bonnet, who carried a copy of the novel *Tom Jones*.

'Good afternoon, Lavender. I understand your son is playing in the match today?'

'Yes, good afternoon to you too, Morton.' He pointed across to Sebastián. 'That's my son, Sebastián.'

Morton nodded. 'He's a handsome young fellow. You must be proud of him.'

'I am. He's a skilled cricket player.'

'I hope so, because the school team is excellent – especially Brewster, the young brute who's their captain.' Morton turned to the young woman by his side. 'May I introduce you to my daughter, Miss Amelia Morton?'

Lavender smiled at the young girl and gave her a small bow. 'I'm pleased to meet you, Miss Morton. I hope you enjoy the match.'

Her scowl deepened and her insipid eyes flickered with annoyance. 'I most certainly will *not*. I've no intention of paying it any attention. I can't think of a worse way of spending an afternoon than watching sweaty boys showing off. I'm only here because Papa *insisted* I came out of the house, but I intend to find some shade, sit on the grass and read my novel.'

Morton gave a wry smile. 'Then don't let us delay your pleasure, Amelia.'

'I won't.'

She huffed and stormed off towards the shade at the edge of the green.

'My apologies, Lavender. She's been moody recently. She misses her mother badly and I'm often at a loss about how to react to her outbursts.'

'There's no requirement for an apology. I know how difficult they can be at this age. Sebastián has developed quite a temper.'

'My late wife was a wonderful woman, and she had lofty ambitions for Amelia. My daughter wants to become a lady author, and her mother encouraged her in this dream.'

'I'm a great reader myself. That's a noble ambition.'

'Mm.' Morton looked unconvinced. 'Her writing style tends towards the swashbuckling amorality of Henry Fielding, rather than the respectability of Miss Edgeworth. She's fascinated by the rougher parts of Brentford and the characters who live there. But enough of that. I'm curious to learn how your inquiries progress.'

A quick glance reassured Lavender that the game wasn't ready to begin yet. The players were milling around the pitch, and Rachel was with her mother, who'd found a small pair of scissors and was slitting the neckline of her dress.

Lavender told Morton what he'd uncovered so far about their suspects. The doctor smiled when he heard Mrs Minskip had suggested Miss Finch might be the author behind the poisonous letters circulating around the parish.

'That wouldn't surprise me. Miss Finch can be a spiteful little woman. I don't suppose I can persuade you to leave Mrs Charlton out of your investigation?'

Lavender glanced at him slyly. 'Are you fond of her, Doctor?'

Morton nodded, and his eyes drifted across to where Elizabeth Charlton was in animated conversation with Magdalena. 'Yes, very. But I suspect my feelings aren't reciprocated. Elizabeth is an independent woman, and her first marriage was unhappy. It's made her wary of men.'

'There's a couple of other things bothering me,' Lavender said, 'that concern *you.*'

'*Me?*'

'Yes. Firstly, why didn't you tell me Clara Langford's baby was born seven months into her marriage – but arrived fully developed?'

Morton stopped walking and had the grace to look embarrassed. 'Ah, did Dora Kilby tell you this?'

'Yes, she did. Is it true? And if so, why didn't you tell me?'

Morton sighed. 'Yes, it's true. I realised the truth when I saw the child the day after her birth.'

'Did you tell anyone?'

'No, I kept my suspicions to myself.'

'What about her husband? Did Langford suspect anything?'

'I don't know. He never asked my opinion or raised the matter with me.'

'So, whose child is it? Is it your brother's? Was she expecting his child when she married Langford?'

Morton averted his gaze and flushed with discomfort. 'I honestly don't know. And if you were wondering – I didn't ask Mark either.'

'If Langford suspected the child was Ashfield's, he would have been seething with anger. It gives him a strong motive to kill her.'

'Yes, I understand. How do you intend to proceed, Lavender?'

'I intend to speak to Langford again tomorrow. Sir James has warned me to keep away from him, but I won't be deterred.'

'Did you know the baron is related to Langford by marriage?'

Lavender sighed. At last things were making some sense. 'No. I didn't know that.'

'Langford's first wife was a cousin of Lady Clitherow. When she died, Sir James gave Langford the living here in Ealing. Their two daughters have been educated in the school room at Boston Manor ever since – along with the other children of the Clitherow family.

'This arrangement was a severe disappointment to my own Amelia,' Morton continued. 'Previously, she'd enjoyed a fine education from their governess. But the arrival of Langford's daughters meant there was no room for her anymore, and she had to leave.'

Lavender followed his glance towards the young girl who was now reading her book, half hidden beneath the shade of a tree. 'That must have been a bitter blow for her.'

'What was the other thing, Lavender?'

'I'm sorry?'

'You said there were a couple of things that bothered you?'

'Yes. I want to ask you about that vile allegation in the letter you received. I need to establish how well our poisoned letter writer knows his – or her – victims. I understand there were unfounded rumours at your former practice in Manchester that you were an abortionist.'

Morton was horrified. 'You've investigated *me*?'

'Yes – and your former colleagues sang your praises. Like I said, I need to establish how intimately the hand behind the poisoned quill knows his or her victims. Is it possible this calumny has followed you here to Ealing?'

'Absolutely not! The matter was dismissed by the Manchester hospital board as unsubstantiated jealous gossip. The whole sorry affair happened over a year before I came back.'

'So how could anyone here know about it?'

'They don't,' Morton snapped. 'It was a stab in the dark on behalf of that scurrilous letter writer. It's an unpleasant and nasty allegation that often haunts men in my profession.'

Lavender nodded but didn't get chance to reply. The players had gathered around Captain Sawyer on the pitch and Magdalena was gesticulating to him to return.

The game was about to begin.

Where the hell was Ned?

Chapter Twenty-Three

There were nine other boys from Great Ealing School besides Bruce, which meant there would be two teams of six. Four of these schoolboys were about the same age – if not older – than Sebastián. The rest were as small as Rachel. Two of the little ones were twins and they both looked terrified.

Captain Sawyer tossed a coin and Bruce, as one of the captains, made the call and lost. The other captain, the boy called Brewster, opted to bat first and picked his team. They took it in turns.

By the time Bruce had called Sebastián and Rachel to his side, Brewster had picked two of the bigger boys. Lavender expected him to go for the last remaining older lad – whom Elizabeth Charlton told them was the son of an ambassador called Thornton. But Brewster opted to leave Thornton for Bruce to pick for his own team. The nervous twins made up the last two members of Bruce's side.

It was obvious from the start that the boys from Great Ealing School were excellent and well-practised cricketers. Brewster hit three sixes and a four and the rest of his team also did well. Sebastián was a good bowler, but every ball was met with the sharp crack of leather on willow, numerous runs and a ripple of polite applause from the spectators. The score on the rickety wooden score board was meticulously kept by the headmaster and rose rapidly.

Bruce was an excellent wicketkeeper, and early in the game nearly stumped Brewster, but Rachel and the young twins were kept on their toes chasing the ball across the green. Meanwhile, Thornton regularly dropped the catches when they came his way. And as he was fielding in the mid-wicket position and all the batters were right-handed, it often came his way.

He missed his third catch because he fell over just before he reached the ball. He was subjected to good-natured teasing from the crowd.

'It's the grass – it's still wet from last night,' he called out to those who chided him. Grinning, he picked up the ball from the grass and threw it back to Sebastián.

Lavender frowned; the grass was bone dry. Thornton was deliberately helping his pals on the other team by dropping those catches.

Fortunately, Rachel had also noticed. She raced over to speak to Bruce and pointed at Thornton. Bruce called to the boy and told him to swap places with her.

'Well spotted, Rachel,' Lavender murmured under his breath.

The grin disappeared from Thornton's face as he sulkily obeyed his captain.

'Don't worry!' Brewster called out to him from the crease. 'It doesn't matter. She's only a girl!'

It did matter. Sebastián bowled again. Brewster hit the ball hard, straight towards Rachel – who darted beneath it like a white-winged swallow and caught it in both hands.

As the applause rippled around the green, Woods suddenly appeared next to Betsy. 'I'm glad I got back in time to see *that.*' He clapped his huge hands together in an encore that sounded like crashing thunder. 'Well done, Treacle!' he boomed.

Rachel grinned in delight at her father's praise.

'Sit down, Ned!' Betsy snapped. 'Your makin' a spectacle of yourself.'

The pace of the game increased dramatically now the school team captain had been dismissed. His team played like the devil was after them. The thwack of the ball against the bats punctuated the air like pistol shots.

But the confidence of Sebastián, Bruce, Rachel and the twins had also been bolstered by Rachel's stunning catch.

Sebastián bowled out one boy; Bruce stumped out another and one of the twins hurled the ball at the wickets before the batsman got back to the safety of the batting crease.

Great Ealing School only had two batters remaining in their team and these last two players took the score up to eighty-nine before one of them made a mistake, caught the ball on the edge of his bat and sent it straight into Sebastián's hands.

The youngsters left the pitch for a short rest in the shade and a glass of cloudy lemonade. The applause from the spectators was warm and well deserved.

Lavender relaxed back in his seat and exhaled heavily. He'd been holding his breath.

He scanned the crowds to check on the whereabouts of his little daughter. Teresa had taken the two little girls away from the murky water of the duck-pond. They were playing with Alfie Bobbin and a ball on the far boundary of the pitch.

Close to them, beneath the shade of a tree that fell on the road, was a stationary carriage with two black horses. Lavender's forehead creased as he tried to remember where he'd seen it before…

But he was distracted by the arrival of Sebastián, Rachel and Bruce. They were flushed and sweaty but grinning from ear to ear.

How were children able to run around in this heat and not care?

'We only need ninety runs to win!' Sebastián announced.

'That's fifteen each,' Bruce added.

'Do you think you can manage that?' Lavender asked, smiling.

'Of course we can!' Rachel exclaimed.

Woods was on his feet again, commending the children for their performance and offering his advice about their batting order. The children turned towards him and Lavender sat back.

Further down the row of chairs, Doctor Morton had joined Elizabeth Charlton and laughed at something she'd said. When she reached out and lightly touched his arm, Lavender's eyebrows rose in surprise; the couple were openly flirting. And this time he didn't need Woods or Magdalena to point it out to him.

Did they plan the murder together? he wondered. *How genuine were their protestations of affection for Ashfield and Clara Langford? Had they sacrificed their siblings for the money Elizabeth Charlton would now inherit?*

He shook his head to clear his mind of these useless speculations. He needed hard evidence to link someone – anyone – to the vicarage at the time of the murder.

Captain Sawyer called the teams back to the pitch and Lavender rose to his feet to join Ned.

'How did it go with Abel Jupp, Ned?'

Woods shook his head and scowled. 'He stands by his claim the vicar were with him at the time of the murder. I tried to shake him and questioned his timin' but the cove is resolute.'

Disappointment flooded through Lavender.

'Were Langford at the funeral service?' Woods asked.

'Not according to the vicar or his sexton.'

'So where were the wheedlin' fella? Do you think he keeps a woman stashed away somewhere in Brentford?'

Lavender smiled. 'I don't know. But in this case, anything is possible.'

A dark cloud flickered across Woods' face and his jaw tightened. 'I'll tell you somethin' though, sir. I've a notion there's more to this Jupp fella than meets the eye. My old nose ain't stopped twitchin' since I met him. For a start, he ain't no sickly old man.'

Lavender's smile broadened. 'That old nose of yours has never let you down yet.'

'Yes, and if it's all right with you, sir, I'll spend some time scratchin' this itch tomorrow.'

'You do what you have to do, Ned.'

'Will the two of you sit down, please?' Betsy called out from behind them. 'You're blockin' our view.'

Thornton and one of the twins went into bat first. Thornton was a cautious but steady batsman – too cautious, Lavender thought. He suspected the young traitor had reverted to type and was aiding his Great Ealing schoolmates by giving half a performance. Meanwhile, the younger boy only managed six runs before he was caught out.

The second twin fared little better, scoring twelve before he was run out by Thornton, who seemed to find this amusing.

Lavender heard Woods curse the boy beneath his breath and comment: 'They're strugglin' to make those fifteen runs apiece.'

Bruce went into bat and quickly scored two fours and a six.

In a final act of sabotage for his team, Thornton gently hit the ball into the open hands of the opposing captain, Brewster. He left the pitch, grinning.

It was now down to Bruce, Sebastián and Rachel to make fifty-two runs between them.

Sebastián joined Bruce on the pitch.

'They're savin' the best player till last,' Woods murmured, with a proud nod towards his daughter.

The speed and excitement of the game increased. Sebastián and Bruce worked well together; their practice over the last few days had paid dividends. They were fast, agile and cautious – yet at the same time confident. The green resounded with cheering and *thwack!* after *thwack!* The opposing team struggled to retrieve the ball as it hurtled through the stifling air. The headmaster was kept busy changing the scoreboard.

By the time Bruce was caught out, their team's total score was seventy-two. He left the pitch to loud applause and cheering.

When Rachel walked towards the stumps there were murmurs of surprise from the crowd, which she ignored.

'Oh, Ned, I'm so anxious for her!' Betsy wailed.

Woods put a comforting arm around his wife. 'Have some faith, wench,' he chided. 'You know she plays better than either of her brothers.'

Once she reached the batting crease, Rachel gave Sebastián a wicked grin and called out: 'You only managed three sixes, García.'

Sebastián grinned back. 'Do you want to make this a competition?'

'I'll wager you two shillin's I beat you on sixes.'

'Agreed!'

Betsy started in shock. 'She's gamblin', Ned! And where's she goin' to get two shillin's from?'

Brewster ran up to the bowling crease and hurled the ball as hard as he could at Rachel.

She swung her bat – and sent the ball hurtling over the boundary.

'Six!' yelled Captain Sawyer.

Most of the crowd were now on their feet in surprise and delight.

But on the next over she did it again.

'Are you still sure about our wager, García?' she teased.

The next fifteen minutes were some of the best cricket Lavender had ever seen. Years of playing together with Eddie and Dan Woods had taught Rachel and Sebastián how to think with the same mind. Their chemistry was instinctive – a quick glance was enough to signal to each other their next move. They gave Ealing a masterclass in rhythm and trust.

At one point, Sebastián changed his stance and switched to batting left-handed. He whacked it above the heads of the startled – and disorganised – fielders on the other side of the pitch. It rolled over the boundary.

'Six!' yelled Captain Sawyer.

The crowd rose to their feet and applauded in delight. Lavender had never felt so proud of his son.

Magdalena picked up Jack, who'd begun to whimper. When he wouldn't settle in her arms, Lavender took him in his own, whispered in his ear and pointed out Sebastián. The baby squealed with delight at the sight of his big brother racing around the pitch. His eyes lit up with excitement.

Rachel was now at the crease. They only needed one run to draw level – and two to win. Lavender knew they'd make it.

Brewster called his team together for a quick discussion before he bowled again. The boys nodded in agreement and went back to their positions.

Just as Brewster was about to make his run up to the bowling crease, one of the fielders from the school team screamed and fell on the grass, clutching his leg. Everyone turned towards him in alarm – including Captain Sawyer.

Brewster saw his chance. He raced to the crease and hurled the ball straight at Rachel's midriff with a force that would have cracked the girl's ribs.

She leapt out of the way and the ball crashed into the stumps, sending the bails flying.

'Out!' Brewster screamed. He leapt into the air, whooping with delight and waving his arms. His teammates and the spectators from the school took up the cry.

'No ball!' Rachel yelled.

'It was a no ball!' Sebastián and Bruce yelled in unison.

They raced over to Captain Sawyer, but the elderly man had been so distracted by the screaming boy he hadn't seen the delivery. He could only nod sadly and confirm that Rachel was out.

Lavender's heart sank. The game was over. They'd lost by one run. The opposition had cheated their way to victory.

The adults rose to their feet to comfort and console their children – but Sebastián didn't return to them. Hurling his bat on to the ground, he stormed off towards the duck-pond.

Magdalena started forward, but Lavender grabbed her arm and handed her Jack. 'I'll go.'

He took his time and walked slowly. Sebastián was dashing away tears of frustration and appeared to be shouting at the ducks. He wanted to give his boy a chance to compose himself before he appeared at his side.

By the time he reached him, Sebastián had slumped down on to the grass and was sitting hunched over with his head bowed. His long, floppy fringe fell forward, covering his flushed and anguished face.

Lavender sat down on the grass beside him. Sebastián's cricket whites were now smeared with grass stains and mud, and his white shirt clung to his back with sweat.

‘That was the best game of cricket I’ve ever seen,’ Lavender said quietly. ‘You were amazing, son.’

Sebastián didn’t look up. ‘They cheated.’

‘Yes, they did – repeatedly. But Captain Sawyer didn’t see that last ball and had no choice but to declare the game over. They deliberately distracted him.’

Silence fell between them for a moment. But it was never totally quiet or still in the countryside, Lavender realised. Two curious ducks glided closer across the water, trailing weed behind them. A crow rose wheeling and cawing from a tree, and a frog croaked in the reeds.

Sebastián tossed a small pebble into the water. ‘Why do people cheat like that, Pa?’ His voice rose angrily. ‘And why do they lie, bully and hurt each other?’

‘Those are huge questions. Riddles I’ve spent my life trying to solve and I don’t pretend to know the answers. All I know is not everyone is like that – and those that are get punished in the end.’

Sebastián grunted in disbelief. ‘They won the match – that’s not a punishment. Now they’ll be lauded as heroes.’

Lavender shook his head. ‘No, they won’t. Their schoolmasters and some of their peers watched them cheat. Yes, they won the match, but they’ll have lost respect. It’s a shallow victory when you lose the respect of your fellow schoolmates for cheating.’

Sebastián raised his head and looked more hopeful. This thought had given him comfort.

‘What was victorious was the brilliant performance you and Rachel – and young Bruce – gave at the end. *That* is what people will remember about this game.’

‘Did I win my wager? I lost count of the sixes we scored.’

‘You owe Rachel two shillings – but you were the highest scoring batsman in the entire match, and I’m proud of you.’

A grin spread across his son’s handsome young face and the light came back in his dark eyes. ‘You’ll have to loan me two shillings, Pa. I can’t welch on a wager with Rachel, but I’m bushed. We’ve family honour to think about.’

Lavender laughed, pulled the coins out of his pocket and tossed them to his son. 'Please don't make a habit of wagering with Rachel; she knows how to place a good bet. You'll lose a lot of money, and I don't want Ned sending round the bailiffs.'

Sebastián grinned again, took the coins and rose to his feet. 'I need to shake Captain Sawyer's hand and tell him there's no hard feelings on my part. The poor fella must be mortified.'

'And that makes me proud of you as well, son.'

Sebastián's grin widened. He sprinted off back towards the crowd, now gathered around the sandwiches and cakes.

Lavender stood up and smiled as he watched him go.

But his smile faded when he saw Sir James Clitherow and Constable Hinge striding purposefully across the green towards him. Both men looked grim.

'Lavender, you'll have to come with us now,' the magistrate said.

'Why? What's happened?'

'You were right about the Snelling woman. Hinge and Norbert have just pulled her body out of the River Brent. By the look of her, she's been dead for weeks.'

Chapter Twenty-Four

While Sir James collected Doctor Morton to accompany them, Lavender went in search of Woods. His constable was standing in a large crowd by the tea tent with his arm round his daughter, munching on a cucumber sandwich.

When Lavender explained that he needed him, Woods nodded, swallowed the last of his sandwich and told Rachel he would have to leave.

Rachel didn't seem concerned; she was basking in the attention and curiosity of the spectators and answering their questions. Meanwhile, Betsy fussed around in the background, handing out plates of sandwiches and pastries.

But before they left, Woods scowled, reached out and grabbed two of Betsy's apple turnovers from the table. He shoved one in his own pocket and gave the other to Lavender with a cryptic comment: 'You'd better hide this. Half the buggers in the district are out to filch them.'

Lavender said nothing. Clearly, the theft of Betsy's apple turnovers would be his next case.

If Sir James was annoyed that there were now *two* Bow Street constables working in his parish, he didn't show it. He was distracted and concerned about this latest discovery. When Lavender introduced Woods, he merely nodded.

Constable Hinge led them down a quiet lane that ran beside the river.

'How did you find her?' Lavender asked him.

The constable's sludge-brown eyes gave him a sly sideways glance. He grinned toothlessly. 'I turned over every stone and rock like yer told me, sir. But it were the cow 'erd, Gregory, who found 'er this mornin' when he came to get his dunnocks fer milkin'. We'd already searched that spot, but I reckon she were trapped under the water by the reeds and the storm brought 'er up to the surface last night.'

Lavender grimaced at the thought of the state of the corpse after such a long immersion in water. He'd helped drag enough dead bodies out of the River Thames to know that after a week or two, the decomposition of the tissue produced foul-smelling gases that made the body buoyant and float to the surface.

Hinge was probably right. The torrential rain of the previous night would have swollen the river, increased the current and dislodged Mrs Snelling's body from the reeds and other detritus that held it down.

'Mind you, when we 'auled her on to the bank and checked 'er pockets, we was surprised she'd come up at all,' Hinge added.

'Why?' Lavender asked.

'They was full of rocks – big 'uns.'

Woods' greying eyebrows creased across his broad forehead in a frown. 'Did she do it herself? Did she drown herself?'

Hinge shrugged. ''Tis 'ard to tell. Either that or some murderin' bastard used them rocks to weigh 'er down. I've a notion she were dead before she went into the river.'

Lavender nodded again. This scruffy man with his shifty eyes and unkempt whiskers was finally thinking like a police constable.

'I'll perform an autopsy when we get her to the morgue,' Doctor Morton reassured them. 'It won't take me long to establish if drowning was – or wasn't – the cause of death.'

'Did you find anythin' else in her pockets?' Woods asked.

Constable Hinge frowned. 'Like what?'

'The housemaid at the vicarage said she'd filched a silver cup before she left.'

Hinge shook his head. 'No. No, there weren't anythin' like that. Just rocks. And the Reverend were clear the gal had made a mistake.'

Lavender and Woods exchanged a knowing glance. Neither of them believed the vicar when he said Flora was mistaken.

'Do you think this cow field is the scene of the crime?' Woods asked Hinge.

Hinge shrugged. ''Tis 'ard to tell.' He turned off the path and climbed over a battered fence into a small overgrown copse. 'It's quicker this way.'

They followed. Lavender frowned as they waded through thigh-high nettles, and a dangling thistle caught and snagged his best waistcoat. He also realised with annoyance that he'd forgotten about the apple turnover Woods had shoved into his coat pocket. The cream had oozed out of the pastry and through the material. It had formed a dark and sticky patch on his coat pocket.

They emerged from the wood into a lush meadow, full of clover, buttercups and grazing cows. The meandering river dissected the field and murmured sadly as it wove silver ribbons in the sunlight.

A swarthy fellow with pockmarked skin and greasy hair stood on the muddy riverbank guarding the bloated and sodden corpse of the woman in a black cloak.

Hinge pointed to the reeds behind his fellow officer. 'That's where we found 'er. She were trapped in them reeds.'

Lavender glanced around the meadow in dismay. If this was the scene of the crime, it would be difficult to find any evidence. If the rain hadn't washed it away into the river, the cows' hooves would have trampled it into the ground.

'Do you want me to have a look around, sir?' Woods asked.

Lavender nodded gratefully and Woods fell back, his eyes scanning the meadow.

They were still fifteen feet away from the body, but it was already obvious that the woman's abdomen was grotesquely distended due to the putrefaction. The skin was peeling away from her swollen and marbled hands.

Then the stench of rotting flesh assaulted their nostrils.

Sir James stopped, turned a sickly shade of green and reached for his handkerchief. 'You go ahead,' he told the others, 'I'll follow.'

Lavender, the doctor and Hinge walked in silence towards the corpse. Doctor Morton pulled a pair of thin cotton gloves out of his pocket, put them on and dropped down on to his haunches to examine what remained of Mrs Snelling.

Constable Norbert, grateful to be relieved of his charge, stepped away from the corpse and joined Hinge. Meanwhile, the cows chewed their clover thoughtfully, swished their tails and watched them through large inquisitive eyes, untroubled by the presence of people – either dead or alive.

Lavender stared down at the woman's hideous and swollen face. Her wide, gaping mouth was locked in a death scream. What remained of her skin after the ravages of the river and its reptile inhabitants was waxy pale and smeared with a substance he suspected was dissolving body fat. He'd heard a lot about the notorious Mrs Snelling over the last few days, and not much of it was commendable. But this woman had had as much right to a long life as any of them, and her baby deserved a mother. He felt sympathy for them – and cold anger for her killer.

He felt even more angry on her account a few seconds later when Doctor Morton turned her head to one side and he saw the damage done to the back of her skull. Morton reached down and pulled a large wooden splinter out of the crushed mass of bone and dark hair.

'There's the cause of death, gentlemen,' Morton said. 'This was no accidental drowning. Mrs Snelling was beaten viciously on the back of her head.'

Morton stood up and peeled off his gloves. 'I'll perform an autopsy when we get her body to the morgue, but I doubt I'll find any water in her lungs. I suspect she was beaten to death with a heavy piece of wood. Maybe a cudgel? I need to examine her closely.'

Lavender remembered the sagging and broken fence. A plank from the fence or a fallen tree branch would both have made good murder weapons, and they were easily disposed of. All the killer had to do was hurl the murder weapon into the water, where it would float down to the Thames and out into the German Sea.

'Can you tell how long she's been dead?' he asked.

The doctor shook his head. 'Decomposition is advanced so it's more than ten days, but I can't tell for sure.'

Lavender nodded, walked across the muddy riverbank and examined the ground. This was where the cows came down to drink. There were drag marks where Hinge and Norbert had hauled the waterlogged corpse across the mud, but the rest of the area was churned up and pockmarked with round hoof prints from the cattle. He cursed his luck. The one thing this damned case needed more than anything was some hard evidence. Yet again it eluded him.

He glanced hopefully at Woods, who was walking across the meadow towards him. But his constable shook his head.

Sir James had recovered from his nausea and appeared at his side. 'This is a bad show, Lavender. A bad show. I don't understand what's happening here. Two murders? Ealing is such a pleasant place to live!'

Lavender knew what he meant. The contented lowing of the cattle, mingling with birdsong and the gentle splash of water against the stones, made it hard to believe this had been the scene of a violent murder. But he had little sympathy for Sir James.

'I think we can assume this wasn't a suicide,' Lavender said coldly. 'I believe the man – or woman – who killed Mrs Langford also killed her wet nurse. For both women from the same household to be murdered – probably on the same day – is too much of a coincidence.'

The baron's pale, round face contorted with anguish. 'But why, Lavender? Why?'

'She saw something – or someone – connected to the murder of Clara Langford and had to be silenced. The maid, Flora, claims there was someone, whom she thought was a man, at the other side of the village green just before Mrs Snelling left. It's likely that in the fog she ran straight into this person.'

'But surely that was Ashfield?'

'He says not. He admits he brazenly rode up to the vicarage, tied up his horse and walked up the garden path to the front door. And in this, at least, I believe him.'

'Ashfield might have tracked her down afterwards.'

'She would have already been back in Brentford by then – but she didn't arrive home that day. You have to broaden your mind, Sir James. Ashfield can't have been in two places at once. He was either here, killing the wet nurse – or in the vicarage murdering Mrs Langford. Or he didn't kill these women and someone else did.'

Sir James's face flushed with anger. 'I've no doubt Ashfield murdered poor Clara Langford.'

Lavender's tone sharpened. 'Exactly how many killers do you have in Ealing, Sir James? One for Mrs Langford – and one for Mrs Snelling?'

The baron opened his mouth to answer but Lavender hadn't finished. 'You'll need to have a good answer to that question for Ashfield's trial at the Old Bailey. Because that'll be the *first* thing his defence lawyer will ask you – and the reporters from the newspapers will record your answer.'

This threat of public ridicule strangled the baron's protests in his throat, and he began to bluster. 'I don't welcome your tone, Lavender!'

But Lavender barely noticed his discomfort. He was struck with a thought. 'In fact, I've a notion Mrs Snelling was the first one to die that day.'

Sir James's indignation died and was replaced by curiosity. 'How so?'

'Let's suppose she met the man who was loitering outside the vicarage – a man who didn't want to be recognised and who was intent on murdering Clara Langford. A few minutes later, the killer will have seen the maid leave. He knew Ashfield was alone with Mrs Langford and suspected he would be with her some time. This gave him ample opportunity to hurry after the wet nurse, bludgeon her to death and dispose of the body.'

'That's a lot of supposition, Lavender,' Sir James warned.

'It's the only thing that makes sense.'

Doctor Morton and Ned joined them, and Lavender continued with his theory. 'I suspect the killer followed her and murdered her – here. Then he returned to Ealing to wait until Ashfield left the vicarage.'

'How would he know Ashfield was still there?' Sir James asked.

'Because his horse was tied up outside. Once Ashfield left, our killer entered the vicarage and murdered Clara Langford.'

'That makes sense,' Morton said.

Lavender shrugged. 'Could a woman have battered Mrs Snelling to death like this?'

'Possibly – but she'd have to be strong,' the doctor replied.

'Young Flora were sure it were a man she saw,' Woods said.

'A lot of vagrants pass through Ealing,' Sir James said.

'But what motive would a vagrant have to enter the vicarage and poison Mrs Langford? And where did he get the arsenic?' Lavender asked.

'So, who the deuce did it?' Sir James exclaimed.

'Frederick Daniels doesn't have a satisfactory alibi for the day of the murder,' Lavender said. 'And he has a motive.'

'I'll question him again – tonight,' the baron promised.

'Elizabeth Charlton doesn't have a satisfactory alibi either,' Lavender added. 'She claims she was riding with her son, but we only have her word – and that of a thirteen-year-old boy – for that. According to her brother, she often wore men's clothing – especially coats – while out riding. If she was the one outside the vicarage, the maid might have mistaken her for a man.'

Sir James nodded. 'I'll speak to her, too.'

'Oh, come now, Lavender!' Doctor Morton protested. 'We've talked about this before – Mrs Charlton loved her sister. And I don't believe she's strong enough to beat this poor woman to death!'

Lavender glared at him. 'Perhaps she had an accomplice? Perhaps it's time we investigated *your* alibi in more detail, Doctor. Where did you say you were on the morning of the murder?'

Morton was speechless with anger.

'What on earth do you mean, sir?' Sir James snapped.

'If Mrs Charlton marries Doctor Morton then he also has a financial motive to kill Clara Langford. What would be more natural than calling on his patient and giving her medication to drink? Perhaps arsenic-laced medication?'

'That's ridiculous, Lavender! I hired you to find the real killer, remember? I'd hardly have done that if I murdered her myself! This is slanderous speculation!'

Sir James held up his hands and his voice boomed with anger. 'Enough of this bickering, gentlemen! The events of this afternoon have upset us all. In the light of today's discovery, I shall reopen my investigation into Clara Langford's murder – and *I'll* pay Bow Street – and Lavender – to track down this evil devil. Ashfield isn't off the hook yet, but we need to make more enquiries. *And*,' he added, turning towards the furious doctor, 'Lavender may investigate and question anyone he wants – including you, Morton.'

Morton turned on his heel and strode back the way they'd come. 'I shall return to Ealing and get my tools for the autopsy,' he yelled over his shoulder.

Lavender took a deep breath. 'Thank you for your support, Sir James.'

'Ha! Don't thank me. I'm impressed with your powers of detection, Lavender – you've opened my eyes. But I'm not impressed with your lack of tact and subtlety around the gentlemen of our parish. You're too brusque with your suspects. I've already had a complaint from the Reverend Langford about your behaviour yesterday. He found it disappointing.'

Lavender bit his tongue and consoled himself that Langford would be more than *disappointed* by the time he'd finished with him tomorrow.

'I need your constable to help Hinge and Norbert carry Mrs Snelling's body to the morgue,' said Sir James. 'Is that acceptable?'

Lavender and Woods agreed, and Sir James walked away to speak to his men.

Beside Lavender, Woods grinned from ear to ear. He tutted. 'Upsettin' folks again, sir? I've warned you about that.'

Lavender managed a small smile. 'I'm merely rattling a few cages, Ned – and you usually approve of that. There's been a nasty complacency about this case ever since the death of Clara Langford. We need to reassess the situation now we've discovered this second body.'

'Sir James appears to be coming around to your way of seein' things now.'

'His eyes are still blinkered when it comes to the vicar. But at least while he's distracted with Daniels and Mrs Charlton, I'm free to interrogate Langford again.'

Woods nodded. 'I'll see you tomorrow afternoon, sir.'

'Ah, yes, you've got some investigations of your own to carry out, I believe. Something about Abel Jupp? And will you continue your search for your father? Magdalena told me about that.'

'Oh, I fancy I may encounter my Pa at some point tomorrow mornin',' Woods said vaguely.

'Do you need help tracking him down?'

Woods scowled and shook his head.

Betsy had told Magdalena that Woods became sulky and defensive every time his father was mentioned. Alby's suggestion that the old man who'd deserted them and their beloved mother was still alive had reopened old wounds for Ned.

'Thank you, sir, but it's a family matter. I need to deal with it myself.'

Lavender was prepared to let the matter drop; Ned would confide in him eventually. 'Thank you for your help today, Ned – I appreciate it.'

'And by the by, sir, don't forget there's a double murderer at large in this fancy parish.' Woods waved a warning finger at him. 'Rattlin' cages is all well and good – until you upset the wrong man. Keep yer pistol primed and in yer pocket.'

Chapter Twenty-Five

Lavender was the last one down to breakfast the following day. He gave Magdalena a kiss and sat beside her.

She smiled and handed him a small, framed drawing. 'Look at what Captain Sawyer has done for us!'

Lavender was surprised and delighted. It was an intricate – and realistic – black-ink sketch of Sebastián leaning over his cricket bat at the stumps, waiting for the ball to be thrown.

Sawyer had captured the essence of their youthful son: the set of his jaw, the concentration and confidence on his handsome face and the taut muscles beneath his shirt sleeves, along with the glossy sheen of his black hair.

'He's drawn one of Rachel for Betsy – and another of Bruce for Mrs Charlton.'

'Thank you, Captain. What a fabulous memento of the match! We shall treasure this always.'

'I sketched the three of them when they were practising the day before,' Captain Sawyer explained. 'I knew there wouldn't be time at the match.'

'It's an incredible likeness. Thank you. What do you think, Sebastián?'

His son paused briefly with his fork halfway to his mouth and said: 'I think I need a haircut, Pa.'

The adults laughed.

'Do you want to visit the village barber today?' Sawyer asked. 'I'll take you if you want.'

Sebastián shook his head, still chomping on his food. 'Thank you, sir, but no. I'm going fruit-picking with Bruce and Rachel.' He shovelled the last of his kipper into his mouth, mumbled something about being excused, and dashed out of the room.

'Enjoy yourself,' Magdalena called out after him.

'I was worried he might be bored and deflated today now the match is over,' Lavender said, 'but it looks like my fears were unfounded.'

'He's having a wonderful time here,' Magdalena commented. 'I haven't seen him so excited and happy for ages.'

And I haven't seen you so happy for ages either, Lavender thought.

'The poor boy would be even happier if Joshua had kept his eye on the ball yesterday,' Lady Caroline said with a pointed glance at her husband.

Captain Sawyer winced. 'Don't remind me, Caroline. I still can't fathom how that young scoundrel delivered such a broadside while I was distracted.'

'You were worried the screaming boy was badly injured,' Magdalena soothed.

'But where do these rum bubs learn such tricks?' the captain complained. 'They're barely breeched.'

But before anyone could answer, the footman entered the room with a letter for Lavender from Sir James Clitherow. The other adults fell silent as he used his knife to split the seal and open it.

Lavender rolled his eyes, put the letter down on the tablecloth and picked up his fork again. He waited until the servants had left the room before he spoke. 'Well, that's solved the mystery of Frederick Daniels' whereabouts on the morning of his sister's murder.'

'Where was he, Stephen?' Magdalena asked.

'Sir James questioned him again last night. Daniels told him he rode out of The Laurels to spend the morning with a woman in Brentford. Constable Hinge visited the woman last night and she's confirmed his alibi.'

Lady Caroline frowned. 'Are they sure? I haven't heard any rumours that Frederick Daniels is courting anyone. And I can assure you, Stephen, this parish is a hotbed of gossip.'

Captain Sawyer gave a great guffaw of laughter. 'You're such a precious – but innocent – goose, Caroline.'

Magdalena smiled. 'This young woman is probably not the kind of female a gentleman would marry, hence the secrecy.'

Captain Sawyer was more direct. 'The lad's got himself an obliging doxy stashed away in Brentford.'

Lady Caroline looked shocked. 'Is this true, Stephen?'

'It seems so. He must have been too embarrassed to admit her existence before. But it's interesting he's still adamant that when they met, the vicar was coming *away* from Ealing. I need to push Langford on that point this morning. Will he be reading the sermon at the church today, do you think?'

'I'm a Catholic,' Lady Caroline reminded him. 'I don't know anything about the parish church. I'll ask the servants.'

'*I* know,' Magdalena said suddenly. 'Mrs Charlton told me yesterday afternoon that the vicar has been nowhere near the church since his wife died and prefers to nurse his grief at home.'

Either that, or the man is scared he'd be struck down with a bolt of lightning if he stepped on holy ground, Lavender thought bitterly.

'The Sunday sermons have been read by visiting lay preachers since Mrs Langford's death,' Magdalena continued. 'A retired vicar called Doctor Carr is to give the sermon today.'

Lavender dabbed his mouth with his napkin and pushed back his chair. 'In that case, if Langford will be at home all morning, I'll walk over to the vicarage and see him now. Thank you for a delightful breakfast, Lady Caroline.'

Lavender's route to the centre of the village took him down a quiet back lane. Amelia Morton was walking towards him with her maid. Her head was bent over her book as she walked, and the shade of her bonnet hid her face.

Lavender frowned. This was as good a time as any to speak to the damned girl. 'Good morning, Miss Morton. Please will you send your maid ahead? I wish to speak to you on a private matter.'

Alarm flashed through her pale, lashless eyes. Her thin lips curled in a sneer. 'No, sir – I won't be thus addressed! My father has warned me about speaking with strange men.'

Lavender bit back his annoyance. 'But I'm not a stranger, Miss Morton. You know I'm in Ealing at your father's behest – and he introduced us at the cricket match yesterday. Send your maid away or I shall say what I have to say in front of her, and I can promise you, young woman, you won't like it.'

Reluctantly, Amelia told the frightened young girl to wait for her at the end of the lane. 'But watch us, Mabel, don't take your eyes off this rude man in case he compromises me!'

'Rude, Miss Morton?' Lavender said when the little maid was out of earshot. 'That's ironic, considering the vile language you've used in those dreadful letters you've sent your neighbours.'

Her pale cheeks flushed. 'I don't know what you're talking about!'

'Yes, you do. And I don't know what your poor father will say when I tell him you're behind these libellous letters.'

'This is not true!' Her voice cracked with fear. 'This is calumny!'

'Of course it's true, girl. Your father asked me to track down the vicious libeller who wrote these distressing letters and it quickly became apparent that *you're* the only person it could be. You were the only person in Ealing who knew about the rumours circulating back in Manchester about your father's illegal surgery with the factory girls.' His voice rose with anger. '*You're* the only person bitter enough to cause such mayhem.'

She dropped her book on the dusty ground and pulled out a handkerchief to dab her tearful eyes and her runny nose. She was an unattractive girl, but he had no pity for her.

'Was it when they banished you from the school room at Boston Manor that your hatred took over? I gather Sir James was one of the first – if not *the first* – to receive one of your letters.'

'You don't understand!' she wailed. 'You can't possibly understand what an education means to a girl like *me*. I *deserved* my place there.'

'What?'

The vicar's silly little brats will get a good marriage because of their family connections with the Clitherows – that's all they're fit for. But I'm clever! I *need* to learn so I can support myself. It's what my mother hoped for me.'

'You could have asked your father to send you to a school for young ladies.'

'I have! But he says he's no money to spare for school fees. He spends it on fine coats; he says he needs to look smart to earn the trust of his wealthy patients. And now he wastes the rest of his money helping my stupid Uncle Mark! *I* am neglected.'

Her immaturity and sense of entitlement were repulsive. Lavender was tempted to arrest the girl there and then and dispatch her to Newgate, to share the cell with her poor uncle for a night or two. If that didn't shock some common sense and compassion into her, nothing would.

'Father said I was to spend my life devoting myself to charitable causes. Can you imagine the boredom of that? The misery?'

'But it didn't stop with wreaking your vengeance on your father, the vicar and Sir James, did it? You got a warped pleasure out of the trouble and upset you caused.'

'That's not true!'

'I think it is.'

'Everyone to whom I wrote deserved it.'

Ah, at last a confession.

'Including my wife, Mrs Lavender?'

That halted her self-pity for a moment. Then she sneered. 'I don't like your son. He's a braggart!'

Lavender stared at her dispassionately. 'I've no intention of discussing my son with you. I need to decide what – and when – I tell your father about this.'

Fear flashed across her face again. 'You… you don't have to. I'll stop. I won't do it again. Please promise me you won't tell him.'

He doubted she'd stop of her own accord; she'd got a taste for malicious libel now. Every time she picked up her quill, the temptation would be there.

'I can't promise you anything. You've broken the law and deserve to be punished. Your hatred and bile have ruined lives. Are you aware of the devastation you caused when you pinned that note to the church lychgate?'

She sniffed and brushed her runny nose with her handkerchief again. 'But I didn't.'

'What?'

'I didn't do that. That wasn't me. Yes, I did the rest – posted those letters – and yes, I sent the vicar one, too. But I didn't write the note they found on the lychgate. Someone else did that. They… they copied me. Look, please don't tell my father – he'll send me away to live with my horrible, boring old aunts in Grimsby!'

Lavender stared at her in disbelief. Then he remembered his discussion with Magdalena. They'd both suspected the note about Clara Langford, her husband and her lover had been written by a different hand.

'You sent the vicar one of your poisonous letters?'

'Yes. Soon after the one I sent to Sir James.'

That's another lie Langford told me.

'And where the deuce did you learn such disgusting vocabulary?'

She shrugged. 'I heard it at the factory gates in Manchester, and I hear it Brentford, down on the wharf and outside the taverns. I take notes for my novella. I shall publish it anonymously.'

A wave of pity for Doctor Morton flashed through Lavender; he faced a life of conflict and disappointment with his daughter. 'I need to continue with my business,' he said coldly. 'I'll decide what to tell your father later.' He turned and walked away.

'No, please!' she begged. 'You mustn't tell him anything.'

But he kept on walking and didn't look back. The damned girl deserved to stew in her guilt and misery for the rest of the day. Birds chirped happily in the trees above his head and the breeze blew the scent of ripe fruit towards him, but none of it soothed his troubled soul.

There was something rotten festering at the heart of this idyllic village – and it was time he tore away the façade and exposed it.

Chapter Twenty-Six

Langford scowled when the maidservant showed Lavender into the drawing room of the vicarage.

He was standing by a cabinet, sorting through the contents of one of the drawers. The room had changed since Lavender's last visit. The mantelpiece, windowsills and glass cabinets had been emptied of their precious ornaments and the paintings removed from the walls. The occasional tables were now stacked in a corner, and the carpet had been rolled up and leaned against a wall alongside a pile of packing cases. In fact, the only things left to remind Lavender of his last call were a pile of dead flies on the windowsill beside a rolled-up piece of newspaper.

'What do you want, Detective? I haven't much time. I'm busy.' Langford didn't offer Lavender a seat or refreshments and remained standing himself.

Lavender looked around. 'My goodness, so I see. It looks like you're ready to leave. I thought you told me it would be a few weeks before you left for your new living in Lancashire?'

Langford's pale eyes glittered with dislike. 'I don't see how it's any of your business, but I leave tomorrow. My furniture is to go in storage. My daughters and I will spend a few weeks with family before we head north to my new parish. I need to get away from Ealing.'

Lavender nodded. 'An understandable decision, considering the circumstances, but unfortunately I can't agree to let you go as you are a suspect in a murder inquiry.'

For a moment, Langford looked like he would explode with anger, then he threw back his head and laughed. 'So, God has forsaken me again? Do you still suspect me of murdering Clara?'

'Yes, I do.'

'This is nonsense. I think you are delusional, sir. And there's no murder inquiry anymore. Sir James closed it when Ashfield was – quite rightly – arrested and charged with killing my wife.'

'You're the one who's mistaken,' Lavender said quietly. 'Sir James reopened the case yesterday evening when the dead body of your former wet nurse was dragged out of the River Brent. I presume you haven't heard about this?'

Langford started with shock – *or was that anger?* He glanced away and crossed himself. 'May the Lord have mercy upon her soul. How dreadful! The poor woman!' He went to one of the fireside armchairs and sat down. 'This is such a shock! Ashfield must have killed her, too.'

'I've persuaded Sir James otherwise.'

Langford's mouth gaped open as conflicting emotions flashed across his face. Then he laughed. 'So, you suspect me of killing both my wife *and* my servant while I was at a funeral in Brentford? You must be desperate to find a resolution to this case if you've come to that conclusion. I've read about the great Detective Lavender in *The Times* – and to be honest, I expected more imagination from you than that.'

Lavender ignored the taunt. 'My problem with *you*, Mr Langford, is that you have consistently lied to me since I arrived in Ealing, which means I find it hard to trust any of your declarations of innocence. For a start, you told me Mrs Langford hired the wet nurse, but two witnesses – who worked here at the time – are both adamant it was you who went out and hired this woman to feed your new child. And what's more,' he added quickly before Langford could interrupt, 'both believe you brought home this drunkard to punish your wife. Why did you want to punish her, Mr Langford?'

'I didn't!' The vicar's voice was strained with anger. 'And as for my memory lapse on that occasion, you'll have to forgive me for being so distracted. I'd just buried my murdered wife! Can a blunt instrument like you even imagine what that must have been like?'

'And did you experience another memory lapse when you told me you'd never met Dora Kilby?'

'Who?'

'Dora Kilby. She's the herbalist in Brentford whom you suspected sent out those poisoned letters. You claimed you'd never met her.'

'I'm sure I haven't...'

'She was the midwife who brought your youngest daughter into the world.'

'Oh, her? That was Mrs Kilby? Again, Lavender, as I'm sure you must know, when your wife is in labour a man tends to be distracted. I spent most of that evening praying to God to ask him to ease Clara's suffering.'

'You also forgot to tell me you'd received one of those vile letters yourself.'

The vicar shrugged and stared calmly at Lavender. 'I didn't tell you that because it would have been a lie. I didn't receive one.'

Lavender paused. He knew differently but decided to keep that fact to himself for the moment.

'Have you finished with your accusations now, Lavender? I appreciate I may have been distracted and forgetful at times when we first spoke, and I apologise for my lapses.'

'No, I haven't finished. You also told me that when you returned from Brentford that day, you saw Frederick Daniels coming away from the village.'

'Yes, I did.'

'He claims it was the other way around. He was travelling to Ealing – but *you* had just left the village.'

'This is nonsense! The silly boy is mistaken – and please don't tell me you prefer to take *his* word over mine! For heaven's sake – there was thick fog – it was virtually impossible to see anything more than a few feet away from your nose!'

'Daniels has a sound alibi for the morning of the murder. He visited an acquaintance in Brentford. This witness told Constable Hinge that Daniels left Brentford just after noon, which ties in with his account of meeting you on the road.'

Langford sneered and laughed. 'Well, it's fortunate I also have a solid alibi for that same dreadful morning, isn't it? You need to leave, Lavender. I find this conversation irksome. I want to continue my packing.'

'You don't have an alibi. You arrived at St Paul's Church in Brentford, but none of the other mourners – or the vicar and his sexton – remember seeing you inside the church.'

Alarm flickered across the vicar's face and his forehead creased into a frown.

'Where did you go?'

Langford sighed and put his head in his hands. With his head still bowed, he said: 'I'd hoped this wouldn't come out.'

Lavender waited.

The vicar raised his head. 'I'm ashamed to admit I couldn't face the funeral service when I arrived. I had worrying matters on my mind and wanted some time alone – to think, and to talk with God. I rode along the canal tow path for a while.'

'Can anyone verify this? Were you seen by anyone you know?'

'Of course not! I was avoiding everyone I knew! And there was the damned fog too. In the end, I found myself close to the home of Mr Jupp and decided to call on him. I didn't mention this before because I knew it was a dereliction of my duty. As the vicar of Ealing, I should have paid my respects to the late Reverend Doctor Finch.' A sly smile flickered at the edge of his mouth. 'I presume you've spoken to Mr Jupp, and he's confirmed my alibi?'

'Yes, my constable spoke to him. But these things on your mind, Mr Langford – is one of them the paternity of your youngest daughter? And the possible adultery of your wife?'

Langford was now on his feet, red-faced with fury and pointing at the door. 'Out! Get out of my home – you uncouth devil! How dare you speak thus about my late wife!'

Lavender rose calmly to his feet. 'I will leave – but before I go, I want to see the silver baptism cup. The one the maid claimed was stolen by the wet nurse, Mrs Snelling. You said last time you'd removed it to a safer place?'

'No! I'm damned if I'll cooperate with you – and trust me, Lavender, Sir James will hear about this disgraceful affront!'

'Sir James can count like the rest of us, Mr Langford. I'm sure he's already realised – like you – that your daughter was born in the seventh month of your marriage.'

'This is absurd! The child came early!'

'Did she? Or was Mrs Langford already with child when she married you? And did you suspect the child was Ashfield's? My goodness! That's a strong motive to kill her.'

Langford leaned forward with his fists clenched. 'This is calumny! Vile calumny!'

Lavender had never been punched by a vicar before, but he knew there was a first time for everything. But he'd faced down worse coves than Langford in his time. He stood his ground and said calmly, 'If you won't show me the silver cup, Mr Langford, then I'll come back with a magistrate's warrant – and I'll bring Sir James with me.'

'It's packed in a crate! God only knows which one!'

'Then you'd better unpack your crates, Mr Langford, and find it. As I said earlier, I can't allow you to leave Ealing while you're under suspicion of murdering your wife and your servant.'

'Damn your interference, Lavender!'

'And if you do attempt to leave – I shall be forced to raise a hue and cry with the help of the constabulary and the newspapers. Good day to you, sir. I'll see myself out.'

The interview with Langford had left Lavender seething with anger.

The man had an answer for everything; no wonder he had been able to avoid suspicion for so long. But Lavender didn't believe a word of the vicar's excuses.

But evidence? Where was the damned evidence to support his suspicions?

He knew he needed to walk for a while to clear his head before he returned home to plan his next move. But his eyes fell upon the bow windows and smart wooden signage of the general store across the green. He stopped in his tracks.

The arsenic.

They still hadn't discovered where it came from.

An idea formed in his mind, and he quickened his pace towards the shop.

It was closed and shuttered for the Sabbath. Fortunately, Mr Blake, the proprietor, lived above the premises and hadn't yet left for church. The small, bespectacled man let Lavender into the shop and opened the shutters. The mingled scents of tobacco and spices seemed stronger this morning and dust motes swirled in the sunbeams that slanted down to the sawdust on the floor.

Lavender asked to see the accounts for the vicarage. Blake gave him a puzzled look but fetched him the ledger, placed it on the counter and turned to the right page.

There, itemised in neat handwriting, were the purchases made by the staff and occupants of the vicarage over the last few months.

Lavender's hopes were dashed at first. He had hoped to see that a second box of rat poison had been purchased. But it hadn't.

And then he saw it. The answer to the riddle of Clara Langford's death by poison.

He sighed with satisfaction, stood up straight and thanked Mr Blake for his help.

It was only circumstantial evidence – and wouldn't get a conviction in a court of law. But at least now he knew *how* the vicar had procured the arsenic that killed his wife.

All he had to do now was prove it beyond reasonable doubt.

Chapter Twenty-Seven

Woods yawned and stretched as he plonked down his small wooden stool and fishing rod on the wharf in Brentford. It was early, and the sun was still low in the sky. The tall warehouses around him cast long, chilly shadows across the locks and the canal basin, but he knew it would be another scorching hot day.

He sat down on his stool, pulled his hat low over his eyes and opened his bait tin.

A couple of fellas were frying their breakfast on a small oil stove on the tow path, and the tantalising aroma of fried ham overcame the other less pleasant smells of oil, coal dust and stagnant water and made his stomach rumble. Apart from a skinny dog on the tow path sniffing at a pile of horse manure, the only other movement came from the empty barges drifting gently out in the breeze. Their mooring lines slowly tightened, then sagged once again.

Big Jim Kilby appeared, limping around his precious gauging lock. It was difficult to guess how old the fella was, Woods decided. He could be anywhere between sixty and eighty, but Woods suspected he was closer to the latter. Dora's herbal remedies obviously weren't working. The fella limped more than ever on his arthritic knee, and he rubbed his bad shoulder often. Woods hoped Kilby had some savings, because his days pulling and shoving that balance beam around and hauling on mooring lines were numbered.

Woods cast his line into the oily black water of the canal and glanced at the dark entrance to the alley that led to Abel Jupp's hovel. There was no sign of the man – or hardly anyone else for that matter. Then Woods remembered it was a Sunday. His brain was slow this morning; he'd arrived home late last night, and he hadn't had much sleep.

What did Jupp do on the Sabbath?

The Reverend Langford claimed the man was a regular churchgoer. Woods doubted this from what he'd seen, but it didn't matter anyhow. If Jupp appeared on the wharf in his Sunday best and spent an hour at St Paul's Church on his knees praying, Woods would be a few pews behind him.

He was glad he'd brought his old brown coat and hat. Both were smelly from years of fishing beside the Thames and ripped and patched from scuffling with the coves of London. But they were different to the clothes he'd worn yesterday, and he needed a disguise if he was to follow Jupp all day.

But his disguise hadn't fooled Big Jim Kilby.

The old sea dog limped towards him, scowling with anger and holding his heavy iron windlass like a weapon in his fist. 'Oi – you! I thought I told you to cast your line elsewhere. I don't allow fishin' on my lock.'

Woods smiled and waited until the man was beside him before he answered. He knew sound travelled over water and he wanted to keep his voice low. 'Easy, Big Fella. I'm only doin' my job.'

The angry scowl vanished, and Kilby eyed him now with suspicion and surprise. Thankfully, he lowered his voice. 'What job? Is this Bow Street business? I know you're a runner.'

Woods nodded. 'I'm watchin' out for a cove who lives round here.'

Kilby's eyes darted across the canal in the direction of Jupp's home.

'Is it Woody? What's the old rogue done this time?'

'Woody?'

'Aye, on account of 'is wooden teeth. 'Is real name's Jupp.'

Woods nodded. 'That makes sense now. What do you know about the fella? Why is he a rogue?'

Kilby's face darkened again. ''E's allus filchin' things from the barges – especially the coal. If you put 'im under the 'atches, you'll be doin' me a favour. I'm sick of watchin' out for 'im. I've better things to do with my time.'

'Does he work? How does he earn his chinks?'

Kilby shrugged his huge shoulders and replied: 'I don't know if 'e's ever 'ad a bloody job. 'E gets by with a bit of this and that – thievin' mostly.'

'A shadowy cove, eh?'

''E's also a charmer with the wimmen and a bammer. 'E cons soft-hearted wimmen of the parish to pity 'im. 'E pretends to be ill, and they bring 'im meals. Mind you, I never 'eard of that bein' a crime.'

'It ain't,' Woods said simply.

Two dark-haired and swarthy men came down the steps from the road bridge and walked along the opposite bank of the canal. One had a moustache and a red kerchief around his neck. The other wore a fraying green coat with brass buttons. They turned down the alleyway that led to Jupp's house.

Kilby frowned again and spat in derision on the wharf.

'Who are they?' Woods asked.

'Foreigners. I've seen them talkin' with Woody before. I've a notion they're crew from a Spanish tradin' ship on the river.'

'Spanish?'

'Aye. I've heard them speak the lingo.'

'You speak Spanish?'

'Aye, I've been all over the world with the navy. I've got a smatterin' of Portugese and French, too.'

'Does our friend Woody speak Spanish?'

Kilby snorted. 'No, the bugger just whines in English.'

The two men reappeared. They retraced their steps back up on the bridge and Brentford High Street.

Kilby still hesitated by his side. Woods sensed the man had something else to say.

'Your daughter's brought 'im stuff.'

Woods nodded. 'I thought that were the case.'

'So, is that's why you're 'ere?' He scowled and added: 'She says 'e's her Grandpa.'

Woods said nothing.

Kilby shrugged and turned to go. 'I guess you know 'ow to care for your own nipper.' He stopped after a few steps and turned back, smiling at a memory.

The old fella's teeth were still good, Woods noticed. The smile lit up his leathery face and his voice softened. 'She's a feisty little gal.'

'She takes after her Ma with her temper. If you want to make a complaint – speak to Mrs Woods. It's her fault.'

Kilby's broad shoulders shook when he laughed. 'I reckon I won't risk it.'

'What did my Treacle say?'

'Your gal told me to mind my manners.'

Woods smiled. 'I've a notion she were right about that.'

'I heard she plays a good game of cricket.'

'Her brothers taught her.'

Kilby seemed surprised. 'You've got sons?'

Woods tore his eyes away from his fishing line and gave Kilby a shrewd look. 'Aye, I've got two great hulkin' lads back in Southwark – and a foster son as well. Their aunt's takin' care of them this week while we're here.'

'A foster son?' Kilby snorted. 'You've taken in another man's son? I didn't take you fer a muttonhead.'

'His Pa is dead,' Woods snapped. 'And *unlike some people* I don't abandon little uns to the workhouse.'

An unmistakable flash of pain flickered in Kilby's eyes. But Woods was too annoyed to stop. 'I reckon you and I take a different view on many things, Jim Kilby. And I've a notion you never brought up any little nippers of your own.'

Kilby's face contorted with misery. 'I buried two daughters – and their Ma with them.'

Woods' knuckles turned white as he gripped his rod harder. His stomach lurched with distress. That news hurt him to the core. He hadn't expected it, and he didn't want to hear it.

He swallowed hard and said as calmly as he could: 'I'm sorry, Kilby. That's hard to bear. You must have suffered.'

Kilby's eyes were moist as he stared across at the other side of the canal. 'Aye, well, it were a long time ago. In Buenos Aires on the other side of the world.' He paused for a second and nodded across towards the alley. 'Your mark's on the move. Leave your fishin' tackle 'ere – I'll take care of it.'

Woods glanced across the canal, just in time to see Abel Jupp slink out of the alley towards the stone steps and the bridge. He waited until the fella's back was to him, then Woods rose to his feet, pulled his hat down further over his eyes and thanked Kilby.

It quickly became apparent that Abel Jupp had no intention of attending church.

He trotted along Brentford's grimy high street, through the dust clouds churned up by the wheels of the ceaseless traffic. He crossed the cobbled market square and turned into a narrow alley.

'He ain't no bloody invalid,' Woods muttered to himself as he struggled to keep up with the sprightly old man.

Woods' nostrils wrinkled in disgust at the entrance to the alley. The looming chimneys of the turpentine factory on the next street blocked out the sunlight here; the passage smelt of damp, mould and human slops.

At the end of the passage were a couple of battered shops with peeling weathered signs and grimy windows. One was a vacant general store – now boarded up against thieves and vagrants. The other's signage was unreadable but the three cracked and faded red globes dangling from a rotten wooden sign marked it out as a pawnbroker's.

Woods pressed himself into the shadows of a doorway and watched. When the door opened, Jupp was ushered inside by an elderly man.

'Now, now, Mr Woody,' Woods said to himself smugly. 'What possible business does a man like you have with a wheedlin' pawnbroker this early on the Sabbath? What's so secretive you can't call when the shop's open?'

There was no way out of the alley except back the way they had come. Woods decided to return to the market square and wait for the cove to reappear. There was a line of empty beer barrels outside the Three Pigeons, which made a handy perch for his backside.

Sleepy Brentford was coming alive. The coaching inns were already busy, and a steady stream of drinkers were making their way towards their open doors. Beggars in tattered rags appeared from nowhere, pestering well-dressed family groups heading for the town's churches.

The whore Peg O'Donnell drifted up the street arm-in-arm with the woman she was belting only a few days earlier. Both still had bruises on their faces from their fight, but now they were sober and the best of friends. Shameless and grinning, they called out lasciviously, advertising their wares, to the men on the street.

Masked by the crowds, Woods felt safe from being seen by Jupp. And sure enough, when the man reappeared, he barely glanced in his direction. Woods watched him head back towards the canal and decided that rather than follow him, he'd pay the pawnbroker a visit; he didn't want to miss him. Most of the brokers he knew in London spent more time in Newgate than in churches, but it would be just his luck if the fella was shutting up shop right now to head out to hear a sermon.

He retraced his steps down the alley and rapped loudly on the battered door, dislodging flakes of peeling paint with his fist.

A few moments later, he heard shuffling and a nervous, high-pitched voice called out: 'We're shut!'

'No, you're not, you lyin' cove,' Woods shouted back. 'I've just seen Jupp leavin'. And I'm a police constable. Open this door – in the name of the law!' He always enjoyed adding this last bit.

The elderly man who opened the door was small with a hunchback and wire spectacles that enlarged his short-sighted eyes to a childlike proportion. He peered up at Woods nervously. 'What you want? I ain't done nothin' wrong.'

‘I’ll be the judge of that.’ Woods stepped forcefully into the cluttered and foul-smelling shop. The stench of unwashed clothes and dirty, mouldy upholstery made his broad nose wrinkle in disgust. ‘Tell me what Abel Jupp were doin’ here – and show me what he’s brought you.’

The man gaped at him in surprise. ‘How do you know Woody brought me anythin’?’

Woods didn’t, but he’d a notion it was a good guess. ‘Stop wastin’ my time and just show me, fella. Otherwise, it’ll be worse for you when I fetch in the rest of the runners.’

‘You’re a runner?’ the man squeaked in horror. He didn’t wait for an answer and scurried off towards the counter at the back of his shop. ‘Woody never said nothin’ about the runners bein’ after ’im!’

He pulled open some drawers behind the counter and rummaged through them.

While he waited, Woods glanced around at the jumble of battered furniture, racks of clothing, piles of old boots and rolls of carpet that lined the walls. He hated these places. Everything here stood for broken lives, misery and desperation.

The pawnbroker piled up a few trinkets on the counter: a broken dirty string of amber beads and a brooch with a broken clasp, some bone pipes among them.

‘It’s the things he finds in the mud beside the river,’ the man wailed.

Woods glared at the nervous man. ‘More likely stuff he’s filched from the barges.’ He took a chance. ‘I want the rest – where is it?’

‘There ain’t no more.’

‘Yes there is. Fetch it out.’

Something flashed across the old man’s face. *Was it confusion or fear?*

The broker’s shoulders slumped. Sighing, he reached below the counter and lifted out a tiny, solid silver baptism cup. Even in the dim light of the shop Woods saw it was a pretty little thing, engraved with swirling flowers – and a name.

'It's the only thing of value 'e brought me!' the pawnbroker wailed. 'I didn't know it were filched! I paid 'im ten shillings!'

'Didn't you see the engravin'?'

'What engravin'?'

It was so dark back here in the bowels of this disgusting shop, Woods believed him. 'Fetch me some light.'

Grumbling, the pawnbroker lit a lantern and placed it on the counter.

Woods traced his finger along the engraving and held it up to the flickering light. '*Thomas John Langford.* Do you know who this is?'

'No.'

'It's the vicar of Ealing.'

The man's eyes widened behind his spectacles. ''Im whose wife were killed?'

'That's right. What you have here, fella, is evidence from a murder inquiry. I'm takin' it to the magistrate.'

Woods turned and left the shop.

Back in the alleyway, with the cup safe in his pocket, he strode towards the sunlight of the high street. He rubbed his old nose, grinning. That itch was now gone. His old nose had never let him down.

He wasn't sure what this latest discovery meant – but he knew the last time this cup had been seen, the wet nurse was dropping it into her cloak pocket.

Had Jupp killed her and found the cup when he stuffed those heavy rocks in her pockets?

Woods frowned. The evidence in his pocket said *yes* – but years of experience had taught him it was a huge leap for a petty thief to move to murder. Jupp was a sly cove – but was he a killer?

But how else had he got hold of the stolen cup?

He took a big breath and shook his old noggin before it became too muddled. It was up to Lavender to unravel the rest of this tangle.

But one thing was certain: he needed an arrest warrant for Jupp – and fast.

Chapter Twenty-Eight

Cedar Court seemed unnaturally quiet when Lavender returned. He couldn't hear the children, or anyone in the house for that matter. Two letters waited for him on a silver platter on the marble table in the hall.

The first was from Magistrate Conant in Bow Street. Conant reminded Lavender his three days were up and demanded his immediate return to London. Somehow, he'd discovered Ned was in Brentford. He wanted both men in his office first thing tomorrow morning to explain what the devil they were up to.

Lavender rolled his eyes, screwed up the letter and promptly forgot about it.

His second letter was from the bishop, whom he'd contacted for more information about the Reverend Langford. The bishop's reply made his spine turn to ice. He cursed Langford as he read.

'Stephen? Is that you?'

Lady Caroline stood at the top of the stairs, leaning heavily on her silver-topped walking cane. Her face was creased with anxiety, pale and tear-stained. 'You must come to Magdalena immediately,' she called out. 'I can't console her.'

He took the stairs two at a time and grabbed her arm. 'What's happened? Is it one of the children?'

'Magdalena will explain. But you must deny it, Stephen! Lie and bluff if you must! Keep this secret – and never, *ever* tell Sebastián!'

He opened his mouth to ask for an explanation, then clamped it shut. He hurried to the bedchamber he shared with his wife.

Magdalena was laid curled up on their bed, sobbing her eyes out. She clutched a letter in her hands. He'd never seen her so distraught.

'I can't do it on my own anymore, Stephen.'

He hurried to her side and gathered her into his arms. 'Do what? What's the matter, *querida?* Is it one of the children? Are they ill? Are you ill?'

She turned her large and tearful violet eyes towards him. She was trembling. She muttered something indistinguishable in Spanish. He bit back his fear and waited until she calmed down. His heart pounded in his chest.

'I've ruined you, Stephen,' she stuttered. 'You're such a good man. I knew I'd bring you trouble. Now I've ruined your life.'

He wiped the tears away from her cheeks. 'Nonsense, *querida.* You and the children are the best things that ever happened to me; you know I love you.'

Mentioning their children set her sobbing again. '*Los niños pobres! Qué les pasará a ellos?*'

His alarm intensified. 'What's happened, *querida*?'

'Antonio has risen from the dead. He's here – in England.'

'What!' Lavender reeled and a wave of nausea shot through him.

'My husband didn't die at Talavera. He was injured – badly injured – and burned. He first wrote to me about two months ago.'

Lavender reeled with shock. He cast a furious glance at her locked writing case on the dresser. He'd *known* there was something in those damned letters from Spain that upset her!

'That's impossible! Antonio died at Talavera. We contacted the War Department. They told us he was dead.' But as the words poured out of his mouth, he remembered that it *was* possible. James Read had confirmed that the body of Don Antonio García de Aviles was never found.

'But if he's still alive, where has he been for the last five years?' he spluttered. 'Why the devil didn't he contact you before?'

'Please don't shout, Stephen,' she pleaded. More tears slid down her cheeks. 'I know this is a terrible shock – and I've brought you to ruin – but please don't hate me and shout.'

'I'm sorry, I'm sorry… I don't hate you.' He pulled her closer and swallowed hard. 'You haven't ruined my life. I love you more than I love myself, *querida*. Tell me everything. Tell me the worst.'

'He wants his son.'

Fear gripped Lavender so tight around his lungs he gasped to breathe. Not Sebastián. Not *his* beautiful, funny and much-loved son. Lavender's world was collapsing around him.

'He claims that in Spain, a child belongs to his father and it's the same in England. Is it true, Stephen?'

He nodded stiffly. His voice still cracked when he spoke. 'And you? Does he want you?'

She gave a short hysterical laugh. 'No! Of course he doesn't! According to him, I'm a spoiled woman, damaged – and damned in the eyes of God for my bigamy!'

Relief, anger, fear – everything swirled round Lavender at once.

'Although he did concede it might help Sebastián to settle back into Spain,' she continued, 'if I took up temporary residence in a small cabaña on the edge of my father's estate in Oviedo. He wants the estate and the rent for himself.'

'And your other children? *Our* children?'

'He says I'm to leave my English bastards with you.'

'He's the bastard!' Lavender stood up and paced furiously around the room. He knew he should stay calm, but his anger with de Aviles was overwhelming.

'Have you told Teresa about this? Is this why Alfie Tummins thought she might return to Spain?'

Magdalena lowered her head. 'Yes, I've told both Teresa and Lady Caroline. I… I needed someone to talk to, while I tried to work out what to do.'

'Telling *me* might have helped. Did you consider taking Sebastián back to Spain and staying with him?'

'No! I'd never give up Sebastián – nor would I leave you and our babies!'

He believed her. He breathed heavily, trying to see a path through this nightmare. Her stubborn refusal to cooperate wouldn't be enough. Legally, she was still the wife of de Aviles – and Sebastián was the Spaniard's son.

He stopped his pacing and returned to her side. Magdalena was on the verge of hysteria and was being torn in two. His heart ached for her suffering.

'Why didn't you tell me about this, *querida*?' he asked gently. 'Why have you suffered this alone?'

'I've been so ashamed, so wretched… I thought you'd cast me out.'

'I'd never do that.'

'I sought advice from the Sisters of Mercy on Carmine Street.'

He was stunned at this turn of events. Magdalena was a Catholic but had never been devout. 'Nuns? Really? You asked some childless virgins what you should do about your two husbands and your three children?'

To his relief, her lips twitched in a half-smile. 'Yes, I knew this was a silly notion the minute I saw their reaction. They told me I should repent to God for my sinful lust; leave you and the little ones in London and go back to Antonio with Sebastián. They told me to prostrate myself before him and beg his forgiveness.'

Whether it was the shock, or just the ridiculous nature of the situation they now found themselves in, Lavender suddenly found himself laughing. He took her in his arms again. 'They don't know you like I know you, *querida*.'

She turned her eyes to him with hope. Her black eyelashes had grown longer with the tears. Even in her grief, his wife was the most beautiful woman he'd ever known.

'You're not angry with me, Stephen?'

'I'm furious with de Aviles and irritated that you didn't tell me anything about this. But, no, I'm not angry with *you*. None of this is your fault – you've nothing to be ashamed about. Don't blame yourself.'

'I tried not to bother you. You've such a difficult job… and so many of us to provide for. I felt it was *my* problem to solve. Lady Caroline invited me here. I was grateful to escape for a while. I pretended it wasn't happening…'

Lavender nodded. It wasn't like Magdalena to run away from a problem, but he understood her desperation.

He wondered about Lady Caroline's advice. Could they bluff their way through this? Keep Sebastián in ignorance about his father and carry on as normal? He shook his head and dismissed the idea. Terrible secrets like this always came out.

Another thought struck him. 'It wouldn't surprise me if other British widows weren't suffering the same dilemma.'

'What do you mean?'

'The war in the Iberian Peninsula has been a bloodbath from start to finish. Almost every battle, from Zaragoza to the final one in Toulouse, led to thousands of casualties. The British army keep meticulous records of their soldiers and allies. But I wonder how many other women have been wrongly told that they're widows. Like you, they've probably remarried and begun a new life. Then, a few years later, they're shocked to see their first husband limping up the road on crutches.'

She nodded thoughtfully. 'So, you don't think this is God's punishment just for my sins?'

'I doubt God has anything to do with this, *querida.* Wars are started by men and mistakes like this are made by men. What I don't understand, though, is why it's taken de Aviles five years to get back in touch with you.'

'He says he was very ill for several years and couldn't remember anything. One side of his body and his face were so badly burned by the fires, it was a miracle he survived.'

Ah, the famous man with the burnt face...

A thought suddenly struck him. 'Did you say earlier that he wants your father's estate in Oviedo?'

'Yes. He says his own estate is burned to the ground and poisoned by the French.'

Lavender nodded. They already knew this from their Spanish agent. Fortunately, Magdalena had inherited an estate from her father, and it had escaped the worst of the French invasion unscathed. They used the income to pay for Sebastián's school fees. One day it would be his.

'Antonio says he needs somewhere to live, and he needs the revenue from the rents for himself and for Sebastián's education – at a new school.'

Lavender gave a bitter laugh. 'No, that's not possible. They don't play cricket at Spanish schools. So, de Aviles wants your son *and* your money, does he?'

She nodded.

Something was wrong – but he couldn't put his finger on it. 'You said he's come to England. When did you meet him?'

'I haven't. I tried... but he won't see me. He says he's so disfigured now he hides away from society.'

Lavender grimaced. 'That won't be pleasant for Sebastián.'

'He wrote me letters to our house in London. I thought if I saw him and pleaded with him to leave us alone, I might persuade him Sebastián is happy and should stay with us.' She hesitated for a moment and added quietly, 'I even thought to give him the estate in Oviedo in exchange....'

'You wanted to bribe him to go away?'

'Yes.'

'But you've not met him.'

'No.'

'So how do you know it *is* de Aviles who's contacted you? Have you considered this may be an elaborate trick? That it's someone else? Someone who contrives to steal from you?'

Magdalena stared at him in surprise. For a moment, hope glimmered in her eyes, then she shook her head and hung it in shame. 'In his letters, he refers to things from our marriage. Intimate things that only a husband would know.'

Lavender braced himself. 'I think it's time you showed me these letters.'

She nodded and went to find the key to her writing case. She opened it and handed him a pile of letters tied up with string.

Lavender's spoken Spanish was excellent, but he struggled to understand some of the written phrases. It didn't help that the handwriting was mean and cramped in style; some words were indistinguishable.

Mean and cramped, he thought. *Just like the man himself.*

He read the letters in the order they'd arrived. The situation unfolded exactly as Magdalena had told him. But her pleading had obviously fallen on deaf ears. In each new letter, de Aviles' tone became more brutal at her refusal to cooperate.

'Where did you send your replies?' he asked.

'He told me to send them to the George and Dragon tavern in Shoreditch.' Her face contorted with misery again. 'I went there once to plead with him. But when I arrived at the tavern they told me the Spanish gentleman paid them to receive his mail, but he and his servants didn't lodge there. I… I gave up trying to find him.'

Lavender imagined her trudging around London with her shoulders slumped and her heart broken, desperately trying to resolve this issue on her own. She'd done everything possible.

He squeezed her hand and returned to the letters, grimacing at the references de Aviles made to the intimacy they'd known during their marriage.

But the idea that this was an elaborate fraud had taken root in his mind and refused to go away.

Some men were indiscreet and talked freely about such matters with their cronies. If this *was* an elaborate deception, then the fraudster knew de Aviles – and knew him well. He probably fought with him in the Spanish resistance against Bonaparte and took part in the Battle of Talavera by his side, which would account for those injuries he'd sustained.

Lavender had little respect for de Aviles and the way he'd abandoned his wife and child to the invading French. He could imagine the man drunk, sitting around a campfire with his fellow guerrillas, on a rocky and freezing mountainside high in the Pyrenees, boasting indelicately and scathingly about his wife and their marriage.

Lavender knew he saw criminals and deception everywhere; after years of working as a Bow Street officer, this trait was deeply engrained in his character.

But just suppose this *was* a trick? The war had torn Spain apart and left it in chaos; many of its citizens were destitute and desperate.

'What's in that last letter? The one you received today that upset you.'

Magdalena handed him the crumpled and tear-stained note, which had fallen on to the carpet.

'It's the only one he's sent to me here. I don't know how he found out I'd come to Ealing. I thought we were safe.'

Lavender remembered the hackney carriage waiting outside his home on the evening his family left. He'd thought nothing of it at the time. *Was that de Aviles?* Did that carriage follow the carriage containing his wife and children?

And what about the vehicle he'd seen parked beside the village green yesterday? *Was de Aviles sitting inside, watching his son play cricket?*

His skin crawled at the thought.

Another memory added to his growing alarm. When he'd first arrived in Ealing, Sebastián told him that he and the other children had been bothered by a pair of Spaniards while they were in the orchard…

He didn't open the letter. He turned to his wife. 'What does he want this time?'

'He threatens to take matters into his own hands. He says I must see my lawyer immediately about transferring my father's estates to him and arrange to bring him Sebastián.'

'What does he mean when he says he intends to take matters into his own hands?'

Her eyes filled up with tears again. 'He didn't explain – but I think he means to publicly expose me as a bigamist. Oh God, Stephen! What are we going to do?'

He reached out to comfort her again. The prophesy of that damned witch rang in his head. *There's danger swirlin' round you and your kin. Great danger...*

'Stephen, what's the matter? Why are you staring at me like that?'

'Where's Sebastián?'

'He's gone out fruit-picking with Bruce and Rachel. Why?'

He rose and tried to compose his expression; he didn't want to alarm her. 'I'm going to get Sebastián and Rachel and bring them here. Tonight, we'll work out how to deal with de Aviles and his threats. In the meantime, I want Sebastián home.'

'But... what about your work, Stephen?'

'The case be damned.'

Chapter Twenty-Nine

Sebastián felt hot, thirsty and annoyed as they approached the Brentford gauging lock. He hated this place, especially its stink. And the smoke-stained, towering warehouses made him feel claustrophobic.

Frustrated, he kicked a stone into the black and oily water of the canal. 'But why me? Why not Bruce?'

'Grandpa said he didn't have the chinks to buy something for Bruce too, so I should just bring you along at two o'clock.'

'I don't want to see him again, Rachel.'

'Stop your moanin', García,' she chided. 'And be grateful. I think it's nice my Grandpa wants to give you something.'

They were both grubby, sweaty and stained with fruit juice from their morning's work. Rachel had quite a collection of leaves and small twigs stuck in her thick, curly brown hair. Both had scratches on their hands and arms.

Sebastián thought of Woody's filthy hovel and grimaced. 'I don't want anything from him.'

When Rachel ignored him, he added, beneath his breath: 'It'll need washing, whatever it is.'

She heard him. 'Don't be mean, García. He can't help bein' poor and dirty – he's had a tragic life, full of misery and bad luck. I'm glad I can help him a little. My Da doesn't seem to care – he ain't even looked for him yet. But Uncle Alby will be pleased with me for carin'.'

Ahead, a church clock chimed the hour, and she quickened her step. 'Come on – he said for me to bring you at two o'clock sharp.'

Lavender was surprised – but damned pleased – to see Ned standing in the hallway, talking to Lady Caroline and Captain Sawyer.

'Good afternoon, sir. I've…'

Lavender cut him off. 'Ned, I need your help with an urgent matter. Captain Sawyer, may Ned borrow one of your horses again?'

'Of course.'

'What's happened, Stephen? How is Magdalena?' Lady Caroline asked.

'I've reassured her, but would you please sit with her until I return? I'll explain everything later. Ned – we need to go.'

He turned to walk to the stables and Woods fell in step beside him without comment.

Once they were alone, Lavender said: 'We need to find our children – fast.'

Woods frowned. 'What's amiss, sir?'

'There's no easy way to explain this, so I'll just say it quickly. A Spaniard has contacted Magdalena. He claims to be her first husband: Don Antonio de Aviles.'

'Gawd's teeth!' Woods stumbled with shock. 'Have you met the cove? Does Sebastián know?'

'Not yet. I've only just found out and Sebastián knows nothing about it – thank God! I want him – and Rachel – back here while I work out what the devil to do. Magdalena is devasted.'

'The poor woman.' Alarm now flashed across Ned's face. 'Did Sebastián tell you about those Spaniards they met the other day? Rachel said they were a rough pair of rogues.'

'Yes, he did. I think de Aviles may have followed my family to Ealing.'

Woods growled and quickened his pace.

Once they reached the stable, it only took them a few minutes to get both horses harnessed and saddled. While they worked, Lavender explained in more detail what had happened.

Woods listened in silence, his jaw clamped and his expression growing angrier and more ferocious with every second.

'Do you think this de Aviles fella would try to speak to Sebastián?'

Lavender swung himself up into the saddle. 'I don't know, Ned. The problem is, I'm not sure this *is* de Aviles. I think it might be a fraudulent trick to get money out of Magdalena. If de Aviles *did* survive the Battle of Talavera, I can't understand why he's waited five years to make contact with his wife and son.'

Woods nodded grimly, tightened the girth on his saddle and swung himself up on to the horse.

'Sebastián was only eight years old when he last saw his father,' Lavender continued. 'But he's not a child anymore – and he can be very emotional and stubborn.'

Woods nodded. 'Just like my lads.'

'I've no idea how he'd react if de Aviles approached him.'

'If it *is* his ruddy Da,' Woods growled angrily.

'We'll go to The Laurels. Elizabeth Charlton will know where they are.'

The alleyway to Woody's hovel stank worse than before, and Sebastián cringed as they ducked below a line of wet laundry strung across the narrow gap. The drying clothes were rags.

Woody waited for them at the door to his home. His beaming smile gave them an excellent view of his worn and stained wooden teeth. 'You came! On time too! Well done, young 'uns.'

'Hello, Grandpa,' Rachel said.

'What is this about, sir?' Sebastián asked.

'I've got a surprise fer you, lad. They'll be 'ere in a minute.'

'Who will? What is this surprise?'

'It's yer Da, son. 'E wanted to meet you 'ere.'

Sebastián frowned. 'My Pa? He's coming here?'

Rachel was also confused. 'Grandpa, why's Uncle Stephen comin' here?'

Woody avoided their questions and pointed back down the alley, over their shoulders. ''Ere he is! Now, ain't this nice? It's your long-lost Da!'

Sebastián turned round, froze and stared in horror at the three men approaching them from behind. They blocked off the sunlight, which increased the gloom in the narrow passage. Rachel moved closer to him.

Two of them were the swarthy Spaniards they'd seen before. Both men were grinning, but their smile didn't reach their eyes.

With them hobbled a third, crippled man. He wore gloves, a hat and a frightening black leather mask over half his face. Behind the small eyehole, Sebastián saw the pale glint of a damaged eye, ringed with pink, raw tissue. He leaned heavily on a walking stick with his left arm, while his right arm hung down, useless, at his side.

He wasn't smiling. He couldn't.

His lips were gone, seared away in whatever inferno had claimed him. The skin around the part of his mouth uncovered by the mask had fused and healed unevenly, leaving behind a permanent, lipless grimace that exposed his teeth.

This grotesque parody of a man walked up to him and said in Spanish: '*Buenas tardes*, Sebastián. It's good to see you again, *mi hijo*.' His voice was hoarse, cracked. Sebastián didn't recognise it.

'Ain't this nice?' Woody gushed. 'How nice to see yer Da again after all this time.'

The crippled man turned his expressionless face towards his companions and nodded. One of the Spaniards pulled a leather pouch of coins out of his pocket and tossed it to Woody, who caught it deftly.

'What's happening, García?' Rachel whispered.

But Sebastián's attention was fixed on the disfigured man. 'Who are you, sir?' he asked in Spanish. 'And what do you want with us?' He tried to sound brave, but he heard the fear in his own voice.

'You know who I am, son, although I'm a little changed. I'm your father, Don Antonio García de Aviles. I've come to take you home to Spain.'

It only took a few minutes to gallop to The Laurels.

Lavender dismounted and opened the small side gate to enter the park. After locking it again and remounting, he set off with Woods at a brisk trot up the long and winding drive.

Lavender was grateful for the shade of the trees, but they had to rein in sharply when they disturbed a bedraggled ostrich in the undergrowth. It lurched across the dusty path, long legs flailing, kicking up a cloud of feathers and dust behind it. It stopped, stared at them accusingly – and hissed loudly. Then it stalked away with injured dignity to the trees on the other side of the path, leaving a trail of scattered feathers in its wake.

'Gawd's teeth!' Woods exclaimed, grinning. 'That's a big feisty bird. I wonder what it tastes like?'

When they drew up outside the house, Bruce ran out of the front door to greet them. It took a moment for Lavender to recognise the scruffy lad in front of him as the same one he'd met yesterday, who'd been resplendent in cricket whites. The boy had a rope tied round his waist, holding up his torn and grubby breeches.

Lavender didn't dismount. 'Where are Sebastián and Rachel?' he called down from the saddle.

'They're not here, sir. Rachel took García to see her Grandpa.'

'Her *what*?'

Woods rolled his eyes and groaned. He gathered up the reins in his hands and turned his horse round. 'Thank you, lad. It's all right, sir, I know where they are.'

But when they prepared to leave, Bruce stepped forward and called out, 'Please wait a moment, sir. I want to tell you something.'

Lavender reined in. He was desperate to find Sebastián but there was an earnestness about the young boy's expression that made him pause.

'Sir James came to talk to us about the day of my aunt's murder. He wanted to know if Mama and I were together all the time. I told him we were.'

Lavender nodded. Elizabeth Charlton had always been the least likely of his suspects for Clara Langford's murder.

'Sir James also asked Mama if she saw anyone in the fog. She didn't – but she wasn't wearing her spectacles, so I'm not surprised. She can hardly see without them.'

Lavender waited for him to go on.

'Sir James doesn't know about Mama's spectacles, so he took her word for it. But this morning, I remembered that *I* saw someone. I don't know if it was important, but please can you tell Sir James?'

'Who was it – and what time was this?'

'It was the Reverend Langford. He was galloping along the lane from Brentford towards the vicarage.'

'When was this, son?'

'I don't remember the time, but it was still early. We'd only just set off from the stables with our horses.'

Lavender nodded. It wasn't exact – but it was good enough. The Charltons' groom had told Lavender his mistress and the young master had ridden out sometime after nine in the morning. If they'd seen Langford soon after that, it gave him plenty of time to be outside the vicarage watching Ashfield arrive and Mrs Snelling leave.

Langford was the man stalking the vicarage on the day of the murder.

Bruce looked troubled. 'Did I do right to tell you this, sir?'

Lavender tousled his dark hair. 'Yes, son. Thank you. I think you've just solved the case of your aunt's murder.'

'I have?' The boy's delight turned to confusion. 'But who did it? Who killed Aunt Clara?'

'I'll tell you tomorrow,' Lavender promised. 'But at this moment, I need to find Sebastián.'

When they trotted back down the long drive, Woods turned to Lavender and said: 'I don't want to alarm you, sir, but the nippers have gone to see Abel Jupp – or Woody, as he's known. My Rachel thinks he's her Grandpa – which he ain't.'

Lavender nodded. 'You've met the man, Ned. Would he hurt them?'

'Not him, sir. But I saw two furriners visit him this mornin'. Big Jim Kilby told me they were Spaniards.'

Lavender's jaw tightened and he spurred his horse into a gallop.

'No!' Sebastián yelled in Spanish. 'You're *not* my father. My father's dead. He was taller. And I'll be damned if I'll go anywhere with you!'

'You'll do what your papá tells you – you young cur!' snapped one of the other Spaniards. 'Or you'll be whipped!'

Rachel clutched Sebastián's arm. 'García?'

Sebastián glanced around for a weapon. A stick. A club. Anything. His fingers found the back of the rickety old chair standing outside Woody's door. 'This man says he's my father. But he's not. When I say "run" – run.'

The burnt man laughed and said in heavily accented English, 'You think I don't understand this stupid language?'

'Run!' Sebastián swung up the chair and hurled it into the masked face of the man in front of him.

They ran.

Sebastián was faster. He'd almost dodged past them when one of the Spaniards leapt forward and grabbed Rachel by her thick, curly hair. He jerked her head back. Her screaming made Sebastián hesitate and turn.

Rachel spun round and bit her captor's hand. Cursing, he grabbed her with one burly arm and pinned her own arms to her sides. Then he cuffed her across her head with his bleeding fist. She screamed again.

Sebastián had hesitated too long. The other Spaniard was on him. He grabbed Sebastián around the throat in a painful and powerful stranglehold that stopped him in his tracks.

'Grandpa! Help us!' Rachel yelled. Her captor slammed his hand across her mouth to shut her up.

Behind them, Woody's door slammed when he went inside his hovel.

'Get them to the coach!' de Aviles yelled.

The children's captors dragged them towards the wharf. Sebastián kicked out, but the powerful man who held him just tightened his grip on his throat. He struggled to breathe. 'You behave,' he threatened in Spanish, 'or I'll squeeze tighter.'

They almost fell out of the alley into the brilliant sunlight of the wharf.

Then they came to an abrupt halt.

Big Jim Kilby blocked their way, scowling.

Legs apart, the huge man had one hand on his hip and was swinging his heavy iron windlass in the other. 'Now then,' he growled. 'What the devil's goin' on 'ere?'

Hope surged through Sebastián.

De Aviles limped forward towards Kilby with another leather pouch of coins in his hand. 'Is not your business, old man,' he said in his broken English. 'Take this. Let us pass.'

Kilby didn't move. His old eyes glinted dangerously below his bushy white eyebrows. 'I reckon it *is* my business when I sees coves tryin' to kidnap nippers.'

De Aviles turned to the Spaniard holding Rachel and said in Spanish, 'Throw the little bitch into the canal. That will distract him.'

'Nooo!' Sebastián's brain screamed.

For a second, the world stood still.

Then Big Jim Kilby jerked forward and headbutted de Aviles on the part of his forehead not covered by the mask.

The Spaniard staggered with shock, lost his balance and fell. His good arm flailed in the air when he fell over the edge of the wharf into the black and oily water of the lock. His walking cane clattered down on to the flagstones at the same time he entered the water with an almighty splash.

Shocked, the remaining two Spaniards loosened their grip on the children. Sebastián felt it and took his chance.

Grabbing Rachel, he tore them both out of the Spaniards' arms and hauled her to Kilby's side. She threw her arms around the lock-keeper's waist and buried her head into his side, sobbing.

Kilby braced himself as the Spaniards cursed and took a step forward.

Swinging his windlass menacingly, he addressed them in Spanish.

‘I wouldn’t if I were you. If either of you bastards lay a finger on these children, I’ll grab you and throw myself into the water – takin’ you with me.’

Startled by the unusual threat, the two men glanced at each other, unsure.

‘I can swim,’ Kilby added. ‘Can you? And I’ve fell in that water more times than I can count, so another dip means nothin’ to me. Your business ’ere is done. Your mate’s dead. The fall’s killed ’im.’

The two men swore, turned and raced off towards the bridge and the road.

Both children were crying with relief.

Kilby pulled Rachel into a tight, protective hug. ‘Pull yerself together, Treacle. Your father’s ’ere now. ’E’ll sort out this mess.’

Sebastián spun round and, through his veil of tears, saw Woods galloping along the towpath towards them in a furious cloud of dust.

Beside him rode Lavender.

Sebastián had never in his life been so pleased to see his Pa.

Chapter Thirty

A noisy crowd had started to gather on the wharf when Lavender and Woods reined in. The boatmen and coal shovellers appeared from nowhere and mingled with the blacksmith and the ostlers from the stables.

In the middle of it all towered a stern-faced old man with pure white hair and a protective arm around their children. Lavender started with shock when he saw the lockkeeper. But that was a matter for later…

'What the hell's happened?' he yelled, as he dismounted.

Woods took Lavender's reins and shoved them into the hands of one of the ostlers. Then the two of them strode through the crowd to their children.

Rachel threw herself, sobbing, into her father's arms. 'They tried to take us, Da!'

Sebastián was doing his best to compose himself, but Lavender didn't hesitate. He gathered his shaking boy into his arms and held him tight.

'Are you all right, son?'

Sebastián gave a strangled sob and nodded into his chest.

But Lavender had seen the red wheals around his throat.

Had some bastard tried to strangle him?

Behind them, Kilby's voice boomed across the wharf as he took control.

'There's been an accident,' he announced. 'A cripple tripped and fell in the cut.' Holding his bad hip with one hand, he bent down and picked up a walking cane from the flagstones and waved it in the air to prove his point. 'This were 'is.'

'Is 'e drowned?' someone asked.

'Yes.'

'Who are the nippers?' someone asked.

‘They saw it ’appen and it upset them. Harris? Get yerself into town and fetch me the constable. Jock – ’elp me open the paddles to bring ’im up. Ted – get some boat ’ooks. We’ll ’aul ’im out when the water’s risen.’

‘Shouldn’t you wait for the law?’ someone suggested.

‘It’s my bloody lock and I’ll deal with it my way, you bird-witted cod’s ’ead!’ Kilby roared. ‘And as for the rest of you idle skelpies – get back to work.’

The crowd dispersed, although several of them took a detour to the lock to ogle at the body floating in the water.

Lavender and Woods led the children to a quieter and shaded corner by a warehouse wall. The colour had come back into Rachel’s cheeks and Sebastián’s tears had been dashed away.

‘Take your time,’ Lavender said, one arm still around his son. ‘You’re safe now. Tell us what happened – but do it slowly.’

Sebastián started. ‘They tried to kidnap us.’

‘Who did?’

‘There were three of them. Spanish.’ He pointed towards the lock. ‘One’s in there. The other two ran off.’

‘He said he were García’s Da, but he ain’t, is he, García?’

Sebastián shook his head – but Lavender saw the agonising doubt in his dark eyes.

‘No. He wasn’t tall enough and he spoke wrong. But… but it was a shock.’

Lavender nodded, and wondered if the fire had damaged de Aviles’ vocal cords along with the rest of him? As for his height, Sebastián had been a small child the last time he saw his father. Even a short man seems tall to a nine-year-old. He knew Sebastián would work this out for himself soon enough and dreaded the questions that would come. ‘Stay with your Uncle Ned a minute, son. I need to see for myself what’s happened to him.’

Woods enveloped Sebastián in his free arm and Lavender walked to the lock.

The water level in the lock was low. A black-coated man floated face down, arms spread-eagled. His hat bobbed beside him. Much of the back of his skull was hairless and badly scarred. His few remaining strands of black hair spread out around him like wispy spider's legs. There were straps around the back of his head that looked like the ties of a mask.

Lavender took a sharp intake of breath. But he felt nothing apart from contempt for this man who'd tried to tear his family apart.

His family was safe. But there was bound to be an inquest, and the children might be called as witnesses. Then the whole damned scandal would be dragged out into the limelight. Magdalena's – their – nightmare wasn't over yet.

Kilby opened the paddles. Water poured into the lock and the body swirled in the frothy tumult as the level rose. Bracing himself, Lavender returned to Woods and the children.

'Grandpa Woody tricked us here,' Rachel said.

'He did, did he?' Woods growled.

'Yes, they gave him money. They'd paid him to trick us,' Sebastián said.

'I begged him to save us, Da – but he just went inside and slammed the door!' Rachel wailed.

'Me and that Woody cove need a word or two,' Woods growled.

'Mr Kilby rescued us.'

Sebastián took up the story, his voice faltering. 'When Kilby stood in their way, the one who said he was my father said in Spanish that they should throw Rachel into the canal to distract him. He called her a little bitch.'

Rachel squealed in shock and Woods had never looked more furious. 'They were goin' to do *what* to my daughter!' he roared.

The wharf was still busy. People were milling around. Heads turned towards them.

Lavender put a restraining hand on Woods' arm. His constable's muscles were tensed like iron bars beneath his jacket. 'Let's hear the rest, Ned, before we react.'

Sebastián stumbled over the next words. 'I thought they'd… I thought they'd do it…kill Rachel. I couldn't stop them. But Mr Kilby speaks Spanish. He understood. He… he headbutted the man and knocked him into the lock.'

'Mr Kilby says he fell, Da, but he didn't,' Rachel stammered. 'Mr Kilby butted him. He saved us.' She started crying again.

'Yes, he saved us,' Sebastián murmured.

Lavender took a quick glance at Kilby before gathering his son in his arms again. The lockkeeper had a large, swollen bruise forming on his broad forehead.

He looked at Woods over the heads of their children.

They were both thinking the same thing. De Aviles might have been unconscious from the blow to his head when he hit the water. If Kilby's actions were discovered, would an inquest rule this was manslaughter? Or would it be murder? Either way, both children would be hauled into court as witnesses.

'No wonder Kilby ain't mentioned the other two coves,' Woods said quietly. 'Do you think we should go along with this ruse?'

Lavender hesitated, then nodded. 'Yes. I'm not sure Kilby will succeed with this pretence – there's bound to be witnesses. But we owe him our silence. It might keep Kilby out of gaol. And our children out of the witness dock.'

Sebastián and Rachel were watching them closely. Sebastián frowned. 'What do you mean, Pa? Why should Mr Kilby go to gaol? He protected *us*. That's not against the law, is it?'

'I'll explain later when we get home, Sebastián. You've been incredibly brave and we're proud of you, but we need to get you home to your mothers.'

'Are you proud, too, Da?' Rachel asked.

Woods smiled and roughly tousled the hair on both of their heads with his huge hands. 'Aye, I am. I've never been prouder.' His voice cracked with emotion. 'Apart from yesterday, when I watched you two play the best game of cricket I've ever seen.'

Both children managed a weak smile.

'I've a notion Mr Kilby don't like the law,' Woods said. 'He delivers his own justice and prefers to mind his own business. He don't like a fuss.'

'But we've got to thank him!' Rachel insisted. 'And Ma will want to bake him a cake.'

'I'll thank him tonight, Treacle – when I buy him a tankard of ale.'

'But what about those other two villains, Pa?' Sebastián asked. 'Shouldn't you go after them? They hurt us.'

Lavender hesitated. There was nothing more he'd like in the world than to grab the throat of the man who hurt his son and choke him to death. But if he and Woods brought these coves to justice, the whole damned story of the attempted kidnapping would come out – and the reasons for it. Besides which, he didn't want to leave Sebastián's side until he got him back to Magdalena.

'That's the town constable's job – *my* job is to get you home.'

Woods clenched his jaw and frowned. 'Aye, but there's another bugger I need to deal with before we go.' He turned to Rachel and looked down into her little face. 'That Woody fella ain't your grandpa, Treacle. His real name's Abel Jupp.'

Her eyes widened with shock, then anger flashed across her face. 'The wheedlin', lyin' bastard!' she exclaimed. 'I gave him the two shillin's I won from García – and one of Ma's apple turnovers!'

'He's a sly fox,' Woods nodded, wisely ignoring her cussing. 'But I've got a warrant in my pocket for his arrest for theft and murder.'

'What!' Lavender exclaimed.

Woods glanced up at him and grinned. 'I've been busy, sir, while you've been rattlin' cages. I've got evidence that ties him to the murder of Mrs Snelling.' He turned back to Rachel. 'Do you want to help me teach the old cove a lesson, Treacle? Do you want to see your old Da haul him into gaol?'

'Yes! I'll help. Can I kick him?'

Woods laughed and led her towards the alley.

Sebastián turned his dark and intelligent eyes towards Lavender and asked him the questions he'd been dreading. 'Who was that man, Pa? And why did he claim he was my father?'

'I believe he was a fraudster. He'd written to your mother a while ago asking for you – and the income she gets from her estate in Oviedo.'

Sebastián's eyes widened. 'Mamá knows about him?'

Lavender stumbled a little over his words. 'She received another letter from him today, a threatening one. I didn't like the sound of it so that's why I've come here to get you.'

Horror and anger flashed through Sebastián's eyes. 'How long have you both known? Is that why Mamá's been so unhappy over the last few months?'

'Yes. She's tried hard to resolve it – she only told me about it today.'

'But I don't understand! My father died at Talavera – he was a great hero! Mamá has been to his grave!'

'You're confused, son. You mother hasn't been back to Spain since she fled the country with you, nearly six years ago. And as for your father's grave… it doesn't exist. There was a horrendous fire at Talavera. It was… it was impossible to identify all the dead. We're not sure what happened to your father's body.' Instinct told him if he wasn't honest with Sebastián now, his son would never trust him again.

Sebastián's face contorted with anger and shock. 'But if there's no grave it *might* have been him!'

'I doubt it. Years ago, when your father didn't reply to your mother's letters, I helped her make enquiries with the War Department, who assured us he was dead.'

'But that… that *monster* might have been my father!'

'I believe it's an elaborate hoax.'

'What if I turn out like him?'

Lavender reached out but Sebastián shook off his hand. 'That won't happen, son. He's not your father. Like I said, I believe this man is a liar and a fraud…'

'I'm *not* your son!' Sebastián's voice rose hysterically. 'That's the whole point of this, isn't it? I was sired by that murdering bastard! You say you *believe* – but you *don't know*! You and Mamá have kept secrets from me and lied to me for months. I can't trust either of you!'

He turned and ran off down the tow path towards Ealing.

'Sebastián!'

He started to go after him, but a large hand grasped his arm. It was Jim Kilby. 'Let 'im be. The lad's in shock from what's 'appened today. 'E'll calm down and come 'ome when 'e's hungry.'

'Are you an expert on parenting, Mr Kilby?' Lavender snapped. He wondered how much the lockkeeper had overheard.

Kilby chuckled. 'Me? No. And my own son will tell you I'm the worst.'

'Yes, he probably will.'

'But I've seen enough of your lad to know 'e's a decent boy. But 'e's flounderin' like a piece of flotsam right now. Just give 'im a wide berth until 'e calms down and when 'e limps back into port, make sure you give 'im a safe harbour.'

I just wish it was that simple, Lavender thought, as he watched his distraught child vanish around a bend on the tow path.

Chapter Thirty-One

An amusing sight met their eyes as Woods and Rachel picked their way back down the rank and gloomy alleyway to Woody's house.

The old man had dragged his battered old chair to the high wall that separated the alley from the graveyard beyond and had attempted to scale it. He'd failed miserably, and in his haste he'd kicked the chair away. He now dangled by his skinny arms from the rough stone, squealing.

Woods bit back his urge to laugh. 'Abel Jupp!' he roared. 'By the power invested in me by His Royal Highness The Prince Regent, in the name and on behalf of His Majesty King George III, I arrest you on suspicion of the murder of Annette Snelling and the theft of a silver cup from the Reverend Langford.'

He wanted to add: *'and for aidin' and abettin' in the kidnappin' of my little Treacle, you bastard.'* But that wasn't written on the warrant, so he didn't.

He reached up, grabbed one of the old man's spindly legs and gave it a sharp pull.

Jupp gave another squeal and fell in an ungainly heap at their feet. 'I ain't done nothin'! I ain't done nothin'!' His wooden teeth clattered together with fear. 'I'm sick. I ain't well! You can't treat an old man like this!'

'There ain't nothin' wrong with you!' Woods roared. 'Get to your feet, you wheedlin' murderin' cove.'

'You're a bad man!' Rachel added furiously. 'And you ain't my Grandpa! You lied to me and sold me to those ruffians!'

'I ain't murdered no one!' Woody protested, but he staggered to his feet. 'I ain't stole nuffin or sold anyone!'

Rachel turned her innocent little face up to her father. 'Can I kick him now, Da?'

'Yes, Treacle, you can.'

And she did. Right between his legs.

Jupp screamed, clutched his nutmegs and fell on the ground, sobbing.

'Did I do it right, Da?' Rachel asked. 'Eddie and Dan taught me how to do that.'

Woods burst out laughing. 'Gawd's teeth, Treacle! I'll have to have a word with your brothers when we get home.'

'They said this was what I had to do with any man who annoyed me.'

'I pity the poor fella who marries you.'

'What do you mean, Da?'

'I'll explain when you're older, sweetheart.' He reached down, grabbed Jupp by the shoulder and hauled the old fella to his feet. Tears streamed down Jupp's face but at least he'd stopped complaining. Woods shoved and dragged the old fella out into the bright sunlight of the wharf.

To his surprise, Lavender was still there – but there was no sign of Sebastián.

Lavender saw the question in his eyes. 'Sebastián needed some time alone. He's gone back to Ealing.'

Woods nodded. Lavender looked worried sick – and young Sebastián must be in one hell of a state. The Lavenders were in the middle of an almighty pickle, and Woods had no idea how they'd unravel this blessed tangle. But one thing he knew from experience: it took a while to get used to the shocking notion that your Da had risen from the grave.

And Lavender needed distracting. 'Come with me, sir. I need help gettin' this cove to the gaol. He fell on a chair while tryin' to escape and has damaged his nutmegs.'

A small, cynical smile twitched at the sides of Lavender's mouth. He nodded, grabbed hold of Jupp's other shoulder and between them they hauled the whimpering old man up the steps on to the high street.

The constables in Brentford kept a few cells beneath a red-bricked house on Town Meadow to lock up drunks, petty thieves and debtors. They took Jupp there. It wasn't far, but dragging Jupp through the curious and shocked crowds on the high street wasn't easy.

While they walked, Woods told Lavender the story of the pawnbroker and Reverend Langford's silver cup.

'I know it's a huge leap from petty theft to murderin' a woman for a silver bauble,' Woods admitted. 'But when I told Sir James what I'd found, he didn't hesitate to sign the warrant. He wanted me to come here with Constable Hinge to arrest Jupp, but I reckoned you'd like to be there. That's why I were there, at Lady Caroline's.'

Lavender frowned. 'We'll question him when we're inside. We're here now.'

They told Rachel to wait outside in the sunshine for a while.

The blue eyes of the elderly and whiskery constable who answered the door widened with surprise when Woods showed him the warrant, signed by Magistrate Sir James Clitherow.

'A murderer, eh?' he spluttered, as Lavender and Woods dragged Jupp down the dark staircase towards the cells. 'We ain't had no killers in 'ere before.'

The gaol frightened Jupp. He began to whine again. 'I ain't murdered no one! I never knew the Snellin' woman – I'd 'eard of the old lush, yes. But I never met her. And I didn't set up your nippers either – they conned me!'

Woods sighed. 'He gets confused.'

Lavender stopped at the bottom of the stairs and turned to the wailing old man. 'Right, listen to me carefully, Jupp. You've not been arrested because of the incident with the Spaniards on the wharf.'

'I ain't?'

'No.'

Woods pulled Langford's baptism cup out of his pocket. 'You're here because of this silver cup, which you took to the pawnbrokers.'

He paused for a moment to let this news sink into Jupp's addled brain. 'This cup belonged to the Reverend Langford, and it was stolen.'

'No, it weren't.'

'Yes, it was. It was stolen from the vicarage by the wet nurse, Annette Snelling, who has since been murdered.'

'The only way it came into your possession is because you had something to do with her death,' Lavender added. 'And if you killed her, Jupp – you'll hang for this.'

Jupp opened his mouth, revealing his ugly worn teeth. Then he snapped it shut again, and his teeth clicked. His rheumy eyes flickered. Woods had the sense that behind them, his wheedling brain was trying to work out how to squirm out of this charge.

'But it ain't stolen.'

'Of course it is!' Lavender snapped. 'The housemaid at the vicarage saw the wet nurse putting it into her cloak pocket on the day Mrs Langford was killed.'

Jupp lowered his eyes and said: 'But 'e gave it to me. 'Ow can it be stolen if 'e gave it me?'

The stress and trauma of the day seemed to rise up in Lavender like a thunderous wave. Woods had never seen him so angry or heard him yell so loud. 'What? What are you talking about? Who the devil gave it to you?'

Jupp visibly cowered. 'The vicar.'

'What?'

''E gave it me on account of the 'elp I'd given 'im. 'E told me the cup were worth a golden boy – but that sly old pawnbroker only gave me ten shillin's for it.'

Lavender seemed to freeze. 'What help had you given Reverend Langford that warranted him giving you this silver cup?'

Jupp sighed. 'I weren't supposed to say anythin'.'

'Tell the truth, you wheedlin' bastard!' Woods snapped. 'Or it'll be the long drop for you!'

''E turned up at mine the night 'is wife were killed. 'E said 'e needed a favour. Said 'e were worried they'd pin 'is wife's death on 'im because 'e'd been ridin' alone on the towpath when she were killed. 'E asked me to tell the constables 'e were with me when 'is wife were killed.'

Even Woods was startled. 'Are you sayin' Reverend Langford bribed you to give him an alibi?'

Jupp stood up straighter, frowned and considered his next words. 'Aye, I reckon that's 'ow it was. I saw no 'arm in it. 'E allus were a decent man, the vicar. A kindly soul. 'E gave me the cup.'

'Aye, he's a decent man all right,' Woods added grimly. 'He'd just battered a woman to death and poisoned another.'

His words had no meaning to the old man. He just smiled and flashed his hideous teeth. 'Well, I reckon that's sorted. Can I go 'ome now?'

Lavender wrenched open the door of the cell and pushed the old man inside. 'No, you can't,' he snapped. 'That's perverting the course of justice. You'll stay here until the magistrate decides what the hell to do with you.'

Chapter Thirty-Two

'You've done well, Ned. Very well,' Lavender said as they made their way back to Ealing on the tow path. Woods had lifted Rachel up into the saddle of his horse and walked alongside her, while she held the reins.

Beside him, Woods' broad moon of a face broke out into a wide grin at Lavender's compliment. 'My old nose ain't let me down yet.'

Lavender was grateful for the shade of the overhanging trees against the relentless heat of the sun. But despite the warmth, the beauty of the surrounding countryside – and the fact his mystery was solved – his heart was heavy with misery. He couldn't shake off the nagging doubt that he'd let down his family and friends. The sweet scent of ripened fruit now seemed cloying to him and even the sight of a small frog hopping along the tow path failed to lift his spirits.

Sebastián had almost been abducted by a gang of dangerous men. Rachel was seconds away from a watery death. And what would those coves have done with his boy once they'd got him back in Spain?

Lavender forced those fears out of his mind. 'Yes, while I've been bouncing around the parish, rattling cages and getting nowhere with this case, you've knuckled down, followed your nose and found the evidence to solve it.'

Woods' grin widened. 'I've allus said – if you think you smell a rat – then you've found a rat.'

Lavender managed a small smile. 'That's sage advice, Constable. I should listen to you more often. You told me at the start that sometimes the simplest solution to a mystery is the right one – and you were right.'

'Yes, but that murderin' vicar covered his tracks well,' Woods pointed out.

'Not well enough. His mistake was retrieving the cup from the dead wet nurse's pocket and giving it to Jupp. I think he panicked when he found it and just wanted to get rid of it. He didn't expect to see it. If he'd just paid Jupp some money to provide his alibi, and left the cup in the dead woman's pocket, he would probably have got away with the crime. He wasn't thinking straight – he didn't know what to do with the cup.'

'Do you think he killed his wife in a passion, sir? Were he suspicious that she and Ashfield were still carryin' on together, do you think?'

He was about to reply when he caught sight of Rachel, who was sitting wide-eyed, listening to them both with her ears straining.

'I'll tell you tomorrow when we arrest Langford.'

'Are we not goin' for him tonight?'

'No, Ned. Tonight is for our families and children. Langford can wait. I'll send a note to Sir James and ask him to call on me tomorrow morning. Then we'll get a warrant and arrest Langford.'

Woods nodded. 'God only knows what state Betsy will be in when she finds out what happened to our little Treacle in Brentford.'

'You'll have to hide her rollin' pin, Da,' Rachel said. 'She might try to break into Brentford gaol and beat Woody.'

'That's a good notion, Treacle. I'll put it on top of the dresser – she can't reach it up there.' Woods glanced up at Lavender. 'Do you want to ride ahead, sir? Young Sebastián will already be at home. You should be there.'

'Yes, I will. Don't bother returning Captain Sawyer's horse tonight, Ned. Bring it with you tomorrow and we'll go together to the vicarage. And *thank you* – thank you again for your help.'

'I'm glad I were there, sir.'

Lavender spurred his horse forward, then reined in sharply. 'And Ned,' he said over his shoulder, 'when you see Jim Kilby tonight, don't berate him. Give him the chance to explain.'

Confusion flickered across Woods' face and his forehead creased in a frown. 'I didn't plan to berate him – he were a hero today. I'll gladly listen to how he saved my daughter.'

'I didn't mean listen to his explanation about today,' Lavender said softly. 'I meant his explanation of what happened forty years ago – when he left you, Alby and your mother.'

Woods came to an abrupt halt and Rachel reined in, too. Her mouth dropped open.

'You've worked it out?'

'Of course I did. He's an older version of Alby – and I'm one of the few people in London who knows what your brother looks like. You must have recognised him too.'

Woods nodded and his face twitched as he tried to control the emotion surging through him. 'I knew who he were the minute I clapped my peepers on him. And it were his voice too. It's harsher and cracked now – but I recognised his voice. There's many a night I cried myself to sleep as a nipper, wantin' to hear his voice again – and that great boomin' laugh of his.'

'Just give him a chance to explain, Ned. I know it's hard – but you've got a second chance. A second chance to know your Da.'

Magdalena, Lady Caroline and Captain Sawyer were waiting for Lavender in the drawing room when he returned to Cedar Court. But there was no sign of Sebastián.

Magdalena looked drawn and tired. She threw herself into Lavender's arms. 'What's happened, Stephen? I've had a note from Elizabeth Charlton at The Laurels. Sebastián arrived there about an hour ago in a dreadful state. He won't tell her what's upset him and has gone off with Bruce into the woods.'

Lavender led her to the sofa and pulled her down beside him. 'He's had a horrific shock, *querida.* But he'll be safe with his friend.'

'You look wretched, Stephen,' Lady Caroline said, reaching for the servants' bell. 'I'll order some tea and coffee.'

Sighing with relief, he explained the events of the afternoon to his shocked audience, pausing only when the maid entered with the silver tea tray and coffee jug. Once she'd left and he'd quenched his thirst, he resumed his tale.

'That man – the one who claimed to be de Aviles – was everything he described to you, Magdalena. Hideously disfigured by fire.'

'And Sebastián believes him to be his father?' Captain Sawyer asked.

Lavender nodded. 'He's distraught. More so, I think, because the fiend wanted to throw Rachel into the canal. That horrified him. But he's angry with you and me too, Magdalena.'

'That's understandable,' Lady Caroline said gently. 'It must have been a dreadful shock.'

'I'm so sorry, Caroline, that we've brought this… this scandal to your door,' Magdalena murmured.

Lady Caroline laughed, making her feathered turban bob about. 'I'm no stranger to scandal myself – as you both know. And to be honest, I find the whole notion that you are a pair of bigamists and adulterers quite amusing. The Gods of Mischief are playing games. I can't imagine two people *less* likely than the pair of you to commit bigamy *or* adultery.'

'And I don't know what the fuss is about,' Sawyer said, chuckling. 'I've known plenty of sailors in the merchant navy – on regular runs between Scotland and London – who thought it was a good notion to have a *wife* in each port. One of them was a captain.'

'Oh, behave, Joshua!' Lady Caroline exclaimed. 'You know things are different for women. It simply isn't the done thing for a woman to have husbands scattered all over Europe.'

'But Antonio is dead now,' Magdalena said. 'So, I only have one husband – the one I want.' She squeezed Lavender's hand.

Magdalena had taken the news of de Aviles' death calmly, he thought. Her relief was obvious. Now her dark eyes narrowed, and her forehead creased, as if she was making a decision. 'I should make sure,' she murmured.

Lavender was about to ask what she meant when Sawyer interrupted him. 'Do you think there's any chance you can keep all this quiet, Lavender?'

Lavender shrugged and turned his palms out in a sign of helplessness. 'I've no idea what will happen. There's bound to be an inquest – but who the witnesses will be, and what they'll say, I don't know.'

'Will they want the children to give evidence?' Lady Caroline asked.

Lavender shrugged again. 'I don't know. The lockkeeper, Kilby, told everyone de Aviles fell into the lock by accident—'

'That often happens,' Lady Caroline observed. 'People will believe that.'

'But I can't ask the children to lie,' Lavender said.

Lady Caroline nodded. 'No, you can't. But if they don't get called to give evidence, you may ask them to protect Magdalena's reputation and keep quiet about the events of this afternoon. I often found that bribery worked well when I needed some discretion from my stepdaughters.'

Suddenly, Magdalena stood up. 'Lady Caroline, I need your assistance.' Her eyes looked strange, haunted – and her determined little chin was raised into the air.

'Anything, my dear. What is it?'

'I need you to order your carriage and take me to the morgue in Brentford. I need to see this evil man who claimed to be Antonio.'

'Magdalena! No! I forbid it!' Lavender exclaimed.

'I need to do it for Sebastián. I need to do it for myself also. I need to know the truth. I'm the only person who can do this.'

'Good heavens!' Lady Caroline said. 'I hope you don't want *me* to come inside the morgue with you. I've seen enough dead husbands to last me a lifetime.'

A tiny smile flickered around the corners of Magdalena's mouth. 'I just need you to gain me entry. You're the daughter of an earl – and no one ever refuses you anything.'

Lavender rose to his feet. 'I'll come with you, *querida.* You don't need to do this alone.'

She shook her head. 'No, Stephen. I shall do this with Lady Caroline. It would attract too much attention if you and I went together. I shall say I once had a crippled servant who went missing. I'd heard about the accident, and I wanted to know if it was him.'

The carriage was ordered, and the maid fetched the women's bonnets and shawls. Lavender stood by the window and watched anxiously as his wife and Lady Caroline disappeared out of the gate of Cedar Court.

He didn't like the idea of this trip to the morgue, but he saw the sense in it. Unless Magdalena identified the body, they would spend the rest of their lives wondering if the corpse on the slab was de Aviles, or not – Sebastián especially.

He was startled from his thoughts by the sudden appearance in the drawing room of Teresa and the children. Alice ran to him and demanded to be picked up. Smiling, he lifted her into his arms.

Teresa's olive-tinted little face was contorted into a scowl. She stood defiantly in front of him, her legs apart. The sunshine of Ealing had brought out the freckles on her nose. 'Is true?' she demanded.

'I'm sorry, Teresa – is what true?'

'Is true Don Antonio is dead again?'

'Yes. The man who claimed to be him drowned in the canal this afternoon.'

'Did you push him in water?'

'No!' he laughed. 'But if I'd got there first, I might have done.'

Teresa nodded in approval. ''Tis good he's dead again. He was bad man. Now we don't go back to Spain.' She stepped forward and pushed his son towards him. 'Here. You look after *los niños*. Tell Doña Magdalena I catch coach to London tonight.'

Surprised, Lavender put down Alice and took Jack into his arms. 'Where are you going, Teresa?'

She was already halfway to the door when she stopped and turned back. She smiled and blushed like a young girl. 'To tell Mr Alfie Tummins I'll be his lovin' wife.'

Lavender put his little ones to bed and read Alice her story but when Magdalena and Lady Caroline returned two hours later, he was agitated, and his indigestion was playing up again.

He met them in the hallway, where they were divesting themselves of their shawls and bonnets. He was delighted to see they'd brought Sebastián home with them.

Sebastián grinned and strode towards him with his hand held out.

'No hard feelings, eh, Pa?' he asked. 'I'm sorry I shouted at you earlier.'

Lavender ignored the proffered hand and pulled his boy into a hug. 'How do you feel now?'

Sebastián flicked his long fringe out of his eyes and nodded. 'Mamá's explained everything.' He yawned. 'She fetched me home. I'm tired though.'

'It's been a long and difficult day for us all,' Lavender said. He was desperate to know what Magdalena had discovered at the morgue.

But Sebastián didn't give him a chance to ask. He turned towards the staircase. 'Goodnight, Pa.' He kissed his mother goodnight, then bounded away up the stairs.

Magdalena came towards Lavender, smiling. She melted into his arms.

'What happened, *querida?*

'It's not him. You were right, Stephen. That man was a fraud. It's not Antonio.'

Chapter Thirty-Three

Woods found Big Jim Kilby in the smoky taproom of the Three Pigeons on Brentford High Street. It was a dirty and seedy place, but it was peaceful tonight, quiet enough for the long chat he needed to have with Kilby.

The big white-haired fella was sitting at a corner table with a couple of exhausted bargees, sipping their ale. They had coal dust engrained into the lines on their brown leathery faces and were uniformly dressed in stained collarless shirts, dirty jackets and those wide leather belts favoured by dockers and boatmen throughout the country.

Woods collected a tankard of ale from the barman and strolled across.

Kilby glanced up in surprise and his broad face lit up with a wide grin. 'Well, if it ain't Constable Woods. 'Ave you come to arrest me, Constable?'

Woods smiled. 'Not this time, Kilby – but watch your manners.' He turned to the other two men and said pleasantly: 'Can you fellas let me have a word or two alone with my Da?'

Both men started with surprise. One of them nearly knocked over his tankard of ale. They cast curious glances across the table at Kilby. Then they rose and left the two men in peace.

Kilby was still grinning. 'Well, that's ruined it, Neddy. No one will drink with me again now they know my son's a runner.'

Woods shrugged and sat down. 'You need a better set of mates, Kilby, if your cronies are afraid of the law.' He gestured to the mob-capped barmaid, who came across with her jug and filled up the tankards of both men. Woods slid the coins across the table.

'I liked it better when you called me "Da".'

'And I'd like it better if you called me Ned.'

Kilby winked, smiled and took a gulp of his ale. 'Thank you for the drink, Neddy.'

Woods rolled his eyes and cleared his throat. 'Before we talk about the other thing that's danglin' between us, I need to know what happened to my daughter this afternoon. She's told me most of it, but I need to know the rest.'

Kilby's face darkened with anger. 'Them coves were goin' to throw my granddaughter in the lock and drown 'er. I'd watched 'er and the lad go down the alley and those furriners follow them. I heard them shoutin' in that cursed lingo of theirs and knew they was up to no good.'

'My little Treacle can swim,' Woods said gently. 'I taught her myself—'

'— like I learned you and Bert?' Kilby asked.

'Well, I didn't throw her into the Serpentine, like you did to us. But, yes, I taught her to swim. I'm grateful to you. You saved her a nasty dunkin' and maybe some injury with your actions. And she told me what you did to that cove who threatened her.'

'Aye, well, those coves weren't no more than a gang of swaggerin' sapheads. They wanted to distract *me*, so I distracted them. And don't thank me. I don't want no fuss about my part in it.'

Woods pulled a couple of large brown paper parcels out of his coat pocket. 'It's too late to be a blushin' moll. Mrs Woods heard all about it and has sent you these.'

Kilby's eyes widened when he unwrapped the parcels and pulled out the soft fruit cake, the freshly baked scones and the meat pie with its golden crust. 'All 'ome cooked?' he asked.

Woods nodded. 'Mrs Woods is an excellent cook.'

Kilby pulled each item to his broad nostrils and sniffed in the delicious aroma, before wrapping them up again. 'Thank 'er. It's been a while since a woman cooked for me.'

'So, what happened when the constable arrived at the weigh dock?'

Kilby shrugged. 'I told 'im the fella tripped and fell in. They took the body away. There's to be an inquest 'ere at this tavern tomorrow afternoon. I'm to give evidence.'

'Do they want to talk to Rachel and Sebastián?' Woods asked.

'No. I told them the nippers passed by after the accident and were upset by the sight of the dustman floatin' in the water. I said they saw nothin' else, and the daft grunter believed me.'

Woods decided not to take offence about this derogatory term for a constable. Kilby – he still struggled to think of him as 'Da' – had lived most of his life in the last century and, by the sound of it, most of it halfway across the world among foreigners. He was a rough old bugger, with bad habits and his own ways. It would take some time for them to get used to each other.

Besides which, Woods was pleased with this news. He knew how grim and frightening inquests were. He didn't want his little Rachel forced into the witness dock.

'I'm grateful – thank you. But were there any fellas there who'll challenge your account?'

Kilby shrugged. 'If there were, they ain't said anythin'. And it were quieter than normal because of the Sabbath. Harry Polkin were waitin' with 'is barge to go through the lock and 'e saw it all. But 'e don't want no business with the law. When I opened the gates, I ain't ever seen a man belt so fast down the towpath. 'Is 'orse 'ad a shock when 'e made it break into a gallop. The pair of them will be back in the Black Country by now.'

Woods nodded, relieved. It sounded like Kilby's ruse might work.

Kilby broke the silence. 'If you want to 'ear the rest, I'll need more ale. It's not a pretty story.'

It took a moment for Woods to realise what the old fella meant. He beckoned again to the barmaid, who refilled their tankards, and braced himself. Kilby seemed to be struggling for the right words.

Woods broke the silence and said harshly: 'So, what happened? Why did you desert us?'

'It weren't desertion.'

'That's how the law sees it.'

Kilby snarled. 'Is that the same damned law that lets the navy kidnap 'onest men and drag them away from their wives and nippers? If so, 'ang the law!'

Woods gasped. This wasn't what he'd expected. 'You were pressed?' He'd heard how families, especially those who lived by the docks, had been torn apart by the navy press gangs. But neither he, nor Alby, or their Ma, had ever thought it had happened to them.

'Aye. One minute I'm enjoyin' a quiet drink in the Dog and Duck. Then I leaves and some bugger shouts "Get the big one!" They slap a sack over my 'ead and drag me to the naval base.'

Kilby paused to take a gulp of his ale. His scowling face had an unhealthy flush.

'I tried to fight them off but there was too many of them. One coshed me on my noggin, and I blacked out. When I woke up, I were in the bowels of a stinkin' ship – HMS *Neptune*. We was just pullin' out of port. I tried to jump overboard and swim back. But they caught me again – and this time they lashed me.'

Woods sat back on his stool and stared at his father, aghast. All these years of hating his Da. Blaming him. Missing him. He didn't know what to think or say – or what to feel. He sipped his ale and waited.

'It were the first time they turned the cat-o'-nine-tails on me – but it weren't the last. I caused trouble – a lot of it. I ain't ever been so damned angry in my life. All I wanted were to get back to your Ma and you lads. They say we live in a Christian country, Neddy – but what gives them the bloody right to filch grown men from their families? I might as well 'ave been a blackie taken for a slave in some 'eathen outback in Africa.' Kilby turned and spat on the sawdust floor in disgust.

'Where did you sail?'

'All bloody over. I were too miserable to take it all in at first. God, I missed you. I were worried sick about 'ow your Ma would cope – and terrified she'd have to take up whorin' to support you.'

Woods bristled at the thought. 'She worked her fingers to the bone in a factory in the day and took in sewin' at night. She ruined her eyes and were blind at the end.'

Kilby nodded sadly. 'Tilda allus were a good woman. I can see she's brought you up fine. For a long time, we was in the West Indies, battlin' with the Frenchies over some poxy little islands. That were a bad place. If the bullets, the cannonballs and the flyin' splinters didn't get you – the fever did. The rest of the crew fell like flies with disease. I were so low at the point, I wanted to die with them.'

'But you didn't.'

'No. God had other plans to torment me. After the West Indies, we sailed down the South Americas and ended up in the Argentine. And that's where the worm turned on me.'

'The worm?'

'Aye, a tiny bloody thing the size of a worm that's part of your gut. They showed me mine when they cut it out. I've never known pain like it, Neddy – and my vomit were green.'

Woods' eyebrows rose in surprise. He'd known people who'd died from this illness.

'I were bad for days, then I collapsed in a back street in Buenos Aires. I knew I were destined for an earth bath this time. But it weren't to be. A priest and a kindly widow found me. They took me to her 'ome and she called out the *curandero* to burn feathers, chant mumbo-jumbo and wave his black, heathen magic over me.'

Woods grimaced. 'Well, you're still here so I've a notion it worked.'

Kilby shrugged. 'In the end they cut the bugger out. It took three men to 'old me down, while I cursed and screamed. I kept that worm for years, pickled in a jar of vinegar. I 'ad fevers after – and it took a long time to get back on my feet – and all the time the widow woman and her priest cared for me, which weren't easy since I didn't speak 'er lingo – and they 'adn't a word of English. By then, the *Neptune* 'ad sailed, and I were stranded.'

'Did the navy know what happened to you?'

Kilby shook his head. 'I doubt it, or they'd 'ave sent their own sawbones along to butcher me. No, I reckon they wrote my name down in their log as a deserter.'

Woods nodded. This wasn't good news – but it made sense. He understood now why Kilby had changed his name and hidden down here in Brentford and why he took a dim view of the law. His Da was probably still wanted for desertion by the navy – although it was the navy who'd deserted him. 'When did this happen?'

'Back in 'eighty-one. I'd been gone fer nearly two years by then and reckoned you and your Ma had given up 'ope of ever seein' me again – if yer were still alive, that is. So, I made the best of it. I learned the lingo and worked on the docks in Buenos Aires as a stevedore.'

'And the woman?'

Kilby gave a rueful smile. 'I married 'er. Seemed like the decent thing to do after all she'd done fer me. She were a good woman,' he added wistfully. 'We had two gals. They were a handsome pair, and feisty – like your Rachel.' He dashed a tear from his eye, crossed himself and muttered something under his breath. He indicated to the barmaid that he wanted his tankard refilled.

Woods decided to brush over that part of his father's life. He still hated the notion that Kilby had had a second family – and the old fella would only get maudlin if he asked him about the death of his foreign wife and daughters. 'When did you come home?'

'About ten years ago. I worked my way back on the merchant ships. It took a year. I went to Rotherhithe to look for yer Ma and you two lads. But none of you was there and I learned yer Ma and yer brother was dead. Some fella told me Bert drowned in the Thames. Drowned?' Kilby snorted and shook his head. 'And after I'd taught the daft bugger to swim! Should have saved myself the trouble.'

Woods blinked but said nothing about Alby. Resentment and jealousy had started to squirm in his mind. His father could suffer his loss a while longer. 'Didn't you try to find me?'

'Oh, I knew where you was, Neddy. I've even seen yer name in the newspaper: Assistant Chief Constable Edward Woods.'

'Why the devil didn't you seek me out?'

Kilby shifted uneasily and looked miserable. 'You've done well, son. Very well. You're respectable, with a fine family. I figured you'd want nothin' to do with an old tar who's wanted for desertion.'

'That sounds like you didn't care.'

'No, lad. There were nothin' I wanted more. It's been 'ard these last few years – knowin' you was there, and I couldn't meet you. It made me miserable, and the loneliness were bad.'

'Gawd's teeth,' Woods murmured, and he took a large swig of his own ale to help numb the emotion pulsating through him. Ten years. The daft old bugger had wasted bloody ten years.

'I didn't want to bring trouble to yer door, so I stayed away.'

'It seems to me that my brother's not the only saphead in this family.'

Kilby frowned. 'What do you mean?'

'For a start, you changed your name to Kilby and got a job beside one of the busiest canals in England. You work the locks where Ma's sprawlin' tribe of Kilby relatives pass through every week. Did it not enter your daft noggin someone who knew Ma would recognise you one day?'

Kilby's eyes widened beneath their bushy white eyebrows. 'Is that what happened?'

'Yes, some fella called Nathan Kilby – our cousin Tod's brother – he recognised you. He began a rumour you were still alive and that's why I'm in Brentford.'

'You came 'ere lookin fer me?' Kilby was delighted. 'You looked for me? And old Nathan's still alive? He were at our wedding – mine and your Ma's. I didn't figure for him to still be alive – nor workin' the barges on the cut.'

'Well, he is,' Woods said.

Kilby shook his head in disbelief at this miracle.

'And another reason you're a muttonhead is for stayin' away from us for so long.'

'I figured it were for the best...'

'Well, it weren't. You wasted ten bloody years of our lives.'

'What do yer mean by wasted years, Son?'

Son. *How long had he yearned to hear that word?*

He suddenly felt hot – and feared he might embarrass himself. His voice cracked when he spoke, and he struggled to keep it calm. 'Now we've met – and you've told me what happened, I feel better about knowin' you.'

'You do?'

'Yes.' He took another pause. 'Besides which, Mrs Woods and my daughters want to know you.'

'They do?'

'Yes. And Mrs Woods allus knows what's best for the family.'

'She sounds a wise woman.'

'She is. So, here's what we'll do. On Sunday week, you're to put on your best shirt and come to our home in Southwark for your Sunday roast. You can meet your grandsons there, too.'

Kilby's eyes moistened. 'That's kind. Very kind.'

'But I need you to bring Rachel with you.'

'Why?'

'Because she ain't comin' back to London with us. Mrs Charlton at The Laurels has asked her to stay in Ealing this summer and help with the animals.'

Kilby nodded rapidly, his eyes wide. Woods got the impression the old fella would do anything in the world he asked at this time. He was desperate for a family.

'I've 'eard about that woman and her menagerie,' Kilby said. ''Tis a strange affair. Do you want me to keep an eye on little Treacle? Make sure she's content and safe?'

Woods smiled at his enthusiasm. 'Yes, you can do that.' He pictured Kilby's scowling old face peering through the gates at The Laurels, watching out for his granddaughter. The Charltons had better treat her well.

'And here's the next thing. If you behave yourself next Sunday – and mind yer manners, like Rachel told you – then Mrs Woods will write favourably about you to Rosie.'

'Who's Rosie?'

'She's Alby's wife.'

'I don't know a fella called Alby.'

'Yes you do. It's your eldest son, Bert. My brother.'

The old fella jerked in his seat, his face creased with hope. 'He's still alive? My Bert's still with us?'

'Yes. He got into trouble with the law when he were young and fled to the Kilbys for help. He changed his name to Alby Kilby. He and Rosie run a tavern in Market Harborough.'

'He didn't drown?'

'No. He swims like a ruddy fish – or more like a giant whale. They've got three grown-up sons.'

'Another three grandsons?'

Woods nodded, downed the last of his ale and pushed back his stool to stand up. He felt too much at that moment, and he didn't want to unman himself in front of his Da by crying like a nipper.

'We're goin' back to Southwark in a couple of days. I'll see you again before we leave.'

Woods held out his hand, stiffly. His father grasped it in his own huge and wrinkled paw. They locked eyes together for a moment and nodded silently. Then Woods turned on his heel and left.

Outside, Woods' breath became laboured as he fought back the tears.

Nearly forty years of aching for his Da and wondering what the hell had happened to him. Forty bloody years! Where was the justice in the world for all this loss? For him and his Ma? For Alby – and for his Da, himself?

Woods hurried away from the high street, down on to the towpath and past the boats and the wharf. When he knew he was alone, the tears finally came – and so did the anger.

He stomped along beside the black water, yelling and cursing. He cursed at the stars in the sky and the moon. He railed against them, against the cruelty of fate – and against an indifferent God.

But most of all he railed at the cruelty of the men who'd torn his family apart. If they stepped in front of him now, he'd choke them to death with his bare hands.

A couple of sleeping ducks woke up and scurried ahead of him, squawking in fear, and launched themselves into the safety of the water. Somewhere, a dog fox barked in alarm.

Eventually, he stopped, exhausted with yelling, and leaned heavily against a wall beneath the overhanging boughs of an apple tree. He breathed in the cool night air and tried to stop shaking. Above his head, a little owl hooted nervously.

Lavender's voice came unbidden into his head: *Well done, Ned. You've got a second chance now. A second chance to know your Da.*

Woods dashed the tears away from his face with his sleeve and smiled ruefully up at the owl. 'Sorry, little fella.' He sniffed. 'I didn't mean to frighten you.'

He'd done right to leave when he did. Part of him wanted to rush home to Betsy – but he didn't want her to see him in this state. His old noggin still swirled with everything he'd heard tonight; he needed to make sense of it.

But it was a grand night. He'd take a long walk in the shadows cast by the moonlight.

When he set off, he remembered the last look he'd shared with Kilby before he left. No doubt the old fella also needed some time to mull it over – especially the news that Alby was still alive. Yesterday, Kilby had no one. Now he'd been welcomed into the life of two sons and eight grandchildren and would have love and care in his final years.

And what do I have? Woods wondered.

He smiled as Lavender's voice came back into his head again: *You've got a mystery solved, Ned. One that's haunted you all your life.*

Chapter Thirty-Four

Brilliant sunlight woke Lavender early. He ate alone in Lady Caroline's sunny dining room until a yawning servant informed him Constable Woods had arrived.

The two men greeted each other warmly and Woods happily accepted Lavender's offer of a second breakfast. While he shook out his napkin and stuffed it down the front of his waistcoat, he told Lavender the gist of Kilby's good news the night before.

'We had a good chat – father to son, like.'

Lavender smiled. 'I'm pleased to hear it.'

'And from what he says, it sounds like the big fella has succeeded with this ruse to temper the events of yesterday afternoon. No one will be askin' for our nippers to appear at the inquest. I don't know if they've identified Don Antonio, but if we can keep Rachel and young Sebastián from their chatterin', I figure we can keep this whole sorry affair about the kidnappin' to ourselves.'

'It wasn't Don Antonio.' Lavender helped himself to another muffin. 'Like I suspected, it was a fraudster. Magdalena and Lady Caroline went to the morgue for a quiet and private visit last night. She's confirmed it wasn't her first husband.'

Woods gave him a curious sideways glance. 'That's good news for all of you,' he said slowly.

Lavender bristled. He knew Ned didn't believe him. And to be honest, he didn't know if he believed it himself. Magdalena would do anything – even lie – to protect Sebastián. Their boy needed to hear that monster wasn't his father.

But did it matter in the end? Whether de Aviles was dead in an unmarked grave in Spain or on a slab in the morgue in Brentford – he was still dead.

None of them had done anything to deserve this nightmare – and, thankfully, it looked like it was finished now.

'Yes, we're all relieved with this news – especially Sebastián. He'd always idolised his soldier father and everything about yesterday horrified him. And I've managed to bribe him to be quiet about the whole thing. Lady Caroline gave me the notion of bribery.'

Woods chuckled. 'Now, why doesn't that surprise me?'

'Yes. I'm now resolved to visit Magdalena's estates in Spain this autumn when the temperature cools a little. We've neglected our Spanish affairs for long enough and this horrific attempt to defraud us is a direct consequence of our neglect. I shall take Sebastián out of school for a few weeks and take him with me. He's delighted about that. I've ensured his silence with this promise of our trip to Spain. Magdalena is happy to stay at home with the little ones. But what about Rachel? How is she?'

'Much better. And she's too excited to fuss about yesterday afternoon. I think she's forgotten it already. She's to spend the rest of the summer here in Ealing with the Charltons and their menagerie. Mrs Charlton has offered to pay her some pin money in exchange for her help.' Woods fell silent for a moment, then added: 'Dora Kilby were right – I've got to say goodbye to my daughter.'

Lavender rolled his eyes at the mention of the Brentford witch but then he saw Woods' morose expression, and said sympathetically: 'But surely she'll be back in London in the autumn to resume her studies at school?'

Woods shrugged. 'Who knows? My Treacle ain't ever been one for learnin'. She's so happy about this chance to work with the animals. I reckon it might be the makin' of her.'

'I know you'll miss her badly. And Betsy?'

'Betsy can't stop snifflin'. She clutches the sketch Captain Sawyer drew of Rachel to her bosom and keeps mutterin' that it's all she'll have left of her daughter.'

Lavender sighed. 'I know you didn't see this on the horizon, Ned, but we have to let them go sometime – and she'll only be a few miles away. I suspect we'll lose Sebastián to either the army or to Spain in a few years – and then I'll be clutching our sketch of him to my own bosom and sniffling.'

Woods nodded, sadly. 'Our nippers are growin' up, sir. Trouble is, we never thought it would be Rachel who'd leave us first.'

He paused to reflect, then grinned and winked. 'Now, if it were one of our lads, I reckon we'd be hoistin' up the Union flag.'

Lavender smiled. 'They'll never leave. You feed them too well.'

Woods chuckled. 'I reckon Magistrate Conant won't like you swannin' off to the continent.'

Lavender grimaced. 'Oh damn, I'd forgotten about him. He sent me a letter a few days ago, demanding I return to Bow Street. And I was to bring you with me – he knows you're in Brentford.'

'How?'

'I don't know, Ned – but I wish the man would spend as much time tracking down criminals in London as he does tracking down his officers.'

Woods burst out laughing but stopped when an ashen-faced footman entered the room. 'It's Sir James Clitherow to see you, sir. He says it's urgent.'

The magistrate had already followed the footman into the dining room, his expression sombre. 'Lavender. Woods? I'm glad you're both here. We need to go to the vicarage immediately.'

'Why, sir?'

'It's Thomas Langford. He's dead.'

The three men strode quickly across the village green towards the vicarage. The trees rustled in the light breeze above their heads. The underside of their leaves became almost translucent in the brilliant sunlight. Lavender realised with a jolt it was only two days since the cricket match on this green. He'd seen two dead bodies since then – and was about to see a third.

'The first I knew about it was an hour ago when Mrs Minskip, Langford's cook, arrived at Boston Manor with the three little girls,' Sir James said. 'She's very distressed.'

'Who found him?' Lavender asked.

'She did – when she went into his study this morning. Her husband has fetched Doctor Morton.'

The magistrate fell silent for a moment, then exploded in anger and frustration. 'I tell you, Lavender, I'm sick to death of all this tragedy in the parish! Apart from Clara Langford and the wet nurse, a crippled man fell into the canal and drowned yesterday.'

'Aye,' Woods said quietly. 'We were passin' by just after it happened. A bad business.'

'It's like there's a damned curse on us! The grim reaper is stalking Ealing and Brentford, just looking for someone to mow down with his scythe. We don't even know the name of this cripple.'

Lavender and Woods didn't reply.

Mr Minskip let them into the vicarage. The old man was pale and strained. Mumbling, he told them Doctor Morton was in the study with the body. They made their way past the piles of packing cases in the hallway and into the room. Sir James immediately recoiled at the smell and stepped back out into the hallway. He pulled out his handkerchief and held it over his nose.

Morton had already pulled back the drapes and the room was flooded with light. Thickly carpeted, with some nice pieces of delicately carved furniture, it would have been a pleasant room if it wasn't for the overpowering smell of vomit and faeces.

Langford was sitting in the chair but had slumped across the top of the cherrywood desk into a pool of his own vomit mixed with blood. His fair hair was soaked in it and his lifeless eyes stared at the fireplace. Rigor had already set in, and his mouth was fixed in a disfiguring death grimace, with the lips pulled back to expose his fine teeth.

Beside him, in his gloved hand, Morton held a small, unlabelled bottle of colourless liquid. 'It looks like it's arsenic again,' he told them.

''Tis a horrible death,' Woods murmured.

'Where the hell is this bloody poison coming from?' snapped the agitated magistrate, from the threshold of the room.

'It ain't ours!' the disembodied voice of Minskip exclaimed from the hallway. 'I've already checked. And after the last time – when the missus died – I put an extra lock on the door where we keep the rat poison.'

Lavender glanced around quickly and stepped forward to examine the scene in more detail. 'I think I may have the answer to the mystery of the arsenic.' He put on his own gloves, leaned over the waste-paper basket and lifted out two long, anaemic strips. 'Fly papers. Langford has soaked the arsenic out of fly papers – and not for the first time.'

'Are you saying he killed himself?' Sir James shouted. 'This is ridiculous! He's a man of God! Why would he do such a thing?' Nausea and anger had turned his florid face a peculiar colour.

'I'm afraid Lavender may be right,' Doctor Morton said gently. He held up a sheet of paper on which was written a single sentence. 'I found this next to the body. It's in Langford's own hand.'

Sir James gasped. 'What does it say?'

'*The lecherous bitch drove me to it...*'

Silence fell on the room.

'Is that a written confession to the killin' of his wife?' Woods asked, his face creased with confusion.

'Yes.' Lavender took the note from Morton. 'We need to sit down and have a long talk, Sir James. Yesterday, we uncovered valuable evidence that Langford is behind the death of his wife. And Abel Jupp has confirmed that Langford bribed him to give him an alibi.'

He turned away from the shocked magistrate and spoke to Minskip. 'When your wife found him like this, did she touch anything in this room?'

'She didn't touch anythin'. She never got over the threshold. She screamed when she saw him – and came rushin' to find me. I told her to take the little 'uns to Boston Manor and I went to get Doctor Morton.'

'Who was the last person to see the vicar alive?'

'I figure that will 'ave been me. 'E were sat in 'ere last night when I were lockin' the doors. 'E said "goodnight" to me, and I went up to bed and left 'im.'

'How was he when you saw him?' Woods asked.

'Quiet, thoughtful – perhaps broodin' a bit. The man's 'ad a lot to deal with.'

Including my allegations yesterday, Lavender thought. He felt a slight pang of guilt and wondered if he'd pushed Langford to take his own life? 'So, no one else apart from you and your wife and the children have been in the house since last night?' he asked.

'No.'

'Then I think we can safely assume he poisoned himself.' Lavender stared at the dead man and tried to feel sympathy – after all, even if Clara Langford had been innocent of everything they suspected, she'd behaved in a stupid and foolish way that was bound to upset and injure the pride of any man. But he didn't feel it. This was no crime of passion caused by a jealous rage. Langford had planned to kill his wife for some time – and thought nothing of murdering Annette Snelling to cover his tracks.

'Is there anything else we can do here?' Sir James asked.

Doctor Morton shook his head. 'Mr Minskip, please fetch the undertaker.'

The servant left, and Sir James suggested they retire to the drawing room to discuss the matter further. The room was still in darkness and looked strange, now most of its contents were packed away in boxes. But it smelt a lot better than the study. Lavender opened the drapes and one of the windows to let in fresh air. Dust mites danced in the sunbeams that poured through the windows, their gaiety at odds with the grim mood of the four men.

As usual, there was a small pile of dead flies on the windowsill. But another exhausted insect was banging against the glass panes. Lavender was relieved when it finally found its way out of the open window and escaped this house of death. That was one life saved, anyway.

Behind him, the magistrate went straight for the brandy decanter and poured them all a healthy measure. It was too early in the morning for such strong spirits, but Lavender took his glass gratefully. Langford's suicide had been a shock for them all. Sir James in particular looked devasted.

Once they sat down, Lavender began to gently explain. 'Yesterday, Langford's alibi for the morning of his wife's murder collapsed – and I found a witness who'd seen him riding back to Ealing.'

'Good God!'

'I asked you to call on me this morning, Sir James, because I wanted you to write out a warrant for Langford's arrest.'

Slowly, he told them everything he knew. He explained how Langford had admitted he didn't attend the church for the funeral service in Brentford; how Bruce Charlton had seen him in Ealing and Abel Jupp had confirmed the vicar had bribed him to provide an alibi.

'His plan to frame Mark Ashfield for Mrs Langford's death was falling apart – and he knew it. That's why he's killed himself. It was either death by his own hand – or by a hangman's noose.'

'But why?' Sir James asked. 'Why did he kill his wife?'

'I believe Langford had become disillusioned with his marriage and obsessed with his wife's continued affection for Mark Ashfield. When their daughter was born seven months into their marriage, he may have suspected the child was Ashfield's. Either way, I think he had planned to kill his wife for some time – the note pinned to the lychgate on his church suggests that. As does the arsenic.'

Sir James looked horrified. 'Good God! Are you saying Langford was also behind that spate of vicious letters?'

'No, I've spoken to the female behind those letters. She admits posting them, but she's adamant she wasn't responsible for the vile note at the church that accused Ashfield and Clara Langford of adultery.'

'Who is this bitch?' Sir James demanded. 'Whether she did it or not, she deserves to be whipped.'

‘I’ll explain later about that. Let’s get back to the murder case. She claims someone copied her style. I’d wondered from the start if it was written by a different hand. There’s a slight difference in the punctuation and the public manner of its disclosure made it stand out as different from the rest. I believe her when she says she isn’t responsible for it.’

‘What I think happened is this. When Langford received his own letter from our poisonous scribbler, it gave him the idea to write the accusation to discredit his wife and cause her distress. I think he hoped it would look like she’d killed herself out of shame because of the public scandal the note had caused.’

‘I struggle to comprehend how a godly man like Langford would even know language like that – never mind use it,’ Sir James protested.

‘I understand his previous living was in Rotherhithe, in London,’ Lavender said. ‘In a parish like that, he’d have heard plenty of colourful language. Like I’ve said, I believe his original intention was to make his wife’s death look like suicide. But Mark Ashfield’s arrival at the vicarage gave him the opportunity to frame his wife’s lover for the crime instead.

‘Langford returned to Ealing that day because he suspected Ashfield might visit Clara Langford while he was at the funeral,’ he continued. ‘He was right. Once Ashfield left the vicarage and she was alone, he saw his opportunity and seized it. He came inside. I’ve no idea if he confronted his wife with his suspicions about her adultery – or maybe he just smiled and handed her the glass of water laced with arsenic.’

Doctor Morton visibly shuddered at the picture Lavender was depicting.

‘None of us knows exactly what occurred,’ Lavender continued. ‘But after she was dead, he left and was riding back to Brentford when he bumped into Frederick Daniels.’

‘What did you mean earlier about the fly papers, Lavender?’ Morton asked.

'It takes a long time and a lot of patience to soak the arsenic off fly papers. That's why I believe he'd planned to kill her for some time. I checked with the village store. Someone from the vicarage has bought a huge quantity of fly papers over the last few months – far more than any other household in the village. And on my first visit here, Mrs Minskip was surprised to find their stocks had been depleted. She had to go out and purchase more.'

Sir James groaned, rested his elbow on the arm of his chair and put his bald head in his hand. 'The idiot, the absolute idiot. There are other ways to deal with lecherous and adulterous women.'

Woods glanced at Lavender, confused. But Lavender shook his head to warn him to be quiet. He had no doubt the magistrate was referring to an asylum. Lechery was considered a valid reason to have your wife committed.

'I still can't believe it,' Sir James continued. 'Lady Clitherow loved his first wife like a sister. She and Langford were part of my family.'

'That reminds me,' Lavender said. 'When Langford told you his first wife had died, what did he say was the cause of her death?'

'He wrote to Lady Clitherow and told her she'd perished with a fever. Why?'

Lavender pulled a letter out of his pocket and handed it across to the magistrate. 'When I first took on this case, I knew Langford should be the prime suspect – husbands always are, in the mysterious deaths of their wives. Magistrate Conant contacted the bishop and asked for more information about Langford. This is his reply.'

Sir James took the letter in an unsteady hand and unfolded it. His face reddened with anger as he read. 'The first Mrs Langford killed herself! The damned man lied to me and my wife!'

'He lied to me constantly throughout this investigation,' Lavender said calmly. 'The bishop doesn't go into details, but I suspect you'll also want to investigate this, Sir James? It seems to me that Langford may have a history of getting rid of troublesome wives.'

Sir James rose shakily to his feet. Whether it was the copious amount of brandy he'd drunk or rage that made him unsteady, Lavender didn't know. But he knew the man needed no more convincing about Langford's guilt.

'You've done well, Lavender,' he said gruffly. 'I'll write to Magistrate Conant, expressing my thanks for your help in this case.'

'I'd welcome it if you'd also tell him Constable Woods gave me invaluable assistance,' Lavender said. 'He's in Brentford on a private family matter and is unpaid. But he found that baptism cup, which is vital evidence linking Langford to the murder of both Clara Langford and Annette Snelling.'

Sir James nodded at Woods. 'I'll make sure you're remunerated for your trouble, Constable. Thank you. And I'll let you both know when the inquest is to be held.'

'And my brother?' Doctor Morton asked sharply. 'When will he be released from Newgate?'

'Immediately,' Sir James snapped back. 'I'll send word to the gaoler that the case against him has been dropped. In fact, Morton, you can take my letter there yourself this afternoon and fetch him home.' With that, he turned and left the room.

Chapter Thirty-Five

Lavender sighed with relief when Sir James left. He glanced across the hearth rug at Morton and realised the doctor was doing the same.

They hadn't spoken since their argument on the riverbank. Lavender remembered the accusations he'd levelled at the doctor and cringed. 'I need to apologise to you for my words the other day, Doctor. I'm sorry I accused you and Mrs Charlton.'

Morton smiled. 'Think nothing of it, Lavender. You were doing your job. I'm pleased you've finally got your evidence, solved this damnable mystery and secured my brother's release.'

Lavender nodded, grateful for his understanding.

'I also want to thank you for your discretion with that other matter.'

'What do you mean?'

'The hand behind Ealing's poisoned quill was my daughter, Amelia, wasn't it?'

'Has she told you?' Lavender asked in surprise.

'Not yet. But after our talk at the cricket match when you pointed out it had to be someone who knew about those scurrilous accusations against me in Manchester, I started to suspect her. And earlier, when you referred to the writer as a *female* – rather than a woman – I knew I was right.'

Lavender smiled. 'I complimented you the first day we met on your detection skills, Doctor – and I need to compliment you again. You miss nothing.'

'Ha! Apart from the fact that my own child has terrorised the parish with her quill.'

'What are you going to do about her?' Woods asked.

Morton shrugged, stood up and glanced out of the window. He looked worried. 'I don't know yet. I might ask Mrs Charlton's advice. Daughters are such a worry for us men, are they not?'

Woods nodded vigorously but Lavender just smiled and wondered when he would hear about the doctor's betrothal to Elizabeth Charlton.

'The undertakers are here, gentlemen,' Morton said. 'I'm afraid I must leave you now.'

They shook hands and parted. Morton went back to the study with Minskip and the black-coated undertakers, while Lavender and Woods walked out into the sunshine.

The birds were singing in the trees and bees buzzed lazily over the dandelions on the village green. The good weather still showed no sign of breaking. For the first time that week, Lavender appreciated the prettiness of Ealing, the wonderful weather and the tranquillity of the place. In the distance he saw the dark, wooded slopes of Hanger Hill. It seemed to be beckoning to him. An idea formed in his mind.

Woods suddenly stopped beneath the shade of one of the trees. 'And if you're feelin' guilty, you can stop it now. That man had the death of at least two women on his conscience. He knew he were headin' for the gallows the minute he heard we'd found the wetnurse and you were questionin' his alibi. You didn't push him to kill himself.'

Lavender glanced at him and smiled. 'You know me so well, Ned.'

'Well, someone needs to look after you. You're a useless saphead on your own. I can't even take a few days away from work without you trackin' me down to help.'

'You're right. I wouldn't have solved this case without you.'

Woods grunted, his eyes on the coaching inn on the other side of the green. 'Good. Then you can buy me an ale and a meat pie to thank me.'

Lavender laughed. 'But you've already had two meals today! I assume Betsy fed you before you came and joined me at breakfast?'

Woods shrugged. 'That were hours ago – and solvin' mysteries makes me hungry.'

'Come on then. I'll buy you a meat pie.' The two men fell into step as they walked across the grass towards the tavern. 'I want to hear more about what your father said.'

Woods grunted. 'It were nothin'. We just chatted.'

Lavender smiled. The ale in the tavern would loosen his constable's tongue.

'I suppose you'll go back to Bow Street this afternoon?'

'No, I won't. I intend to take a few days away from work, enjoy Lady Caroline's hospitality and spend some time with my family. We nearly lost Sebastián yesterday. If there's one thing I've learned from this dreadful experience, it's that our families are the most precious thing in the world and we need to cherish them.'

Woods raised his bushy grey eyebrows and gave Lavender a quizzical look. 'That ain't like you, sir. You live for your mysteries.'

'I know, but I shall change, Ned – and enjoy Magdalena and the children while I can. In fact, I might even hire a trap – like you did – and take them all for a picnic on Hanger Hill tomorrow.'

'Gawd's teeth!' Woods muttered. 'He's even copyin' me now!'

AUTHOR'S NOTES & ACKNOWLEDGEMENTS

Ever since I learned about the horrific fires at the Battle of Talavera, I've toyed with the idea of resurrecting Magdalena's first husband. I can't remember which came first, this idea – or the gypsy girl's prediction about the man with the burnt face in *The Heiress of Linn Hagh.* But those of you who have followed this series will be aware of the connection. I mull over random scraps of information for years in my head before they finally slip like a piece of jigsaw into the right place in a plot.

Then I realised that although I'd occasionally mentioned Woods' mother during the series, I'd never once referred to his father. The thought of Woods and Sebastián both having to deal with the surprising return of their fathers intrigued me. I thought Woods' experience might add a lighter, more amusing subplot and contrast with the shock and horror of the return of de Aviles.

And when I decided to cast doubt on the paternity of Clara Langford's baby, I realised that I now had a novel full of Daddy issues. For a while, I toyed with the idea of calling this book *Who's the Daddy?* But *The Poisoned Quill* sounded more appropriate for the series.

I also took inspiration from the fabulous 2023 film *Wicked Little Letters*, which is set in 1920 and based on the true story of Rose Gooding and Edith Swan. That film reminded me that real life is often more bizarre than fiction and it gave me a fun opportunity to play around with some of the more colourful phrases from Regency cant and slang.

I enjoyed researching Ealing and Brentford as the setting for this novel. Both places have now been absorbed by the great metropolis of London but back in 1814 Ealing was a lovely suburban village, full of orchards and market gardens and home to many distinguished gentlemen and their families including the Duke of York, two generals, an admiral and Sir John Soane, one of Britain's leading architects.

Much to my surprise, I discovered Ealing had also been the home of an eminent American. In 1816, John Quincy Adams moved to the village with his family while he was the American Ambassador to Britain. He later became the sixth President of the United States. Adams wrote extensively about his life in Ealing in his diaries, which has been a great help to my research.

There's also a few incidents from my personal life in this novel. Firstly, I've a friend whose Indian grandfather was a sailor during the 1930s. When his ship docked into an English port, he ended up in hospital with appendicitis. His ship sailed away without him, and he made a new life in England.

Secondly, a member of my own family was once surrounded on a canal tow path by three youths who wanted his watch and wallet. He gave them the same threat Kilby gave to the Spaniards and, surprisingly, it worked. They ran off, muttering. Nobody likes the thought of an unexpected plunge into polluted cold water.

And earlier this year, my nine-year-old grandson, Bruce, asked if I'd write him into this book as a character. Naturally, I agreed. I hope his story makes him smile.

I need to acknowledge the help of Lynn Butler-Ellis, Jenni Davis and Jill Boulton with the editing of this novel. Thank you all. And many thanks must also go to my excellent – and very patient – book cover designer, Jessica Bell. Our cousin, Wayne Charlton, helped me write the scene containing the cricket match – but any mistakes are mine and mine only. And my father, Tony James, assisted me with the research into the Grand Union Canal and the Brentford gauging lock. Thank you, both.

Finally, to you, the reader, thank you for reading my novel. If you've enjoyed it, please leave a review on Amazon.

Karen Charlton
www.karencharlton.com
October, 2025
Harrogate, North Yorkshire

ABOUT THE AUTHOR

Karen Charlton is the best-selling author of The Detective Lavender Mysteries and The York Ladies' Detective Agency Mysteries.

A former English teacher, with two grown-up children and three grandchildren, she lives in Harrogate, North Yorkshire with her two cats and writes full time. She enjoys gardening and dressmaking, a good mystery, and historical dramas on TV.

She's an avid fiction reader herself and loves to hear from her own readers. You can contact her via her website. For the latest news about her fiction, public appearances, and some special offers, sign up for her occasional newsletter on the home page. www.karencharlton.com

ALSO BY KAREN CHARLTON

AGATHA CHRISTIE MEETS FOYLE'S WAR

The York Ladies' Detective Agency Mysteries follow the adventures of two bright young women who set up a private detective agency in York during the Second World War.

Best friends since school and passionate fans of the Golden Age detective stories of Agatha Christie and Dorothy L. Sayers, these enterprising young women quickly discover that their clients have more secrets than the people they want them to investigate.

Perplexing mysteries and unsolved murders abound as they pick their way through the blacked-out wartime streets of their historic city.

Recommended for fans of the highly acclaimed TV series *Foyle's War* and for fans of Richard Osman, Alexander McCall Smith and Agatha and Dorothy – those 'Queens of Crime'.

Printed in Dunstable, United Kingdom

79753454R00167